MW01067356

BEARER OF
BAD NEWS

BEARER OF BAD NEWS

A Novel

ELISABETH DINI

GALLERY BOOKS

NEW YORK AMSTERDAM/ANTWERP LONDON
TORONTO SYDNEY/MELBOURNE NEW DELHI

Gallery Books
An Imprint of Simon & Schuster, LLC
1230 Avenue of the Americas
New York, NY 10020

For more than 100 years, Simon & Schuster has championed authors and the stories they create. By respecting the copyright of an author's intellectual property, you enable Simon & Schuster and the author to continue publishing exceptional books for years to come. We thank you for supporting the author's copyright by purchasing an authorized edition of this book.

No amount of this book may be reproduced or stored in any format, nor may it be uploaded to any website, database, language-learning model, or other repository, retrieval, or artificial intelligence system without express permission. All rights reserved. Inquiries may be directed to Simon & Schuster, 1230 Avenue of the Americas, New York, NY 10020 or permissions@simonandschuster.com.

This book is a work of fiction. Any references to historical events, real people, or real places are used fictitiously. Other names, characters, places, and events are products of the author's imagination, and any resemblance to actual events or places or persons, living or dead, is entirely coincidental.

Copyright © 2025 by Brava Ventures B.V.

All rights reserved, including the right to reproduce this book or portions thereof in any form whatsoever. For information, address Gallery Books Subsidiary Rights Department, 1230 Avenue of the Americas, New York, NY 10020.

First Gallery Books hardcover edition April 2025

GALLERY BOOKS and colophon are registered trademarks of Simon & Schuster, LLC

Simon & Schuster strongly believes in freedom of expression and stands against censorship in all its forms. For more information, visit BooksBelong.com.

For information about special discounts for bulk purchases, please contact Simon & Schuster Special Sales at 1-866-506-1949 or business@simonandschuster.com.

The Simon & Schuster Speakers Bureau can bring authors to your live event. For more information or to book an event, contact the Simon & Schuster Speakers Bureau at 1-866-248-3049 or visit our website at www.simonspeakers.com.

Interior design by Kathryn A. Kenney-Peterson

Manufactured in the United States of America

10 9 8 7 6 5 4 3 2 1

Library of Congress Cataloging-in-Publication Data
Names: Dini, Elisabeth, author.
Title: Bearer of bad news : a novel / Elisabeth Dini.
Description: First Gallery Books hardcover edition. | New York : Gallery Books, 2025.
Identifiers: LCCN 2024024215 (print) | LCCN 2024024216 (ebook) |
    ISBN 9781668063576 (hardcover) | ISBN 9781668063583 (trade paperback) |
    ISBN 9781668063590 (ebook)
Subjects: LCGFT: Cozy mysteries. | Humorous fiction. | Novels.
Classification: LCC PS3604.I4778 B43 2025 (print) | LCC PS3604.I4778 (ebook) |
    DDC 813/.6—dc23/eng/20240702
LC record available at https://lccn.loc.gov/2024024215
LC ebook record available at https://lccn.loc.gov/2024024216

ISBN 978-1-6680-6357-6
ISBN 978-1-6680-6359-0 (ebook)

For my mom and Grammy Mel,
whose kindness fills the world with light.
I am so grateful to be yours.

BEARER OF
BAD NEWS

ONE

Click. It's over in a second and hardly makes a sound, not that I'm there to hear it. While the photo that will torpedo my engagement is snapped at a music festival outside LA, I'm in Las Vegas, mindlessly scrolling social media to kill time during yet another glacially slow day at work. As if fated, that's when the sponsored job advertisement first pops up in my feed.

Seeking Bearer of Bad News!!

The two exclamation points reek of desperation, and the generic sunset profile photo screams either scam or retiree. Nonetheless, the ad intrigues.

> Seeking a professional BOBN to deliver an account of a certain misadventure to my estranged sister, early 40s, last known whereabouts in the Italian Dolomites. All expenses paid to find her and convey said bad news. Generous per diem and $25,000 success fee. Experience with complex family dynamics and immediate availability preferred. Please apply via DM.

Complex family dynamics and a $25,000 success fee? I'm bored enough to journey down the rabbit hole—I haven't had a client all afternoon—but just then a mousy woman with a puckered expression and large sunglasses ducks into the strip-mall cubicle I euphemistically call a salon. She hesitates before asking for blond highlights, eyeing the cracked linoleum and bright pink walls that aspire to cheerful but achieve Pepto Bismol.

I want to say something reassuring, but the truth is that whether from lack of natural talent (my suspicion) or because you can't be good at something you don't particularly enjoy (my best friend Adam's theory), I remain a mediocre hairstylist. Still, it pays the bills until I find a better fit, especially while Julian isn't working. For money, that is—as far as my fiancé is concerned, art is its own reward.

Almost as soon as she sits down and takes off her sunglasses, I realize that the woman, who introduces herself as Vivian, needs a therapist more than a hairdresser. Before I've managed to paint foils on even half her head, I already know that she happened to be passing by my salon while her next-door neighbor, who happens to be an ex, was also passing by. In front of her. But she was not following him because, due to a restraining order, that would be illegal. It would be helpful, Vivian stresses, if I could pretend she had this appointment in advance. Just if anyone asks. Like a parole officer.

Vivian catches my eye in the mirror, and I nod solemnly while making one of the hundreds of noncommittal, oatmeal-bland, could-mean-anything noises that I've mastered to stay afloat in this profession.

"He acts like I've done something crazy, but the apartment freed up fair and square. Is it my fault that it was just what I'd been looking for?" Vivian's eyes bulge to emphasize the injustice of it all. "Really it's just coincidence, don't you think?"

"But you knew he lived next door before you moved in, right?" I try not to sound judgmental.

"I know where lots of people live, Lacey." Vivian's tone drips condescension.

"It's Lucy," I mutter, trying to get through the foils double-time.

"You look nothing like a Lucy." In the mirror, Vivian's expression is piercing. "Did anyone ever tell you that you look just like that old-time movie star, Genevieve Saint?"

"No." I try to keep my voice even. Not even Julian knows that Genevieve Saint is my grandmother. Of course he knows about *a* grandmother who—my mother dead, my father not in the picture—raised me in Switzerland. But her full name never came up, let alone the unforgivable lie that severed our relationship.

I lower my head but can feel Vivian's stare dissecting my reflection before her attention shifts to a different topic. "When's the big day?" she asks, her eyes flitting to my engagement ring, which is honestly hard to miss.

Julian could afford a large stone because it's fake. We agreed cubic zirconia was the right way to go. Blood diamonds, such a tragedy. Also, cost. I don't say any of this to Vivian. "We haven't set a date," I say.

"Really?" She looks surprised. "Did you just get engaged?"

"About nine months ago." I keep my tone casual, but Vivian's eyebrows climb into her hairline. "We'll set a date soon," I reassure her. "It's just that Julian is in the middle of a career change, and weddings are expensive."

Vivian still looks skeptical.

"His parents are super Catholic," I rush to add. "So we have to do Pre-Cana classes and book the church—it's quite involved."

Obviously unconvinced, Vivian makes her own oatmeal noise. "Have you been together long?"

"Almost four years." I don't mention that for two of those years Julian was in the Peace Corps in Senegal. We met at a retro dance party at the University of Nevada, Reno, coming together to Madonna's "Vogue," all hand gestures and gyration. I had felt confident. I had felt beautiful. I had *been* beautiful. With him. Julian had that effect on me.

"And you're only now getting engaged?" Vivian says. "Seems like a lot of red flags."

I open my mouth and then close it again, forcing a tight smile. A woman with a restraining order actively stalking her ex is telling me that *my* relationship has red flags?

In the mirror, Vivian's eyes narrow. I brace myself for another question about my engagement, but instead she says, "You know, plastic surgery has come a long way in the last few years." Her tone is offhand, as if commenting on whether peaches are in season.

The abrupt change of subject is unnerving. The crescent of burned flesh that curls underneath my chin and toward my left ear starts to itch, but with my hands fully occupied, I can't smooth my hair back over my jaw. Twenty-two years, three plastic surgeries, and countless laser treatments have not fully erased the scar I've had since the age of four, nor my self-consciousness.

Seemingly oblivious to my discomfort, Vivian prattles on about a friend whose face had been nearly ripped off by a Rottweiler and the miracles a doctor from Brazil had wrought with illegal stem cells and a mafia-subsidized lab outside of Rio.

"Medicine isn't regulated there," Vivian says. "The fact that she still has a face shows what's possible when the government stays out of it."

"But does her face"—I pause diplomatically—"*work*?" I try and fail to picture the mechanics of little cells magically conjoining like organic duct tape.

Vivian quirks an eyebrow, as if considering the question. "She'll always drink her meals through a straw. But on the other hand"—her tone turns snide—"she has very little scarring."

The smell of bleach burns my lungs. I deeply regret that I've already done my best with Vivian's highlights. They look almost right, which is as good as it gets for my clients.

Also, I steal things, which is how I come to possess a pack of gum from Vivian's purse. But I never thieve unprovoked, and Vivian certainly had it coming after she followed her barbed commentary with the further offenses of no tip or thanks. Even so, I smile with fake warmth and wish her a nice day (of stalking). On her way out, she does in fact look around hopefully, as if her ex/neighbor might still be in the vicinity.

When Vivian is out of sight, I toss the gum into the trash. The things I steal are never valuable enough to miss, and I never keep them for long in case the police come knocking to see what I know about that missing hotel pen, hair clip, lipstick, roll of breath mints, or whatnot.

These are the rules that Adam set for me years ago, after I was nearly expelled from our New England boarding school. When we met in ninth grade, Adam was always dressed in shocking plaids and neon, and I was the awkward kid with the scarred face. We bonded as fellow social pariahs and foreign students—me from Switzerland and him from Uganda—who were both unappreciated and ahead of our time.

My first ill-fated foray into theft was taking an ugly charm bracelet from Madeline, who was not unlike Vivian in lobbing double-edged comments that exploded like hand grenades. With her perfect skin and cupid's-bow mouth, Madeline delighted in whispering about us to her gaggle of friends. Like synchronized swimmers, they would crane their necks to laugh in our direction, gazes scorching like an acid bath.

Without Adam's rules to guide me, I was easily caught. Madeline's charm bracelet, which turned out to be an heirloom, was discovered by the dorm master in my desk. But I was able to boo-hoo my way out of it. Dead mother, facial disfigurement, you get the picture.

Those days are long past, the little voice in my head (or Little Voice, as I have come to think of her) reminds me soothingly, even though we both know my teenage foibles and insecurities still lurk beneath the surface like bog monsters.

Shaking off the negativity of the last few hours, I emerge from the salon just as day softens into twilight, neon lights sparking to life all around me. Even in early May, the temperatures are already peaking in the eighties. The air is a warm embrace, the dry heat pleasurable and entirely unlike the alpine climate of my childhood.

Opting for the long route home, I turn onto the Strip for the distraction of the glam and grit out on parade. Las Vegas is the Zsa Zsa Gabor of cities— too sparkly and brazen for the occasion but hypnotizing all the same. I pass by a woman carrying a teacup dog in a baby sling, both in matching straw hats. Tourists in sneakers and yoga pants clutch smartphones as they snap pictures of fake world landmarks and erupting fountains in rainbow colors. Near the nicer casinos, I move into a riot of high-heeled, gold-chained, fake- and real-Rolexed bling that advertises readiness for a What-Happens-in-Vegas-Stays-in-Vegas Saturday night.

My street brings a seedier array of sights. A convenience store and pawn shop. A woman with a vacant stare walking a lunging Doberman. A leering man in a beret and velvet pants. I take out my phone to look occupied. Sometime during my interminable hours with Vivian, I've missed a call from Julian. I play the voicemail immediately.

"Hey, babe, my work trip is going better than expected." Referring to these LA audition weekends as "work trips" when Julian has never made a penny acting is what he calls visualizing success. To be supportive, I play along.

And Julian has gotten closer to a big break. Just last month, he went viral for his role in a dog-food commercial where he and a Great Dane barked in tandem to Louis Armstrong's "What a Wonderful World." Coined "Hot Dog Guy" by the gods of TikTok, Julian's sort-of big break was overshadowed by his questionable decision to accept payment in a cryptocurrency that we had neither heard of nor managed to access. That's show business.

"They asked me in for a callback Monday, or maybe even Tuesday," the voicemail continues. "Depends on the director's schedule, but I'll be here for a few extra nights." He ends the message in the unoriginally coded way we always say *I love you*: "Sending three."

Disappointed I won't see him tonight as planned, I remind myself that this is why we packed up our life in Reno six months ago and moved to Vegas in the first place. With my Nevada cosmetology license, this was the closest we could get to LA after Julian had a revelation that his calling was not his solid job in accounting but rather life on the big screen. The things we do for the people we love.

Completely oblivious of what's to come, I text Julian a heart emoji before fumbling for the keyless entry fob that unlocks the front door to our loft apartment. Living here wasn't my top choice. A so-called luxury building in an otherwise dodgy neighborhood, its amenities are little more than bells and whistles. Growing up with Grandmother, who found four-star hotels rather shabby, I would know.

"It's like the glitchy spaceship those galactic movie characters are always forced to buy after they escape a kidnapping," I'd told Adam after the viewing.

"Don't you get veto power if you're the one signing the lease?" Adam asked.

This was a fair point—Julian's credit was shot, so our first shared apartment would be in my name only—but Julian had been so excited about the apartment that I hadn't wanted to be a wet blanket. Plus, I'd assumed it was out of our price range. Only it turned out to be barely affordable because not everyone wants to talk to their appliances.

Inside the robot apartment I now call home, I kick off my shoes. The lights are operated by a shoddy voice-command system, but I rarely bother as it's never really dark. Rumor has it that keeping all twelve million lights on the Strip illuminated makes it the most expensive attraction in the world. Living close enough to bathe in the ambient glow, potent despite the barrier of cheap IKEA curtains and the building across the street that blocks any view of the lights themselves, I believe it.

The space is sparsely furnished. A flimsy leaf-patterned privacy screen sections off the bedroom area in a way that I'd hoped would evoke elegance but is more reminiscent of a garage sale, which is indeed where we bought it. Other than that, there is an elephantine living room couch, left by the previous tenant because it was too big to get out the door (how it arrived is anyone's guess), and a huge television that Julian bought over my objection that we couldn't afford it.

I'm glad I lost that fight because it's my only friend most nights. Tonight won't be an exception, though maybe there will be a small cheese pizza in my future to spice up the evening. In anticipation, I flop down on the couch and take out my phone to order.

It's only then that I see the SOS CALL ME!!!! text from Adam.

"Didn't you see my missed calls?" he demands, his aggrieved face filling my phone screen. Video calls have become our thing since the move.

Distracted by Julian's voicemail, I hadn't. I start to tell him about

Vivian's semi-successful highlights and restraining order (no way will I fess up to the stolen gum), but he cuts me off.

"Is Julian off auditioning?"

"Yep."

"Another dog-food commercial? He'd be perfect as the dog."

"Very funny." Adam hasn't been a fan of Julian since the move, even less so as the audition weekends have increased in frequency.

"I'm not kidding," Adam says. "There's—"

He changes phone angles, and I get an unobstructed view of his ugly reindeer sweater. "Why are you dressed for Christmas in May?" I interrupt, partly because the sweater is truly hideous and partly because I don't want to listen to yet another rant about Julian.

"People appreciate that I'm festive year-round." Adam looks down at the googly-eyed reindeer. "My students love this outfit."

"They're six. Not exactly a tough demographic."

"Enough distraction!" Adam holds up a stern hand in traffic-cop fashion. "Did you not see the SOS?"

"Oh, right. SOS." I try to look appropriately receptive to the forthcoming bad news, though Adam's SOS texts have sometimes been about Whole Foods running out of hummus.

"I'm going to send you a picture Maurice sent me—"

"You and Maurice are texting now?" I try to keep the amusement out of my voice. Until Adam recently developed a crush, Maurice was more my friend than his. My old debate partner from college, Maurice had fallen out of touch when he joined the Navy SEALs and did a bunch of top-secret stuff before moving back to Reno last year and reentering our lives (and Adam's heart). For his part, Maurice seems oblivious to Adam's feelings, which doesn't speak well for his spycraft since Adam is about as subtle as a nuclear bomb.

"Yes, we text, but that's hardly the point."

"Fine, what is the point?"

"Do you remember Mr. Chippy?"

"From the Laughtacular?" When Julian first decided he wanted to be an actor, Adam had invited him to join his amateur improv class, and the resulting Laughtacular Showcase was hands down one of the most painful three-hour periods of my life. "Didn't he move to Los Angeles?"

Adam nods his head, looking near to tears. At least now I know where this is going. Aksel Larsen, the statuesque Norwegian who bravely took on the role of Mr. Chippy the talking squirrel, had been the object of Adam's unrequited love for the entirety of Improv Secrets 101.

"I am a better friend to you than Maurice." Adam fans his face. "He sent me the picture because he knew I would do what had to be done, that bastard."

"Can we speed this up? I was about to order a pizza."

"Pizza won't fix this." Adam shakes his head sadly. "I'm going to forward what he sent me, but you need to promise not to freak out."

"Okay," I lie. I am fully prepared to freak out, if only to show solidarity with Adam for whatever his ex-crush Mr. Chippy has done now. But when Adam sends through the photo, I only squint. All I can make out is a passionate embrace between two men. Tousled hair, exposed skin, a surprising amount of glitter . . . but that could be the lighting.

"It's from a music festival earlier today. Maurice was there. He took this photo."

"On the bright side, you were right that Aksel's into guys." I focus on the positive.

"Can you not see who he's kissing?" Adam looks close to stroking out.

I continue to squint. "Lights on," I call. Despite my command, the room stays dark.

"Forget about the lights!"

"Lights on!" I try one more time. In the kitchen, the garbage disposal starts to whir. "This place! It's like living in the opening scene of a slasher movie—"

"Zoom. In. On. The. Photo." Adam's tone is ominous.

With my thumb and forefinger, I enlarge the couple. Eyes closed, expression rapturous, features partially obscured by a baseball hat but—and now it's obvious—so very familiar. And then I freak out.

"Is that—"

"Yes." Adam hisses the word like he's auditioning for the role of an evil wizard.

"Why is Julian kissing Aksel Larsen?" I try to keep hysteria at bay. Probably my first thought should have been one of outrage, but instead I find myself wondering: *Has Julian ever kissed me that way?*

"Oh, honey." Adam's tone is tragic. "Who wouldn't kiss Aksel Larsen?"

Wasserman Bosch Attorneys
Basel, Switzerland
December 18, 1981

Dear Ms. Saint,

As discussed in our meeting last week, I have made discreet inquiries regarding your situation. If you are amenable, I suggest that you—or I on your behalf—reach out to the Department of Lost Things. This institution may be unknown to you, as it is to most, but through various government contacts, I have confirmed that the organization does the quiet work you seek.

To allay your concerns about legitimacy, permit me to recount what I have learned. Most agree that rumors of the Department existing unofficially prior to World War II are unsupported. Officially, the Department was founded in 1942 as an intergovernmental effort, much like the tribunals later established to prosecute war crimes. Though its later evolution is not publicly known, my sources believe that the Department ended up privately funded and populated by agents of government entities around the world. As a testament to the work undertaken, it is rumored that at least some of these agents volunteer their time without compensation or their governments' knowledge or permission.

Despite unusual aspects of its structure (one contact referenced "spies playing Robin Hood"), the Department has historically provided services useful enough to ensure its independence. In many cases, world governments and international institutions cooperate with (and even defer to) the Department. In short, I believe they are best positioned to provide the necessary assistance, though contacting them is not without risk given your situation.

I remain available to further discuss at your convenience. Until then, I wish you and yours joyous holidays.

Sincere regards,

David Bosch

David Bosch
Partner

TWO

Unaware that he had been photographed sucking face with the duplicitous Mr. Chippy, Julian at first denies everything.

I cry and rage-scream and then forward him the photo.

"Oh, shit," Julian says, and then he hangs up on me. When I try to call back, it goes straight to voicemail.

"Get a good night's sleep and then drive straight to Reno tomorrow morning," Adam urges. "How many hair appointments would you have to cancel to spend the week with me?"

"Only two," I sob, crying harder. "My clients don't love me either."

"People don't want hair appointments"—Adam flounders but quickly rebounds—"in spring. Every hairstylist struggles in spring. Summer will be your season, angel. Until then, get thee to Reno. I've already stocked the freezer with your favorite flavors."

Snot is running down my face. "I need to be here when Julian rushes home to beg for my forgiveness." Which he will. Probably.

Little Voice makes an oatmeal noise. Adam clears his throat. I swallow an Ambien to take the edge off heartbreak's rat teeth, currently shredding my insides.

The next morning, my calls to Julian still aren't going through, and my texts remain unanswered.

Are you seriously ghosting me? I demand midmorning.

Three dots appear and disappear under my message, but in the end, Julian doesn't respond.

In retribution, I tear through his side of the closet and nightstand, plus his drawers in our shared desk. I already knew that Julian took his laptop and phone, but now I notice with alarm that his favorite T-shirt, only nice suit, and fancy designer jeans are gone too. As is our largest suitcase, the one that is far too big for a weekend trip.

Seeing the hole where the suitcase used to be is like a punch in the gut. How long have these things been missing? There was no audition. That's evident. What about all the other weekends? For the first time, it hits me that Julian may not be in the midst of a fleeting bi-curious indiscretion, that he might have been slowly leaving me for weeks or even months.

I sit down in the closet and cry against the legs of Julian's shitty everyday jeans, which smell faintly of laundry detergent but nothing like him. The thought that he may never return makes my heart stutter. Then I think about potentially having to date again, and it stops altogether.

"I blame myself," Adam says when I call from my crumpled position in the closet. "I mean, it was never a great sign that his name is Julian. It's a very mercurial name. And then he got too hot for his own good."

"Thanks."

"You know what I mean. Classic story of boy meets theater." Adam sighs. "I never should have introduced him to the Reno amateur thespian scene or suggested that gym membership. It was a recipe for disaster. I mean, I'm the reason he met Aksel, though in my defense, I was sure that if Aksel was going to make out with anyone, it would have been me—"

Call waiting beeps. "It's Julian," I whisper urgently.

"Why are you whispering?"

"I'm in the closet."

"*You're* in the closet? Because that's hilar—" Adam starts, but I hang up before Julian can be diverted to voicemail.

"Hello?" I crawl out of the mess of tangled clothes. The closet is not the right energy for this call. "Julian?" My voice is breathless.

"Are you jogging?"

"No." I haul myself to my feet like a drunkard and move into the kitchen.

"You sound winded."

The conversation doesn't get much better from there. I want to ask about the missing suitcase and if he has left me for good, and if so, why his voicemail pretended he would be gone only a few days, and whether he wants to come back but worries I couldn't forgive an affair, let alone one with a man, and, speaking of that, if he is still attracted to women—scratch that, *to me*—but it all feels too fraught for a phone conversation.

"Just come home and we'll talk about it," I say. The question of whether our relationship has a future is one that should be addressed in person.

"I need time, Lu." Julian sounds as if he's been attacked by the dog in the Hot Dog Guy commercial and then chased barefoot for several miles over rough ground.

But sympathy is beyond me. Instead, rage spikes like quicksilver in a thermometer. Before I can reply, I hear a distinctly resonant voice coming from somewhere terribly close to Julian. Visions of the spectacularly horrible Laughtacular flood my memory, the chattering Mr. Chippy nibbling imaginary nuts in a way that now seems premonitory.

"You're still with"—I hear myself and channel less of a cat-caught-in-bear-trap vocal register—"him?"

The connection goes silent, as if I've been muted.

"How long has this been going on, Julian?" Behind me, the garbage disposal starts up. "Dammit!" I'm not sure which of them I'm addressing.

"Lu, I have to go." Julian's voice comes back over the line.

"Don't go." I hate that I'm pleading but can't stop myself. "We have to talk—"

"Hello?" Julian shouts into the phone. "What's that noise?"

"It's the stupid garbage disposal." My voice is as choppy as the grinding.

"What? Bad connection! I can't hear you."

"I know you can hear me."

"Hello?"

"Julian, I've watched you do this a million times with your mother. I *know*—"

The line goes dead. He hung up on me. Again.

When I text Adam, his response is immediate: Cancel those 2 clients & abandon that glitchy MF apartment immediately. My couch is your couch.

Wasserman Bosch Attorneys
Basel, Switzerland
June 17, 1982

Re: Department of Lost Things

To Whom It May Concern:

    I write on behalf of my client, Genevieve Saint, who has recently come into information about an emerald necklace that, despite extensive investigation on our part, has dropped out of public view. If helpful for your inquiries, this item was previously owned by famed French courtesan Esther Lachmann, professionally known as La Païva, and—my client believes—later passed into the possession of Professor Mordechai Baum, a resident of Berlin who died in the Dachau concentration camp in 1942. Based on our inquiries, the necklace has not been seen since the end of World War II.

    Your organization is known for its discretion in assisting those wrongfully parted from their belongings, and my client wishes to inquire if you have (or can obtain) any information about this item and the person or persons who may currently possess it.

    Should you have, or in the future come into, such information, my client would appreciate hearing from you and would compensate accordingly for your time and efforts.

Sincere regards,

David Bosch
David Bosch
Partner

THREE

I can see you standing, honey, with his arms around your body . . ." I'm belting out Taylor Swift's "exile" when Adam comes home from work. He has an armful of Chinese takeout, which fills me with apprehension. Our most sensitive conversations always involve egg rolls. I immediately fumble for my phone to stop the song, but it's too late.

"How many times has this been on repeat?" Adams asks. Before I can answer, he holds up a hand. "Don't answer that question."

It's probably for the best, so I stay quiet.

Adam sighs dramatically. "Did you at least leave the apartment today?" He tries to sound conversational, but I hear the judgment lurking.

I am tempted to lie but don't have the energy. A week after abandoning my robot abode and driving eight hours to flee soul-crushing heartbreak and take up residence on Adam's pull-out sofa, I have hardly moved.

Adam unloads cartons of takeout onto the coffee table. "As your oldest, dearest, and frankly most spectacular friend, I feel compelled to tell you that you are a hot mess right now. This"—Adam waves a set of chopsticks like Edward Scissorhands around the specter of my unwashed hair, baggy sweatpants, and DO OR DO NOT, THERE IS NO TRY Yoda T-shirt—"is not a hygienic situation."

I brace for a hostile retort, then deflate. It's hard to claim the high ground when I've been wearing the same outfit for three days. "Let's be honest, my looks have never been my strong suit." I try for a joke, but the words come out heavy.

"I did not accept an invite to a pity party." Adam's expression is firm. "You have everything dysmorphia and low self-esteem. Basically, you're an unreliable narrator. The girl at the kitchen sink or whatever. We've been over this—I'm not here to be the clichéd gay bestie where you drip mascara and self-hatred, and I give a sprightly pep talk. Did you watch that Brené Brown video I sent?"

My face must look like I feel because Adam immediately halts his lecture. "I'm way ahead of myself. We need wine." As he moves toward the kitchen, I hear him mutter under his breath, "Like, a lot of wine."

Sharing a small one-bedroom apartment would strain even the best of friendships, let alone when one friend is a shut-in weathering an imploding engagement. The problem with the hardest of times is that you need more than a hug and a cookie to bounce into the next chapter. More like you need to be carried through barbed wire and up a mountain and then allowed to eat all the food in your friend's backpack and hog the fire in the shelter they built single-handedly, and then you need them to do the same thing for you again, day after day, until you manage to get your shit together. In short, I offer Adam little in return for his hospitality beyond my sparkling personality. *Sparkling* being, of course, a euphemism for dark and deeply depressed.

Adam returns with a cheap bottle of red and two wineglasses. He fills both to the brim, lips pinched so tightly that I know he's forcing himself to wait before launching into whatever he wants to say.

I take my glass. "Just say it."

Adam thrusts the egg rolls in my direction.

"Don't try to soften this with an egg roll!"

"Aren't we going to cheers?" Adam puts the carton down and reaches for his own wineglass.

"Fine." We never miss a cheers.

"To honesty." Adam makes the word sound like the gold standard of qualities.

"To being nonjudgmental." I adopt the same tone.

We clink glasses, a little harder than necessary.

"It has to be said, so I'll say it." Adam looks pained. "You know Julian may not come back, right?"

I feel my face contort.

"It may not be the worst thing." Pity radiates from Adam's eyes. "My personal feelings about Julian aside, you never liked Vegas anyway. Have you made a single friend there?"

I shake my head.

"It hasn't even been a year since you left Reno. You can slide back into your life here—"

"Without Julian?" Angrily I shove an egg roll into my mouth. Stress-eating is one of my love languages.

"It's not like you're alone. You have me, your grandmother—"

"You know I don't speak to her. And anyway, I can't get out of the apartment lease for another—" I do a quick mental calculation. "Five and a half months. And the salon lease ends a month after that." I reach for another egg roll as I mentally tally the numbers in my bank account after a week of not working. Rent for both will be tight this month, but the idea of being in that apartment without Julian—now or ever—feels like a mental health death sentence.

"Maybe you can call your old salon in Meadowood and see—"

"Do you know how glad they were to see the back of me?" I grab the veggie lo mein and dig in. "I was barely making ends meet before we moved, and it's even worse in Vegas. I've been living off savings."

I'd never admitted this to Adam before. He had counseled against moving and putting the lease in my name and had been right on both counts. But now he studiously avoids my gaze and utters not a single *I told you so* or *Why doesn't Julian find a way to pay his share?* or *You're an idiot.*

"Maybe it's time to reconsider reaching out to your grandmother. She'd give you the money."

A memory of Grandmother surfaces, the way she looked the last time I saw her four years ago, standing in front of the Swiss chalet she inherited from her late husband like one of Pissarro's blurred pastel figures, the lake a sunset violet spill of paint behind the big windows and manicured shrubs covered in snow.

"If you're leaving, then leave," Grandmother had said. "But don't think you're taking anything of value out of this house."

She had supervised my packing, sternly removing from my hands anything with significant resale value—the sapphire earrings she'd given me as a high school graduation present and the vintage Hermès handbag she had thought looked nicer on my arm than hers and old jewelry from previous marriages that she'd casually thrown my way, plus the small fortune of other luxury items I had in my closet. She must have intuited my plan to sell it all to start my new and independent life. What she did not intuit was that I would not be deterred from starting that life penniless.

In the end, I brought away very little: casual clothing and costume jewelry, a warm winter coat and a few pairs of shoes. So much of my childhood was left behind, and at the time, I didn't mind leaving its remnants to molder. Later I regretted all that abandoned history but not enough to change my mind.

"No way," I say to Adam. "I'm never talking to her again."

"That's a pretty bold statement to make about the person who raised you." Adam's tone is diplomatic.

"Your father raised you too," I shoot back.

Adam flinches, and I immediately regret the words. Adam's conservative father disinherited him when he came out the summer after we graduated from boarding school. I had cried with him after he hung up the phone the night he told his parents he would never marry a woman. He hasn't seen anyone in his family or been back to Uganda since, though his mother still secretly calls him when his father is out. Had he gone home, he could have been imprisoned or even killed for being gay. He wants to believe that his father would never turn him in, but he can't be sure.

Even so, he maintains that it was the price of being honest about who he is, and he doesn't regret it, even though his timing was terrible because his father immediately withdrew all financial support for college. Without his father's connections, Adam also lost his visa to stay in the United States. It was Grandmother who paid for the immigration lawyer who successfully petitioned for Adam's asylum status.

Grandmother's support for Adam did not extend to me joining him at "a state school in the middle of nowhere," as she put it. In actuality, the University of Nevada, Reno hailed from the Biggest Little City in the World, but Grandmother didn't want to hear it. Even before our last big fight, she'd threatened to cut off all financial support if I enrolled there instead of at her top choices: Harvard or the Sorbonne. That I didn't have the grades or speak French were two other things Grandmother didn't want to hear.

There was never a question of what I would do when UNR was the only school to offer Adam a full scholarship. Applying as an orphan, I got plenty of financial aid and joined him. As always, Grandmother kept her word. She didn't give me a cent toward college, but I started taking courses toward my cosmetology license on the weekends and soon cut hair here and there to make ends meet.

"I'm sorry. I'm the worst. I didn't mean that." I offer Adam the last egg roll.

Adam takes a long swallow of wine, seemingly debating whether or not to be angry. As usual, his good nature wins, though he doesn't meet my eyes when he takes the egg roll. His voice is calm when he finally responds. "I don't want to forgive him today, but who knows about tomorrow? Sometimes we forgive the unforgivable, Lu. You don't have to close yourself off to the possibility that you'll change your mind."

I want to argue, but given my cruelty of the moment before, I instead nod in silent penance.

"And also," Adam continues, "the fact that you just went there shows me that you're in an even worse place than I thought. You need to get yourself out of"—again he looks at my Yoda T-shirt—"whatever this is."

He's right. I can't remember feeling this lost since my last stand with Grandmother.

"Pull up the leases," Adam says. "Let's see what they say about termination."

An hour later, I've barely stopped short of licking the take-out cartons, and Adam has read out loud lots of boring legalese on tenant this and landlord that and something called force majeure that he is sure will be our ace in the hole.

Not being a lawyer himself, Adam calls Maurice to weigh in. Though also not a lawyer, Maurice is subjected to long passages of both leases that Adam reads out loud, over my objections that none of this is necessary until we're sure that Julian isn't coming back.

"Of course," Adam says sweetly.

"Maybe offer to pay your way out of the leases?" Maurice suggests. "If you explain the situation, they might settle for a smaller amount."

Adam gives me an exaggerated thumbs-up, as if Maurice has just told us the secret to nuclear fusion.

"Isn't Maurice brilliant?" Adam sounds giddy when the call finally ends.

"Sure." I start to clean up our dinner mess, rooting out the fortune cookies from the bottom of the takeaway bag. "Sounds like this one is for you," Adam says after breaking his open. He reads out loud: "'When I let go of what I am, I become what I might be. Lao Tzu.'"

"Huh. Because I let go of hairdressing and now I'm just loafing on your couch."

"Point taken. What's yours, then?"

I snap my own cookie cleanly in two and read, "'Roads were made for journeys, not destinations. Confucius.'" I grimace. "Not sure I see any journeys in my future unless they're free." I remember the paid ad that had appeared yet again this morning in my feed.

Seeking a professional BOBN to deliver an account of a
certain misadventure. . . . $25,000 success fee. . . .

Probably a scam. But on the other hand, why not outsource delivering bad news if you could afford it? There were quirky wealthy folks paying for far stranger things.

Later that night, sleepless on the sofa bed that squawks like a seagull at my slightest movement, I tally all the things I could do with $25,000, especially if Adam is right that Julian and I are not en route to reconciliation. Sure, it sounds too good to be true, but what if it's not?

It doesn't take long to find the ad in my feed. After reading it through again, I click on the sunset avatar, but the profile for one "Taffy Waters" is set to private. This—along with the obviously fake name—should give me pause but only intrigues me further.

There's no harm in applying, Little Voice says from her annoying vantage inside my head. *It's not like you have to hand over your Social Security number.*

Insanity is doing the same thing again and again and expecting a different result, Einstein (or someone) said, and if anything is true, it is that.

I type slowly with one finger into the little private message window:

> Dear Ms. Waters,
>
> I am writing to apply to your advertisement for a Bearer of Bad News. I am not sure that I am a professional—I do hair for a living, and that is similar to a therapist because people tell you a lot of things: about partners who don't do normal partner things and kids who don't do normal kid things and bodies that don't do normal body things. It makes you wonder what is normal and if it even exists because no one seems to think they have it. Anyway, I may not be a professional BOBN, but I have had a lot of bad news in my life. I'm not sure what news you need to get to your sister, but I would do my best to deliver it. I'm sorry you're estranged. As someone familiar with family estrangement, I know how much it sucks. I haven't spoken to my only known family for . . .

I stop and stare at what I've written. This stranger is not my therapist. I hit delete and try again.

> Dear Taffy,
> I am interested in the Bearer of Bad News position and consider myself an expert in both complex family dynamics and bad news. As for availability, I could leave tomorrow.
> Sincerely,
> Lucy Rey

Applying is not the same as accepting the position, Little Voice reminds me. Quickly, before I can think better of it, I hit send.

Dear Countess Waters,

Thank you for writing to Genevieve Saint. Ms. Saint sincerely appreciates your message. Unfortunately, because of the volume of fan mail Ms. Saint receives, she is unable to personally reply to each letter. However, please accept this autographed photo of Ms. Saint from her Oscar-winning performance in *The Devil and the Doctor* as a token of gratitude for being one of her beloved fans.

Sincere regards on behalf of,

Genevieve Saint
Genevieve Saint

FOUR

wake to a ping. A notification box on my phone screen announces that I have received a new private message from Taffy Waters. Still half asleep, I click and read:

> Dear Lucy,
> You sound perfect. Can we discuss your qualifications at
> 12 pm PST? Video link below.
> In joy,
> Taffy

In joy? I hate Taffy already. With the wine-and-egg-roll insanity of last night behind me, it's clear that responding to a sunset avatar was a mistake. But not one that's too late to undo. I'll simply cancel the interview.

Or should I take the interview? Obviously taking the *job* would be insanity. Wouldn't it? *How can you know unless you get more information?* Little Voice politely inquires. Then I see the time on my phone and leap from the couch. I'm nearly late for my appointment with Miss Mary.

I have Maurice to thank/blame for having Miss Mary in my life. My second night at Adam's, Maurice came over to offer booze and condolences and said something along the lines of: "My friend Mary is breaking into therapy."

As if the two had coordinated beforehand (which they likely had), Adam immediately said, "Lucy, a little therapy would be great for you, don't you think?"

"You would like her," Maurice enthused before I could respond in the negative. "Mary's nontraditional. She's pioneering a different method, similar to Freud but without a medical degree."

I had heard of social workers with strings of letters after their names that meant they could do what sounded exactly like therapy but without prescriptions.

"Her background is in theater," Maurice continued. "Well, that and Nevada's Department of Motor Vehicles. She retired last year after thirty years of cheerful service."

Probably this should have deterred me, but it didn't. I was desperate to get Adam off my back about how I should talk to someone, and an actual therapist was not in my budget. Miss Mary's movement therapy with the friends-of-friends discount, however, was surprisingly affordable.

Movement Moments is a two-room establishment in a shopping complex with mostly vacant storefronts. The walls in the waiting room are covered with so many posters they could be wallpaper. A bumbling cartoon bee buzzes over BEE-LIEVE IN YOURSELF. A rock climber clings to a cliff under a bold DON'T LET YOUR EXCUSES WIN.

Almost as soon as I walk in, the door to the inner sanctum dramatically bangs open. The doorknob smashes into a poster of a roaring tiger haloed by COURAGE ISN'T FOR COWARDS.

"Darling, DARLING!" Miss Mary comes forth, neon caftan swirling. She looks like a sherbet flavor, the outfit taking almost all attention away from her face, which sags. She is old, but her eyes are merry.

However weary her face, Miss Mary's hat is having none of it. The jaunty cloche in deep peacock blue has a little red dragon peeping from behind a large ostrich feather. Nobody puts Miss Mary in a corner.

"My fiancé hasn't called—" I start.

Miss Mary cuts me off. "No talking. Your body does the talking here."

This, I will learn, is the shortcoming of movement therapy. During our intake call, I told Miss Mary the whole Julian sob story and got the spiel on her movement therapy philosophy. The body knows what the heart needs,

Miss Mary believes. Talking comes from the head, which can't be trusted. This might be true, but I still want Miss Mary's head to tell my head that Julian's actions don't mean what Adam thinks.

I try to speak again, but Miss Mary loudly shushes me and waves me into what she calls the Space. Covered with speakers, the room isn't a technological masterpiece so much as a collection of any old speaker from any old junk heap. Small, large, rusted, new, rectangular, circular, octagonal—as if the multifaceted eyes of dozens of different insects were plastered at random over the wall by a mad scientist. For reasons that are not visually apparent, the room smells of overripe strawberries.

"Lights out?" Miss Mary asks.

"Yes, please." The lights go out, though I can still see a seam of silver under the door and the glowing screen of Miss Mary's phone.

The floor of the room has a small trampoline, a king-size mattress covered in throw pillows with deep purple sheets (no visible stains, but it's certainly a forgiving color), and a Twister game board placed over several thick yoga mats duct-taped together.

"What is your theme song?" Miss Mary had asked during our call.

I hadn't had an answer.

"The key to a good theme song is the energy," Miss Mary had advised. "It's not a song you sit on the couch and cry to. It's the song that makes you feel so much *something* that you want to move. Good feelings, bad feelings, whatever, as long as you can't sit still when you hear it." We had spent the better part of the call (longer than one would expect for a free consult) finding mine, mostly through trial and error as Miss Mary piddled her way around Spotify.

"The same one we discussed?"

I nod, and a few seconds later Dolly Parton's "Jolene" blares from the speakers.

"Let your body lead," Miss Mary hollers over the noise.

That's all the encouragement I need to launch into an angry-awkward-flailing-one-person mosh pit. Am I moving along with the melody? Maybe not, but frustration and sadness and fear for my future and whether my relationship is dead and whether I'll ever find the love I so desperately want and a million other emotions jerk my limbs like a rogue puppet.

"Please, don't take my man," I beg along with Dolly.

Miss Mary materializes at my shoulder, frowning. "Maybe it's time for a new song."

Without my input, she pulls out her phone and pokes at it. "Survivor" by Destiny's Child bursts out of the speakers, lyrics projected in large font on the wall. Miss Mary's tech savvy is impressive.

The voluminous folds of her caftan sway, and Miss Mary commands, "Sing!"

It takes me a beat to get the hang of it, but by the time we get to the chorus, I'm game. "I'm a survivor," I come in a bit uncertainly, but after a few lines feel myself cracking open.

"I'M A SURVIVOR," I bellow.

"Yes!" Miss Mary encourages.

I picture Julian insisting that we move to Las Vegas even though I knew no one there and leaving me alone for so many weekends in the creepy broken-tech apartment with the fancy appliances that constantly malfunctioned and running away with Mr. Chippy.

Something blooms in my chest, lava-hot and snarling. I violently kick at the mattress.

"Let it out, let it out!" Miss Mary's voice is approving, gleeful even.

And then I start to sob uncontrollably. My face feels hot and almost blistered. I stand in the middle of the room, hands slack by my sides, tears coursing down my face. My voice catches and wavers pathetically.

"Enough." Miss Mary kills the music. "Shall we close with something less angry?"

I nod. Movement therapy ends so quickly. Or, rather, twenty minutes is all I can afford of movement therapy.

The Bengsons blare from the speakers. Simple positivity and a folksy middle-aged singer with a voice like an angel.

"This is the keep going, keep going, keep going on, keep going on song . . ." The lyrics appear on the wall again, and Miss Mary nudges me until I sing, and then she joins, our voices off-key and equally unlikely to attract any music deals.

The song ends. Instead of feeling better, the huge fissure inside of me sizzles like water thrown into a firepit. I feel more out of sorts than when I came in.

"Do you think Julian will come back?" I ask as Miss Mary runs my credit card.

Miss Mary adjusts the dragon on her hat, which has fallen askew sometime during our session. "Maybe you're asking the wrong question."

I stare at her blankly. "What is the right question?"

Miss Mary cocks her head but doesn't answer, the little dragon waggling as if summoning magic. I battle the urge to punch her hat dragon in its smug little face. *What am I paying you for?* I want to ask, but I'm paying so little that I probably got my money's worth just from the electricity used during my session.

Resigned, I turn to go, my back bowing under what feels like a great weight. Miss Mary sighs, as if she expected more from me. "Only you know the right question, sugar."

But I don't know the right question. I'm not going to find it on Adam's couch either. Given that my options to get off his couch are limited, I squeal out of the parking lot with all the horsepower my ancient Prius can muster. If I hurry, I can still make it back in time for my interview with Taffy.

Department of Lost Things: Case File 1982-024, Record 2
ARCHIVES
Inaugural Case Note

The following background information on the referenced emerald necklace was assembled based on the details provided in Record 1[*]:

Provenance: Emeralds bought by Count Guido Henckel von Donnersmarck (1830–1916) and fashioned into a necklace as a gift for his mistress and later wife, famed French courtesan Esther Lachmann (aka La Païva) (1819–1884), whose son (1840–1882) from a prior relationship is the grandfather of Mordechai Baum (1900–1944). Though there is no official record, La Païva appears to have given the necklace to her son, who passed it down to his descendants. In its last known sighting, the necklace was worn to the opera by M. Baum's wife in a photograph in the society pages of *Berliner Tageblatt* in 1922 (see attached). Currently unknown if M. Baum has any living descendants.

The directors of the Department of Lost Things have convened a meeting and voted 4 in favor, 3 against to open Case 1982-024 into the whereabouts of this necklace.

---

[*] Due to "scheduling" (but perhaps indicating a change of heart in referring this case?), G. Saint (and her lawyer) have so far been unavailable for interview.

FIVE

Taffy Waters shines bright as an artificial light. She could be thirty-five or sixty. Likely sculpted by expensive serums, creams, fillers, freezers, and plastic surgery, her face has the ageless look of Madame Tussaud's wax. Somehow the human eye can still recognize the absence of youth, but there isn't a single wrinkle or gray hair to blame.

Even over video, Taffy's pink tracksuit looks puppy soft and likely to have some sort of adjective on the butt like *Moist* or *Jiggly* or *Scrumptious*. Behind her, a huge tropical plant sits in front of floor-to-ceiling windows, beyond which I can glimpse a little square of lush garden.

My first impression is one of eccentric wealth, and I feel a flutter of excitement behind my breastbone. This was, after all, the best-case scenario—someone rich enough to outsource all of life's unpleasantries, including bad news bearing.

"Hello, hello!" Taffy chirps at me through Adam's laptop, filling the screen with doll eyes and a too-big smile with too-white teeth. She has dimples, but I am not charmed. "I'm Taffy Waters. So pleased to meet you."

Is her name really Taffy Waters? I hadn't been expecting that.

"It's wonderful to meet you too." I try for an equally big smile and resist the urge to tug at the collar of the work shirt Adam reserves for parent-teacher conference days. It was the only thing clean and pressed enough in the house to qualify as interview-ready, and I hope that the torso-up view will obscure the ill fit. At least she can't see my sweatpants. Business on top and narcolepsy on the bottom.

"I don't see the resemblance to Genevieve," Taffy muses, tapping a manicured nail against her plump bottom lip.

My heart sinks. Taffy knows about Grandmother.

"And that scar! What on earth happened to you?"

She doesn't wait for me to respond, which is absolutely for the best.

"You'd think Genevieve Saint of all people would know the best plastic surgeons." Taffy's face freezes in an expression of horror, voice dropping into a whisper. "My God, was that the best they could do?"

As if blinded by the glare of an interrogator's spotlight, I blink rapidly. I must look as speechless and overwhelmed as I feel because Taffy's face morphs into marshmallow sweetness.

"Oh, no!" Her chagrin seems sincere. "There I go again. Open mouth, insert foot, Taffy!" She laughs with the awkwardness of someone familiar with committing and then apologizing for gaffes. "The scar's not that bad! It's really not. And how lucky it's only on the side of your face, just your jaw, really. And the rest of you is simply gorgeous!" Another forced laugh and then Taffy pauses—waiting, I expect, for me to reassure her that it's perfectly fine that she turned my appearance into the first order of business in our conversation.

My desperate search for a response fails, and I feel my stomach cramping. Can I simply hang up on her? I wish we were in person so that I could even the score by snatching a little something from her purse.

Remember the $25,000 success fee, Little Voice reminds me.

"And that scar has *not* been holding you back." Taffy continues to dig herself into an ever-deeper hole. "I mean, I've seen your fiancé—of course I checked your social media before our little chat—and he's quite the looker! And honestly, now that I keep staring at you, I don't even notice the scar anymore. There is something quite striking about you, really. *Just* like Genevieve. I see it now."

Oh my God, how do I make her stop? My face feels frozen. I want to ask her how she knows about Grandmother, but I can't find the words.

"Without the scar, you'd be almost *too* beautiful," Taffy careens on. "It's only fair, honey. Not that I can relate personally; I wasn't born beautiful. But I've been happily married for fifteen years. The secret to that, I don't mind telling you, is *not* marrying for looks." Taffy finally comes up for air with a significant look.

I force out my best oatmeal noise.

Taffy reaches offscreen, her hand returning into view with a crystal glass full of ice water (or vodka, which would explain a lot). "I'm quite parched, and we haven't even started yet!" She takes a delicate sip. "Do you know that some people hate the taste of water?"

I shake my head.

"I know, I can't believe it either. How can you hate the taste of water? It's like hating the smell of fresh air. Do you personally know anyone who hates the taste of water?" Taffy's gaze is frank. From somewhere offscreen, a dog, or maybe several dogs, start to bark.

Again, I shake my head, wondering if "water" is some sort of code.

"Me neither." She sighs. "Maybe it's fake news. Anyway"—another bright smile—"that's more of a sidenote. You are quite easy to talk to. I wasn't sure what to expect, but you're likable, which is a relief."

Taffy appears to jot something on a piece of paper. "So, check for square one. Very good listener. I'm adding the *very* because I really am impressed. You'd think listening would be about the easiest thing anyone could do, but I can tell you from experience that it's one of the hardest. If you knew Coco—well, let's just say that my sister is a talker, but only to the right sort of person. A listening sort of person. And she's not exactly a straightforward communicator."

The barking gets louder, so it's possible I misheard. "I'm sorry, did you say your sister's name is Coco?"

"Taffy and Coco—isn't that adorable?" Taffy looks thrilled. "I came up with the nickname myself."

A laugh is forcing its way up my throat, and it takes all my strength to choke it down. "It's the cutest," I confirm with a straight face. *Who's the actor now, Julian?*

"I have to be honest, I had a feeling you'd be perfect for this position. *Really* perfect. This is not the place or time to air dirty laundry, but it's clear you have dirty laundry and haven't aired it, and that's also attractive to me. *Quite* attractive." Taffy pauses, as if waiting for me to agree, or perhaps throw all my laundry in her face right over the video call.

I decide the strong-and-silent manifestation is working for me. Instead of speaking, I make another of my enigmatic hairdresser-survival sounds.

"Well." Taffy gives me another long look. "Discretion is something I need on this job. Would you say you're discreet, Lucy? Can I call you Lucy?"

"Yes," I say. "And yes."

"Good, that's very good. And not that you need one, but I assume you have a Swiss passport because of Genevieve—you grew up there, didn't you?"

I nod without clarifying which question I'm answering, but Taffy doesn't seem to care.

"Great," she says. "And I have to ask this—you know, lawyers." Taffy airily waves a hand toward the tropical plant. "Are you willing to sign a non-disclosure agreement? Before you answer"—I haven't tried to answer, but Taffy holds up a hand—"you should know that the provisions in the NDA, were you to break it, are a bit . . . almost inhumane. You would end up losing everything," she says matter-of-factly. "Everything you have, everything you might one day have, all of it. Of course, that's *only* if you break it, and if you have no intention of breaking your word, then why wouldn't you sign it?" Another airy laugh. "Am I right?"

"Sure," I say.

Another scribble on the pad. "You'd also need to sign a full release and waiver in case of injury."

I feel my eyebrows rise, and Taffy's eyes widen in alarm.

"Don't look worried! It's not that my sister would hurt you! Coco's delusional, not violent—at least not particularly—but it's the environment. The trekking, you know. It's a warm year, so most of the snow is melted, but it's the *mountains*." Taffy pronounces the word like *flesh-eating dinosaur*.

"Happy to sign a waiver," I say untruthfully. I'd prefer not to sign anything, but Taffy clearly has a checklist of boxes that must be ticked if I want the job. *Do* I want the job?

As if on cue, Taffy appears to check another box. "Okay, so good listener, discreet, NDA, full release and waiver," she mutters to herself. "Ah! How do you feel about Nazis?"

Why is she asking about Nazis? Little Voice bangs an alarm bell.

My great-grandmother was a Jewish refugee who escaped Nazi Germany. I had only been eight when she passed away, and I knew hardly anything about her life. Like Grandmother, I hadn't been raised religiously or culturally Jewish. I only learned about my great-grandmother's origins because I stumbled on a *Life* magazine interview from the seventies, just after Grandmother won her first Academy Award. The article didn't have much detail, and Grandmother refused to answer questions, citing her mother's privacy.

Regardless, there is only one answer to Taffy's question: "I'm not a fan of Nazis," I say. And then I become concerned. "Are *you* a fan?"

"Of course I'm not a fan of Nazis!" Taffy's eyes pop. "It is an absolute prerequisite that you *not* like Nazis."

"Phew!" I mime wiping my forehead. "No worries there, and"—I rush to clarify because even if desperate for a job, I'm not without standards—"I would never work for someone who likes Nazis."

"That's a relief." Taffy smiles. "Very happy to hear we align on the Nazi issue."

Who doesn't align on the Nazi issue? I decide to chalk it up to her paranoia about the type of people who may be inclined to respond to a job advertised on social media involving free international travel and few to no real qualifications.

Taffy looks back down at her checklist. "And the final item." Her pen hovers as she looks at me expectantly. "Do you have any hunting experience?"

"Like—with a gun?" I flounder, wondering if part of the job will involve ferreting out Nazis who have spent the last seventy-five years evading justice in remote Alpine huts, living in squalor but for a Picasso on the wall, snatched from Taffy's family. On the one hand, they're sure to be old and slow at this point. On the other, all I have experience hunting is bargains that look expensive and cupboards for chocolate stashes I may have forgotten about.

"It's just . . . we don't *exactly* know where my sister is. We have an area where she probably is, but you'll have to look for her. As in, hunt for her. Maybe *tracking* is a better word. Do you have tracking experience?"

I try to mask my growing incredulity. "Is your sister in danger?"

"Of course not!" Taffy's face suggests my question is ridiculous. "Not that we know of. And if she is, it wouldn't be your job to get involved in anything dangerous."

"It's just . . . maybe you need someone with more experience, like a private investigator?"

"That's exactly what most people would do." Taffy shakes her head. "My sister will see that coming a mile away. That's why I advertised specifically for a Bearer of Bad News."

"I see," I say, even though I don't. Warning lights start flashing. I consider my next words carefully. "Not to imply anything negative—that's certainly not my intention—but is your sister involved in something illegal?"

"Of course not!" Taffy laughs as if I've said something hilarious. "It's really more of a family drama that's gotten out of hand. My father passed away a few weeks ago, and my sister—" Taffy tilts her head and taps her lip as she muses. "What to say before you've signed the NDA. I wish my lawyer were on the call. Maybe I can text him." She fiddles with her phone but then looks up. "Will you promise not to say anything?"

I nod.

"Great, can you say *yes* out loud instead of just nodding, so it's legally binding?"

"Yes," I say, not at all sure that saying the word out loud makes it legally binding.

Taffy leans closer to the screen. "My sister went a little crazy. Like full-on conspiracy theories. She has this whole story in her head about something that happened with my father, and—" Taffy sighs. "Honestly, I'm worried about her, but we're not on the best of terms right now."

"So you want me to find her and tell her—" I pause, but Taffy doesn't complete the sentence. I decide to be blunt. "What's the bad news?"

"No more questions." Taffy puts a finger in front of her lips. "Not unless you get the job and sign the NDA."

Taffy goes on to outline the particulars of what she calls the "gig": flights to Italy and back, all expenses reimbursed ("like three-star expenses, nothing over the top"), and a per diem of $100 per day. And—best part for last—if I'm successful, I'll walk away with the $25,000 success fee.

My heart quickens in anticipation. With that money, I could pay out both leases, move back to Reno, and then train for another job and get out of hairdressing for good. Not that I'd ever really wanted to be a hairdresser anyway. After graduation, while I struggled to decide what to do next, it had been an easy thing to do part-time in between trying (and hating) other possibilities. Interior design, physical therapy, photography, real estate . . . I'd sort of pursued all of these and more. Basically, I was the Goldilocks of jobs and had yet to find one that was just right.

"You do need the money?" Taffy asks. "Otherwise, I doubt you would have applied for this little assignment. I'm guessing you're estranged from Genevieve?"

I do not want to comment on Grandmother, but I have to know. In a careful tone, I venture, "Can I ask how you know she's my grandmother?" It is not common information.

"A background check, of course." Taffy doesn't miss a beat. "I'm not wasting my time interviewing applicants who clearly aren't suitable."

Would Grandmother's name really come up in a background check on me? Even for professionals, Grandmother's move to Switzerland, where privacy was no joke and records weren't in English, made digging difficult. Not only that, but Grandmother and I never had the same last name. My mother had changed her last name to Rey sometime before I was born. She needed a fresh start, Grandmother said, though how she landed on Rey was a mystery. Grandmother had been supportive, which wasn't surprising, given that she had gone from Sophie Edelstein to Genevieve Saint herself. These were women who believed in reinvention.

"Do you speak with her?" Taffy continues.

"Miss Waters, I don't want to be rude, but—"

"Say no more." Another of Taffy's crystal-bell laughs. "You probably have one of those trust funds that you can't access until you're thirty. Or maybe you were cut off. Was it drugs? Or your . . . alternative lifestyle?"

Alternative lifestyle? "You mean—?" I have no idea what she means.

"Oh, honey." Taffy shakes her head in apparent sympathy. "I can't even imagine. Or I can imagine, but I probably shouldn't. It's something Max and I are working on in couples therapy."

Does she know about Julian and Mr. Chippy? It seems unlikely that a background report ready in less than twenty-four hours could include that level of detail, but Taffy seems to be waiting for me to say something. Since I don't know what she's talking about or whether commenting on her couples therapy would make me a good listener (check) or put me on the wrong side of discretion (un-check), I nod (again). My interview responses are mostly impersonating a bobblehead.

Taffy continues, "I don't want to pry into your personal life, but am I right that you could call your grandmother—if you needed her, I mean?"

I blink. "I mean, I know her phone number."

"I imagine that she would just *die* if she knew I was quizzing you like this. She's always been so private, hasn't she?" Taffy leans forward, her eyes boring into mine through the video screen.

Is Taffy some sort of superfan? I try to think of a graceful way to avoid talking about Grandmother's legendary obsession with privacy, but in the end, I'm saved by the dog. Frantic barking sounds directly into the microphone. "Down, Muppet!" Taffy scolds as a puff of beige fur bounds in front of her screen.

I see a pink tongue and one roguish dog eye. "Hello, Muppet," I say, recognizing at once that Taffy is the sort of dog person who will expect Muppet to be greeted.

"Say hi to Lucy!" A hand grabs Muppet's paw and puppeteers it into a wave. "Hello, hello!" a cartoonish Taffy voice squeaks.

Muppet barks. Taffy's screen lilts sideways. "No, Muppet, no!" I see a polished wood floor. Taffy's face reappears. "Lucy?" She is nearly shouting. "Lucy, can you hear me?"

"Yes," I say.

More barking. Another dog seems to have joined the mix, this one snow white.

"Lucy, it's been wonderful to meet you." Taffy is breathless. "I think I have all the information I need. Stop that! Stop it!" I can no longer see any parts of Taffy, only white and beige fur. "I have a few more applicants to speak with, but I expect you'll be hearing back from me shortly." The barking reaches a crescendo.

"Muppet! Can't you see I'm on the phone?" The screen jumps again. "You can see it's *chaos* here, Lucy. Absolute chaos. Can we agree to chat again soon?"

"Yes," I say.

"Ciao, ciao!" The screen goes dark.

Adam's voice comes from behind me. "Whoever that was, I love her."

"You're like a ninja," I tell him. "I didn't hear you come in."

"I am good, aren't I?" Adam smirks. "Had a half day today and rushed home to try to catch you in bed doomscrolling Julian. It was going to be the *aha* moment that started my intervention, but now you may not need it." Adam spots my attire. "You're wearing my shirt."

"Sorry," I say.

"Are you kidding? You can borrow my toothbrush if it gets you out of the apartment. That was a job interview, wasn't it?"

"For a job I'm not going to take," I say, though my heart contracts as if in disagreement. "Well, maybe I'll take it. Who am I to turn down a free trip to Italy?"

"A free trip to Italy? I'm suspicious already."

I pull up the advertisement and hand Adam my phone so that he can see for himself. "Well," he says, handing back my phone after reading, "if this didn't sound so sketchy, I'd have to concede that you are basically the poster child for a Bearer of Bad News."

"What's that supposed to mean?"

"Come on, Lu. Remember you told that guy at senior prom that his mole was probably cancerous? Or when you informed the diner waitress that she did not look like a natural redhead or when you told Maurice that it did sound like his boss hated him? Too bad it isn't exactly a profession."

"But what if it could be?" I challenge, even though I had been thinking along the exact same lines only moments before.

"Wait, are you seriously considering this?" Adam frowns.

"You know those times when you have absolutely nothing to lose?" When our eyes meet, I make no effort to hide the lower-than-low heartbreak I feel. "I think this is one of those times. And how else can I make twenty-five grand in a week?"

Adam's frown deepens, but then he sighs and walks over to the desk. "Then I guess we better start figuring out if this job is legit. What did you find out about her online?"

"I haven't really looked her up yet."

Adam scoldingly tsks before taking possession of the laptop. "Thank God I'm here."

I follow Adam to the couch and lean over his shoulder to spell out TAFFY WATERS. He obediently types her name into the search bar. Pages of results materialize.

When Adam clicks on the Images tab, Taffy's face framed by two decades of different hairstyles and outfits and jewels stares out at us from the photography archives of dozens of different galas and fundraisers.

"That's her," I say. "At least we know that's her real name."

"She's a career socialite," Adam observes, returning to the search results. "With a Wikipedia page." He clicks on it.

Countess Tabitha "Taffy" Georgiana Wellington Ernst
(née Carter; born July 1, 1973), professionally known
as Taffy Waters, is an American socialite, dog breeder,
actress, model, singer, artist, animal rights activist, writer,
and DJ. She is best known for her roles in the films *Gnomes*
of Venice (2001); *Northy's Pole* (2005); and *Henchmen 2:*
The Legend of Danny Patrick's Crucible (2011).

Adam looks up. "I must know about *Northy's Pole* immediately! How have we not seen these movies?"

"Don't get distracted!" I continue to read. Taffy trains Pomeranians (that explains Muppet and the mystery dog), paints in both oil and watercolor, and is married to Count Maxwell Ernst, a minor noble from one of those European empires that no longer exists. She splits her time between London and Los Angeles. No mention of a family feud, no mention of a sister, and no mention of people who hate water.

"She's fabulous," Adam breathes. "It says here she's vegan, but one of her books is called *95 Ways to Cook with Bacon*."

"Maybe all that bacon turned her vegan?" I look to the little window to the right that normally has biographical information, but other than the noble husband Adam mentioned, the box is empty.

Adam tries Coco Waters and then Coco Carter. No results, other than some adult-only website hits. "*That* could be interesting," Adam says.

"Don't click those!" I stop him. "Coco is a nickname. That should have been obvious. I mean, unless the parents were acid tripping . . ."

"Or rich people. Don't you remember that Madeline's mom's pet name was Pooh?"

I cackle. "I died when you called her Pooh to her face at graduation."

We grin at each other.

"It's clear we need to dig deeper." Adam snaps the laptop shut. "I'll call Maurice."

"Oh, really? You'll call Maurice?" I arch an eyebrow.

"What?" Adam feigns innocence. "Is it my fault that he's amazing at internet research?"

"Right, it's the internet research," I joke as I walk toward the bathroom, already unbuttoning Adam's shirt to change back into my sweatshirt. In truth, Maurice works for an agency with an acronym and can't tell us anything about his job. While I've never seen his internet skills in action, Adam is likely right that they are impressive.

But before Maurice arrives for pizza and sleuthing, my phone pings with a new message from the sunset avatar.

Muppet & I loved meeting u. Can tell ur the right pick. Can u leave Saturday? Taffy

Unilateral Confidentiality Agreement

COUNTESS TABITHA GEORGIANA WELLINGTON ERNST (aka "Taffy Waters") (hereinafter "Disclosing Party") and LUCY REY (hereinafter "Receiving Party") agree as follows:

1. <u>Confidential Information</u>. Receiving Party will not, directly or indirectly—whether through oral, written, or other forms of communication, allusion, or body movements—reveal, suggest, or otherwise disclose, confirm, or deny what Disclosing Party, or any of her Associates, living or dead, may or may not have, or had, in their possession, as it relates to jewelry, jewels, or other items of value. Receiving Party agrees that due to the sensitive nature of her contractual engagement with Disclosing Party, an expanded definition of Confidential Information is required to protect Disclosing Party and that Confidential Information will mean all information disclosed before, on, or after the Effective Date to Receiving Party by Disclosing Party or her family members, friends, pets, advisors, or affiliates (collectively, "Associates"), whether disclosed orally or via written, electronic, auditory, or other means, including body language.

2. <u>Indemnification</u>. Receiving Party shall defend, indemnify, and hold harmless Disclosing Party and Associates from and against all losses, damages, liabilities, deficiencies, actions, judgments, interest, awards, penalties, fines, costs, or expenses of whatever kind, including attorneys' fees, in connection directly or indirectly from a breach of this Agreement by Receiving Party. Receiving Party further agrees that wages, inheritances, and any and all other sources of income can be garnished in perpetuity to satisfy any and all financial obligations to Disclosing Party.

3. <u>Further Terms and Penalties</u>. Receiving Party agrees to the remedies, warranties, and penalties related to any direct or indirect breach of this Agreement attached hereto as Appendices 1–12.

SIX

In the end, I say yes to becoming a Bearer of Bad News because of a photo that Aksel posts to Instagram: two hands intertwined in front of an ethereal ocean sunset. On one hand, a small mole on the outside of the left thumb. Julian's mole. Well, this explains why Julian hasn't texted to ask where I am, as I had presumed he would after returning to the Vegas apartment and finding me gone. But no, he's still with Aksel.

As is often the case, Adam senses my unasked questions about whether I've spent four years being a beard or if any part of my relationship was real. "People can be attracted to more than one gender," he says diplomatically.

I know this is true intellectually—Kinsey's research on sexuality as a spectrum and all that—but I never thought about such nuances in the context of my own relationship. Still, the possibility that Julian is experimenting gives me hope. Couples recover from affairs all the time, don't they?

"Your relationship is suffering from more than this affair, honey." Adam has blown through his diplomacy.

"I have to get away," I say miserably.

"At first I was only twenty percent serious, but maybe you really should take the job. If it's a scam, then hiring a legion of lawyers to draft all those contracts she sent would be shockingly all-in. Crazy as it seems, Taffy might be legit."

"Or maybe she wants to kidnap me and ransom me to Grandmother," I say darkly.

Adam snorts. "Didn't she say you'd have your own rental car? Not a great kidnap plan as far as that goes."

After seeing Julian's mole clasped in Aksel's hand, not even potential kidnapping can deter me. Anything to escape from my life.

Given my family's history with happily-ever-afters, it should have been obvious that I wouldn't marry my first serious boyfriend and sail away into the sunset without a hitch. There was my mother, who had, it seemed, hardly even dated my father, let alone married him. And then there was Grandmother.

The world agrees that Genevieve Saint was very unlucky in love. Married four times to men from four different countries—the United States, Argentina, Japan, and finally Switzerland—all except the last of whom left her.

Grandmother's final marriage—to the only one of her husbands I ever met, a Swiss construction magnate—was the most successful, or at least the longest lasting. The press incorrectly assumed Matthias prompted Grandmother's abrupt retirement from Hollywood when he whisked her away to the lakeside chalet that was left to her upon his death and where I spent my early years. In truth, Grandmother landed in Switzerland well before she met Matthias, when she assumed the role of Reclusive Former Star Caring for her Aged Mother.

Even if Grandmother's romantic history was a rather rocky ride, I have to admire that she never allowed a relationship to hold her life hostage. Maybe I need a little of that energy. I picture Julian finally texting and me archly replying: Sorry, in Italy. Let's talk when I'm back.

And so it is that I find myself at the Reno airport Saturday morning, heading off for adventures unknown exactly two weeks after discovering Mr. Chippy stole my fiancé.

"Do you have your US passport?" Adam mimes holding an imaginary clipboard.

"Check."

"Swiss passport in case that gets you into a shorter line at customs?"

"Check." One of the benefits of Grandmother's marriage to Matthias was that we had both eventually gotten Swiss citizenship.

"NDA?"

"Uncheck. I told you I'm not carrying that thing to Italy!"

The NDA, waiver, and a confusingly titled consultancy contract (role: Bearer of Bad News) had arrived by certified mail within hours after Taffy offered me the job. Together they were as thick as a magazine. Adam and I (and even Maurice) had tried to read through them all once I decided to accept the position, but Taffy was clear that the terms were nonnegotiable so there wasn't much of a point, especially since I wasn't in a financial position to hire a lawyer to negotiate on my behalf anyway. After confirming that the agreement included a $25,000 payment upon "successful location of the sister of Countess Tabitha Georgiana Wellington Ernst (aka Taffy Waters) and deliverance of the bad news specified," I signed everything.

"I'll send you a scanned copy." Adam shakes his fake clipboard at me. In his view the NDA is the most likely of the agreements to be problematic. "If you violate the contract, she won't reimburse your expenses, which sucks, but if you violate the NDA, she can basically ruin your life with lawsuits. You need to take it seriously, Lu. Wasn't there something about seizing your future wages?"

I shrug.

Adam shakes his head. "You're hopeless. Did you at least bring the info Taffy emailed last night? I printed it out for you."

"I did." I give Adam a thumbs-up and haul my backpack out of the backseat. "Guess this is it."

"Don't make me regret my half-hearted support for this crazy venture." Adam gets out of the car and engulfs me in a huge hug. "Find that biatch and get back here. Without your third-wheel energy blocking my mojo, my therapist is going to be out of work."

I give Adam one last squeeze and pull away. "Try movement therapy," I suggest. "That work is never done."

And just like that, I'm off on my first gig as a Bearer of Bad News.

As foreshadowed by Taffy, "all expenses paid" does not encompass four-star travel, or even extra leg room. After changing planes in New York, I end up in a middle economy seat over the wing.

The roar of the jet engine competes with the Mr. Chippy-esque munch noises of the seatmate to my right, who is working her way through a giant bag of trail mix. The seatmate to my left took what I assume was a sleeping pill minutes after takeoff, and her head periodically droops onto my shoulder.

To distract myself, I pull out the pages Adam printed from Taffy's email. At least, Adam and I assumed Taffy was the sender, though the email address was info@bestatallofitllc.com, and the message wasn't signed. Just a subject line, Good luck, and an attachment.

"Shady as fu—" Adam had said when I showed him the email. But by then I had already canceled the last of the hair appointments booked at the Vegas salon and was free as a bird and all in. It was too late to decide that Taffy was shady or the quest ill-fated.

The attachment turned out to be mostly administrative trip details and information on how to submit expenses and receive my $100 per diem. A roundtrip ticket to Verona via Rome, a car rental reservation at the Verona airport, and a hotel confirmation in Ortisei through Friday, which Taffy hoped would be enough time for me to locate her sister. For now, she'd booked me an airport hotel for next Friday evening and an early Saturday morning flight back to Reno.

"We can change the flight if things are going well," Taffy assured me during our last call before my departure. "But you need to update me daily on your efforts, whether via phone or email." There could be, Taffy noted delicately, a temptation by a certain type of person to do no work and collect the $100 per diem. "That's why, as I'm sure you already saw in the contract, we can end this arrangement with no notice and without any per diem or expense payments if it seems like you aren't taking this seriously."

I had noticed that part of the contract but wasn't concerned—I had no intention of giving Taffy a reason to withhold payment.

The next pages were copied from an article about Ortisei and the surrounding region. Adam had read through everything and, as usual, embraced educating me. Some of the information I already knew, like the Dolomites technically being part of the Alps, but the rest of Adam's trivia was new to me.

"Did you know the Dolomites were part of the Austro-Hungarian Empire before being annexed to Italy at the end of World War I?" Adam had asked last night as I attempted to pack from the random assortment of clothing I had thrown into the Prius when I fled Las Vegas.

"We learned about the Congress of Vienna in eleventh grade. Don't you remember?" Adam persisted.

I didn't.

"In 1814? Ringing any bells?" Adam looked exasperated. "It's interesting stuff, Lu. This area has been passed around since the Roman occupation in 15 BC. They still speak indigenous languages, and German is just as common there as Italian, which will be lucky for you."

It was optimistic of Adam to assume I still spoke good German, but I had spent my formative years living in Switzerland, so one could hope.

Adam continued to assault me with information from the packet Taffy had sent, from culture to local foods. The last page was a color photo. The iconic color-shifting pastel stone of the Dolomites protruded like jagged incisors from a verdant green valley, the gigantic scale evident from the miniature white church steeple just visible in contrast. Clearly this last picture was meant as motivation in case I had any doubts about the trip.

"Gorgeous," I breathed, the photo doing its job.

Adam read the caption out loud: "The unique and shifting colors of the rock come from calcium and magnesium carbonate found in the stone—the phenomenon is called *enrosadira*, which means 'turning pink' in Ladin, a language spoken by many of the original inhabitants of the region."

Now recalling the unfamiliar sound of *enrosadira* and the hours Adam and Maurice have promised to spend picking through the internet for the smallest details about Taffy and her family, a spark of excitement flickers to life. Maybe I can really pull this off. And even if I never find Coco, soon I will see *enrosadira* with my own eyes—across the world from Julian and Aksel and whatever they might be doing right now.

After a flight delay on top of an already longish layover in Rome, it's midafternoon on Sunday when I finally land at the rather underwhelming Verona airport. I buy a lackluster sandwich to try to chew myself awake for the two-hour drive to Ortisei. Small airports have their perks, and I walk directly to the rental car agency booth. The itinerary Taffy sent me indicated that my reservation is with Suenos Italia. I thought *suenos* was a Spanish word, but apparently Italians dream in Spanish, or the other way around.

Despite the lines in front of most of the other booths, absolutely no one else is waiting to rent a car from Suenos Italia. The teenager behind the desk is named Franco.

He leads me to a silver two-door sedan, which is at least ten years old. The car is missing a taillight and already has numerous dents and scrapes pre-marked on the form. The inside smells like stale cigar overlaid with the cloying pine of air freshener. "It's not our nicest car," Franco acknowledges, "but it does have Bluetooth."

As I open the driver's side door it sticks, emitting a noise like a badger shrieking from the hinges.

"I already marked that." Franco holds up the form to show me a large X over the driver's side door.

Only when on the open road passing unfamiliar highway signs in Italian, and then both Italian and German, does it hit me that my adventure has begun. The mountains are more ridgelike and looming than those in northern Nevada, the roads narrower, as I wind my way through towns of two-story wooden houses and flowers hanging out of window boxes.

Flower boxes have long made me nostalgic. For years I was sure that I had a memory of my mother in a faux fur hat throwing a snowball at me with red window-box flowers in the background, but it's unlikely the memory is real. Snow and flowers are not often found together, and I was only four the last time I saw my mother—in New York City and not Switzerland—further discrediting the vivid memory.

Even so, my brain persists with such fantasies from time to time. The sound of her singing ("She was a horrible singer, it's a blessing you can't remember that," Grandmother said) and the smell of her perfume ("She didn't wear perfume") and the sound of her and Grandmother screaming at each other ("That you might have heard"). And then, only blank space where memories of a mother should be, ending with the memory of Grandmother telling me that my mother had died in a car crash.

There's even less to remember about my father, who returned to hitchhiking around Europe with his band shortly after I was conceived, according to Grandmother. I was unlikely to ever find him unless I was willing to give my DNA to an ancestry website with a shadowy privacy policy. Of course, Grandmother forbade such things when she had the right to forbid me, and even after she lost that right, I remain hesitant.

I squeeze my eyes shut for a second, bleary from sleep deprivation and the hypnotic winding roads. Thinking about Grandmother is a sure sign of exhaustion. Thank God I'm nearly there. The sun has set, and the mountains around me are now dark shadows, signs of habitation few and far between.

When I finally reach Ortisei—nestled in one of the valleys that wrap around the mountains—it is fairy-tale quaint. Lights twinkle in wooden houses, and the huge hulk of the Dolomites cuts a hard edge against the pearl-gray sky.

I had high hopes for the hotel Taffy booked given its name—the Grand Hotel Ortisei—but these are dashed when I enter. Situated on a small side street in the town's center, the old building looks charming at first, but inside, the hospital lighting and scuffed floors evoke a youth hostel. I'm too tired to care.

I mumble something incomprehensible, but the elderly man behind the front desk still manages to guide me through the process of handing over my passport and reservation number. In German no less, which I'm pleased to find that I still understand. Soon my name is handwritten into a guest ledger—apparently, the lack of technology is part of the hotel's charm—and I receive an old-fashioned key attached to a clunky wooden square with the number 7 painted on it.

Seven could have been a lucky number, but when I open the door, the room is cramped with a narrow twin bed and desk, a faint mildew smell, and curtains so thin that I can see through to vague shapes outside. The shapes are, I learn when I open the drapes, not the mountains like I'd hoped but a small parking lot and what looks like the back of a restaurant. I kick off the combat boots I wore on the plane and collapse onto the bed.

For a moment, it's like I've never left Adam's. This mattress also shrieks like a seagull. That is my lot in life—in this chapter, at least. On the wall across from the bed, a tacky framed poster of a bear in a ruff juggling what look like bowling pins assaults my eyes. I close them to escape the bear's jaunty grin and fall asleep fully clothed, forgetting all about contacting Taffy Waters.

NOTE: The scan quality–a copy of a copy–is poor, with parts difficult to decipher. As a result, the letter will be added to the file in reconstructed parts.

Dear Samuel,

Our journey here was even harder than I imagined it would be, and if I don't survive, you deserve to know how you ended up in these mountains a thousand kilometers from where you were born.

Shall I start with the necklace? For most of the journey from Berlin, a fortune in emeralds was sewn into the seam of my overcoat. Their color was unlike anything I had ever seen—the green of new spring leaves uncurling and lit by the first rays of sun. On freezing-cold nights huddled by the side of a road, I distracted myself by imagining what the miners in Colombia thought when such a color emerged from the brown earth, whether they noticed it before selling the stones on to India for far less than they were worth.

Perhaps India is where the true splendor of the stones emerged, when they were cut and polished. Surely their brilliance was appreciated if they were considered worth sending on to France. Your grandfather always said it was amazing to think of how much was possible more than two hundred years ago—for jewels to journey such distances powered by nothing more than humans and beasts and boats. They landed in the Imperial Crown Jewels of Empress Eugénie, soon deposed when the French monarchy collapsed, and then on to a Prussian industrialist named Guido who became a count. It is he who had the jewels fashioned into this necklace along with a very famous tiara, likely by the famed jeweler Chaumet. I tell you this only so you know the value, even of a single stone. This is your inheritance. Or it was. The necklace should have guaranteed a life of ease and security, but I failed you.

SEVEN

When I open my eyes to the bear's taunting smirk, I remember that I forgot to call Taffy and fumble frantically for my phone.

For possibly the first time ever, I'm grateful to wake up at three a.m. Taffy, nine hours behind me in California, will still be awake. But it's only now I realize that Taffy and I only ever communicated via social media messaging and the video call links she provided. She never gave me a phone number.

This oversight isn't exactly surprising. Even after I signed the NDA, Taffy had been less than forthcoming about her sister and had shut down most of my inquiries about Coco, including her actual name, until I was "in situ." Without more information, my first day on the job will be useless, and I need to hit the ground running if I have any hope of getting the $25,000.

I decide to send a DM to the sunset avatar. While waiting for Taffy to (hopefully) respond, I take advantage of the hotel's surprisingly strong Wi-Fi to video call Adam through WhatsApp. Messaging apps through Wi-Fi are my only link to the outside world until I get a local SIM card, which I'd forgotten to buy at the airport. Fearmongered by Maurice about astronomical fees while abroad, I had temporarily suspended my US number with my carrier before leaving the country.

"You owe Maurice a drink," Adam says without preamble. He is smiling widely in a neon-pink vest.

"I haven't watched *CSI* all these years for nothing." Maurice pops up next to Adam.

"Oh, really, *CSI*?" Adam and I both pretend to believe Maurice when he claims to have a boring desk job.

"Maurice is amazing," Adam says.

I clear my throat, wondering if, with my third-wheel energy out of the way, Adam has moved himself out of the friend zone.

"Let's hear it," I say.

For the next fifteen minutes, Adam and Maurice take turns speaking. I feel like a military captain getting reconnaissance reports from my forward scouts. Arms wave, they talk over one another, and arguments ensue about where "the trail" leads. They agree that the available information is sparse because, it turns out, Coco is technologically savvy. And also, her given name is Catherine.

"That part was tough to figure out," Maurice says. "But we took the photo Taffy sent you"—Taffy had emailed a scanned snapshot of Coco so I would know who to look for, but it was poor quality and presumably quite outdated—"and I ran it through this facial recognition software—"

"Is that even legal?" I interrupt.

"Technically it's unregulated—"

"Let him finish!" Adam commands.

"Anyway, the software found her face in a news article, and"—Maurice hits the table with a loud whack—"Catherine Carter, there you are!"

"Once we had her name, we were off," Adam says.

After observing Adam's years of internet stalking, I knew no stone would be left unturned. But I don't say that in front of Maurice.

Adam and Maurice quickly summarize what they've uncovered: Catherine was trained as a lawyer and devoted herself to human rights law. She has a prestigious job at a war crimes tribunal in The Hague. No active social media accounts identified and no online presence. She and Taffy were the only children of Natasha Bogner, a New York socialite, and John Carter, a much older hedge-fund financier. Neither Adam nor Maurice could find out much more.

"We're emailing you a better photo." Adam holds a color printout up to the camera. "This was in the tribunal's web archives."

Unlike the snapshot from Taffy, which showed a smiling girl with long hair and a carefree smile, the Coco in Adam's picture has cropped hair and intense eyes. The photo was taken at a court appearance, and she is wearing the standard black robe and pleated white bib favored by international criminal mechanisms.

"The caption says, 'Catherine Carter laments the acquittal of Ivan Lukic, accused of overseeing the massacre of two hundred and fifty Roma villagers in the former Yugoslavia.'" Adam looks somber.

"That explains the intense eyes," I say. My phone buzzes with another incoming video call from an unknown number. "That might be Taffy," I say. "Call you later?"

Adam waves me off, and I accept the video request.

"Ciao!" Taffy calls gaily. She is wearing long sparkly earrings and her hair looks professionally styled. In the background, I hear what sounds like a party.

"I hope I'm not keeping you from something fun." I self-consciously brush the rat's nest of hair away from my face.

"You are." Taffy winks. "But obvi I stepped away to see how you're doing."

"I made it here!" My smile feels brittle, but I soldier on, refraining from judgmentally panning the camera around to show the spartan room and tacky juggling bear poster. After all, maybe Taffy had delegated finding my hotel to someone else. And what did I expect? At least I have my own bathroom.

"Wonderful, wonderful!" Taffy seems to be texting while talking to me, leading to odd angles of her face jumping into and out of view, as if she's forgotten the camera is on.

I sense that I'm losing her. "You said that when I arrived you'd tell me where to start looking for Coco. Otherwise, I have no idea how to find her."

I try for a laugh that suggests this is merely an amusing inconvenience rather than setting me up for failure.

"Oh, right." Taffy's eyes refocus.

"How do you know she's in Ortisei?" I decide to start at the beginning.

Taffy taps her lip, a gesture I recall from our interview. "I knew she'd head to Ortisei because it was part of her delusion."

"What delusion?"

"That's not relevant. The point is that she was there, as of last week. At least her IP address was in that area when she logged into her email."

"You can track her IP address?" If I sound skeptical, it's because that sounds illegal, but Taffy nods as if people track IP addresses all the time.

"But honestly it's not as helpful as you'd think—it only narrows things down to an area, and she's hardly checked her email at all!" Taffy pouts. "I also had someone call all the hotels in the vicinity, and she's not registered at any of them, unless she's using a different name. And with all these people renting out bedrooms and cottages and treehouses, she doesn't exactly need a hotel. And there are whole networks of trails that go all over the mountain range. Weeks of trails. Months of trails. A whole rifugio system where you can stay in a different place every night. Maybe she's doing that. It would be just like Coco. That's why we need someone like you on the ground, doing a hut-to-hut search or whatever."

"A hut-to-hut search?" I stare at Taffy, dumbfounded. Perhaps I had been naïve to assume that Taffy wouldn't bother flying me to Italy without more to go on.

"I mean, that's just one idea." Taffy puffs out her cheeks, but the skin seems reluctant to move. "She also mentioned this bar to me—'the oldest bar in Ortisei,' she said. It was the first place I called three weeks ago when I realized Coco hadn't gone home after our father died. Sure enough, the woman who answered had seen Coco. Not that she knew where Coco was staying."

"What did Coco say about the bar?" This sounds like a better place to start than the vague suggestion of hut searching, but as usual, getting a straight answer from Taffy is a Herculean effort.

"Nothing, really. Maybe she read about it somewhere and wanted to see it in person?" Taffy sounds like she's making up theories as she goes along.

"But why Ortisei?" I adopt my most encouraging tone to prompt disclosure.

"She took Daddy's death hard. We all did. His cancer had been in remission, but then—" For a moment, Taffy's mask of nonchalance cracks, and there is real grief on her face. "He went quickly, and he and Coco hadn't really been on speaking terms. I think they both thought there would be more time to reconcile. She made it over to say goodbye, but it wasn't pretty. He was on heavy drugs, and he was saying all sorts of crazy things, and Coco—"

Taffy's head droops as if weighted by an invisible crown. "She took his ravings a little too seriously."

"What was he saying?"

Taffy's face closes. "Look, I have no idea what sent Coco to Ortisei, not really. The truth is that she's been having a hard time. Her husband left her for one of his research assistants. She's deeply in debt—my father hadn't given her money in years, and she ran through her trust fund. Between that and his death, I don't think she's quite right in the head." She looks over her shoulder. "I need to get back to dinner."

"But if I find Coco, what am I supposed to tell her? You still haven't told me the bad news." I'm determined not to get off the phone until I know how to get my twenty-five grand.

Taffy's eyes narrow, her expression turning waspish. "You tell her that she is in legal peril, that she'll end up fired and disbarred if she doesn't return what she stole from me."

"That's the message?" I picture myself cornering Coco in a back alley with a Dick Tracy trench coat and a mouthful of threats. *Give Taffy what's Taffy's, eh, lady?* Maybe I'll chew on a fat cigar for effect.

"No, that's not what you tell her!" Taffy shakes her head in exasperation. "You say, 'Taffy has a police report ready to go. If you don't bring back what you took, your career will be over. The will is clear, and what you told me is a lie.'"

"Hold on," I say, springing up to get a piece of paper and a pen. "I want to write it down."

"Write it down?" Taffy explodes. "Don't write it down! Just repeat it back to me."

I do.

"Not 'what you told *me*.'" Taffy rolls her eyes. "*I'm* 'me'! So when you say it, use 'her.'"

Chastened, I repeat the message back several times until I've committed it to memory and Taffy is satisfied.

"After I give her this news, I get the bonus?" I clarify.

"Well, yes, if you prove you told her," Taffy says.

"But how do I prove—"

"It's all in your contract. Didn't you read it?"

"The contract is like a phone book. I tried, but—"

A man's hand reaches into the frame, wrapping itself around Taffy's bare shoulder. Taffy jumps when the manicured fingers graze her bare skin. It could be surprise, but to my cynical mind, it looks more as if she is recoiling.

"Darling, there you are. People are wondering where you got off to." The man's voice is cultured, with an accent I can't place.

A piece of coiffed hair has fallen into Taffy's eyes, and the man's fingers brush it away. I want to see his face, but only the dark blue sleeve of his blazer and a glimmer of white starched shirt are visible.

"I'm right here!" Taffy's face smooths, and her voice takes on a television commercial finish. She turns and leans out of frame, presumably to kiss the man, before turning back to me. "I'm afraid I have to run, Lucy."

"But—" I still have so many questions.

Taffy air-kisses the space in front of her phone camera. "Ciao, ciao!" The screen goes dark.

Under the unhinged stare of the ever-juggling bear, I text Adam: Can you and Maurice find anything else out about Taffy's recently deceased father? Sounds like he told Coco something before he died. Maybe even gave something to Coco that Taffy wants—hopefully not related to Nazis, but remember how you thought the jewelry reference in the NDA was weird? Could be connected. Also, anything more on the noble Taffy married? His cuticles put mine to shame. No judgment.

Despite my exhaustion, sleep refuses to come. Jet lag is real. My engagement ring, which I haven't yet managed to take off, burns against my finger. Technically the engagement came before the ring, the idea of marrying more a suggestion than a question from Julian during a boozy weekend trip to Vegas at the end of an evening of too many margaritas.

There was no ring then. The cubic zirconia came later. Lucky me. Not that I wanted a fancy ring. Expensive jewelry hadn't made me happy during my years with Grandmother. And I had agreed with Julian that cubic zirconia looked exactly the same (at least, it would have if he'd splurged for a platinum setting). But part of me still thinks that he could have at least sprung for a lab-grown diamond. Maybe I'm being materialistic, or maybe it wouldn't matter if I had otherwise felt valued in the relationship, but in light of recent events, the cubic zirconia feels jarringly prescient.

Unable to resist further poking the still-raw wound, I reach for my phone on the nightstand and pull up Julian's text messages. Nothing new. I expected as much. He had texted me only once after our disastrous phone call. I really do need time. Please, Lu.

My dozen or so responses back insisting with various degrees of begging, anger, entitlement, and sorrow that he owed me a conversation *right now* had been ignored. But surely leaving the country justifies another text, if only so that he knows I'm in a different time zone.

I finally settle on: Long story, but I'm in Italy. Still hoping we can talk. Where are you these days? I write: Sending three, but then delete it and end with a simple Lu.

Dear Ms. Saint,

Forgive my persistence in writing again, but my last letter must not have made it past your screeners, as otherwise I am sure you would have responded. My lawyer likewise had no luck in reaching you directly, so I'm afraid I must now be blunt. You may not be aware that your granddaughter is in my employ and currently en route to Ortisei. The name should be familiar to you, given your family history, but if not, I'm sure you have the resources to discover what I mean. As for why I am reaching out, that is something best discussed over the phone, but let me assure you that our interests are aligned. I want nothing more than to avoid circumstances that would bring your family's connections to Ortisei into the light.

Please contact me at your earliest convenience to discuss.

Yours sincerely,
Countess Tabitha Georgiana
Wellington Ernst

EIGHT

When I wake from my post-calls second sleep, it's nearly eleven a.m. So much for getting an early start. My body believes I'm still in Nevada, where it is now the middle of the night. Bright sunlight stabs my gritty eyes through the cheap curtains. After checking my phone (Julian has not texted back to inquire about my Italian adventure), I stumble toward the shower, stripping out of the travel clothes I slept in. The room is freezing because even in a warm year, May in the Dolomites is more winter than spring. Luckily, the hot water works.

When I emerge from my room at quarter to noon, the breakfast buffet is closed, and the maze of dark hallways is deserted. Not surprising, given that people don't come to the Dolomites to sit indoors. They come to hike and bike or at least to take the chairlift up to the top of the mountain to breathe the fresh air and enjoy one of the most beautiful vistas on the planet.

A little brass bell sits on top of the dark polished wood of the reception desk. Briskly I ding it. Instead of the wizened old gentleman from last night, someone new emerges from the back room. As he comes into view, I feel a pleasant thrum. He is the best-looking man I've ever seen in real life, like the cutest of the numerous famous actors named Chris.

He shoots me a dazzling smile, dimples splitting his face. He looks familiar, like someone I've met but can't place, possibly because of his resemblance to the Hollywood Chrises.

"Why, hello!" His accent is British or Australian or Kiwi, and he sounds absolutely delighted to greet me.

"You don't sound Italian," I muster. And then, to show I'm not a completely uncultured mess (and that I did read Taffy's fact sheet), I add, "Or German. Or Ladin."

A-plus, I congratulate myself. I nailed all the likely languages.

"Well-spotted," he says, but he doesn't offer more.

I smile and nod. He smiles and nods back. His dimples have the hypnotic power of a cobra.

After a moment, he asks, "Can I—help you with something?"

"Yes." I flash a guilty smile. I am, after all, an engaged woman. "I arrived last night."

"Good on you."

"Yes," I say. "Good on me." I'm fairly certain this is an Aussie expression and decide to be bold. "You're Australian?"

The dimples flash. "Yip." He has a friendly, golden retriever energy.

I nod, as if I'd known it all along. "I could use some advice. I'm here for a week, and I want to get an authentic feel for the place, not just the same spots all the tourists go."

"Right-o," says Dimples.

I'm hoping to ferret out some ideas of where to search for Coco, and Dimples is up for the task, orienting me to where I am on a tourist map and handing me a free bus pass that I can use to travel up and down the valley. As he writes and circles things, Dimples narrates advice, like not eating at the restaurant next door (overpriced) or taking the chairlift in the early morning ("It will still be too cold up there—everyone thinks they want an early start, but they won't enjoy it at those temperatures.").

This gives me exactly the intro I need to suss out whether he might have seen Coco around. "There must not be many tourists this early in the season."

Dimples shrugs. "There might be fewer people than high season, but you're in a town with more hotel beds than full-time residents."

"Ah." At this rate, I will never find Coco, a woman I've never met and have only a fifty-fifty chance of recognizing if she were standing right in front of me. I decide to throw discretion to the wind. "I'm actually looking for someone." I lower my voice conspiratorially, holding my head at an angle I long ago perfected so that my hair falls over my scar.

Dimples leans forward. "A particular someone?"

"Yes." I tell him in broad strokes about Coco and even pull up my phone to show Dimples the more recent photo Adam sent me. "Have you seen her?"

"A middle-aged woman of average appearance?" His smile widens. "Can't say that I have."

I wonder if I should add that the woman might be a thief who—based on the bad news I am set to deliver—is at risk of arrest and possibly in possession of stolen property. "How long have you worked here?" I ask, in case he started yesterday.

"For about two months." He picks up a paper clip and passes it back and forth between long fingers. "Initially I came for wintersport, but now I'm staying to hike."

I love the term "wintersport"—the European shorthand for winter activities, all of which include après ski.

"Sounds like you've been here long enough to know the area," I say. "If you were me, where would you start?"

The front desk phone rings, and Dimples puts up a hand while he answers. "Just one sec," he says into the receiver before turning back to me. "Look, tourists pass through here all the time, but if you stick around for longer than a week this time of year, the locals will know your shirt size and what you eat for breakfast. If I were you, I'd start by getting a lay of the land." With one last grin, he pushes the map and bus pass toward me and turns back to the phone.

I haven't gotten through all my questions, like where to find the oldest bar in town, but I can't bring myself to hover awkwardly while Dimples finishes his call. Unleashed on Ortisei, I head out into the sunshine. The spring feels suspiciously like fall, the air bracingly crisp. The tourist map Dimples provided confirms that Ortisei is not very large. Also, it has three names: Urtijëi in Ladin, Ortisei in Italian, and St. Ulrich in Gröden in German. "The Germans really phoned that one in," I mutter to no one.

Whatever its other failings, the hotel is centrally located. In less than two minutes, I am in the main square, a pedestrian zone surrounded by three-story buildings in tastefully muted pastel hues. A church sits at one end, its red onion dome like a Christmas bauble atop the cream-colored steeple. The Dolomites rise tall and formidable in the distance, purplish in this light and still partly snow-covered. The town, like the hotel, feels deserted—perhaps because it's still early in the season, and most people are off doing outdoor activities in the mountains.

Despite the chill, a few optimistic outdoor tables with heat lamps at the ready wait empty in front of cafes. In the center of the square, a fountain surrounded by pink flowers spurts streams of water in four directions. Frozen in bronze, two naked boys climb onto an orb at its center, a third kneeling nearby with a hand extended as if hoping for a tip. A lone elderly man with a cane and a dog on a leash holds a water bottle beneath one of the streams. He is nattily dressed with wingtip shoes and a tweed jacket. The dog less so. With mangy fur and an oversized head, it looks like an unfortunate cross between a wolf and a sheepdog.

"Are you sure you can drink the water?" I decide this is as good a conversation starter as any. When the man doesn't answer, I dust off my German. The words come out in an accent that feels like an unoiled hinge.

"This water is safe to drink." The man replies in German, gesturing to a sign beneath the fountain that says as much.

"Wow." I'm already loving this alpine life. He looks like a local, so I continue. "Is one of these the oldest bar in Ortisei?" I gesture around the square, where I can see at least three establishments that might fit the bill.

He pulls at his suspenders, alerting me to the fact that he is, for reasons unknown, wearing suspenders. "That one." He points to the plainest of the options, which has no outdoor tables and a firmly closed door.

I thank him and am about to ask about Coco, but he has already turned away with his dog in tow.

None of the bars look open yet, so I continue on. In fifteen minutes, I've covered most of the town, which is almost entirely hotels and restaurants and shops catering to outdoor sports. I find a small grocery store, planning to buy a new SIM card with a data plan, but the clerk tells me they are sold out.

Not ideal, but I don't let it derail me. I buy a few protein bars and then head for the upper town, via a series of escalators and moving walkways to mid-mountain. A babbling creek and walking path stretch out into tall trees on either side.

A bit farther on is the entrance to the Furnes chairlift. Dimples circled this on the map with a "Must-see!" notation. According to the ticket window, the lift will take me nearly three thousand feet up to the summit of Mount Seceda.

I buy a ticket and push through a turnstile gate to the loading platform. The closed chairlift cars are red with huge domed windows and bench seating. The oversized bubbles rotate continuously through the station, up the mountain and back down, slowing at zenith and nadir long enough for passengers on the platform to walk on and off. A man in a booth raises a hand in greeting and gestures me toward an approaching car. Four to six people could crowd in during a busy winter season, but today I have the cabin to myself.

The looming mountains are now the shifting color of a dappled trout. Before rising above the town, the lift passes house after house built in the traditional alpine style, peaked roofs and flowers spilling out of planters on balcony rails.

All of it is beautiful but not so different from Switzerland, though Grandmother was not particularly outdoorsy, and we were most certainly not a mountain-peak kind of family. That she chose to live ringed by mountains she would never scale was only one of her many peculiarities. Enough money to live anywhere and do anything, and yet she stayed in a place she claimed to hate, as if the years she spent as one of Hollywood's highest-paid actors simply never happened. Maybe, from her perspective, they hadn't. Experiences were like water in a river: they were there and then gone. When the flower of fame faded, perhaps it was as if you had never been famous at all.

I had no way of knowing. But after only a few weeks apart from Julian,

I already felt as if I might have imagined the minutes and hours and days of the life we had shared. Even the realest things are only ever a handful of moments away from being memories.

The lift reaches the peak, the doors sliding open for me to exit. The cold air hits me immediately, and I zip my jacket up to my chin. Technically, it's Adam's jacket—a bright orange number that normally I wouldn't be caught dead in—but given my haphazard packing when I fled Las Vegas, his was the warmest winter jacket available.

When I exit the chairlift station, I am slapped in the face with the Most Beautiful View I Have Ever Seen. I appreciate why the Dolomites are a bucket-list destination in a new way. Mountains. Vistas. Wildflowers. Blue skies. I am standing on a ridge above a green meadow nestled between peaks. Hiking trails snake out on all sides. Beyond the ridge, the green drops off sharply into a valley, ringed by yet more mountains in the distance.

My mouth drops, just a little.

A man a few feet away chuckles, then says in accented English, "First time here?"

I nod, my interest piquing when I catch sight of the speaker. A muscular man in his late twenties or early thirties, dressed in hiking pants and a navy down jacket, his jaw shadowed with just the right amount of stubble. If picked apart, none of his features would make any bestseller lists in a plastic surgeon's office, but together they form one of the most charismatic faces I have ever seen.

Also, he looks just like Olivier St. Trapezus, my unrequited college crush who took it in turns to blow me off and lead me on. Though it never went further than a few drunken make-out sessions, I pined after him until I met Julian, sure that if I could just be more, brighter, better, Olivier would (finally) take it beyond the "Will you be at so-and-so's party on Friday? See you there!" phase. He never did (nor did he show up to most of the events where he promised to see me).

Trouble, Little Voice warns. *Olivier St. Trapezus was always trouble.*

She isn't wrong.

"I think my mouth did the same thing when I first saw this view," the Olivier lookalike says.

I laugh nervously, reminded by the fluttering in my chest that I haven't had sex in six months. Rejection depressed Julian, each failed audition sucking away his sex drive like a parasite. I told him I understood and then bought a vibrator. Relationships went through ruts. It was all highly normal. ("NO!" Adam had practically screamed when I told him. "NOT NORMAL.")

"I've seen you in town." Not-Olivier snaps his fingers in recollection. "You're staying at the Dolomiti Resort Spa?"

Don't I wish I were staying anywhere else. "No, I'm at the Grand Hotel Ortisei."

He frowns. "I don't know it."

"Probably for the best." I grin self-consciously.

"If not for the lodging, then why Ortisei?" Wolfish eyes stare out from under a brooding forehead with an intensity that reminds me of one of the following: eccentric billionaire, drummer in an emo band, or trained assassin. I could be attracted to any of the above, which is how I know I'm in trouble.

"I'm here for work."

His eyebrows quirk in polite inquiry.

"I'm a Bearer of Bad News." I haven't referred to myself this way before, but I like the ring of it.

"A what?" He leans forward, as if he hasn't heard me properly.

"A Bearer of Bad News," I repeat. "If you have bad news you need to deliver, you can hire me to break it for you."

His forehead wrinkles, as if he finds the idea peculiar. "What kind of bad news are you delivering?"

"It's confidential." I pat at my hair, smoothing it over my scar. Even if I could tell him, how would I describe it? The situation raises more questions than answers.

But Olivier doesn't push. "Okay, then." He offers a half grin, just as wolfish as his eyes, and I wonder what it would be like to—

"Where are you from?" I blurt, partly out of curiosity and partly to distract myself. A flush is creeping up my neck, and I'm tempted to unzip my jacket.

"Everywhere," he says. "My dad is from Mexico but lived most of his life in San Diego, and my mom is French Moroccan. I grew up in Mexico City. Also in Paris." I can now detect the French in his accent, the way the words are clipped and curled. Another of those lopsided smiles. "So who is the unlucky recipient of your bad news?"

I pull out a photo of Coco, feeling better about the conversation now that it's officially work-related. "Have you seen her?"

Running a hand through stylishly windblown hair, he appears to consider. "I don't think I have. What is her name?"

I open my mouth to answer but then shut it. "I really shouldn't say. Sorry."

"Of course."

And then I have the crazy idea that I can smell him, a hint of alpine and something earthy, and I want to move closer. I take a step back. Damn pheromones. "I better get a move on." I look over my shoulder as if I can hear someone calling my name. "I'm getting a late start, and I want to hike, and—" I cut myself off before I can continue babbling and wave my hand goodbye like a demented Miss America. "Nice to meet you!"

Is this what it feels like to be in sex withdrawal? Is sex withdrawal even a thing?

"I'm David," he calls after me as I walk quickly away, drawing out the *i* so it sounds like a long *e*. "It was nice to meet you . . ."

His words trail off in an invitation. I understand that the courteous thing to do is provide my name to complete the introduction, but if I turn back, I might do something certifiable like blow him a kiss.

And why not? Little Voice devils me. After all, my fiancé has strayed. It might make it easier to reconcile if I have an affair of my own to even the score.

But what about the guy at reception? Little Voice nudges. *He's a way better option.* But of course she would say that.

Cold wind blasts against my cheeks, and I consider that if there were a snowdrift, the best course of action would be to throw myself directly into it. Sex withdrawal is, I decide, definitely a thing.

To my left, a path winds down a narrow peninsula to a small grass plateau on the knife's edge of a cliff. In the US, no one would have access because of lawsuits and liability—the whole area would be fenced off and plastered with warning signs. But in Italy, a person is allowed to be the master of their own stupidity.

A small crowd of hikers is concentrated on the plateau, some standing in clusters and some sitting with snacks and water bottles, all turned toward the hazy Morisot outline of the mountains beyond the plateau.

I turn off on the dirt path and make my way gingerly over the rocks toward the first group, all of whom are staring at a solitary figure obstructing the view. As I get closer, the figure sharpens into a woman, clad in black spandex, standing at the cliff's edge in tree pose. Honestly, her form is impressive. Arms in a wide Y, knee at a perfect ninety-degree angle. This is no idle practitioner. As I watch, she turns her back and splays her legs wide while staring boldly out into the great crevasse beyond.

It's then that I see the camera. Propped on a tripod, I hear it click like gunfire, one shot after another. Every minute or so, the woman in black transitions into a new pose, seemingly oblivious to the crowd. Now she is doing a backbend of some kind. The ledge is narrow enough, and her camera tripod propped just so, that no one else can capture a photo against the view without her appearing in it.

A hiker next to me rolls her eyes. She has her arms entwined around a partner, obviously waiting for a turn against the stunning backdrop. Someone behind me sighs, also apparently waiting. In fact, I realize, the dozen or so hikers standing around with expressions of annoyance are all hoping for a chance to take their own photos without the stranger now in Warrior Three photobombing the background. I wonder if the woman in black is unaware or if she simply doesn't care.

Five minutes pass, maybe ten. I start to question the people around me about Coco, figuring that I might as well take advantage of the captive audience. No one has seen her.

Well, I tried. I turn my attention back to the woman in black, still striking poses, the camera faithfully clicking away like an enamored lover. Above, clouds start to move across the sun, the pane of blue narrowing considerably as dramatic cloud cover rolls in.

"You've got to be kidding," someone grumbles.

Moving closer to the camera equipment, I see a backpack leaning against a rock near the tripod. Casually, I keep my eyes trained on the woman as my hand glides along the canvas to the little zip pocket on top. My pulse quickens, but this isn't my first rodeo. Even so, stealing something in broad daylight around a group of people is not a smart move.

Click, click, click, goes the camera. The woman, thin and perfect from this distance, moves into half-moon pose. *Who does she think she is?* Little Voice seethes. My fingers fasten on a keychain of some kind. Keys are a definite no-no under Adam's rules, but I quickly palm them anyway, moving away from the backpack and shoving my hand into my pocket.

And then, out of nowhere, a pebble zings through the air and hits the tripod. Nothing happens. Within seconds, another small rock follows, and the tripod teeters. When the third projectile hits home, the tripod and camera fall, clattering loudly against the rocks. Among the crowd, someone starts to clap. Soon there is a smattering of applause, even an appreciative whistle. The woman in black comes out of half-moon pose with an outraged expression. She glares at me, still standing near her backpack, and starts toward the toppled camera.

Shit. I move away in what I hope is a casual manner. Behind me, I hear expletives from the woman in black and vicious laughter from someone in the crowd.

"Wait!" the woman in black calls. I can't be sure she's speaking to me, but I don't turn around to find out.

I run.

Department of Lost Things: Case File 1982-024, Record 7
Email correspondence

To the kind gentleman I spoke with on the phone (I'm afraid I did not catch your name),

Thank you for returning my call earlier today; I am grateful that the Department of Lost Things will take on my case.

As you requested, I am attaching scans of the three letters that I received by post. The first, dated 1945 and addressed to me, is a rather poor-quality photocopy. Many words are illegible, but my granddaughter— the one who suggested I reach out to you—and I are working to decipher it. I will share our progress, and please do the same as I imagine you may be better equipped for the reconstruction required.

The last two letters sent to me appear to be the originals. Forgive me for not parting with them, but you will see that the scans attached are very high quality. To my untrained eye, they are in the same handwriting and seem to have been part of the same 1938 communication—one a letter referencing a cake and the other a note that was apparently hidden in the cake, as strange as that sounds. You can see for yourself how small that second communication is. The note at the top in blue ink is in a different handwriting. My guess is that whoever sent me these letters was not the original author and added that clarification.

All three arrived in one envelope last week, as I said, along with the photo, a copy of which I am also attaching. The envelope had only my typed name and address with a postmark from Ortisei, Italy. I believe it was sent by the woman who called me a few days before the date on the postmark. Before her call, I had never even heard of Ortisei, let alone been there. It is distressing for an old man to learn that his entire life might be built on lies. I gladly welcome any information that you may come across, about either my mother or the necklace, and will continue my own search in the meantime.

Sincere regards,
Samuel

NINE

don't dare look back to see if the woman in black is following me. Hoping she's still preoccupied with her camera, I hightail it up the dirt trail back to the main path. When I'm over the ridge, I see someone in a white hat with a pompom zigzagging quickly downhill toward a wooden building near the edge of the cliff. The real culprit, I suspect.

I follow, at a labored pace. My greatest regular physical activity is running to the convenience store for ice cream. By the time I reach the building, which commands an enviable view over the valley, I am gasping for breath. The white pompom hat is nowhere in sight.

Gold lettering above the ornately worked wooden door reads HOTEL PANORAMA. I duck inside and stop to catch my breath. The décor is rustic chic, with a huge stone fireplace and wooden chairs draped with tawny animal skins. I keep my eyes peeled for the white pompom hat, but the only other people in the lobby are too elderly to race down a mountain.

Back outside, the sky is nearly black. The pompom hat still eludes me, but the woman in black is lying in wait, which surprises me. It seems impossible that she gathered up her camera and pursued me down the mountain so quickly, but then again, Adam has been preaching about the benefits of yoga for years.

Up close, she looks exactly the way I would expect an influencer—for surely that's what she is—to look. Always a sore spot of comparison for me, her complexion is like something out of a skincare ad. Envy isn't the right word for what I feel, not exactly. It's more like a longing for what I imagine it must feel like to live in a body that doesn't make you worry about what other people think about you.

"You," the influencer screeches, catching sight of me. She is holding court in front of the outdoor tables, cradling her camera against her chest like an injured child. She gestures to a waitress with short hair dyed a vivid and unnatural red, as if she might be an undercover cop who will whip out a pair of handcuffs. "It's just like I said. This woman in the orange jacket assaulted me and broke my camera."

Damn Adam and his love of bright colors.

The waitress turns to stare.

"I didn't—" I start.

The influencer raises her camera and starts clicking.

"Don't photograph me!" I throw my hands up to shield my face. "Your stupid camera is still working, so it survived the fall just fine!"

"I'll have you know that the lens mount is cracked!" The influencer turns back to the crowd. "And if she didn't do it, then how does she know that my camera fell?" Heads swivel my way. The influencer's mouth drops open. "Is that my keychain sticking out of your pocket?"

That's when I start to run again, this time at full speed toward the chairlift.

"Stop! Don't let her get away!" the influencer cries, but no one seems inclined to assist. At least, when I turn to look over my shoulder, the influencer is the only person chasing me.

I can't recall where I've stashed my return ticket. I slow as I near the turnstiles, but a figure is standing there, gesturing me through.

"Quick!" Olivier-lookalike David says. "I'll slow her down." He scans his own ticket at the reader, and I gratefully push through the gate.

"Pretend I dropped these," I whisper urgently, pressing the keys through the metal grille into David's hand. Bad karma is the last thing I need right now.

At a glacial pace, the chairlift inches toward me. The influencer, seeing my imminent escape, is yelling at the attendant to stop me. The attendant is inside the booth staring at his cell phone, unperturbed. Either he doesn't hear or doesn't care. Both work in my favor.

I step into an empty car and turn to see David intercept the influencer. I'm too far away to hear what is said, but I see him gesturing toward me, his face animated as he mimes an issue with the ticket reader. He leans down to swipe the used ticket as the influencer gestures him out of the way. I then see him bend down and stand with the keys in his hand, as if he just found them on the ground.

God bless that sexy, sexy man.

By the time the influencer makes it onto the platform, the car I inhabit is continuing its slow turn, the doors not yet closed. For a moment, I think she will push her way in, and I'll have to defend myself from being beaten to death with her questionably broken camera on the descent.

But no, at last something goes my way. The doors slide closed. The influencer runs over and starts to bang on them. I wonder idly if she really thinks she can pry them apart. Does the magic of yoga know no limits? Even with the expression of rage on her face, she really is flawlessly beautiful.

"Flaws make a person real," Grandmother told me after the subpar results of my third plastic surgery, just before I turned twelve and shortly thereafter left for boarding school. For someone who ended up excelling in an industry obsessed with beauty, Grandmother wanted me to know she did not start life as a particularly beautiful woman. In her early days in rural California, she had big hair and a crooked smile.

"A crooked smile is not a flaw," I told her. "It became your trademark."

Grandmother shrugged. "I'm only saying there was nothing about my looks that made anyone think, 'That woman is going to be a famous movie star.' Some even described me as bland and unremarkable. Of course I'm *not* bland and unremarkable—what a waste to go through life bland and unremarkable!—but that's not because of my looks, Lucinda. That's what I'm trying to teach you. For most, beauty is something claimed, a type of illusion conjured, not something bestowed. Whatever you truly believe about yourself, the world will see."

Though unconvinced, I nodded. I knew even then that the lucky always insist that they have bent the world to their will, while the unlucky know it is the other way around.

And yet, I have pitted my will against that of the yoga-magic-skincare-phenom cursing at me through chairlift doors that remarkably remain closed, and as she tries to move into the next empty car, the attendant emerges at last from his booth, shaking his meaty fists and shouting indignantly in Italian—at her, not me. This time it is my will that triumphs. Just before the car drops from view, I see the influencer giving me the middle finger, and I smile.

Something has finally gone my way.

Long stories are the hardest to start. And where we come from is always the longest story of all, flowing as it does back through the generations. Alas, I can only go back to your maternal grandparents. Your grandfather was a professor at Berlin's most prestigious university before the war, your grandmother an artist who died in childbirth.

She was not the only mother who died that January day in 1923, and I not the only little girl born in that hospital to a professor from that same university. Grief at losing their wives and wonder at being first-time parents united our fathers, and we, their daughters, grew up the best of friends.

Sophie Baum and Liane Terwiel, one Jewish and one Catholic, both with dark glossy hair and big doe eyes. Strangers would constantly mistake us for sisters, and did we ever correct them? Absolutely not! For we were sisters, in all the ways that counted. The world changed around us, but for as long as possible, we stayed the same.

TEN

An honest evaluation of my search for Coco so far is a pathetic two out of ten. I've said too much to strangers, been caught red-handed in criminal conduct I did commit, and been framed for some I didn't. About the only thing I've nailed is an ill-advised foot chase, and that only thanks to divine intervention. I've been on the job for less than three hours. Though I wasn't a great hairdresser, I might be an even worse Bearer of Bad News.

On the ride down the mountain, I feel equal parts disbelief at how thoroughly jackhammering rain has obliviated the sunny skies of an hour ago and worry that—if the influencer has a cell phone and manages to communicate in Italian, German, and/or Ladin—the police will be waiting to apprehend me at the station below.

I hurriedly take off the orange coat and bundle it under my sweater, smooshing the fabric as flat as I can against my stomach. At least the bright orange color won't betray me as I make my exit. And maybe looking slightly pregnant will add to my disguise.

To my relief, the effort is unnecessary. I am alone as I exit the gondola in the now-pouring rain. The chairlift cars I see making their way toward the station behind me are empty, and I don't overthink my luck. As casually as I can, I hurry back down the motorized walkway and escalator to Ortisei's town center and my third-rate hotel.

"How was it?" Dimples asks when I drag myself into the lobby, waterlogged and shivering.

My combat boots squelch. They were the closest thing to hiking boots I had on hand in Reno. "It rained," I say unnecessarily.

"Tends to do that." He comes out from behind the desk. "A bold choice to go out without a jacket. You do know we're in the mountains, yeah?"

"It's a long story."

He looks at the telltale bulge under my sweater, but all he says is, "Let me get you a blanket." He goes to a hall closet and comes back with a large gray mass of folded fabric. It looks like something from the last World War.

"No offense," I say, "but is that clean?"

"Ish." He wraps the scratchy material around my shoulders. "We're not a five-star hotel."

"Odd, since you seem like a five-star kind of guy."

He leans close to me and whispers, "Behind that desk, I only eat caviar."

I laugh, a forgotten pleasure. "That explains the fish breath."

He grins. "If not for fish breath, I'd never get a break."

"From your admirers?"

"Oh, you should've seen the line before I left Australia. Embarrassing, really."

"Where in Australia?"

"Melbourne. Have you been?"

I shake my head. "I haven't really spent time anywhere." Aside from an entire childhood in a Swiss chalet and assorted European playgrounds, but the controlled environment of five-star experiences lent them a certain sameness that makes me feel more equipped to compare thread counts and spa services than different countries.

"You're here, that's a start." He flashes the dimples, and I feel warmer already.

"What's your name?" I ask. "I feel like we should be on a first-name basis after your excellent advice this morning. And the blanket."

"Chris," he says.

My mouth drops open. "You'll never believe it, but when I first saw you,

I thought that you looked like a Chris." I don't mention that my premonition was related to famous actors.

"I get that a lot," he says. "Is your name also Chris? That would really be something."

I laugh again, enjoying the banter. "No, it's Lucy—but my friends call me Chris, so this is rather awkward."

Chris chuckles, but I can't tell if it's genuine or a sympathy laugh. I don't want the conversation to end, so I forge on. "So, are you here on some kind of gap year?" He looks like he's in his early twenties. Younger than me, but not by much.

Another enigmatic smile. "Nah, I never went to college. I'm more a student of life." Now his laugh sounds self-conscious. "I guess every backpacker uses that one, though. And you're some kind of private investigator?"

"No," I say. "I'm actually a hairstylist, though I also have a completely useless college degree in sociology, which basically qualifies me to do nothing." I paw self-consciously at my hair, frizzy from the rain. I am certain I don't look like a hairstylist. "I'm actually in the middle of a career transition."

"Nice." Another slow smile. "Reinvention is a good thing." He dips his chin toward my left hand, which is clutching the blanket around my neck. "Is your partner coming over to meet you?"

My engagement ring. "No," I say. My face feels like a roasted tomato. "My fiancé actually might have left me? It's a little unclear at the moment, but he is definitely hooking up with this guy who played a talking squirrel in his improv class. Mr. Chippy, which sounds one hundred percent unsexy, but when he's not a talking squirrel—" I stop myself midsentence. Why hadn't I stuck with a simple *No*? "Sorry, that was TMI," I say. "I don't get out much and am not fit for polite society lately. Excuse me while I go die from embarrassment in my room."

"Like, actually die?" Chris asks. "Because it's a lot of paperwork if a guest carks it."

"I'll save that for another day, then," I say. "Thanks for the blanket. I'm going to treat myself to a hot shower and stop babbling now."

"You can babble anytime," Chris says. "I'm paid to listen politely."

I raise a hand in farewell, my shoulders drooping under the weight of the day, though it's still only midafternoon.

Back in my room, I strip out of my wet clothes and throw the itchy gray blanket onto a chair so that I can return it to Dimples/Chris later. In the shower, I turn the water as hot as it will go (not nearly hot enough for my taste) and try to maneuver myself under the dribbling flow, water pressure not being a strong suit of the accommodation.

Eventually my bones start to thaw. The power of thought returns. I consider what Taffy has told me. Directly: not so much. Indirectly: perhaps more than she intended. Coco, whose online presence as Catherine suggests she is a respected human rights lawyer, has taken something. Given Taffy's mention of the will and the daddy issues, probably something from their father that was not hers to take. And given the mention of jewels in the NDA, it's reasonable to assume the stolen object might be of that variety. Then again, the NDA also referred to Taffy's dogs as her associates, and she doesn't seem above misleading me.

But if it's jewelry, then what's the connection to a sleepy alpine town like Ortisei? Unless Coco doesn't actually have the item of value yet and what she stole was a means to find it—a letter or a map of some kind? And why had Taffy mentioned Nazis during our interview? If there was a Nazi angle, then could it relate somehow to Coco's work as a human rights lawyer?

Questions swirling, I towel off and dress in my warmest clothes before burying myself under the blankets on the bed, phone in hand. It's time to reconnect to the world, now that I have Wi-Fi once again.

My stomach knots when I see that there is still no reply from Julian. Perhaps, I console myself, he dropped his phone in the toilet. Or was hit by a bus. No, not that. Well, perhaps just a little *tap* from a bus, enough to shake him up a bit, maybe sprain an ankle. It's not like I wish him dead.

Not yet, anyway. I toggle through various apps, scanning social media for anything on his or Aksel's whereabouts, but there is nothing.

Adam, as usual, comes through with a distraction:

Count Maxwell Ernst can't keep it in his (tuxedo) pants, the subject line reads. In typical Adam fashion, there is no salutation or paragraph breaks, only one long stream of thought:

been looking into Taffy's husband and spent the last six hours reading about European royalty. Not sure it's related, but did you know that former royals from Prussia and Russia and Germany and even Poland are fighting to get back property they lost in the last century? Turns out Europe was littered with little fiefdoms that each had a king before World War I, but after World War II, hardly any royals were left, and most were stripped of titles and exiled. Some kept their jewels and fortunes and now just live like regular rich people, but others, like Count Ernst (who I will now be referring to as Count Manicure), don't have the money to live like regular rich people but do a great job pretending. Count Manicure's mom was a famed beauty from Hong Kong—maybe some money there, but if so, seems to be long gone—and his father bet on all the wrong tech companies (think Friendster instead of Facebook, Compaq instead of IBM, Blockbuster instead of Netflix, you get the drift). The family was penniless until our boy Manicure married Taffy—coincidence? Unclear how he funds his lifestyle, but from the hundreds of society pics (almost all without Taffy), it includes Formula 1 races, yachting, and high-rolling in Monaco. Kidding, kind of, about not keeping it in his pants because I have no proof of that, but the photos tell a story, if you know what I mean. A few attached. I'll keep digging. –A

The photos do "tell a story," if said story is about drunken leering and general handsyness. Taffy's husband is flawlessly handsome with a perfect complexion. I hate him already. For a moment I consider whether this whole business might be related to Count Manicure (how can I not think of him that way?) and his family. That would explain the European connection, but then why would Taffy's father's will be involved?

Can you find any connection between Taffy's family and Europe, other than Count Manicure? I type back after including a few choice puns about the most punnable of the photos Adam sent.

In need of some relaxation, I pull up a meditation video. An unblemished quasi-adult who seems to have never had a stressful moment in her life instructs me in a breathy Irish brogue to let go of whatever isn't serving me.

Obediently, I close my eyes and breathe in and out, visualizing light and trying to *om* all the negativity right out through my solar plexus. But as I focus on recognizing my thoughts and then releasing them, Julian's face floats into view.

"Return to your breathing," the Irish brogue instructs, and I try unsuccessfully to clear my head of all the things I miss about Julian, including his imitation of nearly all of Patrick Swayze's best moves from *Dirty Dancing*.

"Breathe out all your negativity," the voice from my phone says. That'll be the day. "Breathe in acceptance." I jab at my phone until the tidy blond ponytail disappears.

Meditation: fail. Lying spread-eagle under the covers, I think irritably that acceptance is an overrated life skill. How do you get the things you want if you accept your life as it is?

Department of Lost Things: Case File 1982-024, Record 10

NOTE: This personal record excerpt obtained from confidential inquiry into Catherine Carter

To: Catherine Carter, Trial Attorney
From: Musa Odongo, Director of Human Resources
Subject: Notice of Administrative Leave Pending Investigation

Dear Senior Trial Attorney Carter,

The Prosecutor has received a report that you have improperly used your position to obtain information and/or records from another international institution in furtherance of a personal matter unrelated to your work duties or responsibilities. Your conduct may amount to unsatisfactory conduct within the meaning of sections 4.1(a), (j), (l), (o) and/or (t) of the Administrative Instruction on Unsatisfactory Conduct.

Accordingly, the Prosecutor has initiated a preliminary investigation as set out in section 7 of the Administrative Instruction on Disciplinary Procedures. In the context of this investigation and pursuant to section 9.1, you are suspended with immediate effect for the duration of this investigation and must surrender your work identification, UN passport, and all work property and/or confidential information in your possession.

As outlined in section 7, you are afforded the right to respond to the allegations of unsatisfactory conduct and to provide any evidence in your favor. You also have the right to be represented or assisted by a lawyer, staff member, or former staff member of your choosing in accordance with Staff Rule 110.2(d), and to appeal this decision in writing within thirty (30) days in accordance with Staff Rule 110.8.

ELEVEN

Harried by hunger pangs, I drag myself out of my hotel room a few hours later, the scratchy gray blanket in tow. Chris is nowhere to be seen. The older front desk attendant with the markedly less sexy German accent from last night is back with nary a dimple in sight. He doesn't even look up from his phone when I return the blanket.

Outside the sky has cleared, as if this afternoon's rainfall never happened. I head back toward the main square, destined for the oldest bar in Ortisei to look for whomever supposedly answered Taffy's call and admitted that she had seen Coco. It's my only concrete clue.

En route, I pass mountainy mannequins showing off sporting attire in the front windows of multiple stores. How does each get enough business to survive when they all sell the same thing? I'm not an economist, but it seems suspicious unless literally every tourist who comes to Ortisei is woefully unprepared for the elements. And yet, if I consider myself as a case in point, then there might be more than enough business to go around.

Most of the stores are closed this late in the day, but one intrepid storefront still has its lights on. I need a new jacket. The orange look might get me arrested. Spontaneously, I walk in and find a boring black waterproof coat that is both warm and nondescript. And then I see the wall of proper hiking shoes and recall the wet mess I made of my combat boots. Today made it clear they aren't going to cut it, and I am too fond of them to further pit their durability against the Italian Alps.

"You take returns?" I ask the clerk.

When he nods, I decide to expense new hiking boots *and* the jacket to Taffy with the justification that conditions are worse than expected and that I won't be able to search without proper attire. Recalling the bright sun, I browse some sunglasses—all too expensive—and settle on a pair of ski goggles with UV protection that are on clearance. Functionality over fashion will suit me just fine. I also pull a drab black wool hat from the clearance bin that is perfect for disguise purposes as well as warmth. I'll leave the price tags on until I'm sure Taffy will reimburse me, just in case.

New outdoor attire in hand, I finally arrive at the square, far livelier now with hikers and bikers returned from their mountain sojourns and eager to unwind. Daylight is fading, and the pavement still glistens with moisture from the afternoon's storms. But with blazing heat lamps to ward off the chill, the outdoor tables are crowded.

Surprisingly, the oldest bar in Ortisei (as reported by the suspendered old man I met earlier in the day) is the least lively one. No outdoor seating or anything to suggest it's even open, though I think I see light shining un-evenly through the thick antique glass of the front windows. As far as I can tell, the bar doesn't even have a name. There is no awning or marquee, only a sign in the window with NO CASH, CARD PAYMENT ONLY handwritten in English, Italian, and German.

Odd and interesting. Though its pale yellow exterior matches the pastel palette of the other establishments on the square, something about it feels more dated. At the door, a small plaque in Italian confirms its status: "The Oldest Bar in Ortisei. Established 1910." When I try the old-fashioned latch handle, it opens. The bar is a small-ish single room smelling of beer and woodsmoke and dominated by a green enameled heater in the center that I can imagine being all the rage a hundred years ago.

Black-and-white photos of people with skis and pints and smiles line the walls, presumably of former patrons from days gone by. Other than a hand-ful of stools under the long wooden bar in the corner, there are two booths against the back wall and a few small tables clustered around the heater.

I am charmed. Then I spot a young woman standing against the bar with distinctive neon-red hair. She turns at the sound of the bell above the door, and my fears are confirmed: she is the same waitress from the Hotel Panorama who witnessed my flight from the influencer.

I duck my head, hoping that she hasn't recognized me. Even if she saw me this morning, the orange jacket was hopefully more memorable than my face.

With professional warmth, she greets me, and I realize she works here too. If she recalls that she saw me only hours ago, she doesn't let on. "Sit wherever you want," she says in German, gesturing around. I start at the sound of her voice, unusually deep and gravelly, as if her words are ground down in her throat before leaving her body. The register is so low that even inviting me to find a seat sounds seductive.

The few tables are mostly free, but I head to a stool at the bar. First things first—I ask Red (kinder shorthand than Phone Sex Voice) for the Wi-Fi password. At the sound of my German, she immediately switches to English. Not the biggest vote of confidence in my admittedly rusty language skills, but fine.

"The password is g-e-t-a-l-i-f-e," she spells with a straight face. "No capital letters."

I assume she's screwing with me, but no, getalife unlocks what might be the weakest Wi-Fi signal I've ever encountered. I order a glass of the house wine. A few minutes later, Red brings me a glass of something orange and sparkling. Not the house wine, as far as I can tell.

"For you, an Aperol spritz." Red's teeth gleam. They are sharp and complement her rocky voice.

I stare at the drink doubtfully and take a hesitant sip. Orange. Herbal. Sparkly. I'm pretty sure Adam insisted on serving this last summer, and I hated it then too, but there's a vicious gleam in Red's eyes, and I'm afraid to send it back.

"Do you serve food?" I'll need something to balance this orange abomination (and quiet my rumbling stomach).

"Not at this moment. We are short-staffed." She shoots me another spiky smile and walks off. So much for dinner.

The other patrons in the bar seem like regulars or misfits, without the monied-hiking-set look of the tourists I'd seen on the square. An intense twosome with matching bowl cuts debate something over shot glasses of clear liquid. A weathered couple shares a table by the heater. Near the sign for the bathrooms, a rowdy group of teenagers are drinking what may or may not be sodas over a card game.

A very stooped elderly man is the only other person sitting at the bar. I greet him in German, and as he turns toward me, I recognize his suspenders immediately, though up close and personal, I realize he is much older than I thought. Like seriously decrepit, one-foot-in-the-mausoleum old. He does not seem to recognize me, nor does he seem inclined to conversation.

At least, not at first. Hairdressers must master small talk because of the forced proximity with all manner of people for the minutes or hours it takes to snip, color, and curl. If nothing else, my stint in the field was a master class in people skills.

Fifteen minutes later, I know that his name is Andreas, his dog's name is Brutus, he used to be a semiprofessional skier, he was born in Ortisei, and he works in the local municipality (at this I raise my eyebrows, because how on earth has he not been forced into retirement?). Then again, Andreas is remarkably lucid for someone who looks like a contemporary of John the Baptist. Perhaps he is only forty and simply weathered by mountain life. The issue of age aside, I have built enough foundational rapport to get down to business.

"Is she a local?" I gesture to Red, wondering whether she could be the woman with whom Taffy spoke.

Andreas shakes his head. "A student from Berlin working here for the summer. She just arrived last week and has two jobs to save for her studies."

"You already know all that, and she just arrived last week?"

Andreas shrugs. "It's a small place."

"Who else works here?" I press on, not wanting to get diverted into platitudes about village life.

Andreas's brow furrows like a storm cloud, and I remind myself to tone it down. Lesson 101 in detecting. I think fast and say, "An old college room-mate of mine works in a bar around here. I thought it was this one." I hope the course correction comes off smoothly.

"I'm afraid the only other person who works here is the owner, and if she ever went to college, it was probably for witchcraft." Andreas practically spits the words.

Struggling to keep my face blank, I wonder whether Andreas is a misogynist or has a particular axe to grind with the bar owner. I choose my next words carefully, picturing what I would say to a snappish client, though it's hard to translate someone screaming, "What don't you understand about shoulder-length?" into this particular context. A neutral question usually works, I decide. "How long has she owned the bar?"

"Since my sister died last year." Andreas grabs his beer, liquid sloshing over the rim on the way to his mouth. "Surprising that she left this place to her daughter. Ingrid left Ortisei as a teenager and always made plain she hated it here."

"I'm sorry for your loss." I ignore the rest, as it sounds perfectly reasonable to me that a woman would leave her business to her daughter.

"We weren't close." Andreas shrugs matter-of-factly. "But I always approved that she kept this place going. Grandfather Adler first opened the doors more than a hundred years ago." He jerks his head to a photo directly above the bar. A tiny old man beams between a young woman grinning widely with a baby and a girl of about ten with a shy smile. "My father took that photo of him with my mother—her name was Luisa—me as a baby, and Giovanna, my sister. Grandfather died not long after and my father not so long after that."

"I'm sorry," I say again.

"My father was murdered."

I gasp, which seems to satisfy Andreas. "In the late 1930s. Probably killed by Mussolini's secret police for his anti-Fascist activities, but he had his hands in a lot of things, so who knows?"

Now that he's started talking, Andreas can't seem to stop. Like a boulder muscled into rolling downhill, he careens on: "I don't remember him.

I was what they call a miracle baby, a decade younger than my sister. After my father died, my mother was not well. She died soon after the war, and Giovanna paid for me to go to school in Milan. The schools were better there, that's what she said. But I think she saw me as a burden." Andreas's face twists with the bitterness of an old wound, but before I can jump into the silence to steer the conversation toward Coco, he is diverted by an equally stooped man with a long beard who comes up to shake his hand.

Red materializes on the other side of the bar. "I found you some peanuts." She thrusts a little bowl toward me.

My stomach feels like it's eating itself, and I descend on the nuts with profuse thanks.

Waving me off, she says, "I recognize you. From today."

I freeze like a deer in headlights. "I didn't—" I start.

"Even if you did, I don't care." The sharpness is gone from Red's grumble. She sounds almost admiring. "I found that woman's Instagram." Red leans toward me. "Full of fake moments pretending she's all alone in beautiful places all over world, doing yoga like a fool. I'm sure her followers feel sad about their own ordinary lives when they look at her photos. It's like experience porn."

"Porn?" I'm both taken aback and intrigued. "Isn't that a little extreme?"

"Is it? They're both orchestrated fantasies, are they not?"

I shrug, running my finger along the bottom of the empty peanut bowl and licking the salt from my fingers.

"What brings you to Ortisei?" Red asks.

"I'm looking for someone." I show her Coco's photo.

"Why are you looking for her?"

"I've been hired to deliver some bad news." It may be a desire to redeem myself or perhaps it's the alcohol, but I find myself leaning forward to whisper, "She's taken something from her sister."

"Something valuable?"

Is it my imagination, or does Red frown? It's only there for a moment, a ripple in the water, and then her face smooths.

I open my mouth to answer, but then the reality of the NDA crashes down on me. Have I already said too much? Probably. "I'm not sure." I choose my words carefully, though Taffy gave me so little information that there's not much more I could share in any case. If I knew what Coco had supposedly taken, it might help narrow down where to look for her, and I wonder again whether Taffy is purposely setting me up to fail. "Have you seen her?" I press.

"She might have been at the Panorama yesterday." Red is staring hard at the photo.

"Really?" I can't believe my luck. "Did you speak to her?"

Red shakes her head.

"What was she doing?"

"If it was her, then she sat and enjoyed the view with a coffee. Who is she?"

Disappointment deflates my elation. None of this will help me find Coco, though I suppose it's helpful to know she may still be in the area. "I don't know much about her, to be honest."

Red smirks. "Not even her name?"

"I'm not at liberty to say." I pause, regretting my moment of oversharing. "But if you see her again, will you—" I'm about to say *call me*, but until I get a SIM card, that's complicated. "Email me?" I finish lamely.

"Sure." Red hands me a pen from the bar, and I write my email address on a napkin. "And now we're closing."

"Really?" I look at my watch. It's not even ten. "Is the owner here?"

"Not tonight." Red pushes some buttons on a payment machine and slides it toward me. "Card only," she says.

As I search for my card, she introduces herself. "I'm Hilde, by the way. Short for Hildegard. My parents are obsessed with Hildegard von Bingen. Have you heard of her?"

"No."

Hilde's gaze is intense, as if I might be lying about not having heard of her namesake, and I laugh self-consciously before returning the introduction and handing her my bank card.

As Hilde moves on to the table of card-playing teens, I turn to Andreas. "Do they always close this early?"

"It's a different time every night. They don't have set hours." Andreas glares, as if this point underscores the owner's unsuitability, which perhaps it does.

Looking up in time to catch Andreas glowering, Hilde reaches down to fiddle with her phone. A song starts to blare out of the restaurant speakers.

"Is that Becky G?" I ask, sort of recognizing the song from a television show.

Hilde nods, then jerks her chin toward Andreas, who is rooting around in his trouser pockets. "He hates this song, so I've started to play it every night at closing time. It's the only way to get him out the door." She grins rather nastily.

"*Oh partigiano,*" Becky G croons. "*Oh bella ciao . . .*"

"He's not a Becky G fan?"

"This song was around way before Becky G. Women sang it to protest their working conditions in northern Italy's paddy fields, and then it became a symbol of the Italian resistance against Fascism and the Nazis—"

"No one wants to remember any of that," Andreas interrupts, thrusting his bank card in Hilde's direction. She swipes it quickly, and he heads toward the door with his bearded friend.

A line has formed to pay, and I wave at the now-distracted Hilde as I rush to gather my bag and follow Andreas out into the night. The square is mostly empty now, those previously at the outdoor tables chased indoors by the cold.

Andreas's companion is already heading off in a different direction. I hurry to catch Andreas, who is untying Brutus from a bench at the edge of the square. He eyes me warily as I pull up Coco's picture and push my phone toward him.

"Have you seen this woman?" I hope the streetlamp provides enough illumination for him to make out Coco's features.

Expression opaque, he stares at the photograph for a long moment. "I saw her looking quite friendly with Ingrid in the bar last week."

"The bar owner?" My heart races. "Your niece?"

"Technically, but I hardly know the woman."

I hold my tongue, no stranger to family drama. Andreas has already made clear his feelings about Ingrid and her inheritance.

"Do you know where I can find Ingrid or the woman in the photo?" After saying too much to Hilde, I'm careful now to stay within the lines of the NDA (I hope).

"I haven't seen either of them since their little conversation." Andreas turns and starts to lead Brutus away, muttering under his breath, "People should mind their own business, poking into old stories."

I'm not sure if he means me or Coco. "What old stories?"

I start after him, and he turns suddenly, jerking Brutus to a stop. "I'll tell you the same thing I told her and the last woman who came around. I don't know anything about a girl and a baby passing through Ortisei after the war. I was only a child then."

So he had spoken to Coco. But who was "the last woman who came around"? I'm not sure what I had been expecting, but it was not a reference to events from Andreas's childhood. Perhaps Andreas hadn't seen the photo of Coco clearly after all.

"So you spoke to her? It would be so helpful if—"

Brutus growls, as if sensing tension. "Who I talk to is my business." Andreas sounds menacing, even if he looks frail enough for me to push over with a finger. Brutus, on the other hand, has very sharp teeth.

This time when he moves away, I don't follow, but I do call out, "It's just . . . her sister is worried." I don't mention that I've been hired to pass on a threat of arrest and total career devastation from said worried sister.

Andreas harrumphs as if validated. "She should be. Meddlers always get what's coming to them." And then he and Brutus disappear into the night.

Department of Lost Things: Case File 1982-024, Record 7(a)(iii)

Excerpt (translated from German): Letter to Samuel, Ortisei, 1945

When Hitler became chancellor in 1933, we were girls of ten, so close that sometimes even our fathers could not tell from a distance who was Sophie and who Liane. We lived not so far from each other on broad tree-lined streets, and other than annual winter ski trips, which our fathers planned separately except for the last year before the war, we tagged along on each other's vacations and split weekends between our two houses. Aside from our mothers' deaths, we had enjoyed lives of relative ease that continued despite the toxic political environment that closed around Germany like a fist. That our fathers shielded us for so long is no small miracle.

To you, with the benefit of hindsight, it must seem foolhardy we stayed in Germany, but one can never underestimate the power of cognitive dissonance. It is like the story of the frog that will jump out if placed in a pot of boiling water but allow itself to be cooked to death if water is only gradually heated to boiling. We are blinded to the things we do not want to see.

The next part will be hard to write, so perhaps first I shall pause and tell you a story of your grandfather. In my earliest memories, he would drive us—his two girls, he said—outside of Berlin to picnic in the woods next to a river so wide we thought it was the ocean.

He liked to stay past sunset, until the last of the light bled from the sky. "You need the dark for the stars to come out," he would say. "It's in the darkness when the light from the stars shines. The moon, she comes and goes as she pleases. Coquettish, she is. But are the nights darkest without the moon?"

"No," one or both of us would answer. "The darkest nights are the ones without stars."

"Just so, just so! The moon is but one while the stars are hundreds, thousands, millions!" I still remember how he would look when he said this, his face animated and arms gesturing broadly upward. "If every star shines, not even the blackest night can hide from all that light. For any chance against the dark, you must choose to be a star and shine. Remember that!"

The night would deepen around us, and he would pat his front pocket for a pipe and then smoke while teaching us to name the constellations, and we would wait until it was very dark before we bumped and jolted our way back to Berlin. That is the first thing you should know about your grandfather and what he believed. At our best, we are all but a star in the night. Here and then gone, our choice alone if we choose to create light.

TWELVE

Back in the hotel, I shower and then climb into bed, my body exhausted but my jet-lagged brain still wide awake. Grabbing my laptop, I decide to tackle an email update to Taffy.

Dear Taffy,

I spoke with two locals who have seen Coco, one as recently as yesterday. The other saw her last week in the bar you mentioned, but he may not be a reliable source, as he thought Coco was looking for a girl and baby who came through Ortisei after World War II?

There was heavy rain today, but to implement your fabulous suggestion of a "hut-to-hut" search, I will head up to the mountains tomorrow to scout some in the area. I needed better gear for the hike and do not have adequate funds in my bank account to front these expenses. Receipts attached. Thanks in advance for wiring the reimbursement today!

I employ Adam's favorite tactic of treating a desired outcome as a foregone conclusion, desperately hoping I can wear the hiking gear tomorrow instead of returning it. Having written few business messages, I struggle with how to sign off and settle on Sincerely yours. After attaching photos of my receipts, I hit send.

Work attended, I check my personal messages. Still nothing from Julian, but I have another email from Adam:

Not much on Taffy's dad yet, but Coco mentions him in an alum interview
from awhile back. Attaching it here. Seems he had PTSD? Will keep digging.
Hope you're getting into the right kinds of trouble! A.

I open the attachment. It's a scan from an alumni publication featuring
law school graduate Catherine Carter and her path to an exciting career
prosecuting international war crimes. There is another photo and an interview, which is painfully sincere and full of clichés like righting the world's
wrongs, giving voice to the voiceless, and seeking justice for all.

The mention of her father is brief: "I grew up seeing the price of war.
My father, who enlisted in the US Army when he turned eighteen, saw firsthand the horrible things human beings did to each other on the front lines
in World War II. He fought a just war, but it haunted him even so. Hitler's
crimes against humanity have since repeated themselves. The human race
has learned little despite promising 'never again.'"

Coco sounds like a true believer. I could see how someone like that
would drop everything to charge off to Italy if the cause were urgent and
compelling. But what sort of cause would fit that bill, and could it relate to
something she stole from Taffy?

None of my questions about Coco concern me as much as the question
of why Julian is still MIA. I had—perhaps foolishly—thought it would make
a difference if he knew I had fled the country for Italy, like the opposite of
out of sight, out of mind. Whenever I have a moment alone, I miss him so
much that it is hard to believe he doesn't miss me too.

"You don't miss him," Adam had told me, quite sternly, only last week.
"You miss the idea of him. If Olivier St. Trapezus hadn't emotionally gar-
roted you just before you met Julian, I doubt you ever would have gone
on a single date with him, let alone decided to spend your life together.
Seriously, Lu, when is the last time you and Julian had a real conversation?
And I don't mean discussing who will pick up Thai or what looks good on
Netflix."

I wanted to give Adam a million examples of deep and meaningful conversations Julian and I had had in the not-too-distant past, but I was stymied. What came to mind were images of Julian on his laptop searching for auditions or watching television while mouthing the actors' lines while I sat next to him scrolling on my phone. We were together but apart. Before the move to Vegas, we still went dancing and out with friends, but even then, we shared the same physical space but not necessarily our inner lives.

Mostly we said *hello* and *goodbye* and *how was your day*, and that was enough. He made coffee, I made dinner. He bought ice cream, I bought our favorite burritos. I couldn't remember our last real conversation.

"You have to separate the idea of Julian from the reality," Adam said. "He's the only guy you've ever seriously dated, so you have nothing to compare it to. Trust me, you're getting a raw deal."

But it's true for all of us that we can only judge against our own context. And in the context of my romantic life—guys in boarding school who asked me out because they knew about Grandmother and my rather pathetic obsession with Olivier St. Trapezus, whom I kissed only a handful of times—Julian was amazing. Maybe Adam was right that I had no idea what was normal in a relationship. If such a thing as normal even existed, which I suspected might be the biggest lie of all.

Department of Lost Things: Case File 1982-024, Record 8
Case Note

Newly available artificial intelligence analyses identified two transactions for emeralds of the approximate size and shape as those believed to comprise the necklace (see Record 2 for additional provenance information):

Sale by John Carter

1947: sale of one rectangular twenty-carat emerald believed to come from the back of the necklace for $100,000 ($1.275 million in today's dollars) via private auction. Auction house will not reveal identity of buyer without warrant. Shortly after this sale, Carter started the hedge fund that earned his fortune, likely using this money as seed capital.
Current location of J. Carter: New York, NY

Sale by Giovanna Vitale (recently deceased, see also Record 7 in its entirety for further context)

1946: sale of one rectangular emerald for 15,000 Italian lire ($250,000 in today's dollars) to a jewelry maker in Milan. Carat information not provided. No further information on emerald available. Records show that shortly after this sale date, Giovanna's brother, Andreas Vitale, was sent to an expensive private school in Milan, and significant debts owed by Giovanna's father, Giorgio Vitale, including a mortgage on the building housing the family's bar and apartment in Ortisei, were paid off (building currently owned by Giovanna's daughter, Ingrid Vitale).

Notes: High price obtained by J. Carter suggests superior quality of gemstone without inclusions. Photo of necklace worn by Frau Baum in 1922 shows diamonds around each gemstone (assumption that this pattern was continuous, though approximately one-fourth of the necklace is not visible in the photograph). Diamonds from necklace not traceable if they were sold as, unlike the emeralds, the size is not distinctive. Likely that Giovanna Vitale did not get fair price, assuming the emerald she sold was of similar or greater size and quality as the one sold by J. Carter. Connection to Ortisei intriguing (see translated letter to Samuel, Record 7(a))—it is for this reason that we conclude the emeralds sold by J. Carter and G. Vitale are from the same necklace.

<u>Next steps</u>: Interview J. Carter, A. Vitale, and I. Vitale. Congratulate M. F. for writing the code that located these transactions as the sales records were missed in previous searches.

THIRTEEN

D oes anyone wake up each day thinking, *Go, me! I'm waking up to the exact life I always wanted!*? Life coaches and celebrities, I guess. Or they fake that reaction for their brand. But I suspect that, like me, most find their existence a little paler and more mundane than the life they imagined.

That is to say, misery loves company, and I feel truly miserable when I wake my second morning in Ortisei to see that Julian still hasn't texted. The sight of that god-awful bear doesn't improve my mood, but there is one sliver of good cheer in my inbox. An email from Taffy:

> Glad to hear Coco is still in the area! Never heard of a girl and baby. Focus on finding Coco. Wiring payment for the receipts you sent, but please save the rest of your expenses for end of week, when we determine if you've made enough progress to stay on. Have a joyous day!

Good news: I can take the tags off my new hiking gear. Bad news: it's Tuesday, and Taffy is already foreshadowing that the rest of my expenses are not a sure thing. Not unless I make progress.

Knowing that I should get up and start looking for Coco, I instead dive into social media. Impossible to stalk directly, Julian was one of those people who avoided social media on principle. Aksel hasn't posted anything since the hand-holding photo. I start to look for friends and friends of friends who may have posted something that inadvertently includes clues about Aksel or Julian.

Pathetic! Truly pathetic! Little Voice berates me.

I pull the pillow over my face, ashamed. But no, that's not fair. Even if I'm mostly crawling, I'm still moving forward. Far from languishing on Adam's pull-out couch, I'm in the Italian Alps, embarking on a bold new career opportunity, seeing the world, living the dream.

Get your ass up, I hear Miss Mary's jazziest voice in my head. It's true that lying here feeling sorry for myself won't fix anything. With a sigh, I force myself to stand and turn on my little cell phone speaker. Sia's "The Greatest" blares.

By the time the chorus hits, my mood has lifted. "Don't give up, I won't give up," I sing into my hairbrush, my eyes falling on that stupid bear poster only to realize the bear seems to be challenging me to a dance-off. I shimmy closer, still singing. He knows how to juggle, but I have some moves up my sleeve. A knock at the door interrupts what may have been the most epic dance-off of all time between a woman and a bear poster.

I open the door out of breath and immediately regret not checking the peephole first.

"When I got a report at the front desk that a stray cat was being tortured in your room, I thought it was an exaggeration," Chris says.

"It's movement therapy." I gesture expansively with my hairbrush to demonstrate that movement therapy is a serious thing. Which it definitely is. I try to explain about Miss Mary but leave out the dance-off.

"Miss Mary sounds made-up." Chris crosses his arms and leans against the doorframe.

"Don't all the best people?"

Chris grins. It lights up his face. "Right. Then can the . . . *therapy* prescribed by the very real Miss Mary be done at a lower volume?"

I pretend to consider it, then sigh as if the answer hurts me as much as it hurts him. "Not really."

Chris nods again, as if I've presented an irrefutable rebuttal. "Carry on, then," he says. "I'll knock twice if animal control insists on breaking into the room. That's your signal to flee out the window."

"The barred window?"

"That's the one."

With a thumbs-up, I close the door and lean against it. Was he flirting with me, or is he just so charming that every word that comes out of his mouth sounds like flirting? It's probably the Australian accent.

You have more important questions to answer, Little Voice chides. Yet again, she's not wrong.

It's probably for the best that Chris is nowhere in sight when I emerge from my room fifteen minutes later, ready for the day and still high on movement therapy. The dregs of the breakfast buffet have yet to be cleared. All that's left is congealed eggs and heels of bread, but beggars can't be choosers—I'm starving after peanuts for dinner last night.

While wolfing down food, I consider my strategy for the day. I need to find Ingrid, the bar owner, whom Andreas (her reluctant uncle) saw with Coco recently. But if Ingrid is not at the bar, then I'll head back up the mountain and check out the rifugios since that's what I'd told Taffy to justify my hiking gear. Plus, I don't have any other leads, so why not venture somewhere beautiful to clear my head?

With my telltale orange jacket replaced by my nondescript new gear, I stop at the bar, which is locked up tight. Plan A foiled, I take the chairlift up Mount Seceda. The sun is veiled behind cloud cover so heavy that the sky appears white. The grass beneath my feet shimmers silver with dew. No influencers are trying to dominate the landscape that I can see—a pro of visiting on a day that doesn't lend itself to photos.

With no real plan except to find a rifugio, I start down one of the hiking trails. There are many, all numbered and signposted with estimated walking times to various endpoints. I choose one that has a destination less than two hours away. With my new boots not yet broken in, even that might be ambitious, but I tell myself to go big or go home.

The trail starts as a brown scratch in the grass, swallowed by mist a few feet ahead. It's like a trust walk of one. Soon the green meadowland gives way to mountain stone, and I am surrounded by a colorless landscape of gray rock and white fog. The hike has the therapeutic effect of a sensory-deprivation chamber. I walk, and think, and walk, and think, my thoughts more random flickers of consciousness than anything lucid. Love. Loyalty. Betrayal. The line between hope and self-delusion, settling and accepting reality, pushing past obstacles to get what you want and recognizing that your dream is not destined to be. Doors close and windows open, so the saying goes, but the difference between a door that is stuck versus sealed shut is not always obvious. At least, not to me.

The outlines of the mountains are just visible, a fuzzy suggestion of reality, like one of Monet's fog paintings. The haunting ring of cowbells sounds in the near distance. I don't pass a single soul until, quite suddenly, two hours have passed, and I am at a rifugio.

My fingers are numb, and the thought of espresso pulls at me. A signpost informs me that in another hour, I'll reach the next chairlift, where I can ride down to Santa Cristina and then take the bus back to Ortisei, but first I'll stop and rest and ask some questions for my report to Taffy this evening.

This rifugio is a simple wooden building with playground equipment and outdoor tables out front. Without the blanket of mist, I imagine there must be a spectacular view. Indoors, the main dining room is cozy with wooden benches and hand-sewn pillows in faded primary colors and the smell of baking apples.

I order an espresso from a young waitress and take a seat near two college-aged women with braids and hiking tights. Each has a gigantic backpack propped on the floor. At first glance, the most distinct difference between them is that one has blue leggings, the other black.

"Cold out there." I make a show of rubbing my hands together as I collapse onto a bench.

The waitress brings my espresso. The first sip is pure bliss. The Italians know how to do espresso, even at altitude. I comment on that as well, and the Leggings agree. Small talk ensues. They've spent the last ten days hiking from hut to hut along the AV2, the most famous of the Alta Via routes that crisscross the spine of the Dolomites. Some huts are within a few hours' walk from a chairlift, but most are inaccessible to me, an out-of-shape mortal with limited gear and not enough experience as a hiker to venture into the remotest of remote areas. The Leggings are making their way off the mountain with a four-hour hike from a remote rifugio where they spent last night.

I have my phone out and am about to show them a photo of Coco when Blue Leggings says in a low voice, "That guy over there is staring at us."

I turn. A windswept man sits at a corner table. Where had he even come from? I hadn't heard anyone enter after me, so perhaps I had simply overlooked him when I first arrived.

And then I recognize him.

David must recognize me as well because he gives a little wave, and he smiles with what appears to be genuine warmth. "Ah, if it isn't the Bearer of Bad News, my fugitive friend from yesterday. I feared the next time we met you would be in handcuffs."

I laugh awkwardly, then turn away. The Leggings exchange a look. It's the look that does it for me—full of judgment. As if they know the half of it. While they start to fish money out of their pockets, I snatch a glove.

Out of control, Little Voice warns. *David may still be watching.* I drop the glove to the floor as the Leggings gather their backpacks.

"Our weather app says it's supposed to rain in a half hour," Black Leggings says. "At this altitude, it won't stop until tomorrow morning. You should get to wherever you're staying tonight."

"You dropped something," I say, holding up the glove.

Blue Leggings thanks me, and I use the opportunity to show them the new photo of Coco, the one from the alumni magazine. It's a candid shot taken in a garden or some other green space. Unlike the serious court picture in the weird outfit, Coco has longer hair and is laughing, hands clasped in front of her. She looks relaxed, even joyful.

The Leggings stare with identically furrowed brows. They really might be twins.

Blue Leggings turns to her companion. "Is she the one Pablo pointed out a few nights ago?"

"That's right! The one with the *emerald* necklace." Black Leggings rolls her eyes. "As if anyone carries a fortune in jewels out hiking."

This was getting interesting. "What do you mean?"

Blue Leggings shrugs. "I didn't see it. She wasn't actively showing people or anything, but she dropped her bag, and Pablo saw this necklace fall out. He's the one who said it was emeralds. He actually makes jewelry, this is one of his bracelets—" She thrusts an arm toward me, and I see colored beads strung around her wrist.

A sharp look from Black Leggings suggests this present from Pablo may have created some discord between them. "Knowing Pablo, he probably grabbed the necklace from the bag. He's like that," she says to me in an aside, furthering my suspicions of a Pablo Controversy.

Blue Leggings sighs. "He's actually a really nice guy. Anyway, he saw the necklace was made of these huge pieces of what was probably green glass and asked about it—professional interest, you know—and she got all weird. From what Pablo said, she was upset that he saw it."

"Or that he tried to steal it," Black Leggings huffs, hoisting her backpack up onto her shoulders.

"You're just saying that because you didn't like him." Blue Leggings glares.

"Is this woman still at the rifugio?" I wonder if I have it in me to somehow sprint there before dark.

"I doubt it. This was three days ago," Black Leggings says.

"Four days ago," Blue Leggings corrects.

"Was it?" Black Leggings shrugs. "Honestly, those days with Pablo really dragged for me."

"You promised not to—" Blue Leggings starts, and it's clear that I'm losing them.

"What was her name?" I interject quickly before the two start to bicker.

"Pablo spoke to her, not us. And he left for Spain today." Blue Leggings looks downcast.

Black Leggings grimaces, then looks at her phone. "We really have to go."

I follow them as far as the door, spewing questions—Could they be sure it was the woman from the photo? Was anyone else talking to her? Did Pablo say anything more about his encounter?—but whether from fear of the weather or of me, the Leggings hurry away. I regret returning the glove.

Defeated, I make my way back to my now-cold espresso. David is staring at his phone, but his fingers are still, and he seems alert, like a rabbit with its ears pricked. Is it strange that we both ended up at this particular rifugio? It is, after all, a very big mountain.

"So what brings you here?" I decide to ask.

"Hiding from the rain forecast," he says, and I immediately regret prying. It's delusional to think he managed to trail me through the fog or, even less likely, somehow knew I would come here when I hadn't even known it myself.

"You made it off the mountain to continue your search, I see." David catches me staring and smiles that wolfish smile. His hair curls over his ears and touches his collar, disheveled as if from hours on a motorcycle vrooming around tight corners and narrow mountain roads. He has that kind of energy.

"Thanks to you," I say. "I owe you for the card swipe." I refrain from asking if he owns a motorcycle.

"Nah," he says. "I convinced the operator that my card malfunctioned." His teeth are blindingly white when he grins. Probably he also kite-surfs and has a dangerous but unusual hobby like axe throwing. After graduation, Olivier St. Trapezus had (almost) qualified for the Olympics in judo. He had also done illegal drag racing on the empty stretches of desert road outside Reno.

Little Voice makes a gagging sound. *Have you learned nothing?*

"Please." David gestures to the empty seat across from him. "Join me."

I nearly protest. I don't know this man. Sitting with him is not a great idea. But then I remember yesterday. After he saved me from probable arrest and incarceration, it would be rude to refuse.

I take a seat across from him. "Why did you help me?" I can't help but think that if our situations were reversed, I would have sided with the glamorous influencer and not the sketchy scar lady with someone else's keys.

"I knew you were wrongly accused," David says. "How could I not help?"

I feel my forehead wrinkle. I want to ask how he can be so sure of my innocence, but I worry this question makes me sound guilty. I settle on, "I would never try to hurt someone."

"Oh, I don't think anyone was trying to hurt her," David says. "More like they were trying to teach her a lesson about her behavior." His hands are loosely folded on the table, his posture open.

"I'm not sure we can know—" I start.

"Trust me, I know." David smirks with a cockiness that suggests he is used to people accepting his version of events. "On another note, nice that you returned the glove today. And the keys yesterday. Do I need to keep an eye on my belongings?"

The color drains from my face. "Yesterday at the Hotel Panorama, she dropped the keys, and I would have given them back then and there, only she started yelling at me, and I was scared—" I start.

He laughs. "You don't have to bullshit me. I thought maybe it was part of your strategy. People trust you if you do them a favor—even if it's helping them out of a situation you created. Know what I mean?"

His eye contact feels analytic, a visual MRI. I'm not sure what he's looking for, but I'll be damned if I look away first.

In the end, he's the one who glances away to flag down the waitress, who is hunched over a book behind the bar. "Can I get another espresso?" he calls out. "And one for my friend?"

Risky, given what he already knows about me, but I can't help myself. *Don't do it!* Little Voice pleads, to no avail. While his attention is diverted, I slide a hand into the backpack leaning against his chair leg. I don't like his cockiness, and I don't like his resemblance to Olivier. It doesn't matter to me what I pull out, so long as I can take something from him to even the score for the emotional imbalance he's causing me.

My hands fasten on a small piece of paper, but before I can pull it loose,

David turns back to me. "I ordered you another espresso since your first is cold, I reckon," he says.

I incline my head, in acknowledgment or thanks. I'm too frazzled to know which.

"We weren't properly introduced yesterday," David says. "I'm David." Again, that long drawn-out *e* sound. His voice is deep and sonorous, perfectly calibrated to do voiceovers for car insurance commercials.

He holds out a hand, but I have no intention of touching him.

"Actually," I say, "I'd prefer an Americano."

"An Americano," he calls to the waitress, dropping his hand casually as he turns, and that's all the time I need to snatch the scrap of paper up from his bag and into my lap.

"I'm Lucy," I say when his gaze once again settles on me. I resist the urge to make sure my hair covers my scar as I notice the small flecks of gold in his eyes.

The waitress brings our drinks. We reach at the same time for the sugar bowl, and our fingers brush like an Italian mountain-hut version of *Pride and Prejudice*. A little zip of electricity runs up my arm, and the sensation annoys me.

I jerk my fingers away, abandoning the bid for sugar. I catch David looking at my ring finger. The band of metal and winking fake diamond have started to feel like wishful thinking. As for what I'm wishing, that is the question. Someone to love me, I guess, just like most everyone.

I reach for my cup, wrapping my fingers around it so that the ring is no longer visible, but it's too late.

"When's the wedding?" David asks.

Probably I should just make up a date, but instead I start rambling and find myself spilling the whole sordid tale, in much the same embarrassing way I did with Chris yesterday. "I guess we'll set a date later," I finish.

David nods unconvincingly, then clears his throat as if at a loss for words.

You're a mess, Little Voice pronounces. I clear my throat too. "So, what brings you to the Dolomites?"

"I'm doing some research for my PhD."

"What are you researching?"

"My dissertation is on the modern origin of community." Perhaps registering my blank look, David continues, "You've heard of intergenerational trauma?"

I make my noncommittal oatmeal noise and sip my Americano. It's still too hot and burns my tongue, but I manage to keep a neutral expression.

"A child with a grandparent who lived through torture, war, famine—really any sort of extreme traumatic event—may know nothing of their relative's circumstances but still inherit headaches, anxiety, gastrointestinal issues—" David gestures to indicate that the list goes on.

"Interesting." I wonder what I may be in for given how little of my family history I know, including that of the father I never met.

"We're only just starting to learn about the impact," David says. "Trauma epigenetically alters the genes, that's the theory."

Probably I should never procreate to be safe. I blow on my Americano, then realize how unsophisticated that looks and stop. "So why the Dolomites? Not to criticize, but this place mostly seems full of tourists. And didn't I read there wasn't much action here during World War II?"

"It depends on what you mean by *action*," David says. "You're right that there wasn't much fighting. South Tyrol had a lot of Germans, and of course Mussolini was Hitler's ally for much of the war. But you're forgetting about the Great War." David raises his cup and sips—with a lot of sophistication, truth be told—from his espresso.

Then he continues, "In World War I, ninety-five percent of the deaths were military, mostly from trench fighting that many regard as the most brutal form of warfare humanity has ever known. A 370-kilometer battle line ran right through the Dolomites, and—" David breaks off. "I'm rambling like a professor, aren't I?"

"No," I lie. "I love hearing about battle lines." That lupine smile again and the bad boy is back, replacing the crusty intellectual from a few moments before. And then David winks.

Warmth rushes to my cheeks. I'd like to ask him more about his research and whether he works out and what his hopes and dreams for life are. Just a conversation between two interesting and attractive people who happen to meet in a mountain hut. But wait, am I supposed to wink back?

Definitely not, Little Voice says.

I'm rescued from the decision as David continues, "I couldn't help but overhear your conversation with the hikers. Is the person you're looking for— What was her name?"

"Coco," I say before I remember the NDA and my pledge to stop saying things that I shouldn't.

"That's right. Coco." He taps on the table lightly with his index finger. "What do you suppose she's doing with an emerald necklace all the way out here?"

I frown. "I have no clue. And that story may not even be accurate. It wouldn't make much sense to hike around the mountains with something valuable."

But of course Coco has something valuable, I think but don't say out loud. *If you don't bring back what you took* . . . The threat was part of the bad news Taffy sent me to deliver. If whatever Coco had was worthless, she wouldn't have hired someone to track Coco down.

Even so, none of it makes sense. Fleeing to Italy isn't the same as holing up in Yemen, or somewhere without an extradition treaty. The Dolomites aren't exactly an intuitive destination for an escape with stolen goods. Unless Coco was meeting someone here? Away from surveillance cameras and witnesses, the mountains could be perfect for all manner of illegal transactions, including off-loading jewels.

"The woman I'm searching for is a respected international human rights lawyer," I say. "It makes no sense that she would be wandering around the Dolomites with valuables stashed in her bag. This Pablo person was obviously trying to impress that girl—not exactly a credible source."

"A human rights lawyer?" David leans forward.

"Forget I said that," I say, wondering whether the NDA covered Coco's profession and wishing I'd read it more carefully.

"Was her family from Ortisei, displaced during one of the wars, perhaps?"

"You're thinking she'd be perfect for your research?"

The cheeky grin he offers in response is disarming. "It's actually quite common that descendants return, often looking for things looted during the war. Some items are even being returned. There is a sort of amnesty. Return what was taken, and you'll be thanked. No one will point fingers about why it took eighty years. And yes, often there is trauma, which is key to my research."

I tell David what is likely an oversimplified and factually incorrect version of a newspaper story about an American thrift store aficionado who bought a marble bust for thirty dollars that turned out to be two thousand years old. The German museum to which she returned it gave her an undisclosed reward.

"Exactly," David says. "The looters themselves are old now—dead or maybe in nursing homes. Their kids come along and go through the attic or finally get that painting on the wall appraised, never thinking that doing so will expose them to a legal quagmire if it comes back stolen. Even the families of Nazis are asking for things to be returned. Can you imagine that? Nazi descendants arguing that their SS father really did legitimately buy this or that painting stolen from a Jewish family. But that's international law. Everyone gets a fair shake."

The front door to the rifugio bangs open and six hikers in the midst of a rowdy discussion in French troop in. Through the open door, I see that rain clouds have purpled the sky. "Not again," I mutter under my breath.

"Has the rain started?" I ask the hikers in English, twisting in my seat to get a better look out the rifugio's windows.

"Not yet," one says. "But if you don't have a place up here for the night, you should get down the mountain."

"Are you also going back to Ortisei?" I ask David.

"Not tonight."

I want to ask him where he is staying but don't want to sound forward. Thunder booms outside like an indignant message from the gods.

"I guess that's my cue." The memory of my miserable hike home yesterday is powerful motivation, and I rummage for a handful of euro coins to cover my drinks. Hopefully it's not too late to make it back without getting soaked.

"I'm sorry to see you go." David does indeed look sorry, and my heart twists at the thrill of someone wanting me to stay.

"Me too." In one quick motion, I shove the crumpled paper from my lap into a pocket, hoping he won't notice it missing from his bag.

As I prepare to head back out into the wild, David stands and offers me a small bow. "Until we meet again, Lucy."

Berlin
16 November 1938

Dear Giovanna,

*I fondly recall our annual ski trips to Ortisei and how Papa
and I would bring you and your family a Berliner Brot to
enjoy for Christmas. I send one along with this letter and our
regret that, as with the past few winters, such travel will not be
possible this year. Papa could not ski anyway. He has broken
his leg and an arm and faces a long recovery, but we remain
hopeful he will be well again soon.*

*I hope this cake reaches you, and please do not worry if
it takes a few weeks (or longer, as mail even inside of Europe
seems slow these days). You will see that I have packaged it
well, and the Berliner Brot remains delicious for months, so do
not hesitate to tuck in.*

*Enjoy it, and my best to your brother Andreas and of course
your mother. I was very sorry to hear of your father's passing.
I remember the song he taught us the last time we were all
together and sing it often.*

And so I say to you my dear friend, ciao bella,

Sophie

FOURTEEN

For the second day in a row, I return to the hotel wet and beleaguered, though less miserable today in my new hiking attire (thanks, Taffy).

"Is there a little rain cloud that follows you around?" Chris is sitting behind the front desk when I enter. "Either you like the rain, or I need to help you download a weather app."

I want to say something coy but only stare at him mutely.

"Only kidding." Chris's dimples flicker into worry. "From your face, it looks like you saw the photos."

Whatever I looked like before, shock and horror must add a new dimension to my countenance because Chris's face falls. "You—don't know about the photos?"

"What photos?"

Chris uneasily runs a hand through his perfectly tousled hair. "I shouldn't have said anything. They're nothing, really."

I am not fooled by *nothing, really*. If someone asks if you've seen a photo, then unless it's a meme of a baby chicken and a puppy growing up as best friends, you can be sure it's something.

"Show me." I'm sure I manage to sound calm and collected, but Chris's placating tone when he responds suggests otherwise.

"Are you sure?" Chris looks from the computer monitor behind the reception desk to me. "Probably hardly anyone will see them. Even I only stumbled onto the article because I always look at anything tagged Ortisei—"

"Article?" I'm ready to hop over the counter to get to the bottom of things.

As if he can sense the containment ship has sailed, Chris swivels the monitor toward me, revealing an amateur-looking webpage.

RECLUSIVE FORMER SCREEN SIREN GENEVIEVE SAINT'S GRAND-DAUGHTER RAGES AGAINST MODEL DURING ALPINE HOLIDAY, the headline reads. Below the headline are four photos, snapped one after the other by the influencer so that they run together like a cartoon strip of motion. My eyes are wide, mouth open, then my hand thrusts out in a threatening gesture, my expression mean, and finally my arm is flung up as I pull the orange jacket over my face. The only saving grace is that the nicked keychain is not visible in my pocket because then I'd have some real explaining to do.

To Chris's visible dismay, I read the opening paragraph out loud:

Popular influencer Cassi Nowak, eighteen, had a nasty surprise while documenting her spiritual journey in the Italian Dolomites when Lucy Rey, granddaughter of Academy Award–winning star of *The Devil and the Doctor*, attempted to murder her at a popular photo stop.

I ignore my strong desire to swipe the monitor onto the floor in a rage, like the panda in the cheese commercials. "I did not try to hurt her! I don't even know her."

"I don't think there was a lot of fact-checking," Chris says soothingly. "It's more of a blog than a news site. And if it makes you feel any better, Cassi herself is not saying you tried to kill her." He pulls up another window and scrolls through a social media feed with dozens or possibly even hundreds of photos of Cassi doing yoga poses against dramatic backdrops in a variety of midriff-baring spandex outfits. Beaches, mountains, sunrises, sunsets—she gamely tackles them all, just as Hilde had said.

"She has 3.4 million followers," I say in shock.

"Her headstand is impressive," Chris says, stopping at Cassi's most recent post.

Chris is technically correct: Cassi does not accuse me of attempted murder. She uses the more moderate **ATTACKED!!! HAVE YOU SEEN THIS CRAZY PERSON?**, illustrated by a photo of my surprised face captured mid-jacket cover-up next to a stunning picture of Cassi doing crow pose on Mount Seceda.

UPDATE, the caption reads, linking to the blog post. **Thanks to all my fans for the luv and helping to identify my attacker. Ur the best, and I am truly #blessed! Lucy, what a dishonor to your grandmother #Genevieve Saint. Please pay to fix my camera!! If u don't come to me, I will come to u. Remember karma. Namaste.**

An alarmingly high number documents how many times Cassi's post was shared. How on earth did she find out who I was? And how had she discovered that my grandmother was Genevieve Saint? I picture one of the mean girls from my high school, possibly even Madeline herself, scrolling through and delighting in finding Cassi's post and identifying me as her "attacker" with the additional informational gem, *BTW, do you know who her grandmother is?*

Grandmother will lose it if this gets back to her.

"I wouldn't worry about the blog post," Chris is saying. "They must know each other because Cassi obviously provided the photos so it's not objective journalism, and soon people will pick up on that—"

"People?" My voice hitches. "Is it just that one blog post and Cassi's social media, or has this story been featured more widely?"

"You know what?" Chris neatly sidesteps an answer. "I think we need a drink. I'm off in an hour. Why don't you get cleaned up, and then we can grab a pint?"

He smiles, and I feel a little warmer, noticing for the first time the lovely caramel color of his eyes. I find myself nodding even though all I want to do is curl up in a ball in my bed. "I definitely need a drink."

"Nice." The dimples burst forth. "Oh, and Lucy?" he calls as I move away. "Don't search yourself on the internet, yeah? Nothing good ever comes from that."

Recognizing the wisdom of Chris's advice, I resolve to follow it. Back in my room and reconnected to Wi-Fi, my phone lights up with a voice message from an unknown number. The fact that I'm intrigued is a red flag. I know as well as anyone that messages from unknown numbers are likely telemarketers or scammers. But Julian used to leave me voice messages—he thought it was easier to talk and walk rather than talk and type. They were often rambling and rarely had a point, but love makes annoying habits shiny.

In the way of wishful thinking, it suddenly seems possible and even likely that Julian has a new phone number I won't recognize (a burner he had used to cover up his Mr. Chippy affair?), and I hit play. My heart seizes in the adrenaline-soaked way that presages moments of great import, like jumping out of a plane before you know for sure that your parachute will open. It is too early to experience elation or its opposite, but you know one or the other will soon be upon you.

But the familiar voice does not belong to Julian. Grandmother, the queen of "My people will be in touch," sounds querulous, like an old woman bickering with home care staff over a small serving of rice pudding. My heart sinks. Of course she has people or algorithms or search bots or all of the above who monitor these things. Of course she would know immediately if her name were mentioned in the press, even a shitty blog. I'm moderately surprised she figured out how to find me on WhatsApp, but as they say, where there's a will, there's a way.

"Lucinda, what are you doing in the Dolomites? And don't you know how dangerous it is to throw rocks, let alone at someone standing on a cliff? What if that poor model had fallen to her death? You know that I've always warned you about the media. The story was blown out of proportion, I'm certain. In any case, please call me back. I need to speak with you about—"

I delete the message midsentence. Of course it's about the media. Grandmother and her precious reputation. Not to mention her unsolicited strong opinions about the million ways I disappoint her.

"You have no idea what I've sacrificed for this family!" she screamed at me once shortly after my great-grandmother died, for some petty offense or another.

The words had never left me, nor those she left unspoken. *And it wasn't worth it.*

Because that is what she thought. It must be. A daughter gone. A mother lost to mental decline long before death. A granddaughter shipped off to boarding schools. Not that I had felt like an outlier—all the other kids were also there because their parents or guardians were too busy or disinterested to parent them at home or honestly believed that boarding school was the best place for posh children to get the best education and meet other posh children, forming friendships that would fuel success later in life.

Possibly this was true for those better than I at forming friendships. For me, boarding school was lonely, especially those first years. It would have gone easier if I had exploited my relationship with Grandmother, but given the choice, I preferred no friends to fake friends. Correction: one friend, because once I started high school, I'd met Adam.

By the time word got out about who my grandmother was—when Madeline overheard part of the dorm master's conversation during the thwarted bracelet theft—my social status was too low to be resurrected. But when I made it to college, I was anonymous again and had stayed that way. Before yesterday, if you searched Grandmother on the internet, there was no mention of me anywhere, not one photo tying us together. She'd even managed to keep my mother under wraps.

Grandmother's obsession with privacy was all part of her reclusive mystique, and though it stung not to be claimed by her, she insisted her motivation was pure: she didn't want any of her family tormented by the media. And now I'd proved her point.

Hearing her voice after so many years causes my heart to bump around my rib cage as if it has been pounded out of shape and no longer fits there. My palms start to sweat as my phone, back on Wi-Fi at last, nearly jumps out of my hand vibrating with a backlog of notifications.

Listlessly, I open my text messages. One from Adam, of course, and Maurice, but it's the top message that captures my attention. I blink, but it's still there when I open my eyes.

Julian.

Rapidly, I tap on his name. The message is like a punch in the face. Your grandmother is Genevieve Saint? WTF, Lu?!!!!!!!!

This is what finally prompts Julian to respond to me? My misshapen heart whooshes full of an explosive anger.

Yeah, I have my own list of WTFs, I respond.

Not that I can blame him for being surprised. When we first started dating, I told him the basics: my mother was dead, and I'd never met my father. Correctly tagging "family" as a painful topic, Julian proceeded thereafter to avoid it entirely. Watching me cut hair to afford tuition, he assumed that whatever family money had paid for boarding school was gone, and I never corrected him. And by the time he returned from the Peace Corps, and we got more serious, I had discovered the truth about my mother and booted Grandmother from my life. I'd always planned to tell him everything. Eventually.

Three dots appear. I wonder if Julian is crafting his own angry missive back and if we are about to prove that we have lost the ability to properly communicate by engaging in a heated text battle.

The dots disappear, and I wonder where Julian is. Finally back in our apartment in Las Vegas? Still with Aksel in California? I need to see him. Without an in-person conversation where he can tell me if I did something wrong and if we can fix it and whether we have a future, I'm not sure how to move forward. For a moment, I consider simply asking Julian where he is and then buying a plane ticket right now, this minute, to fly there and settle this once and for all. If Julian just looks into my eyes, then I'm sure he'll realize— My mind blanks.

I picture myself disembarking from the plane in Los Angeles or Las Vegas and then getting out of a taxi with my small backpack of mountain wear and an orange jacket that implicates me in a camera crime I didn't commit and walking into the robot apartment or ringing the bell of wherever it is that Mr. Chippy lives and then Julian will appear, and—I see it clear as day—Aksel will be there just behind him, hand on the small of his back, looking at me with polite interest.

They will be tan, without windburned mountain skin or bad hair from an international flight in the middle seat or torn cuticles from DIY self-care. Aksel has perfect skin, of course he does, and Julian will be even more handsome than I remember, and his eyes, when they land on me, will be full of—

I know the answer, and it is a little death. No, not the orgasm kind that a French (of course) poet memorialized hundreds of years ago, but an actual death of something very real inside myself. Because in make-believe Julian's eyes, I only see pity.

The dots have not resurfaced, and I know that Julian will not write back. Not now. I pace, clenching my teeth hard enough to splinter in my mouth. It is an old pain, dressed up like Julian and smelling like heartbreak, but its deeper-shadowed face is familiar. Rejection. Not good enough. Not enough. Never enough to be loved.

There's only one thing that can help me now. I pull up the video so that I can see their faces. The song by the middle-aged couple living their dream in a way that was perhaps smaller than they'd hoped. But they weren't done yet, and every day was a new chance. It was so human, so true to the fate of us all, that it stabbed me in the heart every time.

With their clashing shirts and earnest expressions, the Bengsons look happy and beautiful and so full of life, and I wish I could be in that Midwestern living room with them. I give it all I have as I sing along. *Keep going, keep going, keep going on . . .* That's really all there is to it. Three words to live by.

Maybe the third time through the song, a knock sounds at the door. I consider not answering, but there's no way to pretend I'm not here when I'm singing loudly by myself, and then, as if it's fate, the song gets to the part about good company, and I realize that yes, I damn well do need some good company.

I turn the music off, leaving my phone on the nightstand. I open the door with crazy hair and red eyes. I haven't changed or washed my face or even applied ChapStick. For once, I don't even care about my scar.

"You couldn't help yourself?" Chris asks.

I nod, as if an internet wormhole is to blame. "It's a bad day," I say.

His expression is so frank, so full of compassion, that I want to hug him and cry, but instead I cram my feet back into my hiking boots without tying the laces and grab my jacket.

"Ready to go?" he asks.

"Let's get the hell out of here," I say.

And we do.

Department of Lost Things: Case File 1982-024, Record 11
Case Note

Suggesting J. Carter lied during his interview (see Record 9), there is chatter that his daughter Catherine Carter, an international war crimes prosecutor, has made inquiries about the necklace, generating additional attention that complicates recovery. The French government has preliminarily asserted an ownership claim given Esther Lachmann's French citizenship (see Appendix 1) while Germany considers a counterclaim as Prussian Count Guido Henckel von Donnersmarck was made a prince by German Emperor Wilhelm II. The German theory is likely that the count's marriage to Lachmann made her a German citizen.

Intelligence confirms that the connection to Ortisei and the Vitale family, already known to us (see Record 7), may not yet be known to other parties. We will have a head start if we are correct that this is where C. Carter is headed. She has been careful, not using credit cards or leaving other electronic traces, but we can confirm she crossed the border by train into Italy last week.

To exploit this advantage and in keeping with plans to interview Andreas and his niece, Ingrid Vitale, presently believed to be in Ortisei, Agent Wavelength to be deployed into the field undercover.

Appendix 1:

Le ministère de l'Europe et des affaires étrangères
NOTICE OF OWNERSHIP AND REQUEST FOR REPATRIATION

France asserts its ownership over 500 carats of emeralds purchased in 1868 by Empress Eugénie with tax proceeds of the French people and therefore belonging to the French Republic. Circa 1871 this necklace was given to French citizen Esther Lachmann (aka Pauline Thérèse Lachmann, aka La Païva) (see attached photograph of La Païva in 1872 wearing said necklace). Information from a reliable source indicates that the necklace recently resurfaced in the possession of US citizen Catherine Carter. France requests the assistance of the US government in identifying and returning these emeralds to the French people as a valuable piece of cultural heritage.

FIFTEEN

We head to Ortisei's oldest bar. Chris seemed surprised when I suggested that we come here, but he acquiesced and now sits across from me in one of the cracked leather booths. While he nurses a beer, I'm stuck with another garishly orange Aperol spritz that materialized instead of the gin and tonic I'd ordered.

Hilde strikes again, and the oversight is likely intentional. She knew Chris's order by heart, giving him a smile before leading us to the booth closest to the bar. Andreas is again seated on what must be his usual stool, but thankfully he is deep in conversation and doesn't look up.

"A bit awkward, this," Chris says, once we've done a perfunctory cheers. "But if you want to talk about the"—he clears his throat—"incident, I'm here."

"There was no *incident*. Someone else threw the rocks, and I was basically framed." I don't mention the very real bad thing I did, in terms of thievery. The keys were returned, I reason, so no harm, no foul.

"It's totally her word against yours, and I believe you." Chris's tone is cautious, like the jury is still out despite his words to the contrary.

"Let's change the subject," I say. "Anything mortifying about yourself you care to share to even the playing field? Maybe you came here after a torrid affair in Australia went south? Were you catfished? Tinder swindled?"

Chris holds up his hands to fend me off. "Whoa, nothing like that."

My lips pucker at the sweet-tart taste of the Aperol. "What, then?"

He looks uncomfortable. "Initially I was only going to be in Europe for a week, maybe two, but like I told you, the skiing was fantastic, and I had enough money saved to stay, so I thought why not?"

"Is this your first time in Ortisei?"

"Surprisingly, my second time."

"Surprisingly?"

"Well, my mum was born here."

"In Ortisei?"

"Yip. She only moved back recently." He looks sheepish, as if waiting for me to call him out for not saying from the start that he was here to visit his mother, but I understand all too well not wanting to open yourself up to questions about family.

"What made her move back?" I ask instead.

"She inherited this bar."

"Ingrid is your mom?" At his nod, I cover my surprise by leaning across the table to whisper in horror, "That makes Andreas your uncle."

Chris looks in Andreas's direction. "Great-uncle, not that he'd admit I'm a relation. There's bad blood because of the inheritance. And even worse blood because Andreas offered to buy the bar, and Mum refused. No one expected her to move back and actually give it a go. She's never been great at"—he pauses, searching for the word—"working, I guess you'd say, but with the location, this place doesn't take much."

Well, this is getting interesting. "Will she be here tonight?" I crane my head around, hoping I can add to my report to Taffy that I've managed to question the bar owner spotted with Coco.

"Nah, she texted me yesterday that she's gone off for a few days. Hiking, I expect. Not unusual behavior for her." Chris won't meet my eyes. "She's a free spirit."

"You don't cover the bar for her when she's gone?"

"Us working together wouldn't be the best idea." He looks toward Hilde. "Though Mum only hired Hilde like a week ago, so I'm not sure how smart it is to leave her in charge. That's why Andreas is here, I expect. He likes to keep an eye on things." Chris leans back and crosses his arms. "I try not to get involved."

"I completely understand," I say. "You couldn't pay me enough to work for my grandmother either." I want to ask more, like how I can contact his mother, but Chris's expression stops me. An expert in dodging discussions about family, I recognize the signs.

"Your dad is still in Australia?" I change the subject.

"Yip." Chris's face opens at the mention of his dad. "Never left Australia a day in his life and never will. One of the many reasons he and Mum weren't well-matched. They tried, but—" Chris lifts his palms, his voice belying the lighthearted gesture.

I wonder which is worse: Chris with his obvious disappointment in a mother whose faults he knows or me with my belief that my mother would have rescued me from every disappointment if she'd only stayed in my life.

More drinks follow, Hilde shooting darker and darker looks at our table as the evening wears on. My eyes find the framed black-and-white photos around the bar. They are hard to pin in time. Whether from one hundred years ago or yesterday, they show people doing the same sorts of things that people have always done. Striking a pose. Laughing with friends. Memorializing paramours. Struggling to be remembered, every one of them.

"The photos came with the bar," Chris says, noticing my wandering eye. "My grandmother, and I guess her parents before her, used to photograph everyone who came in. That's her as a kid there." He points to the photo behind the bar that Andreas showed me yesterday.

"So this place has always been in the family?" Not that Andreas has a reason to lie to me, but no reason not to confirm.

"My nonna Giovanna's grandfather moved here from Naples and founded the bar in 1910," Chris says. "The family hit pretty hard times after World War I, and by the time World War II rolled around, almost everybody had died, but Nonna was nobody's fool. Never married. Kept the name Vitale and passed it down to Mum. She came into some money after the war, and paid everything off. Even bought some property up the mountain—that's what Andreas inherited. He runs a little rifugio up there and does something for the local government. Not bad for a former mob family."

"The mob?" I cock an eyebrow.

"Oh, yeah. Nonna Giovanna's grandfather and her father too. It was big news how he died in the late 1930s. Like a mob-style execution. Basically unheard of this far north, but maybe it wasn't the mob. There were all sorts of rumors he was supplying arms to the freedom fighters against Franco in the Spanish Civil War right before World War II took Europe over the edge."

"An arms dealer?"

Chris laughs. "I guess. Would you believe I didn't know any of this until Mum inherited this place?" He looks at me as if expecting to see shock.

"Actually, I would." I give him what I hope is an expression of solidarity. "I know hardly anything about my family. There was no one I could ask growing up." I frown. "Or, I guess I had someone to ask, but she had no interest in answering."

"Mum was the same," Chris says. "But my dad is an open book. I know every family story on his side."

"I'm jealous," I say. "In high school, I used to spend hours on those ancestry websites, trying to trace my family tree. I don't know anything about my dad, and my grandmother was an only child of an only child, at least on her dad's side. I have no idea about her mom. She came over after World War II, but I don't even know her maiden name or the name of the camp where she met my great-grandfather. All I know is that she was a Jewish refugee from somewhere in Germany."

Chris cocks his head. "Aren't there organizations that help people find missing relatives from the war?"

"I guess," I say.

Adam had suggested the same thing back in high school, but when I'd raised it to Grandmother, she became angry. "Why are you always picking at the past?" she'd asked.

I hadn't followed through. Even now, thinking about my great-grandmother causes my heart to churn uncomfortably. I have few memories of her, mostly because she died when I was eight and had dementia for as long as I knew her. She hardly ever spoke, and when she did, she communicated more like a sibyl than a normal person. This was, the staff whispered behind Grandmother's back, because she was crazy. If crazy meant that you exclusively wore flannel nightgowns in pastel floral patterns and wandered around speaking gibberish, then Great-grandmother was nailing it.

I always greeted her politely, though our paths rarely crossed. She was often out of the house getting various medical treatments from specialists, and I was busy with tutors in subjects I would never use again in my life, like ancient Greek and concert piano. Now I regret not getting to know her while I could.

"Yeah, I'm not even sure where I would start with one of those organizations," I say, choking on a large gulp of Aperol spritz.

"Are you close with your fiancé's family?" Chris mercifully changes topic.

"No," I say. "And also, I'm not sure we're getting married." It's the first time I've said this out loud.

"Well." Chris's expression is unreadable, his voice cautious. "Is that a good thing?"

"I don't know anymore. I mean, I thought we were happy. We liked each other. We got along. We had a life. Comfortable is okay."

"Is it?"

I stare at the table.

"Sorry," Chris says. "That came out wrong."

"I guess in theory comfortable shouldn't be enough, but to me, comfortable felt pretty damn good after growing up with Grandmother."

"Hard to grow up in the lap of luxury with a famous movie star, is it?"

"I guess the trips were nice," I concede. "And my pony."

Chris makes a noise in his throat that suggests he thinks I'm joking, though of course I'm not.

"You read up on Grandmother, then?"

"It was in the article." Chris looks abashed.

"I guess it was only a matter of time until our relationship became public." I feel like a dirty little secret. "At least she's hardly famous anymore," I say. "It would have been worse if this happened then. Everyone watching you, seeing you, caring about you . . ." I grimace.

"Fame is the worst punishment, that's what Picasso said," Chris says.

"And yet everyone wants to be famous."

"I think people just want to matter, and if you're seen, then you matter, right? As if the more people who recognize you on the street or 'like' your social media post or ask you for an autograph, the more you exist."

I find myself nodding. "Like if we feel seen, all our problems will disappear, but in reality fame is just a prettier playground where your disappointments hurt more because they are always in front of an audience. And you can't stay famous for long anyway, because there are too many platforms with too many people trying to steal away that same attention."

"You're preaching to the choir," Chris says.

"Are you speaking from personal experience?"

"I mean, I wasn't a movie star," Chris hedges, then raises his voice to talk over my attempt to ask a follow-up question. "Speaking of which, your search is mentioned in that blog post. Maybe some clues will shake loose."

My confusion must show because he continues, "I guess Cassi took it upon herself to interview a number of witnesses who said that you were asking questions about a missing woman with a weird name? Loco?"

Oh no. The crowd I'd interrogated about Coco while Cassi struck poses had apparently ratted me out. Would Taffy view this as a violation of my NDA? I play back everything I had asked about Coco. Surely none of my questions had contained confidential information?

It's at that moment that Hilde chooses to bang the bill down on the table. "We're closing."

"Ah, Hilde, can't we stay for one more round?" Chris turns the dimples on her, but she is unmoved.

"Your mom said you don't get special treatment."

Reaching into the pocket of her apron, Hilde pulls out her phone. At the bar, Andreas puffs up indignantly as the now-familiar strains of "Bella Ciao" issue forth.

"Drinks are on me," I say, handing Hilde my card. I feel exhausted and a little tipsy. All I want is to sleep this horrible day off.

Outside, we move through a mist so fine it's as if raindrops passed through the most delicate of sieves until nearly invisible to the naked eye. The tiny droplets catch the lights of the square, reflecting blurred color.

"It's beautiful," I breathe. I stop walking, tempted to take a photo but knowing that a photograph would never capture the magic.

"It is." Chris is close enough that we are shoulder to shoulder. His hands are deep in his pockets.

I turn to look at him, a rainbow corona of diffuse light around his head from the small beads of water caught in his hair. His profile is as perfect as a sculpture by one of the masters, Rodin or Michelangelo. He turns toward me, a little half smile bringing out his dimples, and my heart rat-a-tat-tats. I wonder if he will kiss me. Would I let him? Would it be cheating on Julian given all that has happened?

Before I can talk myself out of it, before what I'm about to do even registers as a decision, I reach up and touch the side of his face with the lightest brush of fingertips.

Chris catches my hand, squeezing it gently before stepping away. "You can't start something real when you're in the middle of something else."

It's only when my abandoned hand catches the light that I remember my engagement ring. "I wasn't—" I stammer. "I mean, I don't—"

"You don't have to explain." There's no judgment in his voice. If anything, he sounds regretful.

Chris resumes walking, and I trail behind, emotions roiling. *You were going to kiss him.* Even Little Voice is too shocked to muster much of an opinion about whether this development was positive (moving-on-and-seizing-the-day power) or negative (getting-back-at-Julian-and-trying-to-feel-desired baggage).

"I've had too much to drink," I say when we stop in front of the hotel entrance. I try to say something more with my eyes, though I'm not sure what. An apology? Regret? Desire?

"Please," Chris says. "I'm irresistible. It was bound to happen unless you really did cark it."

"I guess if it was inevitable, I won't beat myself up." I summon a wavery smile.

"G'night, Lucy Rey." Chris offers a dashing salute, expression inscrutable.

I stare after him as he walks away, taking the light and magic of the night with him.

Department of Lost Things: Case File 1982-024, Record 7(b)(ii)
(translated from German)

NOTE: This scan, received from Samuel, captures intricate creases that suggest the message was once folded into a square roughly the size of a stamp. Though the handwriting is nearly too small to be legible, the penmanship between the below and Record 7(b)(i) matches. The reference to Kristallnacht, in November 1938, further supports contemporaneity. The all-caps introduction is recent, written in unfaded blue ink, and by a different hand.

> *SAMUEL, YOU WILL NEED A MAGNIFIYING GLASS TO READ THIS SECOND NOTE, WHICH WAS HIDDEN IN THE CAKE.*

G, I know you will find this in the Berliner Brot. You always were so clever. Perhaps I'm being overly paranoid, but the censors read everything, so they say. Forgive me that I haven't been in touch. If you follow the news, you know how bad things have been here. Just last week, the worst yet. They are calling it Kristallnacht from the broken glass, but that is the least of it. Papa was beaten, that's how he broke his leg and arm. Our home was robbed, and all the cash Papa had taken out of the bank for our visas was stolen. We are too afraid to return home so do not write me there. Luckily his old colleague has offered us shelter. I say shelter but really it is hiding. We are in hiding, Giovanna. Not for long, because Papa is determined that we will leave Germany as soon as he is strong enough to walk. I fear that will be a long time, especially since Papa refused to go to the hospital. It's better, he says, if everyone thinks we fled. And soon we will. That is why I am writing, dear Giovanna. War is coming, Papa says, and when it does, getting a message to you may no longer be possible. Would we have a place with you, if we can make it out of Germany? We have my great-aunt Liesl and her husband in Switzerland not so far from the Italian border, so it would not be for long. They say it is harder to get into Switzerland than Italy, if we can make it to you at all. I know your father was an anti-Fascist who opposed Mussolini from the beginning. He had the whole bar going with that raucous field song, "Bella Ciao."

I couldn't name the song in my letter—the Italian censors would hate it as much as the German—but in this hidden missive I can admit that the reason I sing it so often lately is not from joy but because I feel as if we are bidding farewell to all the beauty in the world. Do you remember the friend who came with me on the last ski trip, the one you didn't like? I shall not name her in case this letter is discovered, but your qualms aside, she is my dearest friend. It is with her and her father that we are hiding. Send your response in code and through her: talk about spring flowers if we can come to you and winter storms if not. I will understand if your answer is winter. —S

SIXTEEN

Having neglected to silence my cell phone, I wake to the Alicia Keys "Girl on Fire" ringtone I favor. I fumble for the phone, head pounding. It's after midnight.

"Let's see how Cassi likes it when you sue her for defamation!" Adam rants as soon as I answer. "How dare she accuse you! If you were going to throw a rock at someone, it would be Julian, not that attention-monger."

"Technically the rock was thrown at the camera," I clarify. My voice is hoarse.

"Are you coming down with something?" Adam asks.

"No. Just a little too much to drink."

I hear Maurice whispering from stage right: "Is she drinking alone? I hope she's not drinking alone."

"I wasn't drinking alone." I speak before thinking it through.

"Who were you drinking with?" Adam sounds hopeful.

"The front desk clerk." I can't resist adding, "Who happens to be a hot Aussie."

"A hot Aussie!" Adam sounds delighted. "It's like Lu 2.0. Clearly the Dolomites have been good for you. Tell us everything!"

"Hi, Lu," Maurice says, in case there'd been any doubt that I was on speaker.

"Hi, Maurice." I cough, hoping I sound a little less like death with every sentence.

"We've been thinking about you, baby," Maurice says. "Seems we can't let you out of our sight for even a second without you assaulting someone."

"I'm a handful," I agree.

I tell them all about Chris, but when Adam sounds like he might be doing cartwheels in excitement, I realize that any follow-up questions will inevitably elicit the drama of the ill-fated cheek touch.

"There's also this PhD student who looks more like a racecar driver." I abruptly change course, deciding to blow their minds by throwing David into the mix. I give a brief overview, ending with the detail that bothers me the most. "He reminds me of Olivier St. Trapezus."

There is a brief silence, and then they both groan in unison.

"Run away! Do not pass go!" Adam screeches in mock horror. "Do you remember when you bought tickets for *The Nutcracker*, and he said he'd come but then left you standing outside the theater until a police officer stopped because you were turning blue?"

"That's not what happened—"

Maurice chimes in. "What about the time when you told me you couldn't go out because he said he'd call to tell you where to meet up, and then I saw him on campus making out with that flutist—"

"I think you say flautist," Adam corrects Maurice.

"Anyway, she knew how to handle a flute, which I'm sure was a draw—"

"Enough," I speak over them. "I just said he *reminded* me of Olivier St. Trapezus, not that he *was* Olivier St. Trapezus, but how kind of you both to take me on that walk down memory lane. And now I'm going back to bed. You two are impossible at this hour."

"Not until you hear my update," Maurice says. "I got ahold of a contact who works on repatriating missing items from World War II today. Don't worry, I kept it vague, but I asked if she had heard anything about Ortisei or your missing lawyer."

"And?"

"We think Coco has looted Nazi treasure!" Adam blurts.

"We don't know that." Maurice sounds exasperated.

"Maybe not the particulars," Adam concedes. "But Coco's up to something. Why else would she have called the Department of Justice to ask how to return something taken during World War II?" He delivers the line like a reporter reading a dramatic you-heard-it-here-first byline.

"No idea." A little knot of concern twists my stomach.

"The Alps were basically the Nazis' last stand," Maurice says. "They put looted artwork into mineshafts rigged with explosives and threw treasure into alpine lakes, not that far from Ortisei, actually. And it wasn't just the Nazis either. Artworks and valuables were stolen by American soldiers and mailed or smuggled into—"

"Get to the point!" Adam shrieks.

Maurice sighs. "Catherine—that is, Coco—told my contact she was asking about returning looted items for work," he continues. "And her job is prosecuting war criminals, so that could easily be the reason for the inquiry. She's worked on the tribunals for the former Yugoslavia and Kosovo. Plenty of shady mobster types were in the thick of it during World War II, both for and against the Nazis."

"But anyone could lie and say it was for *work*," Adam says. "Asking for a friend, am I right?"

"When you hear hooves, think horses, not zebras," Maurice says. "There's no reason for us to think she was lying."

"Any mention of a necklace?" Suddenly recalling that I have at least a little information of my own to share, I tell them about the Leggings.

"Nope," Maurice says. "But that could explain the NDA provisions. It's also possible that even if there is some dispute over jewelry in their dad's will, Coco might be in the Dolomites for an entirely different reason."

"Like she stole a necklace from Taffy for fun but is in the Dolomites trying to return a different stolen item for work?" Though I can't see Adam, his tone makes plain he is rolling his eyes. He and Maurice seem to have taken up opposite sides on Coco.

"It's anyone's guess," I say, because at this point it's the truth. "Coco could be in the Dolomites for a million reasons—professional or unprofessional—and Taffy could want who knows what back from her sister: a bank account number, a family heirloom—even something that's not valuable to the outside world, like a photo album. People are crazy when wills are involved."

Adam isn't convinced. "Even if Coco is representing someone through her work, what are the chances that they would give her the actual item? And even if they did, wouldn't she store it somewhere secure and not in a backpack on a hiking trail?"

"Unless she's trying to sell it?" I have very little idea of what international lawyers like Coco do. Presumably go after war criminals and genocidal dictators. That would, I imagine, put one in proximity to many a dubious character. Like the sort who would, for example, help one fence a stolen emerald necklace. Probably such types operate in remote locations, like secret caves in the mountains or whatnot. Seems just as likely as anything else.

"I still don't buy that she's a criminal." Maurice sounds thoughtful. "But maybe Coco's work and her personal life are overlapping? I found out her father joined the Army right after high school and served in Europe during World War II. Last month he died at nearly one hundred."

"He must have been ancient when he had kids," I observe. "Did you find out anything else about Taffy and Coco?"

"Her Wikipedia page says all there is to say about Taffy," Maurice says. "She keeps it very up to date."

Adam snickers.

"Coco is harder," Maurice says. "But I can at least confirm she and Taffy are related. Birth records, even a photo of them on a society page that ran a few snaps of Taffy's wedding."

"Coco was *not* dressed for the occasion," Adam says. "Very drab. Just like a lawyer."

"I'll give her that feedback if I see her."

After we've said our goodbyes, I realize (again) that I've neglected to call Taffy. Not exactly employee of the month behavior (add it to the list), but mortification had driven me straight to bed after I'd said good night to Chris.

Now that I'm awake, I consider calling Taffy to ask her directly about what Coco is doing in Ortisei, but almost as soon as I consider it, I abandon the thought. If Taffy has seen the news about Cassi or, even worse, my investigation going public, I am no match for tough questions.

Instead, I send Taffy a quick email update, detailing the Leggings' report about Pablo and the necklace and the unfortunate news that Ingrid, the person Coco likely spoke with at the oldest bar in Ortisei, is out of town. I do not mention that my search made its way online, hoping that Taffy doesn't have the same sort of text alerts Grandmother must employ to track when certain things are mentioned in even the dustiest corners of the internet. More soon, I sign off.

I am tempted to go back to Cassi's post and read whatever comments may have led her to Grandmother in the first place (and if I recognize whoever spilled the beans), but I fight the urge. Grandmother never read press about herself. She had staff who read everything and then reported back to her, though sometimes she would stop them midsentence with a raised hand. "That's enough," she would say imperiously.

I've also had enough. But still, my fingers itch with an equally dangerous urge: to stalk Aksel and Julian on social media to see if I can divine anything new. Julian still hasn't texted me back.

Run your own race, Little Voice counsels. *It doesn't matter what they're doing.*

It totally matters, but I'm already agitated enough, so instead of internet creeping, I stand and start to pace, wishing it weren't too late for movement therapy. "Closer to Fine" by the Indigo Girls is calling my name. Surely there's something constructive I can do to occupy myself? It's then that I remember the stolen page from David, crumpled into my jacket pocket.

It's not that I took it because I thought it would be interesting, because I didn't. But forgetting to destroy it is an unforgivable lapse. Always, Adam's rules were clear. My compulsion could not remain undetected without the rules, and I'd already grown sloppy since arriving in Ortisei.

When I smooth the page on the bedspread, my content suspicions are validated. A receipt from the day before from a clothing store on Ortisei's main street for items similar to those I myself had purchased: gloves, a scarf, a hat.

Like me, he may have found himself woefully unprepared for the elements. It's a relief to tear it into pieces that I flush down the toilet.

Department of Lost Things: Case File 1982-024, Record 5
ARCHIVES
Excerpt from "Leaflets in Berlin: A Conversation with M. H. Schmitz,"
Inside the Resistance: Interviews with Twelve Women, **published November 3, 2003 (translated from German)**

NOTE: See reference to "Flower Girl" in Record 7(a)(v) (efforts to procure an interview failed as Schmitz died in 2005).

Q: *I understand you were part of a resistance group in Berlin?*

A: That's right. Our group was called the Stars, and my code name was Flower Girl. Not the sort from weddings. It was a literal name because that was my cover. I carried around a basket of flowers that I claimed to bring to the sick or, when times got harder, sell. The flowers were from my garden—I had a large garden then—and in the winter, sprigs of evergreen or even mistletoe. In the bottom of the basket, I had leaflets to distribute.

Q: *Can you explain the importance of leaflets to your resistance efforts?*

A: Creating and distributing leaflets was the entirety of the Stars' resistance work. And if you're wondering how leaflets aid resistance efforts, then you probably come from a place where the government doesn't censor your news. Imagine having no accurate source of information. That was Germany in the 1930s after Hitler rose to power. People forget that Hitler did not start out rounding people up and sending them to camps. He started out curtailing smaller rights and freedoms, like abolishing free speech and a free press.

Q: *How did you distribute these leaflets?*

A: When there was money for stamps, sometimes the leaflets would come to me in envelopes, addressed to random people from the phone book. Those I dropped in postboxes around the city. More often, the leaflets were loose, and those I left everywhere: phone booths, U-Bahn stations, benches in public squares, newspaper kiosks, church pews, university classrooms, anywhere people passed by that I could find a way to access. Outside of Russia, Berlin is the largest continental European city–nine times larger than Paris–and I walked around for hours every day doing what I could, leaving information and also flowers. The flowers weren't political, except that in an ugly world, beauty is its own sort of protest. At least, I think so.

Q: *What did the leaflets say?*

A: Sometimes transcribed foreign news broadcasts. Sometimes intellectual arguments against anti-Semitism and Fascism. Sometimes criticism of Hitler and his regime. Sometimes counterarguments against Nazi propaganda. Sometimes news about the war effort. Sometimes active calls for resistance. Sometimes all of these things. I wasn't involved in creating the leaflets, only in delivering the leaflets I was given.

Q: *Who created the leaflets?*

A: Liane, as far as I know, but there might have been others. She told me she had a typewriter hidden in some sort of crawl space in her basement, and the Germans never found it, not even when they arrested her father.

Q: *Why was Liane's father arrested?*

A: I'm not sure. Liane never spoke of it. He was sent to a camp for political prisoners, and she insisted he would be released and come home any day, but he never did. I always thought it was a miracle that he wasn't arrested sooner. He'd already lost his job for refusing to fire the Jews in his academic department, but that was back in the mid-thirties, and his arrest was closer to the end of the war.

Q: *Was he part of the Stars?*

A: I'm not sure. I only ever met Liane. That's how resistance groups were organized–the ones I know of, anyway–you only knew those with whom you directly worked. The groups didn't know each other either for the most part–our efforts were individual and uncoordinated. Religious groups and political activists and university students and labor unions, all with their own reasons and methods for resisting.

Q: *Did Liane have a code name?*

A: If she did, she never told me. I knew her from before so only ever thought of her as Liane. We had gone to school together but were never friends, despite being close in age and practically neighbors. But we were at enough of the same events before the war where I was bold about speaking out about things, at least at first, and I think Liane must have remembered that. I assume that's why she recruited me.

Q: *What sort of things did you say?*

A: I wasn't a political girl, not then. Many people weren't. What was that quote by Plato, that the price of indifference to public affairs is to be ruled by evil men? Something like that. And I was indifferent, at least at first, though I did say often and in all manner of colorful ways that I thought Hitler was ridiculous. I wasn't alone in not taking him seriously, with all his jumping and screaming. Did you know that the term "Nazi" was created by Hitler's opponents and used as an insult in those days? It was a derogatory term for a backward peasant, and Hitler hated it. I don't think he ever referred to himself as a Nazi, which is funny and rather fitting if you think about how that term defines his whole existence nowadays.

Q: *Were you ever in danger for speaking out?*

A: I was lucky, I suppose, that my criticisms were in the early days of Hitler's ascent and didn't attract too much attention. Certainly I shut up once people who spoke out started getting arrested and hauled off to camps. That wasn't for me. It won't make me look good in your book, but I'm an old woman, so I might as well be honest. I never *wanted* to be in the resistance. I tried my best to ignore what was happening. Or it isn't that I *tried* to ignore it–I didn't think of it like that. I was *able* to ignore it because for a long time it didn't affect me.

Q: *What changed?*

A: I saw a Jewish child beaten near to death on the street for some small infraction, the star on the little jacket's armband bloody before it was over. I did nothing. And I do not know if that child lived or died or if I could have stopped it. I didn't even try, and I will live with that forever. But later I asked myself: to silently watch a child die, is there anything less human? And then: Who am I if I do nothing? That's when I decided to help Liane with her leaflets.

Q. *You already knew about the Stars?*

A. Yes. Whether it was coincidence or kismet, Liane had approached me not too long before that. It must have been 1941, when the Nazis started to round up the Jews of Berlin. Liane kept happening upon me as if by chance around the neighborhood or in the lines for rationed supplies. Looking back, it's clear that she had been feeling out whether to recruit me for months, my views on politics extracted indirectly with the skill of a surgeon, the resistance circle she was part of never even hinted at until she was sure. I had said no. But then I said yes.

Q: *How did your work with the Stars progress?*

A: Liane and I met every Wednesday, rain or shine, at five p.m. in the Tiergarten, that sprawling park in Berlin's center. It was not so far from our neighborhood, and there were plenty of remote areas where we could arrange to pass each other. She would admire my flowers, or sometimes offer to buy one, and slip the newest batch of leaflets into my basket with a sleight of hand that made me sure she could have had an alternate career as a magician.

Q: *Was there really a need for such care if you were only distributing pieces of paper?*

A: Absolutely. If either of us were caught, we would have been arrested and then likely tortured for information about other resistance members, and then either sent to a camp or executed. That's how dangerous words can be. Knowledge is power, as the saying goes.

Q: *Did you have a way to communicate with Liane?*

A: Outside our meetings, no. And I don't think either of us ever missed a Wednesday. I suppose I could have gone to her house, but I only did that once, on the day I decided to join. Liane made it clear unexpected visits were not welcome. She had a big house away from the street, lots of tall trees on a sprawling property next to other large properties. I'm sure this helped with her work–not as many neighbors, so fewer prying eyes.

Q: *She was able to stay in the house, even after her father's arrest?*

A: Yes. She would've been nineteen or twenty–we were about the same age–but back then you needed a guardian until you turned twenty-one. Luckily, the war was making strict rules difficult to enforce with so many men at the front, and with the help of one of her father's old friends, she ended up keeping the house. The Nazis had of course already confiscated everything of value–that they found anyway–after her father's arrest. But you're skipping ahead because I got involved in 1941, and her father was arrested closer to the end of the war, so he would have been there when I first went by the house.

Q: *My apologies. Back to 1941. What happened when you first went to the house?*

A: Liane opened the door. And there was someone else behind her, a girl about our age. Allegedly she was a cousin from the countryside who was now under Liane's father's guardianship, but I didn't buy it. Immediately I thought that Liane was hiding her. She looked awfully like a Jewish girl I had met a few times in the prewar days. Sophie something. I remembered her because of this scandalous rumor that she was descended from a prostitute who married into royalty and left the family with a fortune in jewels. You don't hear stories like that every day.

Q: *Did you ask Liane about this girl?*

A: Of course not! In those days, the less you knew the better. And if Liane was involved with hiding people, I didn't want to know about it. Delivering leaflets was already dangerous enough for me. And that's why I never dropped by the house again. But I did wonder about those jewels because Liane once asked me if I knew someone who could get a good price for emeralds, someone who could be trusted. She wanted to trade a stone or two for gold, as the currency wasn't stable, unless you could get US dollars.

Q: *Were you able to help?*

A: No. "Who has US dollars?" I asked her. "And what do you mean, a stone or two?" I was kidding, of course, but she clammed up after that. Not that I could have helped her anyway. I was not much more than a girl, and I had no more idea than she did how to find a reputable jeweler.

Q: *Do you know what happened to Liane after the war?*

A: No. My father managed to get us out of Germany after our house was bombed by the Allies in late 1944. Liane was still making her leaflets, even after her father was arrested. The last time I saw her, she gave me a letter to mail to Switzerland if we made it out. We did, and I mailed it, so at least I did that much for her.

Q: *Who was the letter to?*

A: I don't know. It was so long ago, I can't even recall the town in Switzerland.

Q: *Did you look for Liane after the war?*

A: I did. But by the time I returned, the city was divided by the Berlin Wall. Liane was in East Berlin, I thought, or maybe she had emigrated. She had been so resolute to wait for her father's return, but unfortunately that wait was ill-fated. He died in Sachsenhausen, that was documented, but nothing about Liane. It was only after the fall of the Berlin Wall that I could be sure I had searched everywhere. Some people just disappeared.

Q: *What about the girl you thought Liane was hiding?*

A: Sophie? I have no idea. I don't even know her last name.

Q: *Thank you for your time. I've asked everyone we have interviewed to share one last reflection on their resistance efforts with our readers.*

A: In the end, what I did was small. If you wait until you can do something big, most likely you'll end up doing nothing. It's the same if you think that small things don't matter and so likewise do nothing. All of us doing nothing gets us nowhere. But if there's one thing I've learned, it is this: all of us doing something—small things, good things, kind things, pure things—that's what moves mountains.

SEVENTEEN

Just after 8:00 a.m., a pounding knock topples the framed bear poster to the floor with a thud. Chris stage-whispers through the door, "I came out from the bathroom and saw Cassi behind the front desk. She's apparently been going from hotel to hotel trying to track you down, and she may have been able to see your name and room number on the ledger before I caught her. Don't come out until I give the all clear."

By the time I reach the door, I see Chris's back through the peephole, disappearing down the hallway at a full run. I slide the dead bolt into place just as a familiar black-spandex-clad woman comes into view down the hallway, trailed by a burly man.

"Lucy, are you in there?"

"Ms. Rey?" A male voice this time. Do influencers have bodyguards? The doorknob rattles. Seriously?

"I'm here for the money to fix my camera." Cassi's voice again, high and lilting. "For those of you just joining us, I am live outside the hotel room of the stalker who some say tried to murder me. While many in the comments have suggested she go to prison for life, I am a person of peace and only want compensation for my broken camera because photography is a passion I can't live without. I'll wait as long as it takes, livestreaming everything to my concerned fans."

She's livestreaming? I back slowly away from the door, trying not to breathe.

This shitty hotel room is now my foxhole. Eventually the knocking stops, but when I creep back to the peephole, I see Cassi lurking in wait, her phone set up on some sort of tripod. I wish I had thought to exchange phone numbers with Chris. And also that I'd had the foresight to stockpile food for an emergency. I root around my backpack but come up only with a lone smashed energy bar.

I may as well pack. There's no way I can stay here now. I don't have the money to pay for her camera, and even if she goes away now, she's sure to come back. When Chris gives the signal, I'll smuggle myself into another hotel. Ideally I can use an assumed name and check in without a passport. Maybe I can make it to the chairlift and hike my way to a remote rifugio.

But how will you pay for that? Little Voice asks.

Shit. Could I explain the situation to Taffy in a way that doesn't send her straight to the internet, which—depending how far down the rabbit hole she goes—will alert her that at best I'm accused of assault and at worst my hunt for her sister is now broadcast on at least one website?

As if triggered by my anxiety, my cell phone, still silenced on the night-stand, catches my attention when the screen lights up with an incoming message alert. Against my better judgment, I accept the summons. The lock screen shows it's from Taffy. Lucy, this is urgent! Call me!!!

"Sorry, Taffy," I mutter to the empty room. "I'm in the middle of my own urgent situation."

Throwing the cell phone into my backpack along with everything else, I'm contemplating a shower when a knock comes from the window. Ugh, has Cassi used her magic yoga skills to climb the wall outside? I stare in horror at the thin curtains, wondering if I should drop to the ground in case she and her livestreaming phone can see me through the fabric. But it's Chris I hear from the other side of the single-pane glass. "It's me!"

I open the window to find him standing on a narrow concrete ledge, clutching the thin wrought-iron bar that runs across the window.

"I found somewhere else for you to stay," he says. "Do you think you can climb over this bar?"

I look at him doubtfully. The bar is there to prevent anyone from getting into or leaving the room via the window. The hotel is built on sloped land, and the distance to the ground is about twenty feet. High enough to kill me? I'm not willing to risk it. But then I picture going out the front door in a walk of shame through Cassi, her special friend, and a virtual audience numbering between zero and millions. I'd choose the broken leg any day.

"This is staff parking." Chris jerks his head toward the sad square of asphalt sandwiched between the hotel and the building next door. "Cassi left a couple of people waiting in the lobby. I'm sure they'll think to circle around back eventually."

"Are they all wearing spandex?"

"I think it must be a uniform."

I grab my backpack while Chris works on removing the window screen. Too late, I look down at myself and realize I am wearing pajama bottoms—an old flannel pair with a cheerfully loud elephant pattern—and a tank top.

"We've got to go!" Chris urges. "If you pull the desk chair over to the window, I think you can make it."

"Lucy?" At the door, a thud sounds, as if someone has thrown a shoulder into the cheap wood. No shame, but I guess you've got to give the viewers what they want.

Quickly I don my jacket, hiking boots, and backpack. With my new wool hat pulled low, I could be any other hiker. Any other hiker who favors elephant pajamas.

"Ready?" Chris asks.

It turns out that escaping from the window is not as challenging as one would expect. With the use of the rickety chair and Chris's help, I manage to balance myself while throwing a leg over the metal bar. The concrete ledge is wide enough to sidestep on, especially with the bar for support. I creep after Chris down the length of the building, jumping down onto a dumpster and from there to the ground.

I am grinning when my feet touch the asphalt. "It's like we're in a spy movie," I tell him.

"Umm." Chris pauses uncertainly. "A lot less cool than that, but okay."

He leads me from the back of the parking lot down a narrow alley and through a series of back streets, avoiding the main square. I marvel that he seems exactly the same as he did yesterday, before the Cheek Touch debacle.

Maybe he doesn't remember, Little Voice offers hopefully.

Chris stops walking, and I realize that the building in front of us is the backside of the oldest bar in Ortisei. Not far enough from the action to be incognito as far as locations go, but certainly better than a new hotel I can't afford.

The door is nondescript, a rectangle of chipped blue wood next to yet another sporting goods store. Chris produces a large old-fashioned key.

"You live here?"

"No, it's Mum's. The front entrance to the bar is off the main square, but this back entrance goes up to the apartment above the bar." He pushes the door open. "She has her flaws, but she hates cancel culture, so I think she'll champion your cause. When she gets back, that is. As far as I know, she's still off on her spirit quest or whatever."

The chipped door opens onto a dimly lit corridor at the end of which a steep wooden staircase winds up to a second-floor landing. Fishing in his pocket for another key, this one regular-sized, Chris gestures me inside.

The apartment smells musty, as if unoccupied for weeks or even years. Contributing to a sense of abandonment, the entryway has peeling damask wallpaper with a faded Wedgwood blue floral pattern—elegant but decades past its prime. A drooping golden chandelier buzzes with flickering light-bulbs that don't seem up to the task of modern electricity. An intricately carved wooden console table that would be at home next to a fainting couch is stacked high with unopened mail.

"She hasn't done much with the place," Chris says as we move down a hallway that runs the length of the apartment. Two rooms open off to the left, but Chris doesn't turn into either. The kitchen at the end of the corridor is likewise outdated—white-and-black-checkered floor, bulbous refrigerator, gas stove, and small white-enameled kitchen table. A huge window behind the table looks out over the square.

Before the kitchen, the hallway turns at a right angle, and Chris points out a small bathroom before we reach a tiny bedroom and a back staircase. "Mum's room is up there." Chris gestures up the stairs. "You can sleep in here." The bedroom under the stairs is only slightly larger than a closet with a twin bed crammed under the sloping ceiling. "This was my room for a couple of days when I first arrived. There's still some of my stuff around— just ignore it."

"Quaint," I say.

"It's the warmest room in the house, so at least there's that."

"Did you tell your mom I'll be staying here?"

"I texted her, but she hardly ever responds." Chris leads the way back to the kitchen, where he rifles through mostly bare cabinets. His face pinches in annoyance. "I'll bring food later. I guess she mostly eats out."

"Don't worry," I say, even as my stomach rumbles.

"If you give me your room key, I'll check you out and make sure you aren't charged for the rest of the week." He puts a copper kettle on the stove to boil and extracts a rumpled tea bag from a drawer.

"My boss is paying, but fantastic." I attempt a smile, rooting around in my backpack until I find the bulky key.

Though Chris is starting to feel like an old friend, albeit one who rejected me, I've known him for less than a week. I know exactly what Adam would say if I told him that I'd been offered sanctuary by someone I'd known all of two days: *Have you identified all the exits and the nearest butcher knife?*

"Why are you helping me?" I ask, flushing as I recall that he's certainly not motivated by trying to get into my pants.

"It's my fault that Cassi found your room number, isn't it? We're not supposed to leave the ledger out." Chris leans against the sink, looking contrite.

"Fair enough." I wonder if the nice-guy schtick is all an act. But if it is, then what's in it for him?

As if sensing my doubt, Chris offers, "Plus, I've been where you are. I want to help."

I raise my eyebrows, trying to picture Chris climbing out a window to avoid someone accusing him of property damage.

At my expression, he says, "Not *exactly* where you are."

"You weren't in elephant pajamas?"

"No comment," he says with a laugh. "But seriously, after my parents split, I was failing school. No matter what I did, I couldn't get my grades up. Later they found out I had ADHD, but at the time, everyone acted like I was just stupid. And I was what you might call husky and didn't quite have my confidence up, not a lot of friends—a bit of an outsider all around." He offers his charming, dimpled smile. "Guess you could say I know what it's like to need a win."

"Ouch."

He winces. "Sorry, maybe that came out wrong. Let me try again. I have a boring job. It's still the low season. There aren't a lot of mystery girls coming through competing for my assistance."

"Yeah, yeah," I say. "So did you ever get one?"

"One what?" The tea kettle starts to whistle.

"A win?"

"I did." Chris pours hot water into two mismatched mugs, moving the single tea bag back and forth between them.

"What was it?"

"Coding." He moves to the table with the teas.

"Coding?"

"Yeah, turns out that my brain was shite at school but took right to Java. And then I started running, mostly to get away from myself, and I hit a growth spurt. Suddenly I wasn't so hard on the eyes."

Understatement of the century.

"Wait, you work as a coder?" I try to square this with his current job at what might possibly be the worst hotel in Ortisei.

"I did. Now I'm on sabbatical."

"Why?"

Chris's mouth tightens, almost as if he doesn't want to answer, but then he says, "I created an app that sold a few months ago. I needed a breather."

The penny drops. "You're a tech millionaire."

He grimaces. "I wouldn't go that far. It's mostly in stock, so it's not like I have a lot of liquidity."

"Why do you even have a job?"

"Mum doesn't know about the app. She doesn't know much about me, to be honest." He looks suddenly like a lost little boy. "That was a bit of the point in renting a place and coming out here, to try to get to know her better. Getting a job was easier than explaining why I didn't need one. Plus, it's only part-time and not a bad way to pass the time, pitting my atrophied social skills against the demands of customer service."

"You're a strange bird."

Chris grins impishly. "This strange bird has to finish his shift." He stands, his tea hardly touched. "But I'll come back with provisions after work. Unless you plan to leave before that?"

For a moment, I'm undecided. With the rental car, I could flee Ortisei anytime I want. But where would I go? Run back to Reno and Adam's pull-out couch? Fully commit to stalking Julian? Crawl back to Grandmother? No. What I want is to finish the job I've been hired to do.

"I'm not leaving before I find Coco," I say.

Chris's phone starts to buzz. "Ack, they've noticed I'm gone." He hands me both keys and heads for the door.

Alone in the apartment, I consider how to move the search for Coco forward under these new conditions. When I pull out my phone to search for a signal, there is no internet. Too wet and miserable to search out a SIM card yesterday, I still don't have data. Guess I won't be calling Taffy back anytime soon.

Lacking other entertainment options, I give myself a tour. It doesn't take long. The upstairs seems like an attic converted into a master bedroom suite, but this is an assumption on my part because the door at the top of the stairs is locked.

My room has nothing of interest aside from a chest of drawers that I rifle through without a second thought, empty but for a few items of men's clothing. These are likely the things left behind that Chris had referenced. The bathroom has one toothbrush and generic shampoo and conditioner sitting alongside the claw-foot tub. No perfume or makeup or even a hairbrush, though Ingrid's bathroom could be upstairs.

The narrow rectangle of a living room has two doors inexplicably opening into the long hall—dark wooden furniture, heavy brocade curtains, and worn Persian carpets, all of it dusty. There are no personal touches, no photographs or anything that might make a house a home. And, more pertinent to me, no televisions, computers, or even a radio.

True, Chris said his mother hardly spends any time here, but still. "Creepy," I say out loud. Then I feel guilty because Chris has jeopardized his job (that he doesn't need, but still) and literally climbed up a (small) building to rescue me and lead me to this fusty little safe haven. I should be more grateful.

But also I need internet and some breakfast. Is it safe to venture out? Will Cassi and her squad be prowling Ortisei's few streets livestreaming? If this doesn't die down quickly, Taffy will definitely hear about it. Surely I can manage to lay low for a few hours. It's not like I had a brilliant plan about how to find Coco today anyway.

I unearth some crackers from the back of a kitchen cabinet, so dry they may have been there since World War I. Maybe they came with the kitchen. I sit at the table and munch idly. According to my phone, it's only eleven. I'm at a loss for how to kill more time and decide to investigate whether I can pick up the Wi-Fi signal from the bar downstairs.

Hunting for Wi-Fi is more of an art than a science, and no one has ever complimented my scientific method. Still, I am solid at pushing the network button at regular intervals as I wander the apartment. It's only when I get close to the front window in the living room, the one overlooking the square directly over the bar, that I have some luck.

If I crouch near the floor under the window, a single available network appears, called CellularediGordo. It's definitely not a secure network, but I don't care. If Gordo isn't smart enough to password protect his Wi-Fi network, then who am I to judge? I decide not to overthink phone hacking and other dangers.

When my phone connects to dear Gordo and two bars appear, I feel like I've just discovered potable water. With a bit of trial and error, I determine that lying flat on my stomach, my arm propped up on one of the tasseled pillows from the couch and angled toward the window, boosts me to three bars.

My phone comes alive with bings and pings that herald emails and texts and voice messages arriving from the ether. Probably 99 percent are about my social media debut as a violent criminal—Cassi had used my real name, which no doubt made the story appear in the feeds of anyone an anonymous algorithm determined may know me, even before the livestream. I'm afraid to check any of the messages, but I do owe Taffy something under our agreement. It's now the middle of the night in California, so she should be sleeping, which feels like a blessing.

My email inbox is a mess, and I don't bother to go through it after I confirm that Taffy has not responded to last night's email. Drat, I'll have to respond to her text. Make that texts, plural. I see now that they started coming at intervals last night, all along the lines of "call me, now." My breath quickens. I can't afford to lose this job on top of everything else.

Just seeing your messages, I reply. Do not want to wake you but will report soon on some interesting developments! There are no developments since last night, but I insert a thumbs-up emoji. And then, after a moment of reflection, a happy face for good measure.

Within seconds after I hit send, a request to video chat appears. Seriously, does the woman ever sleep?

"Hello?" I answer cautiously.

Without preamble, Taffy pounces. "Do you want to explain why some backpacking twins are all over social media saying that the Influencer Assaulter—that's you, by the way—grilled them about a search for a lost woman wandering around the mountains with a fortune in jewels?

"You were not, and I quote, to 'directly or indirectly—whether through oral, written, or other forms of communication, allusion, or body movements—reveal, suggest, or otherwise disclose, confirm, or deny what Disclosing Party'—that's me—'or any of her relatives or Associates, living or dead, may or may not have, or had, in their possession, as it relates to jewelry, jewels, or other items of value.'" My phone screen is filled with pink lips and one large, roving eye, burning like Sauron's. "Did you not read the NDA?"

"I did," I lie, though I suppose scanning is a sort of reading. My heart starts to hammer. "The twins are the ones who told *me* about Coco having jewels." I stumble through an awkward recap of my meeting with the Leggings. "I didn't break the NDA," I conclude, unsure whether this is true and hoping she hasn't also heard about the other people I'd questioned.

"Oh, enough, Lucy." Taffy sounds like it's the thousandth time we've gone over this same tired topic. "Do you know your grandmother had to issue a statement?"

I feel faint. For Grandmother to issue a statement, the sky must be falling. To my knowledge, she hasn't spoken to the press for as long as I've been alive.

"A lot of people are speculating she's wandered off with a purse full of jewels and that *she's* who you're trying find," Taffy continues.

"What people?"

"In the comments, where else? One of the gossip blogs has now picked up the story. It's not a major headline, of course—we both know Genevieve is well past her prime—but everyone loves a fall from grace."

I pull the couch pillow over my face, but instead of offering comfort, it smells like mildew. At least it blocks out the light. Even a minor item of celebrity news will be more than enough to infuriate Grandmother. Especially if it proves what I've long suspected is her greatest fear: that the fame of her youth has atrophied into irrelevance. Or worse, crazy old lady. Either development might kill her.

"Oh, Lucy." Taffy sighs heavily. "You're not an ostrich. Putting a pillow over your face isn't going to solve anything."

I had entirely forgotten I was on video. I peek out from behind the pillow, but Taffy isn't visible on the screen. From the flash of brilliant white sheets I see when the phone moves, she seems to be lying in bed. I wonder if that means her husband is out. Or perhaps they have separate bedrooms. I recall the way his hand looked grasping at her and the photos Adam sent of Count Manicure out on the town. Taffy moves back into the frame, and I feel the full weight of her glare.

The view jerks and then settles, as if she's placed her phone on a stand of some sort, and now I can see not only her face but also her torso. She is wearing a silk dressing gown in a bright flower pattern, her cleavage spilling out from a lacy bustier. Not exactly professional attire, but I'm not one to point a finger. "You didn't answer my question."

"Sorry, can you repeat it? I have a bad connection." I wish this weren't a lie. How I suddenly have perfect reception is a mystery.

"I wanted to know if you've heard from your grandmother about her statement?" Taffy leans forward, sounding expectant.

"No," I lie, recalling the message I had deleted midsentence.

In truth, Grandmother has never stopped leaving me voicemails over the years from different numbers, as if I might answer if I weren't sure who was on the other end. But the few times I did, she hadn't said anything in response to my hello, only breathed into the silence until I hung up. At least, I assumed those calls were from Grandmother.

When she left voicemails, on the other hand, she wasn't shy at all, ostensibly calling to check on me but using the opportunity to issue judgments on my life decisions—or at least that's how it seemed from what I heard. Usually I deleted her messages without letting them play through. I had to, because my anger was harder to sustain the longer I listened. Sometimes Grandmother cried. Always she apologized. She wanted to tell me the whole story, she said.

And maybe the whole story is what scared me away. The whole story could easily be more painful than just continuing to hate Grandmother.

Taffy frowns. "That's surprising she hasn't said anything to you," she says. "You may want to reach out, given the circumstances. It must be up-setting for her to be characterized as losing it when her own mother had dementia for years. Started before you were born, didn't it?"

I nod before I can help myself. Taffy nods back, as if satisfied. Little Voice, asleep at the wheel, belatedly chimes in, *How could she know that?* It's true that Grandmother had closely guarded her mother's condition, and it hadn't been known to the outside world. As far as I knew, no informa-tion was publicly available about my great-grandmother with the excep-tion of that *Life* interview I'd found online. "Where did you hear about my great-grandmother?" I ask, unable to keep the suspicion from my voice.

"Don't try to distract me." Taffy shakes her head as if in awe of my nerve. "I know you're hoping I won't enforce the NDA, which you've clearly violated, and you've now drawn attention to my sister in the international press of all things, when I could not have been clearer that this is a highly confidential family matter."

International press seems a bit of a stretch, though to be fair, I have no idea where the story may have spread from Cassi's social media and the blog post that Chris showed me yesterday. Even so, my anger starts to crackle, and my tone is sharp. "Taffy, you've told me so little about what your sister is doing here that I've been stumbling around blindly with no idea about what may or may not be confidential. I only asked around to try to find her, which is what you hired me to do. And, if what you say is true, then no one thinks this is about your sister anyway—they think it's about my grandmother!"

Instead of angering her, Taffy seems to find my response reassuring, even calming. She reaches outside the range of the camera and returns holding a cut-glass tumbler full of amber liquid. She takes a long pull. When she speaks, her voice is tired. "I had hoped that this would work out differently," she says. "I didn't think knowing about the emeralds would help you find Coco because what logical person would let people know that they were carrying around something so valuable? And Coco is usually an-noyingly logical. She's a lawyer, for God's sake."

"Are the emeralds what she took from you?"

"Not from me, from our father. She's under some crazy delusion that—" With an irate expression, Taffy turns, as if someone has come into the room. "I'm on the phone," she starts, then mutes herself and moves out of the frame.

In a moment, she's back—part of her anyway. I see her hand as she grabs the phone and then her lips as she brings it close to her face. "We'll continue this discussion later."

Before I can respond, she's gone.

By the time war officially started in 1939, Sophie and her Jewish papers had disappeared—escaped to Great-aunt Liesl in Switzerland, that was the official story. Only Liane and her German papers remained. But we shared them and our identities with a grim determination to actively resist the bleak reality in which we found ourselves. Initially the Stars was just the two of us and our fathers, and then eventually ten people—friends and friends-of-friends, mostly unknown to each other for their safety.

The inspiration for the name you'll no doubt recognize from the story I told you about your grandfather. As for the idea, it came to us after Kristallnacht, when synagogues and Jewish homes and businesses were vandalized and destroyed across Germany, and thousands of Jews assaulted and arrested and raped. The newspapers were not allowed to print what really happened, what we had witnessed with our own eyes. Your grandfather was dragged into the street and beaten so badly that he never again returned to his home of forty-five years. He feared his name was on a list, that he'd be arrested or worse. Given what happened, he was right to be afraid.

One father broken, the other took him in. And so we all ended up in the big, drafty house surrounded by trees that shielded us from prying eyes—the widow and his daughter and the two dear friends they were hiding. It was luck, really. Who saw what. Who reported what. Whether your neighbors secretly opposed the regime. In so many ways, we were lucky. In others, we were not.

In the months that followed, it wasn't only broken bones that kept your grandfather in Germany. There was the question of where to go. He contacted his aunt Liesl, though he hadn't seen her since he was ten and had never met her husband, as well as other friends in parts of Europe that might be safer. But there was no word back from anyone, including Giovanna. We didn't know whether any of these communications had been received or answers sent, as telegrams and the mail were monitored and censored. And then, once the war started, free communication was nearly impossible.

Permission from German officials to leave was itself problematic, but permission from destination countries to enter became even more of a challenge for Jews to procure, even for those with resources. And nearly all your grandfather's money—which he had liquidated shortly before Kristallnacht to facilitate emigration—was stolen. Even the jewels.

All except for one necklace. Your grandfather had lent it to a friend's wife to wear for some occasion. Such a valuable item to lend and yet his generosity blessed him, that's what he told us when the necklace was returned. It was the last thing of material value that remained in his possession after a lifetime of wealth.

"Let this be a lesson to you, my girls, about what you put out into the world!"

And a lesson it was.

Which brings us back to the Stars. Your grandfather spoke five languages and spent his time recuperating from his injuries hunched over the radio trying to find banned foreign broadcasts. In the basement was an old typewriter, a Remington. Why not, we thought, transcribe the banned broadcasts and try to distribute them so that people would have real news instead of Nazi propaganda?

Our fathers agreed to the idea quickly. Then came one of their wealthy former colleagues, who bankrolled our costs, as our fathers were both unemployed with savings stolen in one case and stretched thin in the other. Our expenses were not insignificant—carbon paper so that we could make two or three copies of an original from a single typing session, as well as ribbon ink for the typewriter and later a mimeograph, which allowed us to make even more copies. Plus train and tram and bus fare so that our eventual couriers could distribute the fruits of our labors around Berlin and beyond.

GOOD PEOPLE, IN THIS TIME OF TYRANNY AND UNSPEAKABLE ACTS AGAINST OUR FELLOW HUMAN BEINGS, DARE TO RESIST!

We always started our leaflets the same way. All in caps, always with an exclamation point. We were young and idealistic, certain of the good in the world, if only we could reach it.

At first we put out one leaflet every few weeks, but eventually we published weekly—not only radio addresses and news but also philosophical arguments against the war, authored by various members of our group or sometimes reproduced from foreign media.

We ran to the radio every time an air-raid warning sounded—the German frequencies would go quiet then as newsreaders headed to basements, and it was easier to hear the foreign transmitters.

The leaflets all blur together, except for one, from a 1941 radio broadcast from Winston Churchill. I remember because it seemed that the universe was smiling on our endeavor when Churchill said—and I'll never forget this until the day that I die—"The stars in their courses proclaim the deliverance of mankind." I wish I could quote the rest of that speech for you, but there is only one more line that I can recall: "Not so easily shall the lights of freedom die."

"This!" the four of us cried, eyes shining as we crouched around the radio, all except for your grandfather who was typing it all down furiously as Churchill's booming voice transported us to a place of steelier resolve and less-varnished hope. "This!"

Did our efforts make a difference? Did we change a single mind or touch a single heart? I have no way to know. But at least we never bent a knee to the thing we hated. There is so much more that I could say about these years and the Stars, but we will have time when you are older.

For the awful things that came next, I can only bear to outline them:

By 1944, both of our fathers were gone: one seized on the street in October 1941 after Berlin began its first deportation of Jews to camps, the other in 1944 when an informant claimed "that old professor" was responsible for speaking out against the regime. We girls were out of the house when he was arrested, and the only evidence of the leaflet-making, which we always carefully hid in a concealed crawl space in the basement, was never found. For this reason, we were sure that he would only be detained briefly, that any day he would be home.

We felt the same about your grandfather, though by then he had been missing for nearly three years with no word. I still hope that when it's safe to return to Berlin, both of them will be alive and waiting for us. Is that naïve? It's often the case with hope, but a life without it is too dark to contemplate.

With the arrest of "that old professor," we at least knew what had happened. That wasn't the case with your grandfather. He never quite recovered from his Kristallnacht injuries. Two years later, he still seemed too frail to survive any kind of journey. Even so, shortly before he disappeared, he began revisiting the possibility of escape.

False papers were expensive and hard to come by, but your grandfather was undeterred. He said the dangers were mounting and spoke with increasing urgency about using the emeralds to get out of Berlin. As to what he was doing when he left the house that last day, we can only speculate. He had just regained the strength to walk unaided and moved slowly with a painful limp. The necklace was still in its hiding spot on top of a tall rafter in the attic, but perhaps he had gone out to try to negotiate its sale. Whether he was turned in or simply stopped by a Nazi on the street, we may never know. We never found his papers, so he must have had them, identifying him as a Jew. Or maybe not.

We made careful inquiries and heard he had been seen with a group of Jews detained for transport, but we couldn't be certain. After he disappeared, it was impossible for us to leave Berlin in case he came back. We did everything to find him. Letters, lawyers, visits to hospitals and prisons. "I thought he left with his daughter to Switzerland in 1938?" people would offer. And what could we say to that? Still, we checked every list, called in every favor, inquired of every contact. He was nowhere. Our fathers had once been powerful and connected men, but nearly all their old friends turned their backs. Only one whispered a horrible word: Dachau.

Three years later, when we came home to news from a neighbor that "the professor was marched away by the Nazis," we at least knew where to start. An arrest meant jail and then court. Taking turns with our one set of papers, we checked the courthouse daily, where execution notices were posted. "I'm looking for my father . . ." But by then, with war in full throttle, so many people were looking for fathers and brothers and cousins and mothers and sisters and aunts. So many people had been arrested or disappeared, but unlike with your grandfather, we eventually got an answer. He was in a camp for dissidents.

Both of our fathers were reportedly in camps, but this meant hope. They were, we thought, we never stopped thinking, still alive.

That the authorities never came for us shows that neither of our fathers said anything to implicate us or our work with the Stars. The

Nazis did come back for a second search of the house, tearing it apart and taking what they wanted, but still they failed to discover that crawl space or the Jewish girl crammed in among the typewriter and the mimeograph and her own papers, heart thumping in her ears. All they encountered was the girl who answered the door meekly, her German papers all in order, all authentic, no more than the shy daughter of a maybe-dissident. The lack of proof was perhaps the reason for a camp and not an execution, but it was hard to be grateful for that.

Though the authorities at our door should have been the end to the Stars, we persisted. Our anger by then was a white-hot, blinding rage. We would do whatever we could to chop off the head of the beast.

To you this must sound very dark indeed, though darkness is rarely the full picture. Once, long before war unfolded across the continent, my father and I were away from the house for the summer. We returned to find that a vine from the garden had wound its way into the living room, twining inexplicably through the doorjamb and up the wall. Such is life. Where it exists, there will always be a blossoming, an expansion into the available space, no matter how small.

Even on the worst days, there were cracks in the darkness that affirmed we are more than just animals. These fissures of light are, after all, the reason that you exist.

EIGHTEEN

Outside, fat drops of rain splatter the square. The network Cellularedi-Gordo has disappeared, Gordo likely moving on—perhaps after an espresso break at one of the cafes or in an effort to stay dry—and taking my connection to the outside world with him.

Great. Now if Taffy calls back, I won't be able to answer. I want to hear what she was about to say and press her about the personal details she seems to know about my family and placate her about the NDA. For the next several minutes, I desperately refresh my available networks and move to other windows in the apartment, but without Gordo, it's a lost cause. The joys of old-fashioned living.

The rain is hammering now, and any illusions I had about continuing my search for Coco today despite the threat of a Cassi ambush vanish. There's no way I'm getting rained on for the third day in a row.

Out of sorts, I head to the kitchen and turn on the kettle for more tea. A memory of the last time I saw my great-grandmother flits across my mind, perhaps because of Taffy's mention or perhaps because the Miss Havisham vibe of this apartment would be a perfect setting for Great-grandmother as she appeared then, wandering around in the pink-rose nightgown she favored.

This would have been not so long before she died, and the conversation we had stayed with me, though I haven't thought of it in years. I was in the drawing room, lined by paintings of Matthias's relatives that his children desperately wanted back but that Grandmother, in a spiteful rendition of an evil stepmother, refused to cede after his death. They had opposed the marriage, and Genevieve Saint never forgets.

That day Great-grandmother spoke to me in German, even though I had previously only ever known her to speak heavily accented English, despite German being her native tongue. Even as a child, I knew that Great-grandmother refused to go into Germany, though I did not find this particularly interesting. It simply existed as a fact in our life that family vacations would be anywhere but there.

"Have you seen Samuel?" she asked.

"Who's Samuel?" Not her husband, that's for sure. His name was Harry. According to Grandmother, her parents had an epic love story, and her mother had never looked at another man after his death. Even at eight, I knew of their fairy-tale romance, the one that was so bright that it burned up the romantic luck of the next two (and possibly three) generations.

Great-grandmother didn't answer me, only wandered from the room and into the garden. I followed and took her tiny hand, the skin so thin I could feel the veins beneath. The jasmine was in bloom, so it must have been summer. The air was heavy with the scent.

"Did you know him in Germany?" I tried to prod Great-grandmother back into conversation, but it was like I didn't exist.

"Who is Samuel?" I repeated, the buzz of bees in my ears and the jasmine smell almost overpowering.

"Where is the baby?" Great-grandmother became agitated then. "Why can't I find him?" She wrung her hands, and her eyes were full of grief. Again and again, she demanded to know where the baby was, at such volume that her nurse rushed out to soothe her, and I melted away, back into the house.

In the years that followed, the drama of that conversation hovered at the edges of my memory—the anguish was the rawest thing I had seen in my short life. But by the time I worked up the nerve to ask Grandmother about it, she was more reticent than ever to discuss our family history—I assumed from the pain of losing her mother.

On the stove, the tea kettle shrieks, and I jump. Only then do I remember that the only option for tea is the twice-used bag from this morning, but I'll settle for anything. Watching the water turn a dirty brown, I consider a question I never thought would cross my mind.

Should I call Grandmother? Since such a call is impossible with my currently unconnected phone, the question feels safe to ponder. For years, I had been sure I would never speak to her again, but the emotional reaction I'm having feels more complex than hatred.

Your head is going to explode, Little Voice notes helpfully.

It's true. I've got enough on my plate without tackling a reunion with Grandmother. With my weak tea, I drag myself back to the living room. What I need is a distraction. The only option at hand is a bookshelf full of brittle volumes, some leatherbound and likely valuable, some hardcover that appear to be first editions. Churchill's *A Modern Chronicle*, Lewis's *Main Street*, Buck's *The Good Earth*, Remarque's *All Quiet on the Western Front*, Wharton's *Twilight Sleep*, Lawrence's *The Rainbow*. Like the rest of the apartment, nothing from the twenty-first century.

Returning to my spot under the window with *All Quiet on the Western Front*, I make a little nest of cushions and crack the book open. I last read this in high school, and it's just as disturbing as I remember in its depictions of World War I. At one point, the protagonist cowers with his comrades as explosions rend the air around them, clinging to life in a cemetery.

Sounds like your relationship with Julian, Little Voice says.

My spot on the floor is cold. I rouse myself to search for a thermostat but don't find one. I decide to make myself some more tea, even if it's not much more than hot water. While waiting for the kettle, I idly thumb through my phone. Still no signal, but I check my text messages (nothing) and then my email anyway. I blink in shock at the new message on top. No subject, but it's from Julian. I open it immediately. Eyes flying across my phone screen, I read what he couldn't say to me in person. It's only once I've reached the end of the email that I slide down to the cold tile floor and cry like a child with my head in my hands.

Sometime later, spent and in need of comfort, I am drawn to the claw-foot bathtub. When I turn the spigot, I worry the water will be gray. But no, clear, hot water gushes into the tub in a decidedly modern way. God bless technology. There is no bubble bath, which is disappointing, but I manage to get a good froth of foam going with the generic shampoo.

Steam feathers the bathroom mirror as I strip out of my pajamas and lower myself into the water. The exposed skin on my shoulders dimples with goosebumps, and I lean my head back and sink as far down as I can into the suds, closing my eyes and trying to find comfort where I can.

I think of him again, of course I do. Not Aksel-kissing, headshot Julian, but *my* Julian. The shy boy who presented me with a horrendous poem our first Valentine's Day as a couple about Lucy being Goosy (read with the cutest furrow between his brows and endearing glances at my face to see whether I liked it), who wrote long letters from the Peace Corps and cared deeply about helping others, who knew a million knock-knock jokes and would tell them to children, who—

Just because it was once good doesn't mean it still is. People change. Relationships change. I try to shove Little Voice somewhere deep and dark, but she won't go. *Lucy,* Little Voice says with regret and wisdom and a compassion I can hardly bear. *Let him go.*

Is there any feeling so deep, so certain, a love so profound that one can be sure it's not fleeting? Relationships are houses of cards, held together by all manner of beliefs about what we have and who we are and the alternatives. Are we soulmates? Is it good enough? Is there someone better out there? Will we be more miserable without them than with them? Is it possible to feel whole alone?

I wish I had the answers.

I reach over the lip of the bathtub and grab my phone from the floor to read the email again.

Dear Lucy,

I should have talked to you before I left. You had your own secrets, so maybe you can understand that some things feel too big to talk about. Where do I even start? I've been thinking about the perfect way to say this to you for weeks, and this letter is all I can come up with.

First, I'm sorry for cheating and for the lies. I know I hurt you, and you didn't deserve that. And second, what we had together was real, for a long time. You'll want to know what changed, but I can only come up with the same tired thing people always say: It's not you, it's me. But maybe people always say it because often it's the truth.

I spent my whole life being told that things are black-and-white, but there is this universe of gray that I never knew was possible. A world where I'm not an accountant, and I don't have to just be attracted to women or to men, and I don't have to spend the next twenty-five years married with a mortgage and 2.5 kids on a planet that feels like it's dying only to retire with my life behind me, too old and tired to figure out who I really am and what makes me happy and what I want to add to this world.

Who am I when I climb out from under the mountain of expectations? I can just be me and see what comes. There's nothing to fix, nothing that either of us did. We were never destined for that picket-fence life, and I think one day you'll agree. Maybe you already do.

This may be naïve and definitely cliché, but I truly hope that one day we can be friends.

Julian

When you die, they say that your life flashes before your eyes. Lying in the bath, my relationship with Julian does something similar. His smell when I nestled into his chest and the way his eyes would sparkle when he winked at me and how his mouth would crinkle in a kind of duck face when I made him laugh, but also the lonely nights and the way he would turn away sometimes when I wanted to be held and how he had insisted on the robot apartment even though he knew I hated it and let me work a job that was going nowhere to support his acting career. Adam was right: it hadn't been perfect or even particularly good toward the end.

I had loved him, and he had hurt me, but he could stop being a main character in my life without becoming a villain. I don't want to spend my energy holding on to him, whether in love or in hatred. At first I had been so sure that the only way I could let go of Julian was by looking in his eyes and speaking to him in person. That impulse, I now see, made letting go contingent on Julian, giving him a say in it, when really the only person required to let go is me.

This time after I read the email, I look at it for a long time, like one of those puzzles that you stare at until a picture emerges from a pattern of dots. When faced with things not going our way, giving up too soon may be folly but so is holding on too long. There is a point when you realize the tiny window you were trying to squeeze through is actually a brick wall.

I twist the metal of my engagement ring around my finger. It feels alien against my wet skin and slides off easily, leaving a circular groove behind. When I exhale, my breath comes out in a shudder.

Placing the ring on the side of the tub, I slide down until my head is submerged. In the womb-like underwater silence, I can feel my heartbeat. I guess sometimes that's all we have—the blood flowing through our veins as a promise that there will be another day, another chance, another chapter.

Up Close and Personal with Genevieve Saint

by J. A. Fitzgerald

Fresh off her Academy Award win last week for Best Actress, notoriously reclusive Genevieve Saint agreed to a rare interview. Dressed in black crushed velvet Yves Saint Laurent cossack pants paired with a burgundy bolero jacket, she sips tea primly and answers my questions in spare, precise language. Was she expecting to win an Academy Award? No. Was her daughter, less than a year old and whose name has still not been released to the public, at the ceremony? No. Is her divorce from her second husband, Argentinian Renaissance man Ricardo Nocioni Hernandez (presumably the father of her child), finalized? Yes. Is she single? To this, Ms. Saint offered only a coy smile. At twenty-eight, how does she approach raising her daughter as an "older mom"? No answer.

Dear readers, I feared that I had taken things a step too far! No woman close to thirty enjoys jests about her age. Ten minutes into the fifteen I had been allotted, and I had unearthed for you not a single new fact about one of Hollywood's most beautiful and mysterious leading ladies. But fear not! I had one last trick up my sleeve. While the death of Ms. Saint's father in a car accident when she was a toddler is widely known, Ms. Saint's humble early years thereafter, when her mother cleaned houses to make ends meet, remain largely unreported.

Lt. Harry Edelstein and Sophie Edelstein née Baum purportedly made a love connection in Europe at the end of World War II. A source in the Red Cross told this reporter that the couple met when Lt. Edelstein's unit was stationed at a displaced persons camp for survivors who had escaped Hitler's clutches. What, I asked Ms. Saint, was her relationship with her Jewish heritage? I could see from the surprise that flickered across her face that I had managed the near impossible: to catch the unflappable Genevieve Saint off guard. "I didn't grow up practicing any religion." As to how her mother ended up in the Red Cross camp or how Ms. Saint's other relatives fared during the war, Ms. Saint said only, "It is a painful chapter in my mother's life, and I respect that some things are best left in the past." With brisk efficiency, Ms. Saint's assistant swept into the room. Our time was up.

NINETEEN

The tinny ring of the doorbell comes after dark. Overly pruned from the bathwater and emotionally exhausted, I have been listlessly reading on the fainting couch much like a Jane Austen heroine.

With a counter aesthetic, I roll off the couch with the grace of a manatee hauled onto dry land and bang my way through the hallway, unable to locate a light switch.

"Who is it?" I call, even though I'm fairly certain only Chris has a key to the building.

"It's Chris."

He has a pizza box in one hand and a grocery bag and bottle of wine in the other. The greasy smell of melted cheese assails me as he passes. After placing the pizza box and wine on the coffee table, he hands me the groceries. "Luckily it stopped raining long enough for me to bring some provisions."

"Thanks," I say. "For everything, really."

Chris waves away my gratitude. "I've really only moved you to a different two-star accommodation." He looks pointedly around and then fills me in on the world outside. "Cassi has been livestreaming for half the day about her campaign for #camerajustice, but honestly I think it's more of a publicity stunt. I told her crew they were trespassing, but she then paid for a room for tonight, so—" Chris raises palms to the sky as if he did his best. "But I did want to tell you that Cassi is directly appealing to your grandma to pay for her camera if you won't."

I massage my temples, imagining Grandmother's fury about this on top of everything else.

"Do you want to call your grandma?" Chris asks.

I shake my head. "We're not really speaking."

Or rather, I'm the one not speaking to Grandmother, not since the postcard.

It was my last Christmas in Switzerland before I graduated from college. At that point, I had been in the US for longer than I had lived in Switzerland with Grandmother—first at the American boarding schools Grandmother hoped would get me into Harvard and then at college (not Harvard, to Grandmother's dismay).

It was a mostly unaffectionate but structured childhood, and Grandmother—when I spent holidays at the Swiss chalet—showered me with brief half hugs and "darlings" and cheek kisses. "You're not even European," I wanted to say to her, but that ship had sailed sometime before I was born.

I wouldn't call it a benefit, but the silver lining of having absent parents is that you can reinvent them to your own design, which meant that I contended with the realities of Grandmother while imagining my mother and father as perfect humans. If they had lived—because I had decided my father must be dead too or else he would have retrieved me from Grandmother's clutches—we would be together in a small house with a yard and a rescue dog, living happily ever after, of course.

The stories we tell ourselves allow us to exist in the little piece of reality we are granted. Even more than the reality, the stories are everything. If my mother hadn't died, I was sure, my life would have been different. I would have been different. Easier to love and befriend, less shy and awkward, more bubbly and confident.

Year after year after year, this narrative of myself crystallized. All of my problems were because my mother had died. Grandmother's deficiencies were forgivable because she had lost her only child and had never been very maternal to begin with.

The day I found the postcard on that last winter break in Switzerland, I was in Grandmother's bedroom. I was not allowed in her suite of rooms, so I shouldn't have been there, let alone rifling through her things, which is what I was doing. Grandmother had ventured out for a walk, and I had sprung into action as if this might be my only chance.

As the only one of my admittedly few friends who had ever visited the chalet, Adam had masterminded this particular search. This little expedition was, he said, my graduation present to myself.

"She knows how to find your father," Adam insisted.

This allegation blindsided me. "Really?"

I had believed Grandmother without question when she told me that my father's supremely dull and common name made him impossible to find. I myself had conducted many an internet search, all equally overwhelming in the sheer number of search results returned. Equally compelling was the fact that of all of Grandmother's terrible traits, lying was—so I thought then—not among them.

"I mean, have you even seen your birth certificate?" Adam asked. "She must have it if she enrolled you in school and got you a passport. Frankly, it's weird you don't have it now. You'll need it for life things."

I had never given my birth certificate much thought, though I felt stupid for not thinking of it earlier when Adam raised this possibility. It was common sense that I must have a birth certificate and that it might contain a clue about my father. Perhaps a middle name or a signature. (Spoiler: after our fight, Grandmother sent it to me, and it didn't.)

"She'll have a safe in her bedroom closet," Adam said. "Rich people are super paranoid." Like me, he did not identify himself as a rich person and never had. Before he came out to his parents, he was the youngest of five children and not likely to inherit the family business. And of course after he came out, he was disowned.

Grandmother hadn't exactly disinherited me when I defied her and went to UNR for college. Though she refused to pay for my tuition, she bought my plane tickets to Switzerland over holidays and covered the same summer and winter vacations we had always taken. Right up until that final holiday when I conducted the search of her rooms that would blow up our relationship.

"Get into her room, search for any papers, and then find the safe. We'll figure out how to crack it when we know what we're dealing with. Take pictures," Adam advised.

As with many of our plans, it was so-so at best. But still, as soon as Grandmother headed out in her walking ensemble, I raced up the stairs and into her wing of the house. Heavy antiques and valuable art that I recognized as Picasso, Chagall, and even what I thought might be a Basquiat. The bedroom had a large four-poster bed with an old-fashioned canopy in gauzy white. Everything smelled faintly of orange blossom with a spicy note of ginger.

There was a small desk in the corner of the room of the sort that fashionable ladies in period dramas sit behind to handwrite invitations to balls. The desk did not look decorative—stationery sat next to calligraphy pens and neatly stacked envelopes.

I decided to start there. My birth certificate, after all, was hardly a top-secret file. The desk drawers yielded nothing exciting—pens, more stationery, and a few signed headshots. Still, I ran my hands along the insides of the drawers, as I'd seen detectives do in movies. The three side drawers were empty, but when I reached deep into the space behind the narrow center drawer, my fingers snagged on an edge of thick paper. I pulled free a mangled postcard with surgical precision, managing not to tear it further. When finally extracted, the front of the postcard looked like any number of generic beach-at-sunset shots. *Bondi Beach* was written in neon-pink cursive across the bottom.

Life is full of moments, days and weeks and months of them, and most mean nothing. Much of our lives is a collection of seconds that individually have no bearing on our future selves—the hundreds of errands we run, the thousands of casual comments we make, the millions of people we pass as we go about our daily business without ever knowing their names. But every once in a while, there is a moment that means everything, and we entirely miss its significance.

That was me, before I turned the card over.

At first I didn't know what I was looking at. The card was addressed to Grandmother, the postmark nearly two decades' old, the writing faded and hard to read in the places where the card was bent and worn. *Dear mother* was written in cramped script.

I dropped the card, then picked it up, then dropped it again. Grandmother's second secret child, an error with the postmark, a cruel joke—all of these explanations ran through my mind. Because otherwise, a year after my mother had supposedly died, she had instead been very much alive and writing Grandmother this postcard from Australia.

I wish I could say that I recognized the handwriting, but of course I didn't. Most of the message was illegible. I strained over the text, willing the smudged and faded letters back to life, but all I could make out were disjointed words, none of which cohered.

I picked up a pen from the desk and wrote the words on my arm in the order they appeared: *am, start, try, can't, sorry, love, deserve, Lucy.* No signature, no explanation, only a handful of words that upended the story of who I was in the world. For several moments, I simply stared, birth certificate and my father forgotten.

"Is this from my mother?" I raged as soon as Grandmother walked through the double French doors. I shook the postcard in her face, and she looked appropriately horrified.

"I—" she started. The words died on her lips, her face white as a sheet. If she had reacted differently, I might have believed that the postcard was something other than what it appeared to be. But even when pitted against a world-famous actress, if you have the element of surprise, you can get an honest reaction if you play your cards right.

"Is my mother really dead?" I was hysterical, nearly screaming.

Grandmother took a moment to compose herself.

"No," she said.

Department of Lost Things: Case File 1982-024, Record 12
Notes on Undercover Conversations with Andreas Vitale
Location: Ortisei bar owned by subject's niece, Ingrid Vitale

Subject claims he has never heard of any of the parties involved in this matter, except for his sister, Giovanna, with whom he was not close before her death. He claims that his sister never told him how she came up with the money used to keep possession of the building with the bar and apartment after the end of the war. He was still a child then, more than a decade younger, and this was around the time that his mother, who "lost her mind" after his father's murder, was dying. His sister was savvy in business, that was always his assumption. In fact, she had a reputation as the "Fra Diavolo* of Ortisei." After the war, it was she who kept many local families from losing their properties or worse, especially war widows and orphans, many of whom she took in.

Speaking of orphans, he does have a memory of various children staying with them in the apartment, both during and after the war. They also hid partisans before Mussolini's fall, as well as a few refugees, but Andreas was too young to remember much about this. His clearest memory from that time is of a big black car—the fanciest car he ever saw at that time—coming to the village when he was a child to pick up a baby who had been staying with them. This would have been at the very end of or just after the war. Andreas can't be sure.

He claims not to remember anything else about who the baby was or whether anyone went with the baby, nor did he see or meet anyone from the car. He only remembers this incident because the car stood out and because he was given the first piece of cake he had eaten since the war started. He assumed the people in the car must have brought it. It was an Engadiner Nusstorte, invented in the Engadin region of Switzerland, and that has been his favorite type of cake ever since.

---

* Fra Diavolo is (in addition to a popular pasta dish) an eighteenth-century Italian brigand who stole from the rich to give to the poor like the English Robin Hood.

On the next topic of interest, I confess to a blunder in raising the subject of the emeralds, as Andreas, who seemed legitimately surprised at the mention, then became suspicious, muttering under his breath that "it would explain a lot" if his sister had a secret fortune in jewels (see above, on her spending after the war). When asked if there was somewhere his sister would hide a valuable item, Andreas seemed to prevaricate, denying knowledge. From his expression, Andreas may well attempt to suss out such a hiding place himself. Though challenging as a single agent in the field, best attempts will be made to keep him under surveillance.

On a final note, I have reason to suspect that I am no longer the only operative on the ground. Please inquire.

TWENTY

Earth to Lucy." Chris is waving a hand in front of my face.

"Sorry, Grandmother brings up bad memories," I say, because "My grandmother pretended my mother died and lied to me about it for years" is too much of a mouthful.

"I shouldn't have brought it up," Chris says.

"Don't worry about it." I keep my voice bright. "Shall I get plates, and we can celebrate my great escape?"

"About that." Chris looks uncomfortable. "Gerard has a stomach bug. Nothing serious, but I need to cover his shift."

Immediately I wonder if this is an excuse to avoid hanging out with me. "Of course," I chirp as convincingly as I can muster as I follow him to the door.

"I'll be back tomorrow," Chris says. "Call if you need anything. It'll probably be slow at the hotel if you're bored and want to talk."

I tell him about my SIM card situation. "Can't you get an eSIM?" He laughs at my blank stare. "We'll sort it tomorrow." He looks like he wants to give me a hug but in the end only waves before setting off down the stairs. Maybe he's afraid of Cheek Touch 2.0 if he gets too close. The familiar acid burn of rejection flares to life inside my rib cage.

Stop being ridiculous, Little Voice says. If Adam were here, I know he too would tell me to stop being that despondent kitchen sink girl and watch a Brené Brown video or five. *It's not a rejection when somebody doesn't want to help you cheat on your fiancé*, Little Voice digs in. Only I'm not engaged anymore, at least I think that was clear from Julian's email. Perhaps I should have shared this news with Chris, but it's too late now.

Resigning myself to dinner alone and a wasted day in which I've moved not a single step closer to delivering bad news to Coco, I head to the kitchen. The apartment doesn't have any plates. Nor wineglasses. Luckily the bottle has a screw top because I doubt there is an opener either. I pour a generous mugful, ignoring the aroma of vinegar, and help myself to a slice of pizza, sitting down at the kitchen table in the dark. The wine tastes much as it smells, and in an insult to Italian cuisine, the pizza is not much better than Domino's.

By the time I'm finished eating, it's only nine p.m. Having slept away most of the afternoon, reversing any progress I made acclimating to the time zone, it will be a miracle if I can fall asleep again tonight at all. The hours ahead loom: me stuck with the thoughts pinballing around my head. Is Coco a criminal? Will Taffy sue me over the NDA? Fire me? How does she know so much about my family? Am I really a single woman now? Will anyone love me again? What would Miss Mary say? Is there even a song for this?

I absolutely cannot stay by myself in this creepy old apartment for another second. I reason that Cassi and her crew would be too cool for the decidedly rundown oldest bar in Ortisei, which is only just downstairs. Not much of an opportunity to run into them even if they are out and about. And if I do, well, I'm at the point where so many things in my life are simultaneously self-destructing that I'm starting not to care.

I will, I decide, only venture as far as the bar. In disguise. This is likely overkill, but part of me always wanted to go somewhere in disguise, and it seems like a useful life skill to master.

Unfortunately my disguise options are limited, which is what happens when one is forced to pack for an overseas trip in a carry-on backpack (my own fault since Taffy's economy-minus ticket hadn't covered luggage, and I'd been too cheap to spring for it myself). Among Chris's old clothes, I find a large flannel that I throw over my jeans. I have the wool cap I bought, and

I tuck my hair inside. And then I recall the ski goggles I'd purchased on a whim but not yet used.

But no, wearing ski goggles at night would draw more attention than it would avert. Considering other face-coverage options, I draw a blank. Correction: almost a blank. There is one rabbit I might be able to pull out of my hat of tricks.

Or not. I've seen the movies where regular people end up making fake mustaches or entirely new faces with a contour brush, but I can say definitively that is not realistic unless you have a lot of makeup and either relevant experience or access to internet how-tos. At least, this is what I conclude after trying my best with eyeliner to dot what I hope looks like stubble over my chin, obscuring my scar.

It looks . . . Well, I suppose it will really depend on the light, won't it? Certainly from a distance, the effect *could* look like stubble. The face in the mirror shakes its head in disapproval. Why didn't I take a makeup class in beauty school?

I throw on my new jacket—black and forgettable—and head down the creaking stairs after carefully locking up behind me. As I exit the building and circle around into the square, I keep my head bowed. The rain has stopped, but I dodge puddles shining on the pavement. Inside the bar, most of the tables are empty. No one I recognize except, of course, Andreas, who sits on the same barstool huddled with two older gents who seem familiar from the previous evening. They are engaged in a spirited discussion and don't look up when I enter.

If I sit in the darkest corner of the bar, with my head down, I figure I should be able to use the Wi-Fi in peace even if Cassi and her spandex crew poke their heads in for a quick scan. Maybe my disguise, such as it is, will also be enough to escape Andreas's notice if he happens to look over. If Chris is being honest about working tonight, then there's no danger of running into him. As for Hilde the waitress, I decide I'm okay if she sees me in light drag.

In the corner is the most hidden table, so small and tucked away that I'm not even sure I've seen it before. Partially blocked by the coat rack, it occupies a nook perfect for hiding. Making a beeline toward it, I don't see the man sitting there writing in a small notebook until I am nearly on top of him. I try to back away, but he turns.

"David!" His name jumps out of my mouth, half in shock, half in greeting.

David smiles warmly, looking not at all afraid that I might be a stalker, which is a relief given that I keep running into him. "Lucy!"

Well, that answers that question. Disguise: fail (at least at close range).

David stands, dressed in a leather jacket and dark pants. When our eyes meet, I feel a slightly unwelcome zip of electricity.

"What's up with the—?" David seems to be struggling for a word other than "beard."

"I'm trying out something new with eyeliner," I say, rather haughtily.

That's right, own it, Little Voice approves.

"Right." David pulls out a chair. "Join me? The last few times I've been here, I was the only person under sixty the whole night."

So he's a regular. Unsurprising, I guess. Ortisei isn't that big, and this hole-in-the-wall has a lot of character—exactly the sort of place an academic might frequent. Given how hard it is to see this table, he may have even been here at the same time that I was the last two nights. David gestures grandly and moves to the other side of the table, as if he knows that I want to sit with my back to the door.

I'm tempted to decline, but this really is the only table in the bar where I can be more or less incognito. The thought of returning to the apartment with no connection to the outside world and spending the evening alone is about as appealing as cleaning toilets in a prison.

I sit down.

David pulls his near-empty glass of beer across the table, leaving a slug's trail of condensation behind. "Are you staying nearby?"

"Yeah, above this bar, actually." The words fall out of my mouth.

Why are you telling strange men where you're staying? Little Voice demands, but there's no putting the genie back in the bottle now.

"Really?" David looks surprised. "Doesn't the owner live there?"

"So I hear. She's out of town."

"I've heard about that apartment a lot this week, oddly enough."

"Really?" Now I'm the one who's surprised.

"Have you met Andreas, the old guy with the suspenders at the bar?"

I nod.

"I overheard him telling Hilde that he has been trying to get into that apartment ever since his sister's death—she was a woman called Giovanna—"

"I know," I interject as if to assert that I'm just as up-to-date with the town gossip as he is.

"Right," David continues. "I just wanted to warn you that if Andreas doesn't already know, you may not want to tell him you have access. He was ranting that it's a crime he can't enter his childhood home—I guess Ingrid hasn't given him a key. He didn't say why he wanted to go up there, though." David's look invites me to speculate.

"Beats me," I say. "Unless he's in the market for old books and even older furniture." And then, finding it far more interesting that David overheard a conversation between Hilde and Andreas, I ask, "You speak German?"

David shrugs modestly.

At that moment Hilde appears with a neon-orange Aperol spritz. "Your usual."

"It's not my usual," I grumble, peeved that she also knew it was me. So much for mastering disguise as a life skill.

Hilde shoots a dark look at David, then turns back to me. "You have dirt on your face."

"It's facial hair," I start indignantly.

Hilde gives me a pitying look before moving away.

I resist the urge to swipe at the eyeliner, instead excusing myself to the bathroom, where I confirm in the mirror that my makeup stubble skills are even worse than I'd thought. To be fair, the lighting in Ingrid's bathroom upstairs was very poor. With a paper towel, I scrub ineffectually at my jawline until it is red, my scar raised and irritated. The hat will have to suffice as disguise enough.

On my way back to the table, Hilde's raspy voice stops me. "How is your search going?"

"Good." I keep my tone noncommittal.

"I—" she starts, but David comes up next to us.

"Can I get another beer, please?"

Hilde nods tightly and moves away. I follow David back to the table, wondering what Hilde had been about to say. Could she have found a clue about Coco?

"No more need for the disguise?"

I shrug but don't answer, fully appreciating how ridiculous I am. David's foot grazes mine under the table as I sit. Is he playing footsie with me? It's the sugar bowl all over again. With the sting of Chris's rejection still fresh, the idea of someone showing interest feels like a balm.

See? Little Voice crows. *People like you!*

The first notes of "Bella Ciao" blare from the speakers.

Can they seriously be closing already? It's not even ten.

As if in answer, Hilde bangs down David's beer and the bill. "We're closing in fifteen minutes."

David hands Hilde his card and motions to my Aperol spritz. "I've got this too."

Hilde sighs, pulling the little machine from her apron pocket to run the card. *Someone's having a bad day*, Little Voice observes.

From the bar, Andreas calls out something in German that I can't quite make out, and Hilde moves away from us.

I take a sip of my spritz. To be honest, it's growing on me.

"You were telling me about the beard," David says.

But I don't want to tell him about the beard. I don't want to tell him anything. I'd prefer to be the one asking the questions. Possessed by a boldness, I grab for his notebook with the speed of someone who has been nicking items for years.

"Let's talk about you instead," I say, flipping to a random page and starting to read out loud.

"Antonio thinks his uncle had a painting that someone took after he was sent to the camp." I look up at David, who swats at my hand in an effort to retrieve his notebook. With the table between us, I easily evade him. I continue reading: "Two flowers on it? One blue or vase was blue? An aunt said it was a van Gogh. A. isn't sure why. Aunt now dead. A. doesn't know who saw painting in real life. No known pictures of it. Uncle died in Auschwitz. Cousins now in America, A. thinks. No way to contact them."

I flip to another page, then another. All appear to be interviews about missing items. David grows increasingly agitated. He stands and snatches the book. This time I let him. "This is part of your research?" I ask.

He nods, his expression now placid as he tucks the notebook into a jacket pocket as if nothing happened.

"Are you trying to help people find things to combat the trauma?" I try to put it together with what he told me yesterday at the rifugio.

"Most of the things that are lost will never be found." He sounds tired.

"Then why are you writing it all down?"

"Because all these people are going to die, and then there will be no one to remember a painting that might have been a van Gogh or gold buried in a vegetable garden or silverware given to a neighbor to safeguard."

"The authorities are looking into this, surely," I say. "And nonprofits. Aren't there databases?"

David smiles tightly. "If you know that something was stolen from you or a relative, then sure, you have places to go. But if you had something stolen and no one knows because you were killed in the war or at a camp or just fell and got amnesia, then no one is looking. A hell of a lot was stolen and is still resurfacing all over the world. If I don't write it down, maybe no one else will either."

"Something was taken from your family." I know it's not a question.

David's jaw clenches.

"Do you want to talk about it?"

"Nope." David stares at a point over my shoulder, eyes dark with an emotion that smolders just beneath the surface.

"So what happens if you find something?" I try to retreat to stable ground. "Then you get the police involved?"

"Do you know the story of the Italian crown jewels?" David answers with a question of his own.

I don't, and also I don't particularly care, but it's clear David wants to switch the subject, and I have just invaded his private research notes and possibly almost made him cry, so I make a polite noise of inquiry.

"Italy voted for a republic in 1946. Goodbye, farewell to all male members of the Italian royal family. They were exiled from Italy just like that." David snaps his fingers. "Three days after the referendum, the crown jewels get deposited in an Italian bank vault, and various parties have argued over ownership ever since."

"They're still in the vault today?"

"Yep."

This does seem extreme. "Why?" I ask.

"Because no one can agree who has the right to them. The House of Savoy says they do, while the Italian government says they belong to the people. This sort of bickering happens all the time. A collector might buy a painting at auction, and it then turns out the painting was stolen. If the painting is stolen yesterday, most of us would agree that the new buyer should return the painting. But what if it was stolen one hundred years ago and sold legitimately several times since the theft? What if the former owners are long dead, and they have no heirs alive to bring a claim?"

"Your research would help?" I offer.

David shrugs. We sit together quietly for a beat, maybe two, before he says, "You're not wearing your ring."

"Nope." I look down at my finger and the circle of pale flesh where it used to be.

David waits, as if expecting more, but I don't want to talk about Julian. My eyes rove the black-and-white photos on the wall while I grasp for another topic. "Oh my God." The words are involuntary. Standing, I move over to the wall, staring up at a photo near the ceiling.

"What is it?" David moves to stand behind me, following my gaze.

On tiptoe, I just manage to grip the bottom of the frame and wiggle it free. Open-mouthed, I stare at two faces I never expected to see in this bar. Grandmother, decades stripped from her face. And next to her a young girl, no more than ten. My mother.

The child in the photo stares up at Grandmother with such love that it's difficult to imagine there will come a time when she will leave without a backward glance. Well, except for a single postcard, if Grandmother is to be believed.

"It's Genevieve Saint," David says. "They're sitting at the same table we're in, see?" From the angle of the wall visible in the photograph, covered in photos even then, I realize that he's right. "Did you know she'd been here?" David asks, as if he already knows about my relationship to Grandmother. If he's seen Cassi's posts or any of the resulting media, maybe he does.

"No," I say, leaving out that I know hardly anything about Grandmother's past.

Peering around, I see Hilde on the other side of the room. No one is looking at us. Quickly, I tuck the photo under my shirt.

David doesn't even look surprised.

Tilting my head, I consider him: motorcycle hair, a jawline that could cut diamonds, and those wild eyes that seem simultaneously like the best and worst idea. It was always the same with Olivier, back when I was too meek to ask for what I wanted, when I let Olivier make all the moves and accepted whatever he gave me. It was the same with Julian. I don't want to be that girl, not anymore. I don't want to wait to be chosen.

David stares with a frankness that promises all kinds of trouble. Tonight, that's exactly what I want. Someone who says yes instead of no, who—after so much rejection—makes me feel wanted, even if only for an hour.

When Julian met Aksel, there must have been a moment like this—energy sparking against energy, filling the space until there was no longer two separate people but only one mass of atoms, little galaxies spinning and colliding and knotting together until what happens next is inevitable.

"Do you want to get out of here?" I ask.

Department of Lost Things: Case File 1982-024, Record 13
Notes on Undercover Conversations with Ingrid Vitale
Location: Bar owned by subject in Ortisei

Over numerous conversations with subject, this agent was unable to extract information about an emerald necklace. Subject claims jewelry was not part of Giovanna Vitale's estate, and my attempts to see inside her mother's apartment were rebuffed.

As subject spent most of her life away from Ortisei and was not close to her mother prior to her death, I nearly concluded that subject did not have additional information relevant to the investigation. However, the last night I spoke with her, subject's unusually morose mood allowed me to extract previously unknown information (where exact wording is illustrative, quotations used from a secret recording I started when I realized the conversation's import, though I have edited out extraneous commentary):

1. Someone subject would not identify came to town and told her something troubling about Giovanna. Together they found some of her mother's old papers today (subject would not say which or where they were found), which "confirmed the worst." Reading between the lines, it seems as if subject has agreed to work with this person to "right some wrongs," but subject refused to provide additional details.
2. Subject shared the following anecdote, which suggests the "papers" subject found may be related to–or even the originals of?–those sent to Samuel (see Record 7 in its entirety):

"The last time I saw my mother, she was already ill. I asked if there was anything I could do to help her get things in order, but she said she'd already taken care of that. Then she made some comment, like 'Should I have stirred things up after all this time?' I had no idea what she was talking about. When I asked her about it, she said that if she'd found him earlier, she would have told the movie lady, but that it was already too late. 'Sometimes you don't have any good choices,' she said, 'but anyway, I was right in the end.' She also kept repeating: 'He didn't want for anything. And I didn't use it for myself. Only what we needed to survive.'"

When I asked subject what she thought her mother's comments meant, she said: "Of course, I had no idea what she meant at the time. Now I do."

I attempted to get subject to say more about this, but she would not. There was a small piece of paper in her apron pocket that she withdrew to touch, seemingly without realizing it, throughout our conversation. At the end of the evening, when she hung the apron, I was able to snatch the paper long enough to photograph it (see attached). Undated, the paper was yellowed and appeared quite old. The message said:

My dear Sophie,

Times are hard, but I always have spring flowers for you, old friend.

Yours,
Giovanna

The handwriting appears to be a match for the blue-ink annotation on Record 7(b)(ii). I surmise it is an unsent reply to Record 7(b)(ii) and further that it was Giovanna who sent Record 7 to Samuel. I will attempt to verify this hypothesis.

I regret that I did not reveal my identity to subject in an effort to get additional information, as I learned today she has left town unexpectedly with no known return date.

Efforts to gain entry to the apartment will continue. Please advise if breaking and entering is authorized.

TWENTY-ONE

My heart is pounding as David follows me into the apartment. Or maybe it's the picture frame digging into my ribs. I'm not sure what possessed me to take it. A photograph of the people at the heart of my most painful memories is not exactly a recipe for joy.

But sometime, long before I was born, Grandmother had been in Ortisei with my mother. *A lot of people have been in Ortisei*, rational Little Voice reminds me. The Dolomites are exactly the sort of place Grandmother might have chosen for a vacation with her daughter. While shocking to see her face on the wall in a bar all these years later, it's not necessarily anything more than a coincidence.

"Make yourself at home," I say to David, nearly running to my little room under the stairs to tuck the picture frame into my backpack. I'll think about it later. For now I need to focus on what the hell I was thinking asking a man I hardly know into an apartment that's not mine in a clear abuse of Chris's hospitality.

That's right, Little Voice starts in. *What are you doing? Get rid of him before—* I make a Herculean effort to gag Little Voice and leave her locked up inside my head. There has already been more than enough thinking today. I just want one night where I can forget.

When I return, David is walking slowly around the living room. Occasionally he stops to look at something, but it's hard to see clearly because the apartment is dark except for the muted light filtering in from outside.

I move toward the window overlooking the town square. Will I have to make the first move? Before I've always been the one who waited to be noticed, kissed, chosen. In some cases, it had meant waiting forever for something I wanted that never materialized. Like Olivier.

But he was bad for you—Little Voice manages to partially untie herself, but I tighten the restraints. Maybe bad things chosen for yourself are better than good things chosen by others. There's only one way to find out.

David reaches around me to pull the curtain fully open. The night is clear, and stars wink above the dark smudge of the mountains. The building across the way is entirely dark, the square empty at this time of night. David's forearm grazes my shoulder, and I can hear the even rhythm of his breathing.

"It's a beautiful view from up here," he says.

"Mmm." He is too close for me to find actual words. The air between us feels alive, little pricks of electricity nipping down my spine. When I turn, I can smell mint on his breath. My nerve endings zing and pop. In that moment, I want him to touch me more than I want any other thing.

But he doesn't lean forward, doesn't make any move toward me at all. His posture is relaxed, confident, as if it's a foregone conclusion that I will step forward and lift my chin up until our faces are nearly touching, and then thread my hands through his hair as I draw his face to mine.

At first I'm not sure that I will. Can I take another rejection? But then, for once in my life, I take what I want as if sure that it will want me back. It's no tentative cheek touch. After weeks of feeling undesirable and victimized by fate, the assertion is delicious, even when, as I pull him toward me, there is a hesitation, and I fear that I might have misread him.

David's fingers lazily trail down the side of my face. "This isn't a good idea," he says, his voice thick, but then it is he who closes the distance between us.

The kiss is the kind of destructive match that starts forest fires, and the blaze burns away my every thought and fear and sadness. We fumble at each other like teenagers, and I feel a keen gratefulness that my body can still feel this way as his lips dance down my neck, and I pull at his shirt, drawing him into the room under the stairs. The next hour is stolen, furtive, in a way that is only possible between almost strangers. By the time it's over, the borrowed flannel—*sorry, Chris*—is missing buttons, we have both nearly fallen off the twin bed, David has bumped his head on the low sloped ceiling, and there has been laughter and yes, maybe even some tears toward the end because, sweet Jesus, I have not been fucked in such a long time and never, ever by someone whispering multiple languages in my ear.

There was a moment, as he nibbled his way down my neck, my stomach, my hips, when he asked, "Is this okay?" and I briefly considered stopping him. Briefly.

But instead I said yes, quietly, and then more loudly. That other little death, how I'd missed it.

Afterward, we lie sated in the darkness, nearly on top of each other to accommodate the narrow mattress with an old quilt pulled up around us. I doze, though not for long. The bed is uncomfortable, and I am no longer used to my limbs tangled around another's.

When I open my eyes, it is still pitch black in the room. As I adjust myself into a more comfortable position, David runs a finger lightly down my arm.

"You really only came here because of a job?" he asks.

"Why else?" I snuggle back into him, enjoying the feeling of arms around me.

David doesn't respond at first. His fingers continue their leisurely path-finding past my elbow.

Eventually, he says, "It's just—didn't your great-grandmother pass through Ortisei when she escaped Germany?"

I go perfectly still. "How do you know my great-grandmother escaped Germany?"

"It was in the news," he says.

"What news?" I feel myself tense, wondering if he dug up the same ancient interview with Grandmother I myself had read. There was certainly no mention of Ortisei there. "I've never heard of my great-grandmother being here."

"I might have it wrong," David says. "I've been following that influencer's posts—not to snoop but just out of curiosity. I guess I felt invested after helping you escape her. Anyway, there were some crazy comments that I'm probably mixing up."

If I had been in David's situation, I probably would have followed the story too, so part of me understands. But how did he come across it in the first place? *There's something he's not telling you*, Little Voice warns.

"Where did you read—" I start, but then David's hand trails lower, and my breath quickens. As his hand moves between my legs, I turn toward him, other thoughts blissfully silenced. There is only hands and mouths and skin on skin, a primal conversation that exists without words.

David nuzzles into my neck, his lips grazing my scar, and I shiver. Since our kiss by the window, I haven't thought about any of my imperfections, not whether David noticed my scar or whether my legs need a shave or if my breath smells like pizza.

What a gift, to simply exist.

We grew reckless, that's the first thing I'll say.

With both our fathers gone and war drawing ever closer to Berlin, our lives had unraveled, not a thread pulled loose from a sweater but the entire sweater set on fire. How to describe this last year? Ill-fitting clothes and not enough soap, nights playing cards by candlelight to comply with the blackout curfew, hunkering in the basement to transcribe radio broadcasts or shelter from air raids and bombings. By the end, Berlin appeared more rubble than not.

We were alone. No word back from Giovanna or Great-aunt Liesl. Friends—ours and our fathers'—gone from Berlin, some of their own volition and others forcibly removed. Those who remained, we had no reason to trust. Even most of the Stars had disbanded, all except for one—a courier we called Flower Girl.

With our fathers gone, so too went the wariness that had kept us safe. After years of working from the shadows, we started taking bigger risks. Sharing the Liane Terwiel identity papers without incident had made us careless. The years of war had further merged our physical similarities: we were both thinner, our skin sallow from a limited diet. No one looked like an exact match to the prewar photographs on their papers, and this realization emboldened us to push the impersonation to ever greater lengths.

Also, there was this: we needed food. With very little money and a ration card for only one person, we relied on potatoes and chestnuts and anything we could grow in our garden but were still constantly hungry.

With the mounting pressures of survival, it wasn't possible for one of us to sit at home, especially if we wanted to continue the work of the Stars. With only Flower Girl to help, we had to distribute leaflets ourselves as well as locate supplies, work odd jobs for a bit of money or food, and stand in long ration lines for increasingly meager fare.

And so it was that a Nazi guard checked the papers of a girl holding a basket of flowers as she passed through the U-Bahn station on her way to off-load the leaflets hidden beneath them. It was a random check, one that could have gone in a very different direction if he had realized the girl with the German identity documents was actually Jewish, or if he had looked in her basket.

He did neither. Instead he smiled, which led to some polite conversation, then a plan to meet. The romance was strategic, at least at first. He had access to food and provided some illusion of protection. Having a Nazi, even one who was hardly more than a boy, seen coming in and out of the house was helpful if anyone were watching.

But then the love became real; at least I think it did. Even outside of war, many a love story is born of necessity, the line between need and want blurred. Would we have survived without him? It's impossible to know. He brought food and firewood and soap to the girl he thought lived alone after her father's wrongful arrest—that was the story.

Did he ever sense the other girl in the house, reading in the attic those first nights that he came to visit and sleeping there on those later nights when he stayed over? Did he know the supplies he brought were shared?

You'll want to know about him, your father, what sort of man he was. At eighteen, Franz Hammann was not much more than a boy with no real choice on whether or not to become a solider and defend a cause that to my knowledge he never openly supported. That doesn't mean he didn't do bad things in that uniform and for the cause it represented—but on the subject of what he did or didn't do, I simply don't know.

Regardless of whether your father was a good or bad man, a baby was never part of the plan. The very idea was terrifying, with the Allies dropping bombs and shortages of even basic provisions. If there had been time, we would have sought out an alternative. But lack of food made menstruation irregular. By the time it was clear you were on the way, there were no other safe options. We prepared as best as we could, finding a sympathetic midwife from the other side of the city who accepted the story that we were orphaned sisters and asked no questions about the father.

Notwithstanding the censors, getting mail out of the country was virtually impossible at that point, but when Flower Girl left for Switzerland, she agreed to take a letter for Great-aunt Liesl. As determined as we had been to wait out the war in case our fathers returned, your impending arrival changed everything. If it hadn't been the dead of winter or if we knew that someone was expecting us on the other side, we might have left as soon as we knew about you.

At least, I think we would have. But also, there was your father. Love—I think it was love—brought hesitation but also increased your chances of survival. Though Franz was gone by the time of your birth—deployed outside Berlin—he had left money and necessities for your arrival.

At nearly a month old, you met him for the first time. He held you in his arms and cried. It is he who had wanted you to be called Samuel. For his father. Had he lived to tell it, there may have been more to your father's story than we ever knew, because Samuel is most often a Hebrew name. "God has heard," it means. It was perfect.

A few days later, he returned to the front, to the last fortification outside the city. Only two months ago now, though it feels like a lifetime, we heard that he died there. As for his family, I know nothing about them, including whether they knew about you. Even if he'd told them of his love affair, he thought until his dying day that the name of his beloved was Liane, not Sophie. I like to think we could have trusted him fully, but the risk—to you as well as to us—was too grave to chance.

Such a blessing, new life. In that bleak time, you were a spot of joy. But outside our cocoon, the war was not going well for the Germans. News came in whispers about the vanquishing Russian forces skulking ever closer to Berlin, eager to take their pound of flesh for their sisters and mothers and wives, supposedly raped and killed by the German forces. We wondered if Flower Girl had mailed the letter, if we would have a place in Switzerland if we could get out of the city, but could we attempt such a journey with a baby? It seemed even more dangerous than staying.

And then word came that Germany had lost the war. We cheered when we heard and had a little party with the last of the provisions left by your father. Hitler and his lunacy beaten. And yet as far as the world was concerned, the Germans were now the enemy, with no way to prove to a bomb or a bullet that one had been part of the resistance or a Jew in hiding. The great reckoning, for both those responsible and those not, as is always the case in war.

It was around this time that we decided to sew the emeralds into the seam of your grandfather's heaviest overcoat. It was important to keep them safe if we had to run in the middle of the night—not that we thought it would come to that. Even after the hell of the previous years, we were still naïve. Or perhaps only hopeful, that surely the madness could not spiral to new lows indefinitely.

In the days after we knew the war had been lost and the Russian army was coming, I hardly slept. We were still in the big house because we had nowhere else to go, but we had barricaded the windows with furniture and stuffed a few sets of clothing, our remaining money, and all nonperishable food into small bags that we planned to carry if forced to flee.

Though we had never been well-connected with other resistance groups, the work of the Stars was known enough to open a few doors. In this way, we learned of the forger, a Jew with such artistry that there was no identity document he couldn't perfectly mimic. With his skills, it was a mystery why he was still in Berlin. Lucky for us, certainly, because he agreed to make the three of us Swiss identity documents— with the right story, our way out of Germany. But when he showed up at our front door in the dead of night, it was not with papers but with the news that his apartment had been bombed.

He ended up staying with us those last few nights in Berlin. Is it possible that was only three weeks ago? It feels like a lifetime.

We were sleeping in the attic because we could draw the ladder up behind us and the risk of a bomb seemed less than the risk of being stuck in the basement as the Russians descended the stairs. We couldn't all fit in the crawl space, and at least from the attic we had an escape route if anyone entered the house during the night. Out the attic window and across the steep roof slates, down the gnarled branches of the ancient magnolia tree and through the back gate of the garden into the alley, the baby tied with a sheet to one of our backs. It was all there, sketched into the dust of the attic floor like a treasure map to a chest of pirates' gold: our escape.

TWENTY-TWO

Dawn light flexes pale fingers through the window when I wake alone in the small twin bed. I want there to be a rose on the pillow next to me, or at least a note, but there is nothing. Perhaps David is in the bathroom.

"Hello?" I call.

There is no response, but I hear the faintest creak. Is it old wood settling, or is he in the hallway?

"David?" I raise my voice and start to fumble on the ground for my clothes.

No one answers. But did I hear the front door close? Screw the clothes. I bolt from the bed wrapped in the remains of the flannel shirt and speed to the front door. The apartment appears empty.

I head to the window where we first kissed, wondering if I will see David hurrying through the square below. I wait for five minutes but see no one. How did I sleep through his departure from such a small bed?

I have a vague memory of David getting up to go to the bathroom at some point, but surely he came back to bed after? Old insecurities creep in. Was I bad in bed? Did he see the scar in the early morning light and head for the hills—or in this case, the mountains?

I push these thoughts from my head. According to Adam, mentally healthy people look at ambiguous events and view them in their favor, whether they are right or not. (A date doesn't call you back? Intimidated by, rather than uninterested in, you, etc.) Life is hard enough, so why not give yourself the benefit of the doubt?

"David was worried I would reject him so he decided to leave before I could kick him out," I say aloud to the empty room. "It's not me, it's him." Heeding Adam's ghost advice in my head is an unsatisfying substitute for the real thing, but I have no way to call him, unless my unlocked Wi-Fi friend Gordo ambles along (unlikely at this hour).

At least, thanks to Chris, there's breakfast—a slightly stale bag of pastries that I recognize from the hotel buffet, but beggars can't be choosers. Munching my way through a croissant, I straighten up the little room under the stairs so it no longer resembles a sex den and collect the buttons torn from Chris's shirt, scouring the cabinets for a needle and thread. No luck.

After showering and clothing myself like a confident success story ready to start the day, the morning stretches in front of me like hot asphalt without shoes. I need to resume the search for Coco and also figure out how to get out of the Vegas leases and otherwise prepare for a life without Julian, but I'm haunted by the headlines of my current situation:

Broken Engagement! Probably Sued by Taffy!
Unemployed! Abandoned By One-Night Stand!
Reputation in Tatters!

I start to pace, my anxiety a whirling dervish. The living room feels too small. And then I stop. I close my eyes and take a deep breath. I count to ten. My pulse slows. I wish I knew if my music therapy would disturb anyone. Surely just a little wouldn't hurt?

Scrolling through my playlist, I know immediately when I see "Chiquitita" by ABBA that this song is the way. Setting the volume to low, I hold the phone up to my ear. My feet start to tap. *The heartaches come and they go . . .* At first I whisper-sing, but by the time I get to the part about the sun in the sky still shining above me, I'm dancing around the room with full intensity.

And then? Of course I play it again.

"More movement therapy, I see," Chris says from behind me.

My jump is Olympian.

"Didn't mean to scare you," he says. "I've been ringing the bell for like five minutes. And you left the front door unlocked."

"I didn't hear the bell," I say. There's no way I'm going to speculate out loud as to why the front door is unlocked. "What are you doing here so early?"

"I knew you were awake." Chris's lips quirk. "The curtains are open, so I could see you dancing around from the square. It's finally great weather. Get your coat."

"Now?"

"Right-o, before Cassi and her crew wake up."

It's hard to argue with that. I tuck my hair up into my hat and grab my jacket and the goggles. For once, I actually need sun protection here. "Do I need hiking shoes?" I call toward the hallway, where Chris is waiting.

"Yip," he says.

I wonder if I should tell him about the flannel shirt, or what's left of it, but decide to save that for another time. Even if he himself is not interested in me, would he hate that I brought a guy I barely knew into his mother's apartment?

Stop torturing yourself, Little Voice commands. *There is nothing to indicate he cares who you have sex with!* For once I agree with Little Voice and decide not to dwell on it. One's head only has so much space for dwelling, and mine is already filled to the rafters.

Outside the sky is an impossible blue, fragile and clear. Crisp air burns my nostrils. We are the only two people outside this early. There is a strange sense of liberation in being on the move with absolutely no plans, very little money, and a new pair of hiking boots. In the distance, the Dolomites are the palest shade of gray with a tint of lavender. I start toward the escalators, but Chris stops me.

"Not that way," he says. "We're going to hike up." He gestures broadly in the direction of the peak.

"The mountain?" If it sounds like I find the idea preposterous, it's because I do.

"Why not?" Chris says. "You know who's not going to hike up that mountain? Cassi."

It's a good point. Hiking up a steep trail for absolutely no reason is exactly what a girl on the run should do to stay one step ahead of any pursuers. Resolutely I pull on my goggles and set out behind Chris without complaint. As we leave the last buildings of Ortisei behind, I stare with no small amount of envy at the chairlift cars gliding on their wires high above, noting with trepidation that the trail seems to follow a nearly vertical ascent.

At first, Chris makes small talk while I struggle along behind him. He is starting to think about going back to Australia. His father misses him. I say very little and am grateful that he fills the silence.

After the first hour, he stops speaking, moving farther and farther ahead. Softly at first, I start to sing "The Keep Going Song." I change the lyrics as I go, from "keep going on" to "keep hiking on" to the "screw Julian song," though I'm breathing so heavily I doubt anyone can tell what I'm saying.

"Are you singing?" Chris asks, stopping to wait for me.

"No."

He seems to notice my eyewear for the first time. "Nice goggles."

"Thanks." I've started to wonder why more people don't wear goggles hiking. In addition to disguise properties and UV protection, there is an impressive amount of polarization that makes the mountain colors pop.

We've reached a vista, not yet the top of the mountain, but a little overhang perhaps halfway up. I can see the narrow ribbon of trail where we started out from Ortisei far below. The air smells clean. A small bird titters. There is an expansive feeling in my chest, a helium balloon that rises and carries my heart with it.

But by the time we start moving again and reach the steepest part of the rocky trail, I feel like I might throw up. Chris hands me a water bottle and an orange and then encourages me to walk just a little farther.

I'm glad when I do. We come to a meadow tucked into a nook between the toothy Dolomite spines. A few bold wildflowers flash a spot of color here and there. The ground is gently undulating, and Chris leads me over to a small grassy mound.

"Natural backrest." He grins and flops down. He pats the grass next to him. "Take a seat."

"Is it wet?" I look at the ground skeptically.

"You're not made of sugar."

"Chris, I'm not really a sit-in-wet-grass kind of person."

"What kind of life are you living?"

What kind of life, indeed.

"Fine," I grumble, pulling off my goggles and taking a seat. "Now what?"

"You lean back like this." He demonstrates leaning back into the little hillock, tipping his head toward the sky.

Why not? I lean back. The long grass is not exactly soft, but it's at least pleasantly springy against my shoulders.

"Look up," Chris instructs. "It's better than therapy, I promise."

"Therapy, huh?" I lean my head back and stare at the half dome of the sky above me. The bright red and yellow parachutes of paragliders circle overhead. I watch them arc around a jagged peak.

Next to me, Chris responds, "My dad had me talk to someone after Mum left. I was thirteen and didn't see her much after that."

I resist the temptation to say something anodyne, like *People we love disappoint us, even if they are doing their best.*

Instead, I dig deeper and say, "I haven't seen my mom since I was four. Not since I got the scar."

"What scar?"

"The one on my face," I say. "You've seen it."

Chris shakes his head, peering more closely at me. "Where?"

Reluctantly I tilt my chin up, brushing my hair behind my ear. This might, I realize, be the first time outside a doctor's office that I have ever drawn attention to my scar on purpose.

With his index finger, Chris traces the damaged flesh under my chin and up to my ear, gentle as a breeze. His eyes take on a deeper cast, as if seeing me for the first time. I shiver, and he drops his hand.

The spell breaks. Feeling shy, I lean away from him. This guy could teach me a thing or two about a cheek touch. "You would have noticed if you were paying attention."

"Not sure that I would have." Chris's voice is gentle. "I guess it depends on if you're the kind of person looking for flaws. Not everyone is, you know."

"I'm not convinced," I say.

"How did it happen?" Chris asks. He is the kind of listener who makes you feel like there is no one in the entire universe but you.

And so I answer. I tell him that my mother left me alone in the kitchen when I was four. This is what I've been told, though I have no memory of it. I'm not sure if she just left the room or if she actually left the building. It was just the two of us in a little apartment in New York City. A frying pan with oil and garlic for pasta sauce was on the stove, and I apparently pulled it down on myself. Grease splashed on my face, and the pan hit me in the head. I was hospitalized for a few days, and then I went to live with Grandmother in Switzerland.

I haven't seen or heard from my mother since, unless you count the postcard.

Chris doesn't make things up about how my mom probably felt responsible and thought she was doing the right thing leaving and no doubt loves me very much, blah, blah, blah. He just holds me with his eyes and says very quietly, "I'm so sorry."

"She was young when she had me. I'm not sure she really wanted a kid, you know? To be honest, I'm not sure Grandmother ever wanted kids either." I look away, unable to bear the eye contact. "I don't normally tell people—" I start. I decide not to mention that Grandmother pretended my mother died in a car crash or that I believed the lie for most of my life. For all I know, my mother might actually be dead by now. "Grandmother would kill me if any of this got out," I say instead. "She's big on privacy."

Chris puts one large hand over mine and gives it a squeeze. "I'm not going to tell anyone. And if you want, I can give you a rundown of my therapeutic highlights on maternal abandonment." There's a twinkle in his eye.

"By all means." I gesture deferentially.

Chris takes on a high-pitched voice and stares over his nose at me as if wearing owl-eyed spectacles. "When people leave, the first thing you have to do is ask if it's you. Did you do something bad, like punch them in the face or spend their life savings on porn? If the answer is no, then the person left because of them, not you. And if you're a kid, then the answer is always that it's about them, not you." Chris tuts like a schoolmarm.

"Is that all you've got?"

"Tough crowd." Chris steeples his fingers and closes his eyes, as if getting into character. This time he affects a deep, trilling baritone in a posh British accent. "Love requires us to work in that space of what we want from someone versus what is possible for them."

"Better." I pretend to examine my nails. "But not enough to jolt me out of a lifetime of bad habits."

"You can't let go or you won't let go?" Now Chris sounds like an American drill sergeant hustling a recruit to do more push-ups. "Don't you tell me 'can't' when you can but just don't want to! Let that shit go! Let that shit go!"

"Now *that* got me motivated." I bow in appreciation. "I guess I too could have such insights if I could afford real therapy."

"But movement therapy is such a delight to everyone around you, as I myself have experienced," Chris says in his regular voice, giving me a small bow in return.

We laugh, the heaviness of the previous moment evaporating as if it had never been there, and then go back to staring at the sky, alone with our own thoughts. I think about Julian, not only the hundreds of disappointments but also how much worse our sex life of late seems after my hot night with David. And as for my mother, I know fake-therapist Chris is right. Certainly a child isn't at fault for a parent leaving. Who was at fault?

"I don't know where your mother is!" Grandmother had shouted after me the last time I'd seen her, as I'd stormed out of the chalet with my bags loaded and the driver waiting. The postcard was clutched in my hand. She seemed surprised that I was actually leaving, as if the last hours of packing had been performative.

"I didn't know how to tell you." Grandmother followed me down the wide marble staircase, under the chandelier dripping crystal in a house far too big for two people. Only now that I was actually leaving was she willing to give me answers, but by then my heart had hardened, and I only wanted to get away from her. "For years, I didn't tell you anything about your mother. I hoped she'd come back, Lucinda. I was sure she'd come back! But she didn't, and I couldn't find her. I tried everything. Everything!" Grandmother's voice trembled. She looked frail, inhabiting all of her years in the space of a moment.

"But she sent a postcard," I said, as if it were a trump card.

"What good is a postcard? There was no return address. And when you were old enough to ask where she was, when I could no longer push off the answer, there hadn't been word from her for years."

"You should have told me the truth." My voice was a ragged thing.

"Your mother—my daughter—may well be dead." Grandmother had eyes like a wounded animal. "Every day it kills me not to know. I didn't want you to spend your life hoping for her to come back. That kind of wondering kills you slowly, I've seen it happen. Do you understand me?"

I hadn't understood, not then.

"I simply couldn't do that to you." Grandmother sagged like a puppet with snipped strings. I turned away from her without answer.

Then and after, I felt that Grandmother had stolen something critical from me and that if she hadn't lied, my life would have been easier. At first I was sure that if I had known my mother was alive, I would have done what Grandmother had not and found her.

But as I lie in Dolomiti grass staring at a blue sky not so far from the Swiss chalet of my childhood, I've had years to come to terms with the fact that Grandmother wasn't hiding me in some remote cottage like Sleeping

Beauty. My mother knew where to find me. If she had wanted to come back for me, she could have. And though I had tried, and even put Maurice on the case, I had not been any more successful in finding her in the intervening years than Grandmother had.

"Does it matter that I only lied because I love you?" Grandmother had called after me as I threw open the front door into the Swiss winter air and prepared to return to a very different life across the ocean. I hadn't answered her.

The red parachute lazily glides past the yellow, turning down and down and down for a landing somewhere behind the mountain I can't see. Miss Mary's voice comes back to me. *Only you know the right question.* The questions I've been asking—why didn't Grandmother do a better job raising me, and why did my mother and then Julian leave, and why hasn't anyone ever, in the history of my life, loved me the way that I want to be loved—might have answers I'd never considered. Maybe it wasn't that they wouldn't, but rather that they couldn't have done any better.

Above me, the sun shines warm on my face. Alabaster clouds scuttle by, wispy ghost ships headed somewhere I can't follow. I track their progress, the way that the shapes shift and reconstitute. On the horizon, a larger cloud mass hovers, purple-tinged and promising rain. On the other side, the mountains are limned in a deep blue, a corona of silver separating earth from sky.

"After the rain of the last few days, that sunshine feels amazing," Chris says.

"It really does," I agree.

All will be well, and all will be well, and all will be well. The repeating refrain from one of my online meditations seems designed for moments like these, when a very small person looks up at the very big world and realizes that despite everything, it's all so fucking beautiful. Painful and chaotic, never constant, always changing when we least want it to, but then there is this, sitting on top of the world.

God, what a view.

Department of Lost Things: Case File 1982-024, Record 9
Notes from Interview with John Carter
Location: Upper East Side, New York City

Assuming the cover identity of a technician sent to service subject's oxygen machine, I gained access to subject's penthouse residence. Subject's daughter, Tabitha Ernst, was present but on a phone call in another room. Based on observation and a medical records' hack, subject is in last stages of decline from pancreatic cancer. Death expected within the month.

Identifying myself as a representative of an organization attempting to reunite legitimate owners with looted property, I asked subject how he came into possession of the emerald he sold at auction in 1947. Subject denied knowledge until I produced paperwork and threatened to show daughter. Subject then related the following narrative, synthesized for clarity:

In the spring of 1945, subject was a sergeant in the US Army 10th Mountain Division, stationed in South Tyrol. His unit was tasked with maintaining law and order and monitoring the demilitarization and disarmament of former Axis soldiers after their surrender to the Allies, as well as to assist in humanitarian efforts.

For a period after the Axis surrender, subject was assigned to an infantry squad that did night patrols over the Brenner Pass between Austria and Italy to intercept Nazis escaping south. Given the difficult terrain, each night patrol consisted of only three soldiers. One night, his patrol came upon a young woman with a baby. She was searched, and he found her German papers.

The two men on patrol with him, one who lost two brothers on D-Day and the other who the subject described as an "unsavory sort," wanted to detain the woman, possibly worse. The soldiers spoke in English, which the subject later realized the woman understood. She claimed he had the wrong papers and produced another set, this one showing her to be Jewish. She said she was traveling to stay with friends in Ortisei after losing all her family and the baby's father.

Subject felt sorry for the woman, but his comrades less so. Anti-German sentiment was high, and German refugees found little sympathy. The woman was pretty. The unsavory soldier returned to his ideas about what to do to the woman, this time more aggressively, and the other didn't seem inclined to stop him. According to the subject, he intervened and saved the woman.

Subject claims he personally drove the baby, who appeared in good health, and the woman, who was in bad condition, wearing dirty men's clothes and shoes that didn't fit, to Ortisei. In exchange, she gave him a necklace of emeralds ringed by diamonds to show her thanks. He protested this was too generous of a gift, but she responded that he had saved her life and, more importantly, the life of the baby. He did not know the baby's name nor ask about the father. He returned her identity papers, both sets.

Subject maintains he does not know who the woman was meeting in Ortisei or what became of her. He dropped her at a bar in the center of town after he allegedly secured food and clothing for her. Subject denies asking the woman why she had the necklace in her possession. He never, he says, encountered the woman or the baby again.

Trying a different tactic, I told subject that it looked to me like he was running out of time to clean up any messes that he may have made in this life before he left it. At this point in the interview, subject's daughter returned to the room, and the interview was terminated.

TWENTY-THREE

We return to Ortisei in time for Chris's evening shift, taking the easy way down via chairlift. Though I am vigilant on our walk from the escalators, I don't see anyone in black spandex and feel comfortable enough to stop to buy a sandwich.

"Cassi may have assumed you moved on," Chris says when he drops me at the door to his mother's apartment. I hope he's right. "I'll let you know if she's still a guest in the hotel when I start my shift," he promises. I'm glad that he doesn't suggest I go back to the hotel. Décor aside, his mother's apartment is much more comfortable.

Inside I kick off my boots and remove my jacket. Another day nearly gone, and my prospects of finding Coco before my flight home are slim. After the staggering beauty of today, with my legs burning pleasantly from physical exertion, I'm ready to count the trip as a success even if I go home with nothing more than my new hiking gear. I said yes to an adventure and took back at least some ownership over my shitty life situation, and as one of Chris's therapy voices would (probably) say, that's a win in and of itself.

I head to the kitchen for a glass of water, taking my phone out of my pocket. Miraculously, it starts to buzz as messages come in. Perhaps it's the fair weather or a boosted signal—whatever the reason, the Wi-Fi from the bar downstairs is suddenly available. I immediately call Adam.

He answers before the phone even has a chance to ring. "Did you hear about Cassi and your grandmother—" he starts, but I cut him off.

"That is seriously old news," I say. "A million things have happened since then." I don't know where to start. Taffy threatening me over the NDA? Julian's email? The photo of Grandmother and my mother in the bar? I decide to start with what Adam will be most excited to hear. "I slept with someone," I announce unceremoniously.

"Sweet Jesus, there is a God," Maurice says.

"Am I on speaker again?" I don't mention that it's early morning Reno time and therefore notable that Maurice and Adam are together.

"Now that the conversation took this exciting turn, yes." Adam sounds ecstatic. "So how was Chris in bed?"

"Not Chris," I say. "David."

"David?" Maurice says.

At the same time, Adam groans. "Not the guy who reminds you of awful Olivier? Chris was so much bett—"

"Chris kind of rejected me first," I interrupt, shaking off the specter of Cheek Touch and recalling the decidedly non-date-like climb up a huge mountain today (there had been his own, much improved, version of a face touch, but I don't linger on that—spending the night with David surely closed the door on Chris, didn't it?). Disappointment prickles, but I ignore it.

"David sounds like a much better choice for a rebound," Adam says loyally.

"He left before I woke up this morning without saying goodbye."

"Clearly he's a loser," Adam pivots.

"Let's focus on the positive," Maurice chimes in. "You're back in the game. And don't rule Chris out yet. No reason to stop at one rebound if you can have two."

"Maurice is right," Adam says. "But do you want to talk about everything else? With all the Cassi drama, I was prepared for a little sob sesh."

"She doesn't want to cry," Maurice says. "Right, Lucy?"

"Then do you want to come home?" Adam asks. "I kind of think you should come home."

"I think I should see this through," I say. "It's only two more days." And if I can find a way to pull Coco out of thin air, there are a lot of ways I can spend twenty-five grand. Getting off Adam's couch. Enough money to live on while I start a job search. Time to figure out what kinds of jobs to search for. All I know for sure is that I have no intention of returning to life as a hairdresser.

"In that case, I found a little something out about the necklace," Maurice says. "I asked a few friends if there'd been any chatter about a necklace recently, and one got back to me today—unofficially—that I'm not the only one who's been asking lately. According to them, the Department of Lost Things might be involved."

"What's that?" I ask.

"I'd never heard of it either," Adam says.

"Very few people have," Maurice says. "Unofficially, no one knows much. Officially, it started in 1942 when World War II was still in full swing, and there was enough of an idea about the scale of the looting to conclude that governments needed to cooperate with each other if they wanted their citizens' stolen art and other valuables returned. It was basically a volunteer effort with representatives from different agencies agreeing to serve as liaisons. Since those days, the Department has evolved into a sort of gray zone. Almost like a secret society. They attract a lot of spy types, looking to be heroes. Most have day jobs with places like the CIA or the French Ministry of Justice or MI6, but moonlight with the Department."

"For an organization that isn't an organization?"

"Exactly."

"Like those quasi-illegal justice leagues in the movies," Adam provides helpfully. "Maurice says they'll go after anything—or anyone—that's missing if the cause is just."

"Don't the police do that already?"

"Yeah, if your laptop gets stolen," Maurice says. "But when you're talking about items worth millions with disputed ownership across international borders, you'd much rather have the Department. Far less red tape. And they seem unconstrained by particular countries' rules when making sure things end up in the right hands. You know what they say, possession is nine-tenths of the law, so their way avoids years of expensive legal fights."

My mind is spinning like a bicycle wheel. "If they're involved, then does that mean they don't think the necklace belongs with Coco?"

"No idea," Maurice says. "Maybe Coco went to Europe to get the necklace. For all we know, the Department is the one who gave it to her. Maybe she's even one of them. I'll try to find out more."

My phone pings. The battery is low. I had forgotten to charge it last night in all the excitement. "I have to let you go," I say. "My battery is about to—" Before I can finish the sentence, my phone dies.

As I plug my cell phone into its charger, I hear a scraping noise above me, as if someone is inside the locked bedroom. "Hello?" I call for the second time today.

Could David have somehow not left after all and been in the apartment this whole time? Has Cassi broken in? Or Andreas? Is Chris's mom back? The last seems the most likely. Stricken, I wonder if I was speaking loudly enough to be heard upstairs.

But then the feeling of embarrassment at being overheard is replaced by one of unease. If someone is upstairs for a non-nefarious reason, wouldn't they have heard me come in and then come downstairs to say hello?

I start toward the stairs, knowing as I do that this is the wrong move. The right move is to run out of the apartment and call the police, only I doubt police respond quickly in these mountain towns. And what if it is only Chris's mom? Calling the police on her wouldn't make the best first impression. Still, better safe than sorry. I double back to the kitchen, wishing I had a taser or some pepper spray. I settle for a butter knife.

Armed but likely not dangerous, I start up the stairs. "Is anyone there?" I call more loudly.

No one answers. Did I imagine the noise? Could it have been a creaky beam or water moving through the pipes? Old houses are notorious for their sighs and groans, everyone knows that. I move toward the locked door. When I try the knob, it turns.

In a way, I feel relieved. If the door is unlocked, then chances are that Ingrid has come home. Ingrid, who has every right to be in her own apartment. Ingrid, who hopefully knows to expect me here because Chris texted her and may even be able to help me find Coco.

Only, why didn't she answer when I called out?

Wearing headphones, perhaps. Or maybe hard of hearing. I decide I should investigate, just to be sure. Also, I want to know what's in the room.

"Ingrid?" I knock and then push the door open when there is no response.

The room is large with high ceilings and an old-fashioned window seat. Unlike the rest of the house, it doesn't feel neglected. The bed is queen-sized with an elaborately carved headboard, flanked by nightstands and covered with a thick down duvet in a neutral beige. There is a television mounted on the wall across from the bed next to a bookshelf, an antique vanity next to the window seat with a mirror so old that the glass wavers, and an old-fashioned standing wardrobe against the remaining wall.

No one is there. Part of a toilet is visible through an open bathroom door on the other side of the room, but it's also empty except for a claw-foot bathtub like the one downstairs and a modern shower. Women's toiletries are cluttered around the sink—a tube of mascara and an expensive brand of face cleanser I recognize.

The bathroom is small, nowhere to hide. I must have imagined the noise. Perhaps Ingrid came home while I was out with Chris, unlocked her room, and then headed out for an errand or to the bar.

Back in the bedroom, I scan the space. There is nothing personal on the nightstands, no photos or journals or even a lip balm. The bookshelf has a more modern selection than downstairs: mysteries, popular fiction, an English-Italian dictionary. If I'm going to be stuck in this apartment with no internet, then perhaps I will borrow something better to read.

I'm about to grab a Margaret Atwood when I see it. Behind the row of books, flat against the wall, is a photo album. The spine is cracked with age. I shouldn't take it out, but curiosity gets the better of me. It's so old that it's unlikely to belong to Ingrid. It's possible she never even saw it.

Glued onto yellowing pages, the photos are faded. Penciled captions in a neat cursive name the subjects under some. Others are unidentified, almost as if the person who made this album did so from photos she inherited rather than appeared in.

I thumb through quickly. There are about twenty pages of photos, all annotated in the same cursive hand. The earliest year is marked 1911, the last 1936. The bar features prominently in many of the photos, as do people I can only assume are Ingrid's forebears.

A jovial man leans on his elbows behind the bar in one image, grinning at whoever is taking the photo, a small girl propped on his shoulders with her chin resting on his head. He looks like a younger version of Andreas's grandfather in the photo above the bar. *Adler and Luisa, 1911.* The Luisa in the photo must be Andreas and Giovanna's mother as a child.

The man and girl appear often in the pictures that follow, though many are unlabeled. Little Luisa never appears with a mother, at least not in an obvious way, though some photos feature family gatherings with several possible candidates.

Hardly any photos between 1912 and 1914 and then none until the end of 1919, which makes sense given World War I. In a wedding photo, Luisa stands next to her father in front of a small stone church in a simple drop-waist gown, clutching a small bouquet with the Dolomites towering behind. Next to her, a handsome man makes a first appearance. *Giorgio and Luisa, 1922.* This must be the anti-Fascist gangster, the one who would go on to be murdered.

Giorgio and Luisa look young and happy in several undated photos, the main square of Ortisei visible behind them in one, the two holding skis in another. In a photo without a caption, the two sit around a table at what looks like a holiday of some sort, a baby in Luisa's arms and Giorgio's arms wrapped around them both.

When I flip to the next page, a few loose papers fall out. One letter is written on paper so thin that I worry it will tear as I unfold it. It is written in German, which my brain translates automatically as I start to read:

Dear Samuel,

Our journey here was even harder than I imagined it would be, and if I don't survive, you deserve to know how you ended up in these mountains a thousand kilometers from where you were born. . . .

Before I get past the first few sentences, a heavy groan sounds behind me. In amazement, I turn to see the antique wardrobe open. Quickly, I shove the letter and pictures back into the photo album and place it on the nightstand, trading the album for the butter knife I had abandoned there.

Assuming a threatening stance, I try to remember anything I might have read on how to defend oneself with a butter knife. Nothing comes to mind.

And then, a hunched woman twists herself out from the wardrobe as if returning from a visit to Narnia.

When I see her face, I gasp dramatically, straight out of a telenovela but unable to stop myself. The woman is Coco.

Excerpt from *My Badass Zeyde Forged Identity Papers for Underground Jews in World War II Berlin*, **published on Steindogblog.com on October 9, 2010**

This is for all you haters who thought I was exaggerating that my zeyde (Yiddish for granddad, if you're not in the know) is an honest-to-G-d hero. He died in my Illinois hometown last week, and on our last visit, he agreed to tell me about how he got out of Germany during the war.

The family already knew he was a member of the resistance. As the equivalent to a graphic designer in those days, he forged perfect fake papers for those on Hitler's shit list. He barely made it out of Berlin after the Red Army swooped in, killing first and asking questions later (did they give a flying f*ck if you were a Jew in hiding vs. a German? Hell no). But we didn't know much more than that.

I said that the world needs to remember. I guess my zeyde agreed, or maybe they had him on the good stuff at the hospital because he made me a little tape. Seriously, he had a little pocket recorder and everything, so I could share it with the family. Anyways, this is what he said:

> Nowadays there are books and movies that leave little to the imagination about that horrible time. The ugliness is true. The cruelty is true. The deprivation is true. But boy, was I lucky to have German identity documents. And I made them for as many others as I could, for other countries too. If I could get the right supplies–the right stamps and paper and ink colors to fake them–I could forge anything. Even with good fakes, though, we were always afraid of being found out. The neighbor-against-neighbor climate of renunciation that later thrived behind the Berlin Wall was already present, and you didn't know who you could trust.
>
> It was April of 1945 when rumors started to spread that Germany

had lost the war. That month was the final wartime performance of the Berlin Philharmonic orchestra, and they say that Hitler Youth held baskets of cyanide capsules at the exits and offered them to departing concertgoers. Hitler killed himself at the end of April, his key supporters also dead or on the run. We weren't sure who was coming for Berlin at that point. The joke in the city was that optimists were learning English and pessimists Russian.

And then we started to hear horror stories from the towns and villages that the Russians were decimating in their wake. While it's now confirmed by history, it was only rumor then. We didn't know how much we should fear their brutality, in the same way that villagers in the far-flung reaches of Russia had not known how much to fear the brutality of the Nazis. Within a week of Hitler's death, the first of the Russian soldiers entered Berlin, carnage in their wake.

I was almost too late getting out of the city. It was a weariness that kept me rooted. Bone deep. I was so tired of surviving by then. It took my apartment being bombed to shake me from my stupor. I thought I was ready to die, but when faced with death, it turned out I wasn't.

But even with Hitler dead, I was still a Jew in Berlin. I couldn't just waltz into a neighborhood air-raid shelter and hope for the best. Most of my friends had been smarter and were gone, but there were two girls from a group that distributed leaflets who took me in. One was a girl called Liane Terwiel. The other was her Jewish friend, Sophie Baum, who was hiding in the house with her baby, Samuel.

Liane had come to me a few weeks before to ask for Swiss papers. The two girls looked alike enough to share Liane's papers, which is how they had gotten by, but they each needed papers to leave together, and of course German papers wouldn't get them into Switzerland. I was surprised they hadn't fled earlier, but Liane told me both of their fathers had disappeared, and they had been waiting for one or both of them to come back. But with news of the Russians coming, even they were persuaded to take their chances.

I said I would help them, of course, though in the end all my forging materials were destroyed along with my apartment. When I went to tell Liane, she said they had plenty of room. This was just after word came that Hitler was dead. We thought it was over, or nearly over. But the fighting continued. The only "soldiers" left to defend Berlin were boys younger than sixteen and men older than sixty. You can imagine how that went. It was an ugly business, the Russians fighting street by street into the center of Berlin.

We were hiding inside the house, making a plan to flee, which wasn't easy to do. That's why so many people stayed put. You have to imagine yourself in a time before internet searches and smartphones, faced with the dilemma of finding your way not only out of your city but also your country when it was surrounded by a hostile enemy, and you had no weapons and very little food.

And the city was already a minefield. Most of the windows had been blown in from the bombing, and soon we could hear women screaming at night. That was only the start of it, the very beginning as the Reds and what was left of the Germans battled for the city.

Now of course we know about the rapes—some say the largest mass rape in history. Millions of German women and girls between eight and eighty were raped as the Red Army moved through Germany in 1945, many multiple times. Hundreds of thousands died from their injuries or by suicide. But I wasn't around for the worst of all that. I told you, when I heard the Russians were coming, I knew that I had to get out. And I did.

But first I wanted to help those girls. And the baby. Sophie had this necklace she'd inherited from her family. Huge emeralds worth a fortune. I had some contacts and thought we could sell the jewels if we made it to Switzerland. For me, it was as good a place to go as any. And Sophie had family there, even if it was only a great-aunt she'd been unable to contact and never actually met, named Liesl just like my own great-aunt, which was a coincidence that gave us a laugh. Wartime humor doesn't take much.

Then, the day we planned to leave, a bomb hit the house and took half the roof off. Glass was everywhere; I was knocked out from the force of it. When I came to, my ears were ringing, and I was covered in dust and debris. The house was on fire, thick smoke all around, and when I managed to dig myself out, I couldn't see the girls anywhere, or the baby.

When I got outside, I passed out. Smoke inhalation, I reckon. No way to say how long I was unconscious, but the next thing I knew, I was lying in a bush, and the second floor of the house had caved in on itself. There was no question of going back inside the house to look for them. I wanted to call out their names, but there were soldiers in the street then, and I couldn't risk making a sound. Or staying put.

I headed south, like we had planned. Even as a man alone, I almost didn't make it. War doesn't just end. Negotiations between all the countries, all the sides, about borders and penalties and retreats were still ongoing, and even when decisions were made, news was sometimes slow to filter down to troops on the ground.

Meanwhile there were still Nazi soldiers afoot, more desperate and unpredictable than ever before. And the Russians. You didn't want to get caught up by them, no matter which side you were on. It was a dangerous time at the end of a dangerous time.

The Alps was one of the last areas to fall. You'll have seen the shows about the Nazis frantically stashing their stolen treasure in lakes and mines, but it was a better place to be than Berlin, in the fresh air with plenty of places to hide.

In the end, I made it to Switzerland. I'm not sure how that trek would have been possible with a baby. It's awful to say, but if they'd come with me, I may not have made it because I wouldn't have left them.

In the last few years, with more and more records online, I thought about trying to find out what happened to them, but I didn't want verification. I like believing that the three of them made it out somehow. There was one small reason to hope: I had a rucksack of supplies hidden in the garden that was gone when I looked for it. Sure, it could have been stolen or destroyed by the blast, but I like to think that the girls took it and that they made it with Samuel out of that hellscape alive. B'ezrat Hashem.

TWENTY-FOUR

All those wet hours scouring the mountain and ineffectually interviewing everyone I encountered, plus two days I basically wasted, and in the end, Coco has come to me. Though I did not expect our first encounter to involve her hurtling toward me like a professional wrestler.

"Drop it!" She barrels into me, and I fall over, luckily not onto the butter knife. Coco is on top of me, twisting my wrist in what seems like a practiced move, but then she appears to notice I'm not exactly brandishing a lethal weapon.

I'm not sure what she was expecting, but she is off me in an instant, looking sheepish. "I heard someone moving around in here and assumed—" She trails off. "But you're obviously not who I thought you were."

Coco helps me to my feet. She is taller than I had imagined, with longer, wilder hair than in her last photo. She wears hiking clothes and a small backpack, which certainly didn't slow her down in attack mode. Her eyes evoke a bird of prey. A hawk, or maybe even a bald eagle. She must have killed it in a courtroom. "Are you all right?" she asks.

Reaching a hand up to my head, I feel a cut. I must have hit the nightstand on my way down like the proverbial sack of potatoes. "I-I think so?" I stammer. Things are not off to the best start.

"To be fair, you did have a knife," Coco says in lieu of an apology.

"A butter knife," I clarify. "I thought you were a burglar." And then I think: I should tell her the bad news right away, before she runs off and takes my chance at $25,000 with her.

"What are you doing here?" Coco demands, with the natural authority of a head nun at a strict Catholic school. Though I don't see a ruler at the ready, I notice that her left hand is near her waistband, just like in movies before someone pulls a gun.

Even though I have just as much right to ask the same of her, I find myself quickly answering, "I'm Chris's friend Lucy. He told me it was okay if I crashed here for a few days."

At this, Coco visibly relaxes. "Ingrid texted me that he had invited someone to stay, but I didn't expect you home in the middle of the day, nor did I expect you to be snooping around your host's bedroom."

"The door was open. I heard a noise." I cross my arms over my chest defensively. "And you were the one in her closet. What were you doing?" Flipping the tables, I try to bring her down a peg.

"Ah, that's right. I haven't introduced myself. I'm Ingrid's friend, Catherine Carter." Coco (I can't help but keep thinking of her that way) offers no further explanation and turns to shut the still-open wardrobe. But before the door closes, I see that the back is diffused by a soft light. I realize that Coco has emerged not from the wardrobe but from a space behind it.

"Is that a . . ." How does one describe a possible portal? "Hidden room?" I finish lamely.

Coco's lips thin. She's clearly not pleased I have spotted whatever it is. "Shall we get you cleaned up?" Without answering my question, she herds me toward the bedroom door.

"Wait!" I go back for my knife. I can't just leave it lying on the floor.

"Why don't you keep that in your back pocket?" Coco asks. "I'd hate to think of you falling on your way down the stairs."

Is she threatening me or being pragmatic? I can't decide. Obediently, I put the knife in my back pocket. My head is throbbing.

From her jacket, Coco takes out a key and locks the door to the bedroom. Does that mean she has permission to be here? I wonder if I should call Chris to check. But first, the bad news.

Before I can say anything, Coco asks conversationally, "Why are you staying in Ingrid's apartment?"

"I'm being stalked by an influencer who thinks I owe her money," I respond with my usual lack of filter. "Chris thought I'd be safe here."

"Stalked by an influencer?" Coco nods toward the stairs, inviting me to walk down in front of her. Smart, not to put her back to the butter knife.

With Coco on my heels, I descend, considering my answer. Or rather, not answering and jumping straight to the bad news. Then I recall that Taffy mentioned something about proof. Recording the encounter seems the most irrefutable way to prove I've delivered the news, but for that I'll need my phone from the kitchen. I have to buy time. Start with something we have in common. That's the easiest path to rapport.

"It's a long story," I say. "My fiancé recently broke off our engagement; I guess that's how it started. Actually, he only officially broke off the engagement yesterday, but it started before that. First he cheated on me with a guy who played an annoying squirrel in his improv group." I veer into the kitchen, hoping Coco will follow.

"My husband was screwing his teaching assistant, so I sympathize," Coco says, taking the bait and following me. "Now he's living with her in the house on Costa Brava he pressured me to buy with the last of my trust fund and all my retirement savings. He'd convinced me to put it in his name since he has Spanish citizenship. My lawyer says I can kiss that goodbye."

Hearing about her husband makes me feel better about my own situation. Misery loves company, as the old saying goes. Though that's not quite right. More that you feel less abused by fate when you realize you aren't the only one without a perfect job, a perfect relationship, a perfect life.

But also, Coco certainly had motive to steal an expensive necklace from her sister's inheritance. Is that what she has in her backpack?

Stay in your lane, Little Voice reminds me. I don't get paid more if I recover the necklace.

"Your husband sounds like a real jerk," I say, quickly palming my phone from the table.

"It took me a long time to realize that," Coco says. "When you give up so much to make it work, what does it say about you if you wasted all that time and sacrifice on someone who wasn't worth it? It's easier to believe they're amazing. Cognitive dissonance is a real bitch."

"Amen," I say, wracking my brain for a distraction. "I could really use a glass of water." I put my hand to my head as if feeling faint.

Obligingly, Coco turns to the sink, and I frantically try to find the record function on my phone. Is it Voice Memo? Before I can locate the app, which I recall seeing but have never used, Coco is coming toward me with a glass of water and a wet paper towel.

"For the cut on your head," she says, looking contrite. "Though it's barely bleeding. And now I need to be on my way."

"No!" I blurt, toning it down with, "What if I have a concussion? Can you stay for at least a few minutes in case I pass out?" I gingerly dab at my forehead. It's true the wound isn't gushing blood, but a sort of painful lump has formed, and I wince as if I'm being decapitated.

Coco looks alarmed. "Do you feel dizzy?"

"Yes," I lie. Anything to keep her in the apartment until I've finished the job.

Dramatically I collapse into a chair, relieved when Coco takes the seat across from me, maintaining a disturbing level of eye contact as if she is medically trained to spot signs of head trauma. Maybe she is.

"Sorry to hear that your dad died," I say to break the ice with a probably more upsetting topic so that my bad news will be better by comparison.

At the narrowing of Coco's eyes, my mistake is obvious. "Ingrid told Chris," I add with forced nonchalance.

And apparently Coco had told Ingrid about her father's death because she accepts this explanation. Even more, she responds as if she's either starved for company or committed to keeping me awake at any cost lest I fall into a coma.

I keep the conversation going for longer than I'd intended, out of curiosity that turns into genuine interest. If I weren't about to stab her in the back, I'd call it bonding. Ten minutes later, I know that Coco's mother died when she was young, and she and her father hadn't been on speaking terms for years for reasons she doesn't disclose, not until March, when her sister called to say he had cancer. Things were going poorly, and her father wanted to see her.

"He was pretty far gone by the time I arrived," Coco says. "There was a full-time nurse, and Taffy and I were tending to him day and night. Me more than my sister. I wanted the chance to make things right between us, but he was barely coherent. He was talking about things that never happened, like he and my mother playing together as children, though she was twenty years younger, things like that. I was hoping for a moment of lucidity, and eventually I got it."

Coco's still holding my water glass, her knuckles white and strained around the crystal. "You're very easy to talk to," she says. "I can't believe I just told you all that."

"I should have warned you I'm a hairdresser. People tell me everything," I say, though I doubt Coco would have told me anything if she hadn't felt guilty about the maybe-concussion.

"I guess I needed to get it off my chest." Coco looks irritated. She pushes the water glass in my direction, and I take it, realizing I'm parched.

It's the nerves. I am, I realize, going about this interaction all wrong. Get in and get out. That was my first intention. Maybe my brain really is addled. I try to gather the pieces of my plan, tattered like a homework assignment the dog got into. Give the bad news. Get proof of me giving the bad news. Get paid. Start new life.

"Coco," I start, pulling out my phone.

"Please, call me Catherine," Coco cuts in. "My sister is the only one who insists on calling me Coco. Do I seem like a Coco to you?"

Does a grizzly seem like a teddy bear? I want to ask, but I settle for shaking my head.

"And how is it you know Taffy's nickname for me?" Suspicion sparks in Coco's expression, as if she had been right to tackle me after all.

"Speaking of Taffy." I clear my throat, feeling my palms start to sweat. "I haven't been totally honest with you. I'm in Ortisei because she hired me as a Bearer of Bad News."

Coco's eyes turn sharp enough to see through my skin to the muscle beneath. "I don't know what that means." Her voice becomes detached and professional, switching into lawyer mode.

"Sorry," I apologize, fumbling with my phone to start recording. "I need to record this." I then say in an overly loud voice:

"Taffy, I am here with your sister. Coco, can you confirm?"

"I told you to call me Catherine."

Coco's glare makes clear this is as much as I'm going to get from her, and I hurry on with the message. "Taffy hired me to tell you that she has a police report ready to go. If you don't bring back what you took, your career will be over." I'd memorized the message, and I go over the words again in my head, adding the final line: "The will is clear, and what you told her is a lie."

There, I've done it. Bad news delivered. Twenty-five grand coming to my bank account. It doesn't feel as good as I had hoped, especially not with Coco staring at me in obvious dismay. My face twists in sympathy and something like guilt. I like Coco, probably more than her sister.

I stop the recording. Coco stands and moves to the window. In shock, I suppose. Before she turns around, I text the recording to Taffy, typing quickly: Good news. I found Coco (bizarrely in the attic closet of the apartment over Ortisei's oldest bar) and delivered your message. Proof attached. Please wire payment. With any luck, the Wi-Fi gods still smile upon me, the message with attachment will send, and money will be in my account by tonight.

"Granted, I knew she would try something, but I thought she would hire someone to snatch it back, not try to reason with me." Coco turns toward me, her face tight. "When a Spanish kid tried to rob me at a rifugio last week, I thought that was Taffy's goon. Poor kid didn't expect that I'm a black belt."

"Yeah, I noticed," I say drily.

"I was sorry that I broke his arm."

She doesn't sound sorry. And though the Leggings hadn't mentioned Pablo's broken arm, Coco's account implies that Pablo had indeed seen the necklace in her bag.

Trying for a casual tone, I ask, "What were you doing traipsing around with the necklace anyway?"

"I thought someone working in one of the rifugios might be—" Coco stops herself. "Oh, you're good. So friendly, so unthreatening, so very easy to talk to. That my sister sent someone after me isn't a surprise. That it was someone like you, I confess I didn't see coming. But now that I know you just faked a head injury to win my confidence, I'm starting to think I underestimated you."

"I'm bleeding for real!" I protest. "But thank you."

"It wasn't a compliment. In fact, you're in over your head, Lucy. If my sister didn't warn you, she should have."

Seeing my confusion, Coco apparently feels obligated to issue the warning herself. "Look," she starts. "It's cost me a lot to get to the bottom of this. I'm on unpaid leave from my job for not being as clear as I should have about whether I was seeking certain information in an official capacity."

I remember that Maurice had alluded to the possibility that Coco had abused her position in making certain inquiries, and her unpaid leave sounds like a confirmation of questionable behavior. It doesn't exactly inspire confidence in Coco's ethics.

"I was too free with information about the necklace in certain circles," Coco is saying, whatever that means. "I thought I was being circumspect, but I miscalculated the interest in this particular item."

"What are you trying to say?" I ask, because I've never been the sort of person who can pick up hidden meanings when people talk around things.

Coco lets out an exaggerated sigh. "I'm saying that now that the word is out, I have no idea how many people—whether sent by my sister or a government or any number of other more nefarious possibilities—are in Ortisei at this very moment looking for the necklace. And if they aren't here yet, they very soon will be. It could be dangerous to be in the way."

"Noted," I say, trying to sound grave. If she expects me to be scared, then she needs to get a lot better at issuing warnings.

Coco purses her lips, as if considering. "I'd like you to give my sister a message back from me."

"Really?" My eyes widen. "Like a reverse Bearer of Bad News?" I wonder what it says about that in my contract.

"No, just tell her what I'm about to say. Wouldn't you do that anyway?"

I pause to consider. Other than the NDA, which apparently expires never, Taffy hadn't mentioned my obligations to her extending beyond delivering the bad news. Coco and I aren't exactly enemies, nor are Taffy and I friends. Of the two, I prefer Coco. "Now that I've given you the news, I don't think I work for your sister anymore," I conclude.

"Tell her this anyway." Coco glowers like a thundercloud. "The information that may have cost me my job was a name: Giovanna Vitale. That's who sold a stone from the necklace after World War II. Tell her to check my work and take her head out of the sand."

The necklace is missing a stone? And wasn't Giovanna Ingrid's mother's name? I recall the little girl from the photo above the bar. Things have taken an unexpected turn, but Coco is still talking.

"That led me to her brother Andreas, who was decidedly uncooperative. But then I connected with Ingrid, and, despite her lack of discretion when Taffy called and caught her off guard, she's become a real partner."

"A partner in what?" I'm still trying to parse Coco's intentions.

"In trying to return the necklace to its rightful owner." At my expression, Coco laughs. "I'm not a criminal. What did you think I was doing?"

"But didn't you steal the necklace?"

"From my perspective, you can't steal something unless it's from the rightful owner."

"Who is the rightful owner?"

"That's what I came here to find out. I knew so little, only what my father told me, but then Ingrid and I made a remarkable discovery. Giovanna had hidden a letter, and the answer was there all along."

Could she mean the letter in the photo album? If only I'd had time to read it.

A ringtone sounds. Coco pulls a phone from her pocket, frowning as she stares at the screen. She starts toward the door.

"But what about Taffy's police report?" I trail after.

"She can go ahead and file it." Coco doesn't turn around. "She thinks I'll fold to save my reputation. She knows I love my job, but my career is already in the toilet. Being accused of thievery won't help the situation, but I'm not sure it will make it worse."

"Wait," I call, as she opens the front door. "I have more questions! And I'm feeling faint!"

"I'm not falling for that again."

"At least tell me what's in the fake closet!"

"It's just a regular closet," Coco says, as if I hadn't seen proof to the contrary with my own eyes.

Before she disappears down the stairs, Coco turns around. "And one more thing: tell my sister that she knows damn well I'm not a liar."

To: g.saint@gsholdings.com
From: taffy@bestatallofitllc.com
Subject: Your granddaughter, Lucy Rey

Dear Ms. Saint,

   Perhaps my previous communications lacked clarity. Or, if you never received them, please find both letters attached. Now that I've managed to get your email address, I won't mince words: My father told me about your mother. There are certain people with an incorrect narrative about the necklace, one that harms us both were it to become public.

   I beg you, can we join forces to keep our reputations from coming to ruin?

   Call me, please.

Taffy

TWENTY-FIVE

As soon as the door closes behind Coco, exhaustion sweeps over me like a plague of locusts. That's what jet lag, a nearly sleepless night of hot sex, a day of mountain climbing, and a head injury will do to a girl.

And then it hits me: I am a Bearer of Bad News, and the bad news has been delivered. I've done it! Just like that, I turn my frown upside down. Whatever my personal and family dramas, I now have twenty-five thousand reasons to smile. I do a little happy dance in the kitchen and sing some Lizzo because the occasion calls for it. *Feeling good as hell . . .*

I run over to my phone to check that the recording sent to Taffy (miraculously, it did—today is my day). Odd that she hasn't responded yet, but I don't dwell on it. We have a legally binding contract, after all. I decide that Coco's message to her sister is too much to type but that I'll relay it as soon as I get Taffy on the phone.

And then, even though the mystery of the necklace isn't mine to solve, I try the door to the room upstairs, curious about the wardrobe. And that letter. *Dear Samuel*, it had begun. While the world is full of many people named Samuel, I remember my great-grandmother's agitation the day she asked me about a baby with that same name. Could it be related to the photo of Grandmother and my own mother in the bar? Coincidence, surely, but a sense of unease starts to build in my chest. Maybe this is my mystery after all.

The door is locked tight, so unless I learn how to pick locks, I'm out of luck. But . . . could I learn how to pick locks?

Between slices of cold leftover pizza, I take advantage of still having internet and spend the next two hours trying to teach myself exactly that with the help of online videos. But without a lock-picking kit, the going is slow. The closest I can find to an appropriate tool is a paper clip, but the metal bends too easily inside the lock to be effective. Or maybe it's not the tool but the wielder that's the issue.

Before I achieve anything close to success, a series of thumps comes from downstairs, loud and insistent. At first I think something must have fallen, perhaps a book from the bookshelf, but when I go downstairs, the sound comes again. *Thump, thump, thump.* It's coming from beneath me, as if someone in the bar is banging a broom against the ceiling.

I check my watch. Just after ten, about the time the bar is usually closing. Could someone be *signaling*? I run through the list of people who know that I'm here: Chris, Coco, David. Chris has the night shift, and if he wanted to reach me, surely he would just come upstairs as he did this morning. Coco, as demonstrated, also has a key.

And if it's David, I'm done with him. Aren't I? I'd wanted a remedy to feeling undesirable, and he had delivered. So what if he hadn't waited around to say good morning? *Now you're getting it.* Little Voice gives me a high-five.

The sound comes again, and I decide I may as well investigate, if only to get it to stop.

"We're closed," Hilde's throaty voice says in German when I enter the bar, but when she sees me, she grins. "I wondered if you'd come down." She is washing glasses, some sort of house music that sounds suited to a rave playing loudly over the speakers.

A snow shovel leans against a barstool. "Were you banging on the ceiling with that?"

Hilde nods. "I heard you tell David that you're staying in the apartment upstairs. I wanted to talk to you." She sounds serious.

After Coco's warning, and with my job here done, I'm not sure I want to be involved with anything more weighty than a last Aperol spritz and a few more hours of ineffectual attempted lock-picking. Surely now that I've completed the job, Taffy won't pay for me to stay in Ortisei any longer, which means this is my last night.

"Does Ingrid know you close the bar this early?" I ask lightly, hoping to steer the conversation in another direction.

"We never really discussed operating times," Hilde says. "I was interested in working here, so I came by and, as it turned out, she needed to get away for a few days. We talked for a while, she said I had good energy, then gave me the key and showed me how to use the card reader. The hours never came into it."

"After she just met you?"

"I have a trustworthy face." Hilde frames her face with her hands and offers a sweet smile.

"Maybe she figured that with only card payments, not much could go wrong." I struggle to picture someone entrusting her business to an almost-stranger.

"I could let people pay cash if I wanted, so she was right about my face." Hilde sounds annoyed, as if she wished stealing were her thing. "Anyway, I hope she comes back soon. I don't have forever."

"You're tired of working two jobs?"

"Oh, the Panorama?" Hilde squints at me. "Yesterday was my last day. I need to go home next week."

"I thought you were here for the summer?"

Hilde shrugs, as if to say that plans change. "Why are you staying in her apartment?" she pivots in a conversational tone. "Ingrid seemed quite possessive over her space, not wanting Andreas inside and telling me it wasn't convenient when I asked to come up to see the view over the square."

"Honestly," I admit, "I'm not sure Chris got her permission before letting me stay." I widen my eyes in what I hope is a charming "oops" affectation.

"What happened to your face?" Hilde asks, staring at my forehead.

I touch the Band-Aid I put over the small cut from Coco's attack. "I was accosted by a creature in the closet," I say.

"Lucy, you're a gem. Just say you bumped into something if that's what happened." Hilde laughs, throaty and full.

I laugh too, because why not? Hilde turns her attention to something behind the bar. "Anyway," she says, the laughter gone from her voice. "David left this for you." She slides a sealed envelope toward me.

There is nothing written on the front, and it is so light when I pick it up that I wonder if it's empty. Desire to tear the envelope open wars with an equal desire not to do so in front of Hilde. Caution carries the day, and I fold the envelope in half and tuck it into my back pocket.

"When?" I ask.

"Just before closing. A half hour ago?" Hilde shrugs.

Even though not a half hour before I had felt sure *I* was the one who never wanted to see David again, it pinches that he apparently didn't want to see me again either.

My reaction must show because Hilde glares. "Don't be upset over that guy," she says. "I tried to tell you last night—he's the one who got you in trouble with the influencer."

"What do you mean?"

Hilde starts to pour from various bottles into a silver cocktail shaker. "When that spandex yoga creature came into the Panorama complaining about a lunatic who almost knocked her off a cliff, he was the one who said it was someone in an orange jacket. I heard him."

My mouth drops. "Why would he say that?"

"You can come clean," Hilde says. "I think it was a public service."

"But it wasn't me! I followed the person I thought did it down the hill but never got a good look, except for a white hat with a pompom."

Hilde's eyes slit. "Are you sure?"

"You know who that was?" My interest piques.

"You're not going to like my answer." Hilde's mouth tightens, as if tasting something sour. "When I took out the trash at the end of my shift, there was a hat like that in the men's room—not that it meant anything at the time, except that I noticed because it looked too new to throw away. And before he spoke to that woman, I saw David come out of the men's room." Hilde vigorously shakes the silver container.

It's not exactly a bulletproof accusation, but enough to snag like a barbed-wire fence. I speak loudly to be heard over the collision of ice. "But he couldn't have known that I would be blamed . . ." I trail off when I remember the timing of the rock, striking the camera when I was already getting intimate with the influencer's bag. "He couldn't know that I'd follow him down the mountain," I try again.

Hilde stares at me without speaking, perhaps waiting for me to reach my own conclusions. "Though I guess most people would run away from an angry influencer," I conclude. "But David is the reason I got off the mountain without her catching me." There is a pleading note in my voice, and I realize how desperately I want Hilde to be wrong. "Why would he frame me only to help me get away?"

"Classic emotional engineering." With a flourish, Hilde pours a stream of red liquid, almost as bold as her hair, into a glass and hands it to me. "It's my version of a Negroni," she says. "Sorry that I don't have any orange for garnish."

"What do you mean by emotional engineering?" I ask, taking a sip of the drink. Bitter and sweet, which seems on point for a holiday in Italy when life is falling apart.

"I mean that he put you in a bad position only to rescue you from that position so that you felt grateful, or trusting, or like you owed him something." Hilde chews on her bottom lip. "Could be all three."

"But—" I splutter. "That was completely unnecessary. I *like* David. I would have liked him without the rescue."

"Would you?" Hilde comes around the bar and perches on the stool next to me, her own Negroni in hand.

I consider my suspicion of strangers, which is currently at an all-time high. Would I have been so open to chatting with David at the rifugio or bringing him home last night if I hadn't felt positively toward him for saving me from potential arrest?

And then my mind seizes on David's comment at the rifugio: *People trust you if you do them a favor—even if it's helping them out of a situation you created.*

"You think he went through all that just to sleep with me?" I cradle my forehead in my hands. "I'm such an idiot!"

"You slept with him?" Hilde looks disgusted. "I guess he has a sort of sexy-nerd thing going on, but—"

"I'm going through a lot right now," I say defensively.

Hilde's face twists in sympathy. "It happens. Maybe I shouldn't have told you, but if it were me, I'd want to know."

"I guess it doesn't really matter," I say, thinking about how many times Olivier St. Trapezus had done something that should have been the last thing, only it wasn't because I kept opening my heart to his lame excuses and infinite chances. Those days are over. "I wasn't planning to see him again anyway, and I'm leaving tomorrow night."

Hilde nods in approval. "For a second I thought you were going to be the self-destructive type."

I try to muster a convincing *Who, me?* look.

"Not that I'm here to judge," Hilde continues. "People like to blow it all up. We can't help ourselves. I blame it on entropy." She pauses, as if considering. "Or maybe the human condition, supposing the two are different."

I have no idea what she is talking about. Maybe she means irrational behavior, the things we do that we can't explain to ourselves. That I understand. Although sleeping with a hot guy after months of deprivation wasn't exactly irrational.

"What are you, a philosophy major?"

"*Jurastudium*, actually. I want to be a lawyer. My interest in philosophy is just a hobby."

"Your English is fantastic."

"I was a high school exchange student in Colorado for a year. That's where I learned to ski." Apropos of nothing, she changes the subject. "What's the apartment upstairs like?"

"Old," I say. I sip at my Negroni, considering. Why not give the girl a view of the square? "You seem to know how to do a lot of things. I don't suppose your skill set includes lock-picking?"

Department of Lost Things: Case File 1982-024, Record 7(a)(vi)
Excerpt (translated from German): Letter to Samuel, Ortisei, 1945

People plan and God laughs, isn't that what they say? Or maybe that the fate you fear most is unlikely to be what gets you in the end. For me that wasn't true.

When we were forced to flee, there wasn't time for the planned escape from the attic. The bomb came out of nowhere. Luckily I was wearing the overcoat with the emerald necklace. Since the Red Army entered the city, one of us had it nearby at all times, outfitted with the bare essentials for a worst-case scenario: both sets of identity papers sewn into the left pocket and a small cup stuffed with a cloth pouch of powdered baby formula in the right.

Just that afternoon, we'd added one last addition to the coat after the forger had used his drafting skills and our vague memories to construct a rough map with Great-aunt Liesl's address in the southwest of Switzerland on one side and Giovanna's bar in Ortisei on the other. Switzerland, which had been neutral in the war, seemed safer than Italy, plus a blood relation was much more likely to be forced to welcome us, but the route to Ortisei was shorter, and the border likely easier to cross. Not much to go on, but it was all we had.

But then, the bomb. Afterward: dazed and bloody and unsure of what to do, the forger nowhere to be found, Russian commands coming from the street, such a terrible fear that we would be found, that you would be hurt. Just do the next thing, just do the next thing. That's what I was whispering out loud to give us strength. Voices coming closer, sounds of moaning, shouting, gunshots. We had to get away, that much was clear.

The forger had a rucksack hidden in the garden with a few supplies. Should we wait, search for him? There had been no sign of him after the explosion. Too dangerous to stay, and we needed the rucksack. I was in shock but managed to find it. Creeping through back gardens, away from the voices, from the sounds of war. Eventually dawn colored the sky bloody pink, and we stopped outside a partially destroyed house at the edge of the city on a mostly bombed-out street. Broken windows, the front door ajar. It looked abandoned, and thank God it was because we collapsed with exhaustion.

Anyone could have come in and found us and the same was true the next night and the next and the next. Wherever we stopped, whomever we encountered, it was a roll of the dice, when or if our luck would run out. I learned that fear has a taste, acrid and metallic in the back of your throat, and that when your heart pounds hard enough, you can hear a river of blood rushing in your ears.

The plan was to head to Switzerland, but without the forger as a guide and dodging soldiers and roadblocks, we ended up closer to the route to Ortisei. From Berlin to Gera to Salzburg, we traveled over the Brenner Pass, avoiding cities and people as much as possible. War is chaos, and the end of war even more so. There are no longer clear sides. No one is safe.

The forger's pack was like something out of a myth: several emergency rations that he must have obtained from a contact in the military. More baby formula, which the war had made dear. A tent. A warm blanket. Matches. It's no exaggeration that we could not have survived without it, not without venturing into towns where we would not have been safe. And you, somehow seeming to know that our survival depended on keeping quiet.

We traveled almost eight hundred kilometers in fifteen days, from sunup to sundown as fast as we could go, you in a sling fashioned from a strip of cloth. Thank God for the bicycle stolen just outside Berlin. When the pack was heaviest, those first few days, it journeyed in the bicycle's basket. That was of course no longer possible when we reached the mountains.

Forced to abandon many of our supplies, we continued only with what could be carried. Two days to Ortisei, based on my calculations. The thought of going directly to Switzerland without stopping to recover our strength seemed impossible. Before the mountains, the spring nights had not been too harsh, but once we climbed higher, it was frigid.

We would freeze to death, that's what I feared. And so I made a fire. We had just settled in for the night, finally warm, when, with a snap of twigs and the nasal twang of English, the soldiers came upon us.

As fearful as I had been of the Nazis and then the Russians, I was just as afraid of these soldiers, their intent just as ill. One day, I will tell you more of what happened. It is sufficient to say that the leader stopped something worse and even drove us to Ortisei, sparing us the final kilometers in that awful cold.

But he took the necklace in return. He had searched me thoroughly for weapons and found it. What a stinging regret that we had not disassembled the necklace and hidden each jewel separately. Before the others could see, he had slipped the necklace into a pocket.

He may well have saved our lives. Does that make it a fair trade? If he had insisted that I give him the necklace before he helped us, I would have. Does that mean it wasn't stolen?

"Please, it's all that we have to start over," I pleaded as I climbed from the car in front of Giovanna's door, emboldened by our arrival to beg.

"What's this?" Giovanna came outside, exclaiming over the state of us, whisking you into her arms.

Still, I held on tight to that open car door and even tighter to that soldier's gaze. "Please," I said again, forcing into that word the keening desperation of all that had been lost. "It's the only thing he has from the past." I turned to look at you, now screaming as if in relief that finally the worst of the danger was behind us.

The soldier's shoulders hunched then straightened. He pulled the necklace from his pocket and used the knife at his belt to pry out a single jewel that he pressed into my hands, all without meeting my eyes.

"Dirty German." His voice was low, as if he were speaking to himself, but full of such conviction that we both knew it was what he needed to believe to put the rest of the necklace back into his pocket.

Some say that history will be the judge, but I feel sure that God alone can fill that role. God sees what history does not, and I am certain that God wept at the fate of the innocent German women and children of Berlin just the same as at the fate of the Jews and Roma and dissidents and gays and disabled and all the others viewed as subhuman by the Nazis, just as the Red Army viewed the unarmed civilians of Berlin as subhuman, just as every army everywhere views the casualties of war as subhuman because the business of war is otherwise impossible.

TWENTY-SIX

As it turns out, Hilde does know about lock-picking. I can't say I'm surprised, though she is vague on the details as to where she picked up this particular talent.

Hilde locks the bar behind us, and we head into the night. In the square, the red onion dome of the church is visible in the low light, the fountain's frolicking children in shadow. Our feet ring out across the cobblestones as we set off for the apartment.

I jump when a voice shouts shrilly: "Lucy!"

The slightly hysterical undertone. The dramatic delivery. The hint of breathy huskiness. I'd know that voice anywhere. Like a siren song, it claws at me. I can't help it. I turn around. There, in the flesh, wearing the pink velour sweatsuit I'd always imagined her in, stands Taffy Waters.

"Thank God I've found you!" Taffy strides toward us. "Not that the hotel I booked for you was any help at all. What a rude clerk! He tried to convince me you'd left Ortisei, but of course I knew that wasn't the case."

I stare in open-mouthed horror. A small dog nestled in Taffy's arms eyes me malevolently from under a shag of dog bangs. Muppet, I can only presume.

"Don't look so stricken." Taffy's smile matches Muppet's eyes, as though they are auditioning for the role of spirit familiars. "Though I guess if I were you, I might look the same way. Not the *same* way because, my God, Lucy, you really do have a face that twists into the most unpleasant expressions. It's like a Halloween mask. What I mean to say is that I'd be similarly fearful if I'd broken a contract and were about to be sued for a small fortune." Muppet barks, as if to highlight that the struggle is real.

While I wasn't entirely certain I had stayed within bounds when it came to the NDA, I had assumed that finding Coco would be enough to put things right. "But I delivered the news." I try to sound confident. "Didn't you listen to your messages?"

"I did," Taffy says. "But I was already in the air by then. Our last conversation did *not* reassure me." Taffy sighs dramatically. "What choice did I have but to come here and find Coco myself? That you found her first is, I'm afraid, too little, too late. Confidentiality was a material term in your contract. *Material.*" She juts her chin toward me. "That means that once you violated the NDA, the whole contract went bye-bye."

I stare at Taffy in horror.

"Who is this woman?" Hilde's deep voice carries an air of authority.

Taffy turns to Hilde. "I'm Countess Tabitha Ernst, Lucy's boss—or rather, ex-boss."

"But I did what we agreed," I sputter. "You owe me—"

"Oh, Lucy, don't be that way! I don't owe you anything. The contract is crystal clear. If you didn't read it, that's your problem." Taffy rolls her eyes at Hilde, as if she's sure to take Taffy's side. "Even so, out of the pure goodness of my heart, I'm not going to make you pay me back for your plane ticket or the rental car. You'll have to pay for gas, of course, and I don't plan to reimburse any additional expenses, but let's not pretend that I'm the evil witch here."

"You just said you were going to sue her." Hilde's voice is deadpan. The fountain burbles placatingly.

"Oh, that," Taffy says airily. "Honestly, I might change my mind."

I'm suddenly exhausted. "Thanks for clarifying," I say, turning to trudge away. Part of me knows that the smart move is to make nice with Taffy so she doesn't sue, but the greater part of me gives zero fucks.

Hilde falls into step behind me.

"Wait!" Taffy shrieks. Muppet starts to bark.

I keep walking.

"You have to tell me where Coco is." Taffy keeps pace with us as we round the corner, and I pull out the ginormous building key.

I start to say I have no idea, but Hilde gets there first. "Actually, she doesn't need to tell you anything."

The door to the building squeaks open. Later I'll curse myself for unlocking anything with Taffy at my heels. Hindsight is, as they say, twenty-twenty.

Taffy shoves in behind us, just as Andreas comes down the stairs. His eyes dart to the side, almost as if he is looking for somewhere to hide.

"I thought Ingrid said you couldn't be in here," Hilde says. She is turning into my de facto mouthpiece, but she's so good at it that I don't mind.

"That's ridiculous." Andreas pushes past me in his haste to get through the door. "I have a key." He reaches into his pocket and waves the large outside door key that appears to be the twin to the one in my hand. He says something else, but Muppet starts to bark viciously, and I can't make out the words.

Hilde looks troubled. I want to ask her what she thinks Andreas was doing but not in front of Taffy.

"Who was that?" Taffy asks as the door slams behind him. Ignoring her, I head up the stairs with Hilde close behind.

"I think you should go," Hilde says when Taffy starts to follow, as if reading my mind. "You weren't invited in."

"I'd be happy to show myself out," Taffy says pleasantly. "As soon as Lucy tells me where to find my sister."

"Until you pay me, you can find her yourself." I'm at the top of the stairs now, but I don't want to unlock the apartment until Taffy leaves.

Hilde stops behind me and Taffy behind her. We stand there, scrunched together in the semidarkness. The stairwell light on the first floor offers little illumination.

"It wasn't free to fly you to Europe or buy your hiking gear," Taffy says. "Your trip and expenses were in exchange for your efforts to find my sister. It's all in the contract."

"Except you said the contract was broken," Hilde says. "As we say in German, what is right for one is fair for another. If you have no contractual obligations to her, then she has no obligations to you either."

"What are you, her lawyer?"

"Just a student from Berlin," Hilde says.

Perhaps on a timer, the stairway light downstairs blinks off, plunging us into total darkness. Either I left a light on inside the apartment or Andreas had more than one key, because the door is limned in gold.

"I can stand here all night," Taffy says. Muppet growls low in his throat. We seem to be at an impasse.

Hilde turns to me. "May I make a small suggestion?"

"Be my guest."

She turns back to Taffy. "Lucy will tell you everything she knows about your sister's whereabouts—"

I open my mouth to protest that everything I know about Coco's whereabouts could fit on an ant's bare behind, but Hilde elbows me in the dark, as if she knows what I'm thinking. I keep my mouth shut.

"—if," Hilde continues, "you agree not to sue and to pay what you owe her."

"No," Taffy says.

Hilde sniffs as if she had been expecting this response. She feels for my hand and grabs the key. I let her take it, and she shimmies past me, shielded by the gloom. "Fine," she says. "But you're not following us into this apartment." With a quick twist, she unlocks the door and releases a blast of light as she shepherds me inside, using her body to block Taffy from following.

"Good day to you," she says, edging backward into the apartment and then shutting the door onto Taffy's arm, which shoots out to block this very move.

"Ouch!" Taffy calls.

"I will break your arm if you don't remove it." Hilde's voice betrays no emotion. "There are no personal injury lawsuits in Europe, not like the US."

A brief tug-of-war over the door ensues, Taffy at a decided disadvantage due to Muppet.

"Fine," she says breathlessly. "I won't sue you if you tell me everything you know, Lucy. In good faith! And assuming there aren't other violations! And—"

"You won't sue her, period," Hilde says. "That's nonnegotiable."

The sliver of Taffy's face I can see through the door is murderous. "I won't sue." She sounds as if she is choking. "But I am not paying another dime."

Hilde, like some sort of Bavarian street fighter, viciously stomps on the sneakered toe Taffy has wedged inside the door. "If you find your sister because of her help, you pay her everything."

Taffy's lips compress until it looks like she is eating them from the inside.

Hilde again tries to close the door, eliciting a yelp—I hope of surprise— from Muppet. "If you know someone else here in Ortisei who has seen your sister, go ask them," Hilde says. "This is an expiring offer."

"Enough," Taffy gasps. "We have an agreement."

When the door opens, Muppet tears into the apartment like a bat out of hell. Taffy must have set him down.

"Oh, you poor thing! He's afraid of the dark," Taffy says as Muppet finds his way into the living room and careens in frantic circles, yapping as if coming out of a drug fugue. "Can you both be dears and just calm him?" Taffy asks. "I'm afraid I just *must* use the ladies'!"

"Taffy, wait—" I start after her.

"Don't worry, I'll find it," Taffy says over her shoulder.

"Come back!" I call, but Muppet is now nipping at my ankles.

I start after Taffy, and Muppet changes direction, cornering Hilde. "I'm afraid of dogs—Lucy, get him, please." She lets out a guttural shriek of pure terror.

"He won't hurt you," I say, though I have no idea what Muppet may be capable of and hope Hilde has on thick socks. "Muppet," I call, trying to sound authoritative. "Muppet, come here." I crouch, hoping that being at eye level might make me approachable. Muppet stops yipping at Hilde and turns to me. Hilde jumps to the relative safety of the couch.

With one ear cocked, Muppet looks like an adorable little tyrant. "Come here," I cajole. With a little yap, Muppet seems to consider it. "I'll scratch your ears," I promise.

This, as it turns out, is the wrong thing to say. Muppet charges like a bull, butting me in the chest with his head before I even register he's on the move. Off-balance, I topple, and he pounces.

"Muppet, you jerk," I gasp as he stands on my chest and barks into my face like a drill sergeant with the ferocity of a dog ten times his size.

When Taffy comes back into the room, Hilde is still cowering on the couch while Muppet and I face off from the corner where I retreated after rolling out from under him.

"Muppet," Taffy coos. "What on earth are you up to?" Immediately quieting, he scampers over to Taffy, and she scoops him up.

Seizing my chance, I follow after Muppet, slipping a hand deftly into Taffy's handbag and extracting the first thing my fingers happen upon. A small rectangular envelope—a hotel key card, by the feel of it. Surely this is something she will notice missing, but I don't care. In a single motion, I shove the card in its envelope into my back pocket.

"I think your dog is possessed." Hilde shoots Taffy a venomous glare, rummaging in her bag for paper and a pen.

Fifteen minutes later, Muppet is asleep on the couch next to Taffy, apparently exhausted from trying to maim us, and Hilde has made quick work of drafting an agreement between me and Taffy. In the one-page document, Countess Tabitha Georgiana Wellington Ernst, aka Taffy Waters, agrees to drop all claims, known and unknown, inclusive of any NDA violations, real or imagined, related to a contract with me, Ms. Lucy Rey, in return for everything I know about the whereabouts of one Catherine "Coco" Carter. Plus, Taffy will not dispute, and will immediately pay, the $25,000 earned from delivering the contracted "bad news" (but only if my information leads her to Coco).

Given that I have no information and no realistic way to force Taffy to pay me, it's enough to know that she won't sue. It's hard to be up in arms about it when my efforts to find Coco were so mediocre—mostly I feel lucky to have escaped Reno and processed a painful chapter in such beautiful surroundings. And I do get to keep the hiking gear, goggles and all, so there's that.

Hilde signs the agreement as a witness, takes a photo of it with her phone, and emails me a copy. Taffy refuses to give any of her contact information, but Hilde doesn't seem bothered. She tries to slip the "contract" to me, but Taffy is fast, springing out of her chair and grabbing it.

"I'll keep that for now," she says.

Hilde frowns, but I hold up a hand—I've had enough of the two of them fighting.

"Look," I say, "if you try to break our deal, Taffy, feel free to sue me. I have no assets, nothing that will make it worth your while, but I'm not above going to my grandmother to make use of her lawyers. They're ruthless and expensive and would probably counsel me to sue you right back for breach of contract, emotional distress, false advertising, the whole nine yards. Let's just say it's in your best interest to view that piece of paper as binding."

Taffy's eyes widen as if I've molted, a little Gremlin emerging with gnashing teeth from my innards. I feel a bit like that, truth be told. Hilde looks smug. Definitely approving. Before I can lose momentum, I tell Taffy everything I know about Coco and where she might be. In short, somewhere in the area, as of five hours ago.

Hilde listens with apparent interest, even asking questions from time to time. What was Coco carrying? How had she gotten into the apartment?

"Ingrid gave her a key," I say. "They're friends. And that's really all I know." I give Hilde a pointed glare. Whose side is she on, anyway?

"Who is Ingrid?" Taffy asks.

Since Coco said I could, I relate the information about the Vitale family, such as it is. "She said you should look into it," I tell Taffy. "Oh, and also that you know damn well she's not a liar."

Hilde excuses herself to go to the bathroom. Taffy shows no sign of being done with her questions, from why I am staying in this apartment instead of the hotel (she's seen Cassi's posts herself so no real brainteaser there) to what (for the fourth time) Coco and I talked about.

When I finish, Taffy shakes her head at me like a disappointed mentor. "You think that's enough for me to forfeit my right to sue you?"

"Our agreement was that I tell you everything I know about where your sister is," I say. "Which I just did. I never promised that I knew anything useful."

"Do you have any idea what it took to get here?" Taffy jabs a finger in my direction. "Or how much it cost to buy a ticket for day-of travel? And I could only bring one of my dogs. Even in first class. That means I had to leave one of my best friends behind, fully half of my emotional support network, and Muppet may not have been the best choice. Nerves, not his fault. But here I am, being perfectly reasonable, and you're sitting there with that smug little grin telling *me* about contracts?"

"That sounds hard." I adopt one of my most useful hairdresser go-tos.

A creak comes from upstairs, and I realize Hilde has been gone for a long time. Should I check on her?

"It is hard." Miraculously, Taffy seems mollified. "By the way, have you spoken to your grandmother lately?"

"No." I frown at Taffy, who is frowning at me.

Just then Hilde returns to the room, face tense, hands balled at her sides. "I'm going," she says, walking straight to the door.

"But—" I still want her help picking the lock. Irritated, I follow her to the door.

"We'll talk tomorrow," she says, leaning closer to me to whisper, "The door is open for you." But this gesture isn't enough to stifle my annoyance that she's changed the plan.

"Just a moment." Taffy has scooped up the sleeping Muppet and follows Hilde out the door. "Don't go anywhere tomorrow," she says to me. "Stay put until I find Coco."

I revert to an oatmeal noise, grateful that she's leaving and trying to hide the envelope I've just snatched from Hilde's bag behind my back. As for Hilde, she will have no trouble getting rid of Taffy if she doesn't want to speak with her, of that I'm sure. The second Taffy is through the door, I close it behind her. Sliding the dead bolt into place for good measure, I immediately head to the second floor, envelope in hand.

The door to Ingrid's bedroom is indeed unlocked. Why had Hilde ventured upstairs without me? Perhaps she had only picked the lock in case we couldn't easily get rid of Taffy. She had been gone for at least twenty minutes if not longer, but given the wasted hours I had spent on the lock earlier in the evening, that didn't necessarily mean anything.

I'll ask her about it tomorrow, I decide. For now, I'm desperate to read the letter. *Dear Samuel* . . . The nagging sensation that my connection to this situation goes deeper than being hired by Taffy is only accelerating. And from the way she brought up Grandmother again tonight, Taffy knows more than she's saying.

I flip the light switch. Everything looks exactly as it did this afternoon, right down to the photo album left on the nightstand. I'll bring the letter downstairs, I decide. I don't want to stay up here longer than I have to.

But first, curiosity gets the better of me. When I open the wooden wardrobe doors, undiluted darkness greets me, as if the open space I'd seen this afternoon was my imagination. With my cell phone flashlight, I stoop to step up into the wardrobe. It's more than six feet tall, and once inside, I can stand at full height. There are no clothes or other items inside, but even with an unobstructed view, it is difficult to make out the hidden door. Only when I feel along the wood with my fingers can I distinguish the break in the grain.

When Coco came out of the closet, this back panel was open. It must have been for me to see the light coming from the space behind. Had someone been in since and shut it while I was down in the bar with Hilde? My blood runs cold.

Even though I know the door is there, it takes me the better part of twenty minutes to figure out how to dislodge it. There might be an easier way, but I resort to clawing at the seam in the wood with my fingernails until the panel miraculously slides open.

Beyond, there is a tiny room, perhaps once a walk-in closet that the wardrobe was cleverly rigged to conceal. I step down, the space narrow enough that I can touch both walls if I spread my arms but at least ten feet deep. A twin bed frame missing its mattress takes up most of the space. The windowless walls are covered in a peeling floral wallpaper and a series of wooden shelves, as if for storage, though they are empty now. I shine my phone's flashlight at the ceiling and see a vent that presumably lets in some outside light when the sun is shining. But you wouldn't be able to see the sky.

I back out of the little space, feeling claustrophobic. My breath is coming in rapid bursts, but I don't know why. There doesn't seem to be a way to lock the panel, so at least it wasn't a prison. Even so, I can't imagine spending even a single night in such a tiny space.

Back in the bedroom, I go quickly to the nightstand, grabbing the album before heading downstairs. Knowing now that Hilde unlocked Ingrid's room as she'd promised, I feel a tinge of guilt about the envelope, an item that yet again fails Adam's criteria. Also, my second theft of the evening, which speaks to my stress level. Not that I regret depriving Taffy of her key card; picturing her rooting around in her purse before eventually being forced to visit the front desk for a replacement is delightfully satisfying. Hilde, on the other hand, deserved better from me.

Reckless, Little Voice chides.

And it had been. But given what I'm about to discover, perhaps some intuitive force had been at work, guiding my hand. I'll return the envelope tomorrow, I promise myself. But I can't resist taking a peek. It's not sealed, so it can't be that personal. Inside, there is a single photograph. When I see it, I stumble backward, and it flutters to the floor. Now, more than ever, I need to read the letter. But when I open the album, it's gone.

HIGHLY CONFIDENTIAL

Notes from Interview with Sophie Edelstein (née Baum)
Location: G. Saint's home, Hollywood Hills
August 5, 1982

Interview conducted in response to letter received at behest of G. Saint (see Record 1), who refused to be interviewed herself because, she asserted, "I defer entirely to my mother in what or whether to share with you."

Subject reassured that this interview is confidential. Subject continually expressed concern about third parties, in particular those who would seek to use certain information to hurt her daughter's career. To gain subject's cooperation, agreed to classify this interview as Highly Confidential, accessible only by agents Level D-1 or higher. Even with this assurance, subject was reticent, and her account may not be fully accurate.

Subject related the following narrative, synthesized for clarity:

Sophie's best friend was Liane Terwiel, whose father led the department at the university where Sophie's father Mordechai worked. Years after the war, subject learned both men were killed in concentration camps. She had been active in a resistance group called the Stars but claims efforts to find former members failed, and she does not know what became of any who may have survived the war. Sophie is Jewish but did not grow up religious and has not connected with the Jewish community at all since immigrating to the United States.

Subject refused to say more about her early years, nor the war years in Berlin, citing the memories as too painful. Subject relates that after she fled Berlin, there was an "incident" (subject's word) with Allied soldiers as she attempted to cross the Brenner Pass. One American soldier convinced the others not to harm them. Subject refuses to provide more detail. During the "incident," the soldier in command discovered the necklace and commandeered it.

Subject was en route to the home of Giovanna Vitale, known to her from her younger skiing days in Ortisei. The soldier drove her to Giovanna's home in Ortisei, above a bar run by the family. Giovanna was initially kind but then "betrayed" them. Subject refuses to elaborate.

As for the necklace, subject relates that she begged the soldier to return it to her, but he gave her only one jewel, which subject believes is with Samuel. As for Samuel's location, subject does not know and became too distraught to continue. Interview terminated.

FIVE-YEAR FOLLOW-UP NOTE, August 5, 1987: Further attempts to contact Ms. Edelstein failed. Ms. Saint claims her mother has not shared anything about her past with her. Ms. Saint insists that her lawyer's letter (Record 1) misrepresented her own personal knowledge about this matter. This claim is surely false. Suggest that follow-up attempts with both continue.

FIVE-YEAR FOLLOW-UP NOTE, August 5, 1992: Further attempts to contact Ms. Edelstein failed. Ms. Saint claims that she has no new information to share and that due to her mother's health deteriorating, they are moving to Switzerland to take advantage of the mountain air. Suggest that follow-up attempts continue.

FIVE-YEAR FOLLOW-UP NOTE, August 5, 1997: Ms. Edelstein and Ms. Saint continue to refuse to cooperate. Ms. Edelstein is living in Switzerland full-time with her daughter. Suggest that follow-up attempts continue.

TEN-YEAR FOLLOW-UP NOTE, August 5, 2007: Ms. Edelstein deceased. Cause of death: pneumonia complicated by dementia. Ms. Saint requests that we do not contact her again.

TEN-YEAR FOLLOW-UP NOTE, August 5, 2017: Phone number last used to contact Ms. Saint has been disconnected. Efforts to reach her through her lawyers failed.

TWENTY-SEVEN

My last day in Ortisei. Outside the sky is an inviting velvet blue, the early morning sun warm on my face. Where the light hits, the jagged peaks are salmon pink, like pastel shark teeth. I stare out the living room window, unmoved by the peaceful landscape. I've hardly slept, haunted by the photo in Hilde's envelope.

If I want to be on the road for Verona before dark to make my morning flight tomorrow, then I have just over twelve hours left. I've abandoned hopes of getting paid and moved from curiosity to a desperate need to figure out what the F is going on. Now it's personal.

Should I call Grandmother?

Not yet, I decide. And certainly not from this antiquated apartment. Also, the fickle Wi-Fi reversed course last night, revoking connectivity after (hopefully) one panicked text went out to Maurice. This morning I still have zero bars and decide that I will definitely not be remaining at Taffy's disposal twiddling my thumbs.

I want to ask Hilde about the photo, but I have no idea where she lives, and the bar is closed up tight. Inside a little drug store off the square, I buy a SIM card (better late than never) and a protein bar, then decide I may as well see the mountains up close one last time while I collect my thoughts. It's a Friday, and the lifts are more crowded than they have been, perhaps from people here for a long weekend. Still, I manage to find a quiet corner to install the SIM and restart my phone before I disembark at the peak.

There have been a few moments in my life when my body and mind have been on autopilot, a decision already made without my conscious awareness. This is one of those times. Off the gondola, my feet take me back to where the week began—the overlook where Cassi's camera lost the battle against David's well-aimed rock.

There are fewer people today; I suspect the viewpoint is harder to spot without the spectacle of influencer yoga. Whatever the reason, I savor the solitude, finding a flat rock with a gorgeous view over the valley. To put the rest of my plan for the day into motion, I need all the intel I can get and fervently hope Maurice has come through for me.

It is nearly midnight in Nevada when I call, but Maurice sounds wide awake. I want to ask whether he is with Adam but resist the impulse. There will be plenty of time for me to be nosy when I get back.

"I got your text," Maurice says. "Wasn't sure why you wanted me to look into your great-grandmother—did you know she registered at a Red Cross camp not too far from Ortisei in 1945?"

My mouth opens and then closes. Ortisei?

Maurice doesn't wait for me to answer. "She entered the US in 1946 as a Jewish refugee. I saw a copy of the papers. You never said you had a relative who escaped Hitler." There is a note of recrimination in his tone.

"I don't know much about it," I say truthfully. I knew that she had escaped World War II and married an American soldier stationed at a displaced persons camp, but, when she bothered to answer my questions at all, Grandmother had claimed she didn't know which camp. I had assumed it was somewhere in Germany.

"Do her papers say who she arrived at the camp with?" I think about my great-grandmother in her nightgown, searching for Samuel.

"Let me check." I hear the ruffle of pages, almost as if Maurice has made a file. Knowing him, he has. "Alone," he says.

My heart drops. "You're sure?"

"There's a write-up from the caseworker. She was alone. Had burns to her arms and a concussion. This says she was treated for her injuries, but I can't find those records."

"Does it say anything about where she was before or how she ended up there?"

"It's only a paragraph, Lucy. I wish there were more. A lot of camps kept poor records, and many of those were destroyed. We're lucky I found anything."

I wonder how much Grandmother knew and if she had been on vacation when she was photographed in the oldest bar in Ortisei, or here for another purpose. Great-grandmother would have been alive then—had she come along? Remembering David's work on intergenerational trauma, I think of my mother, wherever she might be now and whatever she ran away from.

"Hold on," Maurice says. "There is something. At the end of the paragraph, it lists a previous residence in Ortisei."

He reads me the address, and I recognize it right away.

"I have to go," I say.

Grandmother answers on the first ring.

"Hello?" I start, as if I hadn't been the one to call her.

"Lucinda, thank goodness!" Grandmother's voice still has the theatrical quality I remember, as if projecting to an audience. "I hoped it would be you. Are you well? Tell me you're not working for this horrible countess! But not to worry, I have my lawyers on call."

My throat closes. After everything, Grandmother is still in my corner. I ask how she knows about Taffy, feeling my blood pressure skyrocket as she mentions "menacing letters." In response to her questions, I sketch out my search for Coco and how it coalesced around the mystery of an emerald necklace. I want to see what she will tell me before I ask about her own trip to Ortisei.

"There was a baby," I say, recalling my great-grandmother's lament all those years ago, feeling certain that this is true. Will Grandmother be surprised that I know? Will she feign ignorance? Is it possible that she *is* ignorant? Our family is no stranger to secrets.

But no, Grandmother knows what I mean and doesn't pretend otherwise. "Samuel." In her mouth, the name sounds like something sacred.

"If—" Grandmother starts and stops. "Mama never gave up hope." Her voice is strained. "Have you found him?"

"No." My mind drifts to the letter in the photo album. How had it ended up in Ortisei? Is it addressed to the same Samuel my great-grandmother was looking for? I was hoping that Grandmother would know.

I want to ask who Samuel is to our family, though I'm starting to suspect that I know the answer to that too. Grandmother is rambling, and I have trouble focusing.

"—Ortisei was where she ended up after fleeing Berlin. She had known Giovanna from before the war and was offered a little room in her apartment. That was before the displaced persons camp where she met my father."

"But what about Samuel?"

"I didn't find out about him until after I made my first film. I had offered to buy Mama a house. She still lived in the same moldy shoebox of an apartment where we'd moved after my father died. But she didn't want a house. The only use she had for my money was finding Samuel. Not that she told me about him right away. It dribbled out in fits and starts over several years. She was so ashamed. It wasn't until her mind started to go that she told me everything."

"And then you looked for him?"

"Of course we looked for him!" The feisty Grandmother I know rears her head. "Even when I had the full story, I couldn't find him. The years went by and technology got better, resources to reunite families separated in World War II improved, and still we couldn't find him." Voice choked, she stops speaking then.

My heart crimps in sympathy. If I had known about Samuel back when Grandmother and I had our last terrible fight, would I have felt less angry? She had seemed to me then as someone arbitrarily deciding to keep life-changing information from me for her own equivocal reasons. Whether wielded selfishly or not, no one should have that power over another person.

But now I know that Grandmother had not been able to find Samuel for her mother in the same way she had not been able to find my mother for me. I feel an ache in my chest. A softening, the part of me frozen toward Grandmother starting to thaw.

She begins talking again, as though a dam inside her has burst. Years of saying nothing, of holding everything inside, and now it seems she wants to tell me every detail of her and her mother's efforts to find Samuel. Investigators and various law enforcement agencies and NGOs and anyone else her expensive lawyers had been able to think of.

"I even tried the Department of Lost Things," Grandmother says, and I recall Maurice mentioning them during one of our phone calls. "But that was a mistake. I hadn't realized they would insist on interviews—Mama was so fearful about the consequences—and then they wouldn't leave us alone. Not that they got anywhere either." Grandmother sounds annoyed.

"Did Great-grandmother come with you to Ortisei?" It's not that I'm trying to trick her—more that I want to confirm that Grandmother's days of lying to me are over.

Sure enough, she answers without hesitation. "At first the three of us planned to go—me, Mama, and your mother. Less than a day's drive. At the last minute, Mama wouldn't get in the car. She couldn't go back, she said. I still went—at that point she'd told me about Giovanna—but without her there, Giovanna had no shame about lying to my face. She and her brother Andreas both said they had never heard of Mama or an emerald or a baby."

"You brought my mother?"

"Yes."

That explains the photograph. "So she knew about all this?"

"She did," Grandmother says. "I never lied to her the way Mama lied to me." *Or the way I lied to you*, crackles unspoken over the connection.

"Of course Mama said Giovanna had lied, that she knew where Samuel was," Grandmother continues, "but she refused to confront Giovanna directly. Now you would call it post-traumatic stress disorder, I suppose. And given that Mama was already in the early stages of dementia then, I wasn't even sure I could rely on what she was telling me. It was recently I became aware of a record that showed Giovanna had sold an emerald, but by then both of them were dead."

"But why was Great-grandmother separated from Samuel in the first place?" I ask. "And what do you mean that Giovanna sold an emerald? Was it from the necklace?"

"It's all a very sad story." My flurry of questions seems to overwhelm Grandmother, and her voice is pinched. "That was the last thing she asked about before she died, you know." Now her voice fractures. "She knew she was dying, and half the time she was raving about stars and once what sounded like part of a Churchill speech, but always she came back to Samuel. She couldn't go peacefully, not with the mystery of what happened to him still out there."

I stare at the mountains, the clouds, the sky. "What did you tell her?" My voice is almost a whisper.

I can hear Grandmother breathing, but she doesn't answer right away. Finally, she says, "I lied. When those last moments came, and I was no closer to finding Samuel than I had ever been, I held her hand and gave the performance of my life. I told her the only thing that would bring her peace. The details I invented—Samuel had become a doctor, I said. Three children and five grandchildren. He had never wanted for money, not for a moment. One jewel had been more than enough. That was before I knew that Giovanna likely sold it for her own gain."

One jewel? Little Voice queries. *What about the rest of the necklace?* But I don't want to interrupt Grandmother.

"It would have killed Mama to know Samuel never got that emerald." Grandmother sounds near tears herself. "I assured her that Samuel had looked for her too and was on his way to see us, right at that minute. 'Did he read my letter?' she asked, and I had no idea what she was talking about, but I said, 'Yes, Mama, oh, yes. It meant so much to him.'

"'So he knew about his mother,' she said, and she cried. Tears of joy, not sadness. And then she died with a smile on her face, thinking that her Samuel was about to walk through the door."

Grandmother stops. I wish I knew what to say, but I don't have words. Can lies be beautiful things, or are they always ugly?

Almost as if she can hear my thoughts, Grandmother says, "I don't regret that lie. Unlike some I've told."

There is a pregnant pause, ample opportunity for me to say something forgiving, something magnanimous, but I don't. I stare up at the huge blue vault of sky above me, vast enough to contain the entirety of human suffering. Deep breath in, deep breath out.

"I do have other regrets." Grandmother sounds old then, threadbare.

"Me too." It's all I can offer at that moment. An odd feeling throbs in my lungs, spasming with each breath.

The line crackles. Grandmother is saying something that I can't make out. I frown, straining to catch the words. She is talking about Taffy, I realize. "—countess . . . her father . . ." I then hear what sounds like "extorted money from me," but that makes no sense.

"What?" The rickety connection falters. "I can't hear you."

Clouds are gathering in the sky, and I wonder if that blocks reception. Probably my fault for going with the cheapest data package I could find. Maybe I burned through the fast data with Maurice and am now stuck on 3G.

"My mother—" Grandmother starts.

"What?"

"Email . . . letter—" Grandmother says.

"What letter?"

The connection is too garbled for me to make out her reply. The call disconnects.

"Damn it!" I want to throw my cell phone off the cliff but refrain.

Keeping hold of my treacherous phone, I haul myself up, dust off my pants, and start back toward the chairlift, hoping for better coverage back in Ortisei. When I near the gate, my phone vibrates in my hand, the signal apparently strong enough for text messages. A text from Grandmother: Check your email.

Miraculously, my email loads. Grandmother's note has no subject or text, only an attachment. Excitement or apprehension—or both—floods my system, and my pulse thrums. Could this be a copy of the "Dear Samuel" letter that had disappeared from the photo album?

Fearing that the attachment won't download, I click, expelling a breath I hadn't realized I was holding when it opens. I am disappointed when the letter from Grandmother is in English, not German, no *Dear Samuel* in sight.

My precious daughter, it begins instead. As I read on, my emotions roller-coaster from shock to grief to wonder and back again. The scan is two pages and ends abruptly without signature: *How could I know she would take him from me forever?*

I try to scroll to the next page, but Grandmother only sent the first two. Given that she probably never used a scanner before, I guess I shouldn't be surprised.

Desperate to call Grandmother back and get the rest of the story, I hurry to the lift, pausing when my phone again buzzes. I expect Grandmother, but a text from Chris flashes on the screen.

Down in square & see you in window. Can't find my key. Can I come up?

I stare at the message, perplexed. Chris most definitely does not see me in any window. And if it's not me, then who is in the apartment?

TWENTY-EIGHT

Tall enough to stand out, Chris is immediately visible when I disembark at the terminal point. I'm surprised to see him. After texting that I was not in the apartment and that whoever he saw inside was not me, I wrote him again from the lift after trying unsuccessfully to call. He hadn't responded, and I had expected to race to the apartment to find him with whatever passed in Ortisei for a police presence. A cop with a St. Bernard carrying whiskey? Maybe there would be an arrest, the intruder in hand-cuffs.

Instead, Chris is waiting for me. My heart flips unexpectedly at the sight of him. If there had been more time, and I hadn't met him while still engaged or had resisted David's sex spell and the old patterns of Olivier St. Trapezus . . . Oh, the roads not traveled.

I can't decode his expression, but I hope it's a good sign that he's here, suggesting that the issue of the intruder has been sorted. If someone really did break in, I'll have to come clean about the parade of random folks I'd entertained during my brief guest tenure, and I'm not looking forward to that.

As I exit the turnstile, I see that Chris is not alone. Much shorter and invisible from a distance, Coco stands next to him, grim-faced. At the sight of me, she lunges forward and grabs my arm.

Not again.

With a squeal, I channel the self-defense course I took in college and try to twist free, but I'm no match for her.

"Did you take it?" Coco's grip tightens.

"Take what?" Taffy was right about her sister. She's a raving lunatic. "And if you draw blood again, I'm going to sue." The last I add even though the scratch from yesterday is nearly healed. Better safe than sorry.

Chris says, "Let her go, Catherine. You said you wanted to come with me to apologize for the false alarm, not twist her arm off." Chris turns to me. "Catherine was the one I saw inside the apartment."

Coco, meanwhile, shows no sign of releasing me. "Someone took the necklace." Her voice is urgent. "We don't have any time to lose if it wasn't you."

"It wasn't me," I say truthfully.

For a long moment, Coco's eyes laser into my own. Then she says, "When I went to get the necklace this morning to move it somewhere safer, it was gone. Someone took it from the apartment after I saw you yesterday."

"It was in the hidden room?"

Coco nods. "Ingrid convinced me it was the safest place after the rifugio incident. But the apartment was supposed to be empty. When she texted me that Chris invited a friend to stay"—here she shoots a dark look at Chris—"I checked on it as soon as I could manage. It was still there yesterday. Why didn't I take it with me?" she mutters, almost to herself.

Shock hits me like an ice bath, but also understanding. I had, after all, wondered what Coco was doing in the wardrobe.

"There's a hidden room in Mum's apartment?" Chris sounds perplexed.

"What's going on?" Hilde materializes from the direction of the chairlift. She looks pointedly at Coco's hand clamped stubbornly around my arm.

"It's none of your business." Coco's voice is terse.

"If it's about the necklace, then it is." Hilde boldly holds Coco's gaze.

So Hilde knows about the necklace too. And she had been very keen on getting into the apartment. Hadn't she said Ingrid refused to let her up to look at the view of the square? Not to mention the picked bedroom lock last night and her convenient appearance here now. She must have been following either Coco or Chris.

Well, well, well, we have a suspect. I make an educated guess, turning dramatically on Hilde: "You went into the hidden room last night. Did you take it?"

"No!" Hilde glowers, and it takes all my resolve not to shrink away from the force of it. "But if I did, I have every right!"

"Why do you say that?" Coco's tone is clinical.

"Because I'm Samuel's granddaughter," Hilde says.

The name hits me like a punch to the gut. Something like surprise also passes over Coco's face, but she quickly shutters it.

"Opi would have come himself," Hilde continues, "but his days of travel are behind him. After he contacted the Department of Lost Things, I came as soon as they informed us the necklace may have surfaced in Ortisei. Not that I told them I was coming. They were very 'We'll take care of it' and 'Leave it to us,' but their main concern seemed to be the necklace. And if the necklace was in Ortisei with someone who knew about his history, then Opi didn't want to rely on some agency to get answers."

"Opi . . ." I repeat slowly, recognizing the German. "That's what you call your grandfather?" As the information clicks into place, a glimmer of the full picture comes together. I wonder if this makes Hilde my cousin and what Grandmother will say, and I want to ask her about all of this, but first the most pressing question:

"Samuel is alive?"

"Of course he is!" Hilde looks almost offended.

Elation rolls over me, and my throat closes. I've found him. I will be able to tell Grandmother that I've found him.

"You know Ingrid is on her way to see your grandfather now?" Coco asks Hilde. "For the last few days, she's been going from town to town in canton Graubünden, the area where the Engadiner Nusstorte cake originated, and looking at birth records from 1944 and 1945 for a baby named Samuel Baum."

"Why the Engadiner Nusstorte?" I ask.

"Ingrid overheard Andreas telling David about a baby who left in a big car around the end of the war. Apparently the people in the car brought a Nusstorte. You can't get them in this area."

"Hmm . . ." While I love that cake is a clue, it seems like a bit of a stretch.

Forget about the cake, Little Voice intervenes. *Why was Andreas telling this story to David?*

Why, indeed. But I can think about that later. Andreas was already on my radar, and David is already in my rearview. The focus now is Samuel.

"Ingrid was never going to find a baby with the last name of Baum," Hilde is saying. "Opi grew up as Samuel Wyler."

"Thank you, Hilde." Coco's tone drips sarcasm. "If only you had shared that earlier, you could have saved Ingrid the trip."

"Maybe I should have told her who I was." Hilde looks chagrined, if only mildly. "But she left before I could get to know her, and we already had reason to suspect her family."

"Suspect us of what?" Chris looks baffled.

"Of having the necklace, of course," Hilde answers. "After we got the letters, it took us nearly a year to figure out what was said about the necklace—we had to research the timeline and even reconstruct what was written because the quality of some parts was really bad. My grandfather and I called every agency and NGO and government office we could find to get information on missing people and missing heirlooms, and eventually we were referred to the Department of Lost Things. They helped decode the letter. They're also how we know that Giovanna sold an emerald—the same one referenced in the letter, we assumed. But when we heard the necklace was back in Ortisei, we started to wonder if the American soldier had returned it. Maybe his conscience forced him to do the right thing, only Giovanna kept that for herself, too? For all we knew, Giovanna may have passed the necklace on to someone in her family, like Andreas or Ingrid. Otherwise, how did the necklace end up back here?"

"I can answer that," Coco says. "My father was that American soldier, and I'm the one who brought the necklace here to look for Samuel."

My head is spinning. Though I try to keep up, it's clear that Coco and Hilde have far more pieces to this puzzle than I do.

"No one was supposed to know that secret room existed, let alone the hidden compartment inside it—the necklace should have been safe," Coco is saying.

Echoing my thoughts, Chris asks, "There's a secret compartment in the secret room?" He sounds amused. "Was whoever built that place a magician?"

"I never found the compartment," I admit, though to be fair, I hadn't looked for one.

"Giovanna mentioned both to Ingrid on her death bed, but even Ingrid couldn't find it until she let me help look." Coco sounds smug. "I think Giovanna only told her because she wanted Ingrid to find the contents—a letter to Sophie that it seems Giovanna never sent, plus a very old letter addressed to Samuel—that's how we learned his name."

Hilde nods as if this all makes sense.

"Ingrid thought her mother might have reached out to you. Is that how you knew about the secret room?" Coco asks.

"From the letter to Samuel, yes, but I didn't know to look for the necklace there. I only wanted to see where my grandfather had stayed right after the war. Finding that room—" Hilde's voice trembles. "Seeing how small it was, how dark . . ." She trails off.

Surely now is the time for me to chime in with my family's part in this story, but I'm overwhelmed and unsure of what to say, especially when I still don't know the basic facts of why Great-grandmother and her baby were parted in the first place.

Tell her later, Little Voice implores. *For now, help find the necklace.*

Little Voice is right. I decide to wait to find a private moment with Hilde to discuss what is shaping up to be our shared family history. But there is one detail that could be pertinent to the search.

"I saw a letter to Samuel yesterday in the photo album on the bookshelf.

I didn't have time to read the whole thing, but when I went back for the photo album last night, the letter was gone."

"The photo album wasn't in the secret room?" Coco looks aghast. "That's where we found it. Maybe Ingrid wanted to look through the photos and forgot the letter was inside."

"Did you see the letter when you were in the bedroom?" I look to Hilde, who shakes her head.

"I barely had time to find the secret room," she says.

At this, I frown. "Couldn't you see it clearly when you opened the closet?"

"That's right." Coco catches on quickly, her tone self-recriminatory. "I left the panel door open when Lucy startled me, didn't I?"

"The door to the secret room was closed when I opened the closet," Hilde says.

Coco looks troubled, but she says, "We can talk about all this later. Now we need to find the necklace." She sets off at a brisk clip toward the escalator.

As I race to keep up, I hear Chris ask Hilde, "What's all this about a necklace?"

I can't hear Hilde's response because Coco is asking me for a list of who has been in the apartment since, according to Ingrid, all the keys are accounted for between me, Chris, and herself. I know Coco will lose it when she hears Taffy is in town, but there's nothing for it. I start my list with Hilde and Taffy, and Coco interrupts before I can go further, her bird-of-prey stare piercing.

"You let my sister into the apartment?"

"She basically forced her way in."

"Did you tell her that I'd been in the apartment?"

I don't deny it.

Coco's slow head shake is full of judgment. "And I imagine she found a way to be alone upstairs?"

As we step off the escalator, I relate the Muppet attack and Taffy's trip to the bathroom. Coco looks furious. "She sicced her dog on you? That's the oldest trick in the book!"

"I had no idea the necklace was upstairs," I shoot back. "And probably the only reason she found the room is because anyone could see it if they opened the closet after you left the panel open!" I don't mention that I'm the one who texted Taffy that I found Coco in said closet.

"She must have gotten into the room somehow and taken it," Coco says bleakly. "We have to find her before she leaves. It might already be too late." She picks up speed, nearly jogging toward the town center.

Near the fountain, Coco stops and waits for Hilde and Chris to catch up. Hilde, at least, seems to have followed our conversation because she asks me, "Did you tell them about David?"

"Who's David?" Chris asks.

"Lucy's rebound," Hilde says.

"I didn't—" I fumble. "He wasn't—" I feel Chris's eyes on me but can't bear to look at him. "Plus, that was the night before last. Coco saw the necklace there yesterday, so he can't be the one who took it." I look up. Chris's eyes are steady on mine, full of what might be disappointment or even hurt.

"If Taffy was in the apartment, then she was there for one reason and one reason only." Coco seems not the least bit interested in David. "We need to figure out where she's staying."

Grateful for the change of subject, I'm all too eager to volunteer, "I think I know."

Six eyes bore into mine. Coco looks suspicious, and I realize my mistake. How can I explain how I happen to have Taffy's room key ensconced inside a paper sleeve embossed with a hotel logo, the room number written in pen on the front?

I name the hotel—the most expensive one in town, of course—but don't elaborate further. To deflect attention from myself, I ask Hilde, "Did you go anywhere with her last night? Am I right about the hotel?"

"I got away from her as quickly as possible." Hilde's voice is gruffer than usual. "She wanted to know all about my family—I think she suspected

I was more involved than I was letting on . . ." As if thinking back on the night has jogged loose an important detail, Hilde asks, "What about Andreas? We saw him in the building last night, with a key."

"And you said he was talking to David about baby Samuel," I say, pleased to connect these dots.

"Andreas has been bugging me to let him into the apartment ever since Mum left," Chris muses. "They don't get on, he said, and he just wanted to relive a few childhood memories, but I put him off."

"Strange. Andreas doesn't seem the sort to have the connections to know that the necklace had resurfaced or even that it existed in the first place." Uncertainty flickers across Coco's face. "But he did manage to get into the building last night."

"I couldn't find my key this morning." Chris shares this information reluctantly. "It was in my coat in the staff room at the hotel last night. It's not exactly a fortress. Of course if anyone had told me that there was something valuable in the apartment, I would have been more careful." He says the last as if to ward off expected criticism, but none comes.

"We can blame each other later," Coco says. "For now, let's find Taffy and Andreas. If Taffy has the necklace, she'll be on the first flight back to the US. And if it's Andreas, I'm sure he's not going to waste any time either. Let's divide and conquer. Lucy and I will go find Taffy. Hilde, you and Chris talk to Andreas."

I cringe, preferring Team Andreas to another confrontation with Muppet. But then I remember my contract with Taffy and conclude that bringing Coco to Taffy's hotel room could be worth twenty-five grand.

"Let's do it," I say, and off we go.

Have the necklace. Request immediate extraction.
Will attempt to avoid detection until it can be
arranged. —AW

TWENTY-NINE

Coco boldly pushes into the opulence of Taffy's hotel lobby. Huge glass windows, sparkling chandeliers, wood paneling, and thick rugs do not divert her as she storms past the reception desk and toward the elevators.

"Do we need a plan?" The events of today feel surreal, and I'm not sure I'm ready for what comes next.

"Knock her out, grab it, and run." Coco radiates a dark zealousness that I hope I'm imagining.

"Or," I counter, "you could tell her what you've learned. If you're right that she has the necklace, surely she'll give it back when—"

Coco laughs like a cynical clown hardened by the kid-party circuit. "I've tried to tell her. It's not that she doesn't know, it's that she can't afford to care. Do you have any idea what my sister spends every month on clothes and cocktail parties and vagina spa therapy?"

"Vagina spa—" I start and then stop. "Is that a thing?"

"Yes, it's a thing! And it's expensive. And Taffy's husband is worse than she is with his gambling and hair plugs. They had a fortune, mostly from my father, and Taffy has blown through it supporting the two of them. This necklace is their meal ticket, and she knows it."

Coco doesn't ask how I know Taffy's room number, perhaps sensing that I don't want to talk about it, nor does she mention it when I produce the room key to tap on the elevator panel to authorize our ascent. When the elevator dings open on Taffy's floor, she strides forward and raps smartly on Taffy's door. When no one answers, she puts her hand out wordlessly for the room key. I give it to her, expecting that the card won't work as Taffy surely reported it lost last night.

But no, the lock clicks, and Coco pushes her way inside. The room smells stuffy, and the curtains are drawn. Coco marches over and pulls them open. Sunshine spills into the room.

"Hey!" Taffy's bleary voice comes from the bed.

I scurry inside and close the door behind me. A pile of designer luggage is on a stand in the corner next to a gleaming wooden desk and a queen bed with tousled sheets—that's about it. Sure, there is an Impressionist painting instead of a juggling bear and proper curtains, but I still would have expected something grander from what I know of Taffy's tastes. Maybe Coco is right about her finances.

"It's the afternoon, Tabitha," Coco says. "I can't believe you're still asleep." She starts to rummage through a suitcase open on the luggage rack. "Where is it?"

"Stop that, Coco!" Taffy comes alive, leaping from the bed in silk pajamas, her hair disheveled.

"I've asked you a million times not to call me that. It's Catherine and has been for years." Coco begins to toss things out of the suitcase, and Taffy moves to physically intercept her.

"I know you took the necklace," Coco says, "and I'm not leaving here without it."

"Took the necklace from whom? I thought you had it!" Taffy's voice rises in pitch. She's either a fantastic actress or innocent.

The tension in the room causes my anxiety levels to spike. Knowing exactly how to help, I open my music app and search for Kelly Clarkson's "I Forgive You" so we can really commit to dancing this shit out. Miss Mary would be all for it. Maybe life really can be so easily sorted—the right song and some cardio together time.

Both women turn toward me with death stares as the music blares. "Turn that off!" they say in unison.

"See? You have a lot in comm—" I start, but then a knock comes from a door in the wall connected to the room next door. A man's voice says, "Good to hear that you're up, Countess. The necklace is packaged for transport. We'll head to the airport within the hour."

That shuts me up. I even mute Kelly. Coco looks vindicated.

Taffy's affect completely transforms. "Puck, Lazlo, can you come in here please?" She sounds tightly wound, like a cuckoo clock ready to explode.

The door between the rooms opens, and two looming shapes appear, sucking all the air from the space. I press myself against the wall nearest the desk, hoping to avoid the middle of whatever is unfolding.

At the sight of Puck and Lazlo, Coco's face pales. Perhaps she really had planned to resort to physical force and now understands she can't possibly succeed in wresting the necklace away from these two.

"Bring the package, Mark," Taffy calls to a figure hovering behind Puck and Lazlo.

The package? Not for the first time, I feel like I'm in a spy film with D-list stars.

Taffy sinks onto the bed and pats the spot next to her. "You might as well sit"—she pauses and then carefully articulates—"Catherine."

The gesture seems lost on Coco, who remains standing. Taffy sighs. "Look, if I could afford to give you the necklace, I would, but Daddy lost almost everything in the 2008 crisis. After we sell the penthouse and pay off his medical bills, the necklace is all there is, truly." She leans forward, then says in a pained whisper, "You know Max will leave me if I run out of money."

If she thought the confession would soften her sister, Taffy was incorrect. Coco stands impassively, arms crossed. "He's an asshole, Tabitha. Leaving would be doing you a favor."

I think about Julian and the many ways Adam had hinted and even said outright that I would be better off without him. I couldn't hear it, not until I saw it for myself. That is the way of the truest things—they fall on deaf ears until heard from within.

Taffy clearly isn't there yet. With a sound of disgust, she stands abruptly. "Repack my luggage and take it down to the car," she says to Puck. "You watch her," she says to Lazlo, jerking her head at Coco. Puck climbs awkwardly across the bed to collect the items Coco had thrown to the floor.

Mark, a tiny balding man with chapped lips and a halting walk, emerges from the connecting door with a thin box. At Taffy's impatient gesture, he hands it to her. She flips open the lid, revealing a flash of green rectangles, a sparkle of diamonds. Taffy carefully takes the necklace from the box, holding it up for Coco to see.

My first impression of the necklace is that it is uglier than I'd expected. Gold filigree connects roughly twenty emeralds, all edged with diamonds. The stones in front are the largest, roughly the size and shape of a credit card but more rectangular. Toward the back, the pieces shrink to the size of a thumbnail. On either side of the clasp, an empty setting sits where an emerald should be.

Coco's eyes are fixed on the necklace, her face frozen in a curious expression I can't read. "I thought Daddy must have shown you," she says after a pause. "But you never saw it before Ortisei, did you?"

A complicated series of emotions plays over Taffy's face. Sadness, regret, resignation, defiance—the range implies her relationship with her father was not as pristine as the will suggests. "There's no reason we can't be close again." Taffy ignores the question. "Other than Max, you're the only family I have left."

"Then do the right thing." Coco's tone is imploring. She takes one step toward Taffy. "It's—"

Taffy talks over her. "I don't know why you and Daddy argued, and I don't care. I had nothing to do with the will—"

"This has nothing to do with the will."

"Fine." Taffy holds up a hand. "I'm just trying to say that I want to make things right."

"You'll return the necklace?" Coco sounds hopeful.

Taffy rolls her eyes. "I mean right with you. The necklace is far more valuable than I was expecting, so of course I'm not returning it. It's apparently worth fifteen million dollars." Taffy looks like she's won the lottery, which she more or less has. "According to Mark, the same emeralds were used for a tiara for an actual princess! It was sold at auction in 2011 by Sotheby's for nearly thirteen million dollars, the most expensive tiara in the world."

Taffy looks intently at her sister, as if to gauge a response. When Coco appears unmoved, Taffy says earnestly, "The necklace is ours. It was given to Daddy! And when you hear about the provenance—I mean, it was made for a woman who might have been me in a past life. What was that quote you told me?" Taffy air-claps in Mark's direction.

As if he's repeated this story dozens of times, Mark intones in a voice so dry that I instantly want a sip of water, "When the count promoted her from mistress to wife, La Païva said, 'All my wishes have come to heel, like tame dogs.'"

Taffy shakes her head in a wondering sort of admiration. "That's exactly how I feel about my life, Coco. Just look at Muppet!"

"My wishes are the opposite of tame dogs," I mutter. "More like a tangle of Dobermans trained to kill me."

Taffy and Coco both turn to look at me. "Oh, Lucy," Taffy says. "You are in such a *pathetic* chapter of your life. And what are you still doing here anyway? Actually, no need to answer that. I really don't care."

She should care because you brought her Coco, and now she owes you 25K, Little Voice says, but on that point, I'm biding my time.

After letting Puck pass with the repacked luggage, the one called Lazlo positions himself in front of the door. No one can get in or out without going through him. Taffy turns her attention back to Mark.

"Mark, tell her what you told me after you examined the necklace. Mark's an expert," Taffy tells Coco, as if that's enough to certify his skill set.

"Emeralds of this size and clarity are rare and extremely valuable," Mark rasps.

"You examined the necklace?" Coco sounds surprised. "The gems are real?"

Mark looks offended. "Yes and yes. It's a truly extraordinary piece." He holds his hand out to Taffy, who gives him the necklace. Angling it up to the light and moving so that Coco has a better view, Mark points out various features. "Fake gems look like glass, but see the color and the way the light penetrates?" He holds the biggest emerald up to demonstrate. "Hardly any inclusions. Very high quality."

Coco leans forward, close enough to touch one of the emeralds herself. She peers into the stones as if she may find answers there.

To me the jewels don't look any different from huge pieces of glass, but to be fair, I don't have a good eye. I squint, trying to see what Mark highlights. The emeralds don't sparkle like the diamonds, even when Mark adjusts the angle. Instead, the light seems to enter and pulse from the inside, like a flashlight at the bottom of a forest pool of the deepest green.

"You'd be surprised what they can do in a lab these days," Coco says.

"Don't be bitter." Taffy reaches out to run a finger over the largest stone as if a message is engraved there. "I was sure that the necklace would be missing more than just two stones. Daddy showed restraint."

She doesn't know about Giovanna selling the other stone.

"Daddy should never have taken this necklace." Coco reaches out to grasp Taffy's hand. "The last time I spoke with him, he wanted to make things right."

Taffy yanks her hand away and gestures to Mark. "Bring the cutters." Obediently, Mark hands the necklace back to Taffy and leaves the room.

To Coco, she says, "Mark can remove one of the emeralds for you right now. Not one of the big ones, not today, but one of the pretty little ones in the back, as proof of my intentions. If we sell each emerald individually, we'll get a better return."

"Better return?" Coco's voice is laced with scorn. "You mean you'll avoid uncomfortable questions about how you got the necklace—"

"And if you stop all this nonsense"—Taffy raises her voice to talk over Coco—"I'm willing to give you half, Coco—" Taffy catches herself. "Catherine."

Coco stares in disbelief. "You think that I want anything to do with a necklace that our father stole from a refugee?"

Taffy's smile freezes and then splinters in pieces like glass falling from a broken window. "He did not steal it!" Her voice is just short of a screech. "He was given this necklace because he helped a girl escape a fate she deserved. A German!"

"So what?" Coco matches Taffy's antagonistic tone. "Not all Germans supported Hitler."

"I'm not saying all Germans supported Hitler." Taffy faces off against her sister. "I'm saying that from what Daddy told me, what he did was nothing short of heroic, and that woman thanked him for it. How can you tarnish his name when he's the reason she wasn't raped and then killed along with her baby? Honestly, it was wartime. And a German girl sneaking around the mountains? You couldn't have blamed him if he'd shot her!"

They don't know that Sophie was Jewish, that much is obvious. Should I interrupt to correct Taffy? Would it change her mind? Should it?

"Excuse me," I say, but neither acknowledges me.

"Of course you can blame a soldier who shoots an unarmed woman." Coco is shaking her head with more and more vehemence, as if she can't believe the words coming out of her sister's mouth. "The whole point of human rights is that there are certain things one human being should never do to another no matter what. It's irrelevant whose side they're on or whose side you're on or which side has done the worst things or whether the victim or perpetrator is personally evil or righteous. Human rights have to be universal or else the whole concept is meaningless."

"Spare me the ivory tower lecture," Taffy says. "You idealists are blind to how things work in the real world, Coco." Mark comes to the door, presumably with the cutters, but Taffy waves him away. "Meet me down at the car. We're leaving."

Coco doesn't even look in Mark's direction. "This isn't about my idealism, Taffy. It's about what Daddy told me before he died. He may have saved her, but she didn't give him the necklace. In fact, she pleaded for him not to take it. It was for the child to start a new life. He regretted never finding out what had happened to the baby, if he had been okay. He said that he could not leave this life in peace without returning the necklace to its rightful owner."

I remember that Taffy's father served in World War II, an enlisted man and not an officer. Yet somehow, after the war, he acquired a fortune. Like a magnifying glass that brings a blurry picture into focus, a new understanding dawns on me as Coco speaks. With Great-grandmother dead, is Samuel the only rightful owner? For the first time I wonder whether Grandmother has a claim to the necklace herself.

"The last moments we had together, he could hardly speak." Coco clears her throat as her voice thickens with emotion. "Every word robbed him of breath until he was gasping out each syllable. He asked me to find that baby if I could, to give him what remained of the necklace and beg for his forgiveness. 'Enough, now,' I said, because I thought there would be time.

"He was clenching my hand, insistent on making one last point. 'No saint,' he managed, the machines monitoring his vitals going haywire with his effort. The last words he said to me were about his own failings, his way of conveying that the money hadn't been worth it, at least that's what I thought. He was haunted, Taffy." From the weight of the memory or the journey since, Coco's shoulders sag and she sways on her feet as if deeply fatigued.

"No." Taffy shakes her head. "You're lying!"

"I'm not," Coco insists. "Our father did a bad thing, and his dying wish was to make it right. How do you think I found the necklace? He's the one who told me the combination to the safe where he kept it. He told me where he left the girl and the baby in Ortisei, after he took the necklace. That's how I knew to come here."

"I don't believe you."

"You can't afford to believe me because then you'd have to do something you don't want to do," Coco says. "If Daddy had trusted you to do the right thing, then maybe he would have gone to you instead of to me."

Taffy looks like she's been slapped. Flinging the necklace back into the box with more force than necessary, she starts around the room, throwing a hairbrush, a tube of hand lotion, and other loose items into her handbag. Finishing her sweep, Taffy pulls a pair of velvet flats from under the desk and slides them on.

When she speaks again, her face is mottled, but her voice is calm. "I don't want to hear any more of your bullshit, Coco. I'm taking the necklace. And if you do anything stupid, I have paperwork to show Daddy left it to me in his will."

I'm surprised when Taffy next turns her attention to me and even more surprised when she says, "And I suppose you want your money. You did bring me Coco, just like we agreed last night."

When Coco looks at me, her face is full of fury.

"Ah," Taffy says archly. "I see you thought you had an ally. Lucy's been working for me all along."

"I wasn't—" I start.

"I never would have found that secret room if you hadn't given me the idea to look in the closet." Taffy smiles at me vindictively. "And I am a woman of my word, which means I will pay you twenty-five thousand dollars as promised." As if to prove a point, she takes out her phone and pokes at it. "Done!" she announces with a flourish.

I wonder if she actually wired me money or if the gesture was purely for show. The last thing I need is bad karma from blood money, but I don't stop her. I take a deep breath. It's not my nature to come out swinging, but there is a bolder, braver part of me that is longing to break free. And if I don't ask now, I may never have another chance.

"Why did you bring me here?"

Taffy blinks. "You took the job—"

"Come on, Taffy," I say. "We both know that I was the only one you wanted for the 'job.'" I aggressively employ air quotes.

Taffy shrugs. "It's true you can target ads on social media very narrowly these days. Hairdressers in a certain strip mall, for instance. Even so, it took some time to fine-tune the algorithm. I was close to flying out to see you in person."

Grandmother's choppy words from a few hours before come back to me: hadn't she said that the countess's father "extorted money from me"? I'd assumed I misheard, but what if I hadn't? Fear of the press, living almost as if in hiding—Grandmother's actions certainly matched those of someone being blackmailed. While I have no idea what on earth these people could have over Grandmother, I decide to take a gamble.

"You and your father were trying to extort my grandmother," I say with more confidence than I feel. "And when you couldn't get a direct line to her, you decided I was your way in."

"My, my, our Lucy is growing up." Taffy sounds almost proud. "Only you didn't go to your grandmother the way I thought you would, even after I turned up the heat."

"You're the one who leaked my relationship to Grandmother online." If I had little knives, they would be coming out.

Taffy waves a hand dismissively. "Hiring you seemed like an expensive mistake. But then you actually found my sister and led me to the necklace. Extraordinary, Lucy. Truly."

"But how is my grandmother involved?" *Other than to talk her out of asking for a cut of that necklace*, I think but don't say. It's obvious that I'm missing something important, but I have no idea what.

"I needed someone on my side about what really happened, someone incentivized to agree that Daddy was the rightful owner, just in case," Taffy says, her explanation as clear as mud. "And Daddy had a file . . ."

"But he only had files when—" Coco visibly blanches, as if coming to an unwelcome conclusion. "Daddy was blackmailing Genevieve Saint?"

"Calm down," Taffy says. "Genevieve was the one who tracked *him* down. He was only defending himself, defending us, Coco. He might have needed to sell off another emerald or two for your fancy law school if he hadn't been so successful as a businessman. That necklace was his insurance, and now it's ours."

"But surely he didn't tell you—?"

"That he was blackmailing a movie star? Surely not." Taffy looks miffed. "But he left enough of a paper trail lying around after he died for me to figure it all out. Even some records on your great-grandmother, Lucy." She turns to shake a finger at Coco. "Of course, I never would have thought of contacting Genevieve, or looking for a way to get to her, if you hadn't taken the necklace in the first place. All of this was only to get it back. And now I have it." Taffy pivots back to me. "So you and your grandmother are in the clear. As long as Genevieve doesn't plan on saying anything stupid, of course."

"But what's in your father's file on my family?" My mind is like a hamster on a treadmill, unable to bend this jumble of new facts into coherence.

"You really don't know?" Taffy sounds delighted, and Coco gives her a sharp look.

"I'd like to know the answer to that question too," Coco says.

"The car is ready," the block called Puck rematerializes at the door to announce.

"Alas, our time is up," Taffy says. "But it's not that hard to figure out. Muppet, come!" In true demonic familiar form, Muppet zips from under the bed and springs into Taffy's arms. Taffy starts toward the door, Lazlo reanimating in time to hold it open for her.

"Don't do this, Taffy." Coco sounds surprisingly unemotional, as if going through the motions when the outcome is already decided.

"Oh, Coco." Taffy turns to her sister with a pitying look. "You've been a real bitch about everything, but we'll always be family. Do come to ours for Thanksgiving this year. Kiss, kiss!"

With the box holding the necklace clutched close to her chest, Taffy sweeps past us and out into the hallway, still wearing her silk pajamas.

After Lazlo closes the door in our faces, Coco and I stand motionless. Dust motes dance in the rays of light coming through the window. I feel like I'm observing the situation from outside my body. First things first.

"Should we go after her?" I ask. "Call the police? Intercept her at the airport? Have Grandmother's lawyers start filing papers?"

Coco has a strange look on her face. "Let her go," she says.

"Let her go?" I repeat, unsure I've heard Coco correctly. "You're going to let her get away with it?" I'm surprised at how angry I sound. Furious, even. "She gets a fifteen-million-dollar payout to fund her stupid vagina therapies and her deadbeat aristocratic husband, and Hilde goes home empty-handed, and I just have to hope that she leaves me and my family alone?"

Coco doesn't even blink an eye. "Taffy isn't getting away with anything. That necklace is fake."

My precious daughter,

So much between us remains unsaid, and my mind is not what it once was. Like a half-built house, my life does not feel finished, but I know better than anyone that we are not guaranteed the time we want or need. And no one should die with secrets, not if they can help it. A braver woman would already have told you everything, and I still might. But if I don't get the courage before my body—or, perhaps the bigger danger, my mind—fails, then at least there will be this.

Starting with your father. You know already that Harry found me, half-frozen and unconscious, in the woods a few miles outside of Ortisei and brought me to safety. I woke to a kind nurse bandaging my head at Camp Sarnthein, Harry next to my bed in his US Army uniform. Over the coming days, he came to check on me regularly—a Jewish boy from California who hated the Germans but saw from the papers in my pocket that Sophie Baum was Jewish too.

I woke up with only one set of papers. What happened to the other I'll never know. Had the soldier, who I now know to be John Carter, taken them along with the necklace? Did they fall out of my pocket?

"You're safe now, Sophie." Harry had your same crooked smile, with kind eyes and wild hair. Nothing in the short years we had together would ever tame that hair! Right away, I wanted to take a comb to it. Such a strange thought to have, grief-stricken as I was, but it's all I could think about whenever I looked at him in those first hours of our life together.

I said nothing out loud. Not then, not for days. There was nothing to say. Samuel was gone. Your father brought me tea and pieces of chocolate and newspapers and sat with me quietly, almost as if he knew what would happen if he said a single word. I think I might have screamed or banged my head against the wall or run away into the woods again, even though I knew Samuel wouldn't be there, not after what Giovanna had told me. He's better off, she'd said. Now I know she was wrong, but then I couldn't be sure. And I was so ill.

The next day was the same, and the day after that too. I had nothing at that point, just the clothes on my back. On the third day, Harry brought me a clean pair of pants and a faded green shirt. They were men's clothes and didn't fit well, but I was grateful. On the fourth day, he started talking about his prewar life: a farm and a runt pig that he had nursed back to health after two weeks of touch and go. I was surprised that I understood him—despite my years of English lessons, I don't think I had ever spoken with a native English speaker except for those soldiers on the mountain. But his words were the clearest I'd heard since the bomb in Berlin.

On the fifth day, he told me about the rolling hills of California and how they looked like scorched gold in the summer, and how oak trees grew huge and round-topped like green leafy mushrooms that one could sit beneath and stare up and up at a patchwork of green and blue. One was planted over the graves of his parents. He had no living family. He would often pass whole afternoons beneath that oak, in silent conversation with the blue sky dappled by the leaves.

Had I ever passed a day like that, beneath a tree? he asked me. You've traveled enough now to know the shock of realization that people who don't speak your language or live in your country are still people in the same way that you yourself are a person, experiencing the world much as you do, with the same hopes and dreams and desires for love and safety, beauty and meaning.

I told him yes, though of course he likely knew that's what my answer would be. Sitting under the same sky is something that every single person in this wide world has done. It's as if he knew that my yes would tether me to a world larger than the country I had left behind, and because I could picture his oak tree and that sky and that silence, it did. Later, he said that we would speak of the war years when I was ready. I never was. And then, of course, I lost him in that car crash, far too soon.

It grieves me to this day that I never told him the truth. But even if he'd lived, perhaps I wouldn't have found the courage. Would he have still loved me if he knew? It was unfair to him, but I could not risk finding out. I didn't think I could survive losing anyone else, not then.

But that day in the tent, the taste of chocolate on my tongue, we were two souls who had grown up in different countries and cultures with this experience in common—the sun and sky, the sheer beauty of this earth.

And so instead of recounting all I'd gone through, I told him about a grand old tree in Treptower Park and how we would all go there for picnics, my father spreading a blanket beneath the boughs, and how I would lie on my back and stare up and up, wondering what lay beyond the sky and contemplating how small I was against its expanse. My English was stilted at first, but speaking that foreign tongue made me feel like a new person. And I needed to feel new to survive after all that had happened.

He must have been shocked to hear me speak more than a word, but he only said, "You're not small to me." Then he took my hand, and I felt the tears sliding down my face for all that was lost to me, to Samuel, to Europe, to the world. All those loves that would never bloom, thoughts that would never transform, lives that would not be lived.

It would be a long time before I believed the world could be anything other than ugly, but the memory of a beautiful day with people I loved, even if they were gone, was the start. I could still recall beauty, like the memory of sunshine in winter, and that meant it was not lost to me forever. It was enough to keep living.

And live I did. Sometimes I think you must have guessed my secret, even before I finally told you about Samuel. But you never asked. Perhaps you already know why I refused to go with you to Ortisei, why I cannot stand to see or speak to Giovanna. She took everything from me.

And yet she also saved the most precious thing in the world to me at that time.

There had been no way to get word to her in advance, so she was not expecting us to land on her doorstep so soon after the war. When we arrived, it was clear she was not in a very good position herself. Her mother was nearly catatonic, rocking in a corner, and her little brother was quite thin. As I came to learn, there was very little food—hardly more than what we had in Berlin.

She could have turned us away, but she didn't. For that, and even after the rest, I will always be grateful. When I gave her the map with the details of Great-aunt Liesl in Switzerland, she found a way to contact her. If only I had insisted on getting that paper back, or if Liesl's last name were Baum, or if there were any record of her marriage or married name, or if I'd memorized the address in the first place, I may have found Samuel years ago. The thought of that lost opportunity torments me as much today as it did then, especially now that I am in Switzerland, looking for him in every face that I pass.

This you already know. And that I was hidden away in the secret room, drugged with valerian and whatever else Giovanna gave me, though it's true that I hadn't recovered from the confrontation with the soldiers over Brenner Pass and was quite weak. Maybe she intended only to aid my recovery. And perhaps she really did fear that any German would be lynched—or worse, the baby harmed. I was in no position to protest when she started to take Samuel from me while I slept.

How could I know she would take him from me forever?

THIRTY

W hat do you mean the necklace is fake?" I demand, but Coco opens the door and strides out into the recessed lighting of the hotel hallway without a backward glance to see if I'm following.

It's all I can do not to yell in frustration as I trail after her. She won't answer any of my questions about her theories on why her father was black-mailing Grandmother or why she is sure that the necklace I saw with my own eyes isn't worth a fortune like Mark the expert claimed.

"I need to think." Coco bypasses the elevator and pushes open the door to the stairs, clattering down the concrete steps at high speed.

Heading back to the square, she walks so quickly that I'm nearly jogging to keep up. I'm not sure how to interpret her mood and wonder if she's mad about me being Taffy's alleged collaborator.

"I wasn't working with her," I say. "I only mentioned finding you in a closet in passing, way before I knew there was anything hidden there. And you were the one who wanted to see her today—I didn't trick you into it."

"But you told me where to find her. You had a key to her hotel room." Coco stops short of the fountain in the main square.

For a moment I debate making something up, but trial lawyer Coco will see through that in a heartbeat. "Last night after she pushed her way into the apartment, Hilde was trying to get her to agree not to sue me because she said I'd violated the NDA, and I said I would tell her everything I knew about where you were in exchange, but I knew nothing, so that was why I agreed, and—" I take a deep breath, having saved the worst for last. "Then I stole the room key from her bag."

"A thief instead of a liar." Coco appears to be reassessing her opinion of me. "I'm not sure that's much better." Her gaze shifts to something over my shoulder.

When I turn, I see that she is looking at the two boyish figures adorning the orb in the fountain's center, one trying to pull the other up. "They look like brothers," Coco says, apparently ready to move on from my perfidy.

"I guess." The sun is bright, and I shade my eyes, wishing I had my goggles.

"I really hoped she'd do the right thing."

"But you knew she wouldn't." I remember Coco's rants about her sister. She had been right about everything.

"With people we love, we never stop hoping that we're wrong."

The words hit uncomfortably close to home. "Why did your father stop speaking to you?" I ask to distract myself and also because I have a personal curiosity about other people's reasons for cutting off family members.

I don't expect her to answer, but perhaps she hears my deeper question. After a moment, she says, "Something I said to him about my mother's suicide being his fault. He worked too much. She was unhappy. I still thought then that it was possible to be responsible for another person's happiness. It was a stupid fight, but my words must have cut deeper than I intended. And neither of us were good at admitting we were wrong." Without another word, Coco turns and marches toward the bar.

More layers than an onion, Little Voice observes. *Maybe she meant this as a teaching moment?*

I flip Little Voice off in my head, though the parallel to my own relationship with Grandmother isn't lost on me. And I hadn't known about Coco's mother. I feel a rush of sympathy for her and even Taffy, though empathy isn't the same as pardon.

I hurry to catch up with Coco, who is already at the door. There is a handwritten CLOSED sign, lettered in English, Italian, and German, taped to the bar's entrance, but Coco is undeterred. Ignoring the sign, she tries the latch, and the door swings open. Chris and Hilde are at the bar with a bottle of whiskey and shot glasses.

"See?" Hilde elbows Chris. "I knew they'd ignore the sign."

"Whiskey straight?" Coco beelines toward a vacant stool.

"We're not feeling civilized," Chris says.

"Any luck with Andreas?" Coco asks.

"He doesn't have the necklace." Hilde hands Coco and me each a shot glass filled to the brim. "He remembered Genevieve Saint coming to Ortisei and asking him about a baby who had been with them just after the war, but he followed his sister's lead in saying nothing. He didn't remember much about it anyway, nothing that could help us. He was only a kid."

"So what was he doing in the apartment?" I ask.

"Looking for treasure, just like everybody else," Chris picks up the story. "He got it into his head that Giovanna had a secret cache of jewels. He wasn't clear on what exactly gave him that idea, but given how slighted he feels by his sister, it wouldn't take much. Having grown up in the apartment, he knew about the secret room, even if Giovanna thought he didn't. His father used to hide bootlegged goods there, and later partisans. Andreas had a whole theory about how his mobster father had squirreled away a fortune that Giovanna had hidden from him. He wanted to get into the apartment to check for himself."

Chris pauses to take a sip of whiskey, and Hilde continues, "When Andreas saw Lucy go into the bar last night, he snuck into the hotel to take Chris's keys and then searched the secret room. He didn't have a key to the bedroom door, of course, but he found a way around that."

"He's been taking lock-picking classes on YouTube too." Chris laughs.

"Not as easy as it sounds to learn," I mutter.

"He didn't know about the compartment in the hidden room. He left in a rush when he heard us out in the square—he can't be sure he properly closed the panel behind him," Hilde says.

"That must be how Taffy got in," Coco observes. "Did Andreas take anything?"

"Only the letter from the photo album, and he was persuaded to return it." Hilde pats a manila folder lying next to her on the bar.

"He probably couldn't make much of it with the missing words," Coco says. "It took Ingrid and me days to reconstruct."

My fingers itch to read the letter for myself, but before I can ask, Hilde turns to me and Coco. "From your faces, I guess you didn't have any luck either?" She sounds resigned to bad news, and I wish we had something else to offer.

I decide to let Coco do the honors. I don't envy her position. After ruining her relationship with her sister and her professional reputation to return the necklace to Hilde's family, she has failed.

"I would have seen it," Coco starts, "if I took the necklace out of the compartment yesterday to look at it properly. In my defense, you interrupted me." She shoots a pointed look my way.

"Seen what?" Hilde looks baffled.

Coco pans our faces with a general's stare. "The real necklace is still missing. Taffy stole a fake out of the compartment."

With all of us riveted, Coco relates the moment Taffy took the necklace out of the box, and she saw that the empty settings were in the wrong place—one on each side of the clasp instead of together on the left side.

"I've had that necklace with me for weeks," Coco says. "I spotted it right away. But the fake was good enough to fool Taffy's expert, and whoever orchestrated the counterfeit was sophisticated enough to know what the necklace looked like, not to mention about the two missing jewels."

"Who would bother replacing the real necklace with a fake one?" I ask.

"Someone who doesn't want to get caught," Chris says.

"It has to be one of the governments." Coco expels a long, exasperated breath. "Who else would have the resources? And if they bothered leaving a dupe, they must have needed time to get it out of the country."

"When did you last see the necklace?" Hilde asks. "The real one?"

Coco's cheeks color. "Ingrid and I put it into the secret room together before she left."

"But that was last week!"

Coco looks ready to melt into the floor. One ill-fated decision about where to keep the necklace, and now it's gone. "I wish—" Coco starts, and I can see how much she wants to go back into the past with a smarter version of herself.

You and me both, sister. But we'd still be ourselves and that moment would still be that moment, so we'd just do the same stupid thing again, from paying the bills for a fiancé who's cheating to choosing the wrong hidey-hole for fifteen million dollars' worth of emeralds. We've all been there. So it goes with life—for better and worse, just a series of choices and their consequences.

"Don't blame yourself," Hilde says kindly.

"This isn't over," Coco declares. "I'll help you make inquiries. If a government took the necklace, it won't stay quiet. There are many legal tools at our disposal—"

Hilde puts a hand on Coco's arm. "Let's leave that for another day. For most of Opi's life, he didn't know the necklace existed. What he really wants is to find out about his family."

I feel my throat go dry.

"All we have are the letters and this photo that was mailed with them." Hilde reaches into her bag, and I know she is looking for the envelope when her fumbling becomes frantic.

It's too cruel to let her keep searching. I pull the envelope from my jacket.

Hilde's eyes widen. "Where did you get that?"

"It must have fallen out of your purse last night," I lie. Coco looks suspiciously in my direction but doesn't contradict me.

Carefully, Hilde slides the photo free from the envelope, and we all huddle around to examine it. The photograph is black-and-white, faded, water-damaged. The edges have worn away, the background muted to a soft gray. But the subject is clear enough. Two girls, arms wrapped tight around one another, caught amid a fit of giggles, each next to a pair of skis.

"It's my great-grandmother." With great reverence, Hilde's fingertips hover over the photo. "Sophie." She says the name like a prayer. Maybe it is.

"When I first saw the photo, I knew who it was right away," I say. "She looks just like my grandmother."

"Genevieve Saint?" Coco squints at the photo, but then her eyes widen. "I see it." Then so softly I barely make out the words, "No Saint . . . So that's what my father had on her." And even though later, I will boast to Adam that I'm the one who figured it out first, it was Coco, in this moment, who put all the pieces together. She shakes her head. "Why didn't I see it before?"

"I'm not sure who Genevieve Saint is," Hilde says.

"We should call her," I say to Hilde. "Like right now. She and my great-grandmother never stopped searching for Samuel. Grandmother will be so thrilled to know her brother is alive."

Hilde has been staring at the photograph transfixed, but at my words, she looks up with a startled expression. "Brother?"

"Well, half brother, I suppose."

Coco—the only one who understands the magnitude of the disconnect Hilde and I are navigating—speaks carefully, as if searching for just the right words. "What do you know about your great-grandmother, Lucy?"

It doesn't take long to summarize. The displaced persons camp, her emigration and marriage to the American soldier who saved her life, his tragic death in a car crash when Grandmother was small. And though this information is new to me, I state it with confidence: her great obsession in life had been finding Samuel, her son.

As I speak, Hilde starts to tear a coaster into small pieces with increasing speed. "You're saying your great-grandmother was Sophie Baum?" Her tone is aggressive. "Because that was my grandfather's mother's name."

Coco holds up a hand, her years in the courtroom such that we all quiet immediately and look at her. "Lucy," she says, "I think you should read the letter to Samuel, the one your great-grandmother left with Giovanna along with this picture. Hilde, if you don't mind?"

Without a word, Hilde slides the folder toward me. Inside, I recognize the aged pages from the album. As everyone watches, I start to read.

Department of Lost Things: Case File 1982-024, Record 7(a)(vii)
Excerpt (translated from German): Letter to Samuel, Ortisei, 1945

*From the little room behind Giovanna's wardrobe, I have been
writing this message to you in starts and stops over the past few days
when I've felt strong enough. At night I can hear people in the bar below,
or sometimes out in the square. The war's end is still sinking in, soldiers
coming home every day and the town celebrating. Sometimes I can hear
the same partisan song that Giovanna's father played on his fiddle the
last time I was here. Sad but strong. Resolved. That is how I feel too.*

*And yet Giovanna says that the raucousness is the reason I
must stay hidden. There are soldiers who have not come home. The
anti-German sentiment after losing so many sons and fathers to the
war is high, and if they discovered Germans of any kind here, they
might turn us in. Or worse.*

*According to Giovanna, soon Great-aunt Liesl and her husband
will arrive. You and I will both be away from here, safe and together.
When I am strong enough, I will build a life for us. And when you are
older, I will give you this letter because I do not think I will ever have
the strength to speak out loud this last, hardest thing.*

*When Giovanna asked why it was only the two of us, I stared at her
mutely. I could not say the words. But I told her enough of that day
that she put it together herself. And that was the first time I cried.*

*That last day in Berlin, she was holding you when the bomb
struck and half the house seemed to disappear in an instant.
Beams collapsed in the attic, the ceiling falling in, parts of the floor
disintegrating into a gaping hole. Smoke and flame, a boom like the
sound of the world cracking in half. Miraculously, you were safe.
Among the rubble, I heard your cries. She had shielded you with her
body, of course she had.*

*The air smelled like smoke and burned hair and death, and it was
hard to breathe without choking. I dug frantically, tearing off one of
my nails, covered in dust and blood—whose, I wasn't sure. My ears
were ringing, and blood was trickling into my eye from a cut to my
temple. I hardly noticed, so crazed was I to get you both unburied.*

It felt as if time had stopped, as if it were just the three of us alone in a horrific parallel world to which we had been transported against our will. I'm not sure how long it took me to dig you both out. You first, screaming. I tucked you into the big coat against my chest. You squirmed and wailed, but I needed my hands free.

Where the strength came from to move the planks and plaster and pieces of brick, I'll never know. I couldn't stop, I didn't stop, until I had uncovered her face and then her legs. It wasn't enough. I couldn't pull her free. I had never felt such deep and searing agony as I felt right then staring down at the blood seeping through the pale blue of her shirt, one leg bent at an odd angle and the other still trapped under a crossbeam I could not budge.

How was I standing unscathed while she was so battered? We had been together, just before the blast. Our fate should be the same. And if only one of us could be spared, it should have been her.

Her face was white with dust, her eyebrows powdered with it, and I wiped it away as best I could. Her eyes flickered open, but otherwise she didn't move. But for a moment, she was lucid. Her thoughts were only for you. You were safe, I assured her. I had checked your little body as you wailed, but there was nothing—no bruises, no blood.

I put you on her chest, where she wrapped an arm around you while I returned my efforts to the crossbeam, pulling at it and then scrabbling beneath it to free up space.

"Pull your leg free!" I urged her. I knew we had to go. "I need you to be strong," I said. "I'll carry you as soon as we get you out, but I can't lift the beam. I need you to move your leg."

She didn't respond. I knelt next to her again and reached for her hand. Her fingers were cold, but I pressed them as hard as I dared, trying to will life into her fragile, battered body.

Take me instead, I prayed as I had never prayed before or since. If I could have died for her, I would have. Please, God, spare her.

But there was no God in that place, not there, not then.

She roused herself to run a finger down your tiny nose, your chin, as if to memorize the contours and reassure herself that you were well. When she spoke, her voice was hoarse and weak. "You have to save him," she said. "Promise me."

"We'll all go, Sophie." My voice was broken glass. Hot tears pooled in my eyes, splashed down my cheeks, but I ignored them. "You just

need a moment. Gather your strength, and I'll find a cart, something you can lie on with the baby, and I can—"

Sophie's hand fluttered toward me, landing on my face as soft as the wings of a butterfly. She shook her head, her eyes full of sorrow. My beautiful friend, my only companion these last long, dark years. Her fingers caressed my cheek before falling back to her chest as if even that effort was too much for her. "Liane, you know I can't."

And I did. But I wouldn't leave. My head bent in despair. It's possible that I would have stayed there until the Russians found us or the house burned to the ground—all the strength had gone out of me. I had lost too much. I couldn't lose her too.

Sophie's voice rattled as if her chest were full of marbles. "Do you remember what my father told us?"

Of course I did. All those summer evenings, lying amongst the trees bathed in soft insect sounds and starlight. We cannot control the path set before us. Sometimes we walk in the light of the sun, sometimes the darkest of nights. And in the dark, we always have a choice. Do we let it consume us, the vast expanse of nothing? No, never that. We come from stardust. We will return to being stardust. But until then . . .

"On the darkest nights, be a star and shine," I whisper.

"Yes." Sophie struggled for breath. "Always that, my sister. Now go. I don't want him to see me—"

She couldn't finish the sentence, but I knew what she meant. You had stopped crying and were looking at her with such intensity that it seemed as if you knew it was for the last time. I held your face close to your mother's, your cheek against hers as she seemed to breathe you in, her eyes closing, her face peaceful in your presence.

The smoke was getting thicker and I knew we had to go then, but it seemed impossible to leave Sophie alone in that place. You screamed as I drew you away from her face, and I wanted to scream with you, to rail against Nazis and Russians and war and bombs and fire and fate and God and the bloody stars, all of them.

But there was no time. There was so much more I needed to say, but the smoke was stealing the last of the air in my lungs. You too went silent. And it was that realization, that if I could no longer breathe, it meant that you could not either, that finally got me to my feet and to the ladder, miraculously still intact, through the flames and down the stairs, and finally into the cool night air, the sky bright with stars as the only home I'd ever known burned behind me. Alone, I could never have been strong enough, but for you, I could do anything.

There are so many human desires. To understand and be understood. To love and be loved. To find meaning and purpose. To know who we are and where we come from. I hope this letter leaves no doubt about how much your mother loved you, though you will grow up knowing this and everything else about her because I will tell you myself, every day.

And now I feel stronger, certain that I will be able to give you this letter when you are older along with the precious little I could save of your legacy—the emerald and my most beloved possession, the only photo I have of your mother, the two of us as girls right here in Ortisei. I discovered it in the pocket of the jacket, next to the map, that first horrible night. One last gift from your mother.

Running away with you in my arms was the hardest thing I have ever done. But I did it. To save you. And because your mother asked me to. That's how much I love you both.

Yours,
Liane

THIRTY-ONE

Things that disappear are not uncommon. Socks. Life savings. Friendships. Species. People.

Disappearing is an interesting business. Your name, your appearance, and any trail left behind can give you away, but if you can fly under the radar on all fronts, you may never be found. Especially if records are not sophisticated. And not online. Oh, and bonus if you have someone else's papers and look enough like them to pass, particularly after a war where few came out the other end looking the same as they had at the beginning.

The answer, when it comes to me, was there all along. It's always the things we don't want to see that muddle our thinking and obscure the obvious. Even with the letter's missing words and faded ink, I had made out enough of it to finally understand.

Everyone's eyes are on me when I put the letter down carefully on the bar, next to the picture of two teenage girls, so similar yet so different. Undeniably the taller one is my great-grandmother. But now I see what I hadn't before. The other girl looks very much like Hilde.

"Do you recognize the other girl?" Hilde asks. "Because if you know how we can find Liane, if she's somehow related to your grandmother—"

"I do know who Liane is," I say. "But as for finding her—" My throat closes as I picture my great-grandmother, always roaming, searching, agitated in my memories. If only I could call her right now with the news that her search was finally over. I can only hope that if there is life after death, she has reunited with Sophie long ago and already knows.

When I recover my voice, I tell them the whole story. There is a moment of silence when I stop speaking, and then everyone explodes at once:

Coco: "My father knew all along who your great-grandmother was—that's what he was trying to tell me, not to mistake your family for Sophie's."

Chris: "If only Nonna fixed this while Liane was still alive. We're too late to put it right."

Hilde: "Opi's Aunt Liesl told him that his mother was dead, without much more detail than that. He never fully understood how he made it to Switzerland. Certainly he had no reason to look for a Sophie Baum who survived the war. We read about Liane in the letter but couldn't find any trace of her." Hilde sounds dazed.

"That's because she took the identity of her dead Jewish best friend and moved to the US." Chris shakes his head and mutters under his breath, "Not a good look."

Chris's words are the ones that register, and I bristle. It's suddenly quite clear what Taffy's father had in his file, and why Taffy thought she had leverage over Grandmother.

"What's that they say about people in glass houses not throwing stones?" I look at Chris tartly. "Your family doesn't exactly come out of this smelling like roses."

Chris looks taken aback. "I wasn't criticizing you." He sounds sincere. "None of these people are still alive, Lucy. Your great-grandmother's choices aren't a reflection on you."

"But I don't think she did it on purpose," I say. I pull up the partial letter Grandmother emailed me on my phone and pass it over to Chris. Hilde leans closer to read over his shoulder.

Coco doesn't seem interested. "Even if she did, I'm not judging." She pours herself more whiskey. "Don't you think Sophie would have wanted her best friend to use her papers and her name if it saved her life, especially after she just risked everything to save Sophie's child?"

None of us have anything to say to that.

It's as good a time as any to gather my things. While I'd like to change my flight to a later one, I can't afford the change fees, nor am I sure how that would work, given that I'm not the one who booked any of it. In less than an hour, I need to be on the road.

Promising everyone I'll be back, I head up to the apartment to pack. It takes less than ten minutes, shoving assorted possessions into my backpack and tidying up the apartment. I wrap the new jacket around the framed photo of my mother and grandmother I stole from the bar. I have no intention of returning it.

I fold Chris's torn flannel shirt neatly, wrapping the loose buttons in a fifty-euro bill. *Sorry,* I scrawl on a piece of paper. I want to write an explanation, but what can I possibly say? Night terror? Possession? *Maybe next time you can be the one to rip the buttons off my shirt,* I write.

Too much, Lucy! Little Voice lectures. And it is. But I don't have another piece of paper, so I have to settle for crossing out the words with a heavy hand. Then there's only room to write my name, in small letters beneath the scrawl marks. It will have to do.

My engagement ring is still where I left it on the edge of the bathtub. I consider flushing it down the toilet but know that Adam will be angry if I deprive him of a closure ritual, which will probably involve me tying the ring to a helium balloon with some sort of "Fuck you, Julian" haiku. But actually, I'll probably just return it to Julian. Why waste a perfectly good fake diamond? I slide the ring into the pocket of Adam's neon-orange jacket, back from purgatory.

Mug washed, bed made, clothes packed, and ring retrieved, I consider going up into that secret room where my great-grandmother last saw the baby she loved as her own blood but decide against it. That room is full of ghosts.

Downstairs, the scene remains unchanged—Hilde, Chris, and Coco lined up at the bar with the bottle of whiskey.

"You really need some new clothes," Chris says at the sight of the jacket. "You mentioned a gay best friend, but I'm not seeing it."

"Not every gay guy is good at fashion," I retort. "He's more into clashing plaids and kitschy reindeer sweaters. This is actually his jacket."

"Ouch," Hilde says.

"I won't tell him you said that." I laugh weakly, aware that this is the start of goodbye and unsure how to bring closure to this surreal week.

The mood in the room shifts, as if the others feel it too. Hilde says she will break the news to Samuel about Liane's passing, and then we can discuss how to put him in touch with Grandmother, perhaps later in the summer. Her grandfather, she relates, has been rethinking many things since Giovanna's anonymous missive arrived, including whether Aunt Liesl and her husband kept the news about Liane from him on purpose. They, after all, had known about her and his time in Ortisei but never told him.

"He thinks they were worried Liane would come back for him," Hilde says. "They didn't have children of their own, and he was like a son to them." She relates that her family had also started to search for relatives of her great-grandfather, Franz Hammann, the Nazi soldier who'd loved Sophie and died in the war. "It's a lot," Hilde concludes.

"Everything about this situation is a lot," I say. It will take years of movement therapy to even scratch the surface.

I hand Chris the apartment keys. "I'm happy to return the hosting favor if you ever find yourself in Reno."

"Not Vegas?" Chris asks.

"Guess that depends on whether I can get out of some leases." I sigh, not yet ready to leave this mountain paradise and descend back into real-world concerns like rent.

"Didn't my sister pay you?" Coco asks.

"I doubt it," I say, because nothing about Taffy piddling with her cell phone had looked like a legitimate bank transfer. But everyone is staring at me, so I pull out my phone and check my bank app. The balance is $25,132.54.

I want to dance or cheer, but then I remember Taffy and her father and ethics.

"I have to return this, don't I?"

Coco shrugs. "She didn't get the real necklace. And you did what she hired you to do. Besides, who are you going to return the money to, if not Taffy?"

"Orphans?" I hazard. "Blind rescue animals?"

"Do that," Coco says. "But not now. First get yourself sorted, and you can pay it forward later to the orphans or rescue animals or whatever other cause strikes your fancy."

"This calls for a toast." Chris raises his shot glass. "To fake emeralds."

Hilde shrugs but seems game. "To family."

"We're really doing this?" Coco shakes her head.

"Humor us," Hilde says.

I have the impression that if Coco decides to do anything, whether it's taking out the garbage or taking on a war criminal, she does it 100 percent. And so it's not surprising when she pauses, looking at the ceiling as if considering her next words. When her voice comes, it is quiet. "To trying to do the right thing."

Everyone looks from me to the still-full shot glass on the bar. I knew my turn was coming but still haven't settled on what to say. "I have to drive," I offer.

In short order, Hilde hands me a shot glass full of tonic.

This week feels like it's been a month, a year, a lifetime. But when it comes to one thing I want to toast, the answer is clear. "To letting go."

Four almost-strangers clink glasses, downing our respective shots and sharing smiles. I can't say if I will see any of them again, though we all exchange contact information and make promises to stay in touch.

"Let's do this again, yeah?" Chris is in front of me, arms open for a hug. I hold the embrace a little too long. Or maybe he is the one hesitant to part, because Hilde is suddenly elbowing her way in for a hug of her own.

"Thank you," she says. "If you hadn't come, I don't think we ever would have known what became of Liane." Her eyes mist. "I think Coco is right—Sophie would gladly have shared her identity."

I feel my own eyes fill, but at this point, there are so many things I could be crying over that I can't identify the source of the emotion that floods me.

Coco stays seated, alone with her thoughts and her whiskey, but when I'm almost to the door, she stands suddenly and moves to intercept me. She holds out her hand, which is a blessing of sorts. An embrace from Coco would be like taking an ice shower.

"I can't endorse your kleptomania, but there might be something to this Bearer of Bad News thing," she says. "Taffy always did have a gift with marketing. She may have invented a fake job that you can actually turn into a real one. You"—she pauses as if searching for something encouraging to say—"could be worse at it."

"Thank you." I squeeze her hand. "I hope you get your job back. And the house in Spain."

"I'd settle for the job," Coco says.

"I'll testify on your behalf," Hilde says from behind us. "Certainly a human rights court shouldn't fire you for trying to protect human rights. But that leads me to another question: Are you going to tell Taffy that she doesn't have the real necklace?"

"Maybe." Coco looks pensive. "But if she can pull off selling fake emeralds to keep Count Bald Spot in booze and women, who am I to interfere? Though it's bound to come out when we find the real one. Because we will."

"We can use the money Taffy paid me for the search," I say. "And I'm sure Grandmother will help."

Hilde puts a hand on my arm. "That's kind, but we don't need your money. Giovanna was right about that—Opi inherited quite a sum from his Aunt Liesl and has made a nice living in his own right. For us, the necklace is about family history—"

"Wait, what do you mean, Giovanna was right?" Chris leans forward. "She's been dead for—"

"I haven't told you." Hilde's eyes widen. "Before the letters arrived, before Opi had any idea that they even existed, Giovanna called him."

"And?" Coco gestures impatiently.

"I'm not sure—" Hilde darts a look in my direction, looking deeply uncomfortable.

"Tell us." Coco's lawyer voice brooks no nonsense.

Hilde, no pushover herself, nonetheless wastes no time in complying with Coco's directive. "Opi said she called out of the blue—from the hospital, if I remember correctly. She said nothing about the letters, at least not until the very end. He had no idea who she was, so the call was quite confusing, but eventually he understood that Giovanna—though he didn't know her name—had been the one to reunite him with his Aunt Liesl after the war. 'Why didn't you tell me this before?' Opi demanded. He has never had trouble holding people accountable."

At this, Coco nods approvingly.

"Giovanna said she had tried to find him before but eventually admitted she hadn't tried very hard. Apparently there had once been a map of some sort with Aunt Liesl's name and address in Switzerland that Giovanna had used to find them in the first place, but she claimed she had destroyed it back in 1945 and so had no way to easily locate him. But now she was dying, and it was important for her to get in touch before she died, she said. She credited the advent of online searches for making it possible—she must have at least remembered the name Wyler, but I suppose there's no way to know.

"Anyway, she asked my grandfather if he knew how he had come to live with his aunt and uncle, and he didn't, not in any detail. She said she had known his mother, that she and Sophie had become fast friends during winter ski trips Sophie took to Ortisei as a girl. Once, she brought a friend with her—Liane—and that's who showed up with his baby self at Giovanna's bar after the war. Apparently Liane and Giovanna hadn't gotten along particularly well. Not to make excuses for her." Hilde looks between Chris and me as if expecting that one or both of us will be offended.

"Nonna was a pistol," Chris says, "and she definitely had her own ideas about right and wrong. If she did something questionable, I won't be surprised."

"Well," Hilde continues, "Opi was floored by all this, and he tried to ask questions, but Giovanna said she needed to confess something but that she couldn't get through it if he interrupted. And then she proceeded to tell a story that made no sense, not until he got the letters—"

"Lucy has to go," Coco interjects. "Get to the point."

"When Giovanna wrote to Aunt Liesl after Liane and Samuel arrived on her doorstep, Aunt Liesl wrote back that they were coming for the baby. When they arrived in Ortisei, Liane was sleeping upstairs. She had been ill, and Giovanna had been giving her valerian to help her sleep and caring for baby Samuel herself, so she had the baby when she answered the door. The couple seemed kind and immediately fell in love with the baby. Giovanna could tell from their clothes and the driver waiting in the car outside that they were also wealthy, which was important because so many families had lost everything. People were starving and struggling to get by, including Giovanna and her family.

"Giovanna was ready to wake Liane, to bring her downstairs, but Aunt Liesl said no, that they had never had any intention to bring 'that German' with them. They had come to take the baby, their blood relation, the only one from their extended family who was known to have survived the war. It was not a point of discussion: they were taking Samuel, that very moment, back to Switzerland. Without Liane. And if Giovanna tried to stop them, they would call the authorities immediately and have Liane arrested for impersonation, for kidnapping, for existing as a German—whatever they could make stick.

"According to Giovanna, she protested. She told them that Liane had arrived with Sophie's papers, which she claimed showed that Sophie had sent her with Samuel. News of the papers only made things worse.

"'But where is our Sophie?' That's what they said. 'How is it that this German woman survived, and with our Sophie's papers?'

"They were convinced that Liane had chosen her own life over Sophie's, that she could have saved her, but she stole her papers and her son to protect herself. 'No one would hurt a refugee mother and her baby, but a German woman alone? That's a different story,' that's what they said." Hilde looks away, jaw clenched.

"But Liane had just saved Samuel's life!" I am appalled.

"So Giovanna was forced to make a choice," Coco says.

Hilde nods. She looks near tears. "And even if Giovanna had liked Liane, which she didn't, she still thought the baby would be better off in a stable environment with blood relations. It wasn't necessarily untrue—would Liane as a German refugee be able to find work and build a life for Samuel? It never occurred to her that Liane could use Sophie's identity."

"She let them take Samuel." My face crumples.

"Yes," Hilde says softly. "They left with only the baby. There wasn't time to get the letter or the emerald, so she said—both were with Liane, and she knew that if she accidentally woke her, Liane would never let Samuel go—"

"Which conveniently meant Nonna kept the emerald for herself?" Chris guesses.

"When Samuel was safely away, Giovanna crept into the little room and took the letter, photo, and emerald while Liane was still sleeping. When Liane woke up and found Samuel gone, Giovanna meant to comfort her with assurances that all had been sent with Samuel. Only Liane wasn't comforted. Liane became hysterical, asking again and again for the paper with the address where Samuel had been taken so she could go after him. Only Giovanna knew that Liane was never going to be able to get the baby back from Sophie's aunt and uncle. She had no legal right. She would be arrested. It would ruin her life. And Samuel was better off. Giovanna firmly believed that. So she destroyed the map for Liane's own good, that's what she told Opi."

"And how convenient that if Liane never found Samuel, she would also never know that Giovanna kept the emerald." Coco's voice is caustic.

"I'm just the messenger." Hilde holds up her hands. "Anyway, Liane was crazed. She ran out of the house barefoot in the middle of the night and never came back. Giovanna went after her but couldn't find her. Decades later, Giovanna learned that Liane had gone to America, where, according to Giovanna, she had a fantastic life. Giovanna eventually sold the emerald, but she said she didn't think Sophie would mind. And she didn't regret her choice to give Samuel to Sophie's great-aunt and her husband. They were family."

"Liane was family." My voice has a tremor.

"I agree," Hilde says soothingly.

"And what about the letters?" Coco asks.

"Right before she hung up, Giovanna asked for my grandfather's address to mail something that she said she should have sent a long time ago. Waiting was something she regretted, she said. Samuel had a right to know his own story. 'It's some correspondence between me and your mother,' she said. 'And a letter from Liane. I'll send the original of that one to her family.'" Hilde looks in my direction. "But if you didn't know about it, then obviously she didn't."

"Can I take the letter now?" I ask. "Can I give it to my grandmother?"

Hilde hands me the folder. "Of course," she says. "And I'll email you the reconstructed version as well."

"I'd like to see the other correspondence you were sent," Coco says. "I've only seen the letter to Samuel."

"It's Sophie's letters to Giovanna right after Kristallnacht," Hilde says. "Sophie asked if Giovanna would take her and her father in, but it seems Giovanna never responded."

"Ingrid found a reply to Sophie that Giovanna never sent," Coco says.

Hilde speaks carefully. "In the phone call with Opi, Giovanna sounded as if not sending a response was one of her biggest regrets. It's just that she was already responsible for so many people."

"It likely wouldn't have made a difference even if she had responded," Coco says dismissively.

"That's an easy out," Chris says. "It was still a choice she made and had to live with."

Coco, ever practical, shrugs.

"How did the call end?" Chris turns back to Hilde. "And you'll have to repeat this story to Mum when she's back tomorrow."

"We can call my grandfather, and he can tell her directly," Hilde says. "But I'm afraid there's not much more. Giovanna asked for his forgiveness, something about not being brave enough to answer his mother's message, but she didn't apologize for taking him from Liane.

"'Your mother was my dear friend,' she said, the only time during the entire call when Opi said she showed emotion. 'I had only a second to make the choice for her child that I would have wanted her to make for mine.'

"When she composed herself, she asked if he'd had a good life. He said he had. A very good life. Giovanna seemed pleased by that, but then Opi started to push for her name so they could stay in touch. She refused to tell him and hung up before he could ask more questions." Hilde looks around the room. "And that was that." Her phone pings, but she ignores it.

"To lose that baby after everything else." Coco shakes her head. "Poor Liane."

I feel the same, a clenching in my chest at this weight my great-grandmother had carried her entire life.

"But can we be sure Samuel wasn't better off?" Coco continues. I glare at her, as does Chris. Hilde looks thoughtful, perhaps contemplating the effect of an alternate ending on her family while I wonder the same about mine. None of us answer.

I look at my watch. There's so much more to say, but I'm late. "I really wish we weren't leaving on this note"—I start, already turning toward my bag where I'd left it at the door—"but I'm crap at driving in the dark."

The atmosphere is heavy, and we've said our goodbyes, so I trudge toward my backpack and hoist it onto my shoulders. Rather guiltily, I stare at the empty place on the wall where the photograph of Grandmother and my mother had been. Should I demonstrate personal growth and resolve to be a better, non-thieving person by returning it after all?

Not today, I decide.

"You need a better exit than this." Hilde manages a weak smile and reaches for her phone, searching for something.

Up on the mountain . . . The song pours from the bar speakers, familiar from Hilde's closing routine, but it now has a new significance.

Bella ciao, bella ciao ciao ciao . . .

Goodbye beautiful, indeed.

Glancing at her phone, Hilde suddenly covers her mouth and bends at the waist as if overcome.

"What is it?" The song isn't that good.

Wordlessly, Hilde holds up the screen. From this distance, I can see a string of text messages, but I'm too far away to read them. Hilde starts to laugh and then to cry. She repeats the same word in German again and again, but I can't catch it. She seems to be expressing amazement bordering on the miraculous.

"What?" Coco asks. On her face, there is such hope, almost as if she knows what Hilde will say before she says it.

"The doorbell just rang," Hilde starts. "Opi went to open the door, but no one was there. He looked down and saw a fat manila envelope, the padded kind, with no postmark, nothing written on the front at all. He took it inside, at first afraid to open it, because weren't there all those stories about people mailing powders and bombs and dangerous things? But Opi is too old to care about all that.

"Inside the envelope—" Hilde pauses. Her eyes shine, and she holds up her phone for us all to see. "See for yourselves. He sent a picture."

We crowd around, the object in the photo impossible to mistake. It's the same necklace I saw earlier today, except the two empty settings are next to each other on the left side of the clasp.

When I look at Coco, she is blinking rapidly, as if something is in her eye. Chris is shaking his head in amazement. Hilde has tears streaming down her cheeks. My own face is wet, and I struggle to control the sob that rises like a bubble in my chest. Amazement. Joy. Sheer disbelief that some-times, just sometimes, things turn out all right in the end after all.

Coco tries to say something, but the words seem to stick in her throat.

It's Hilde who finally speaks. "There was a note. 'Dear Samuel, We be-lieve this belongs to you. Kind regards, The Department of Lost Things.'"

THIRTY-TWO

My busted-up rental is right where I left it. After tossing my backpack into the trunk, I lean against the car's hood and look up. Even from an unremarkable slab of asphalt behind a hotel that deserves zero stars, the Dolomites in the distance are a million-dollar view. The mountains are so tall that the sun sets far earlier than its actual descent behind the horizon.

I need to get on the road to avoid driving in the dark. But first, there's something I need to do, one more act of closure, and no, it's not paying Cassi for her camera. For all I care, she can camp outside my empty hotel room for eternity.

The number rings and rings before the voicemail message Julian has had for as long as I've known him clicks on: "This is Julian. Leave a message."

"Hi." Too late now, but I should have thought about what I would say in advance. I stare at the mountains for inspiration, realizing that I am well on my way to leaving a recording of solid mouth-breathing.

"Feels weird to say this into voicemail," I start, "but here goes. I'm calling because I read your letter. My life has been way too full of letters lately. It's a long story, but I've been in Italy doing some soul-searching and also looking for this necklace as part of what I can only call a family saga. Or an international mystery, or something even more thrilling, like a spy mission, and I'm playing the role of James Bond, only without guns. Seriously, you'll think I'm exaggerating, but I'm not.

"Maybe I'll tell you the story one day. But first I think we should have a talk. I'm not going to ask you to come home, so don't worry about that, but we need to sort the apartment and of course I'll give you back the ring." The last comes out awkwardly. What else is there to say? "Do voicemails still have time limits? Feels like I'm going to get cut off any minute, so I'll wrap it up. Hoping that you're well, and—"

I pause. Always before I would end our calls with "sending three," our code for *I love you*. Can you say this to someone who dumped you? Is it appropriate or clingy or desperate or will it send the wrong message? But then I imagine what it must have been like for Julian, carrying this big secret around about who he loves or wants to love, and I remember the times that he rubbed my feet when I was tired and danced with me to cheer me up and gave me his beautiful sleepy smile the first thing after he woke up.

I do still love him. Maybe part of me always will. And also, he lied and cheated and hurt me. But you can love someone imperfect. You can love someone you have parted from. You can love someone for who they were to you then and not who they are to you now. In this crazy fucked-up world, there are so many different kinds of love, and we need them all.

"Sending three," I say. And then I disconnect the call.

My emotions churn. Sadness, yes, it's still there. But then I think of my great-grandmother Liane watching her best friend Sophie die and then saving Sophie's baby by hauling him over a literal mountain range in the ashes of a war. And then losing that baby too.

Jesus, Lucy, have some perspective. And I do, but I still feel sad because hey, I'm just a person. I close my eyes and fill my lungs with the chill mountain air, and I feel peace ripple through the sadness, smoothing its edges. And I think to myself that if trauma is intergenerational, so too is strength, and I am descended from the strongest.

And then, there at the periphery, is a little fizz of butterfly wings that beat against the darkness I've been living with these past few weeks. I've felt it before, of course I have, but it takes me a moment to give it a name, so infrequently has it made an appearance these last years as I took one job I hated after another and tried to be happy in a life that fit like a too-small shoe.

It's hope.

Another day, another chapter, another chance, and damn if I'm not going to seize it for all it's worth. God bless Taffy Waters and her demon dog Muppet because she's given me a ticket to somewhere beautiful when I needed beauty in my life, and she's also given me a business idea that I plan to launch as soon as I get back stateside. Lucy Rey: Bearer of Bad News.

This first assignment has been tough, and I haven't exactly been a natural, but I found Coco and gave her the bad news and frankly that was a success story given my usual effort-to-reward ratio. Sex, intrigue, new faces, and new places—there has been a lot to like. And surely there are many more ordinary cases of bad news that would be far easier to deliver: routine breakups, firings, and disinheritances that I could finesse with a spritz of "You'll get through this" and the listening skills I perfected as a hairdresser.

I unlock the car door. The sun is nearly touching the mountain peaks, blurring their hard edges with a golden glow. It's time to go. Back to Verona, then Rome, then New York, then Reno. Soon I'll be back in Adam's apartment telling him everything over a bottle of cheap wine, and hopefully he'll confess that he and Maurice are an item now, and I'll act surprised, but it's frankly been obvious.

I'll tell him about Hilde and Chris and Coco and how I hadn't swiped anything from any of them (well, only the photo from Hilde, but that practically belonged to me). Anyway, it's progress. Adam will of course ask about Chris (missed opportunity, shit happens) and falling into the old St. Trapezus black hole, aka David—

At the thought of David, I stop. With all that's been going on, I'd forgotten about him entirely, but now I remember that he left me a note that I'd shoved in my jeans pocket because I didn't want to read it in front of Hilde. I've changed shoes and jackets but not pants, and sure enough, the note is still there.

I may as well burn through this last mystery before I leave Ortisei behind. The note is crumpled, and David's handwriting is a mess—jagged lines and ink pushed too hard into a corner of paper likely torn from his notebook.

You were not part of the plan, the note reads. *But I couldn't resist. Everything I told you about the notebook was true. Wish I could have been there when you woke up, but I needed to return something. I'll look you up the next time I'm in Reno. —D*

Thank God I didn't read the note in front of anyone because I can feel my lips quirking into a little smile that reveals more than I want it to. I wonder if I know enough about David to put Maurice on the case and what, if anything, he would discover. Is David even his real name? Did he really frame me for the Cassi camera assault? Was he working for the Department of Lost Things? I remember the creak I heard above my head the morning he disappeared, the way he never convincingly pulled off a PhD student vibe, the avid interest he had shown in me and my family. But maybe not knowing for sure is better—a little mystery never hurt anyone.

As I'm about to refold the note, I see something written on the back.

P.S. I look for lost people too. Think about it.

Well. Sleeping with a spy, that's a new one. And think about it indeed. Does he mean my mother? And had I even told him about her? Unsurprisingly, he seems to know more about me than he should.

As I throw the car into reverse, the wheels squeal. My stomach is doing the same thing. I have one last call to make, and I put the phone on speaker. Despite my disappointing data plan, coverage in Ortisei is better, and I have a good ten minutes until I reach the edge of civilization.

"John Carter, still causing trouble from the grave," Grandmother says when I tell her about Taffy. "When Mama told me the story of the soldier who took the necklace, I was incensed. She told me not to do anything, but I eventually found him anyway. The emerald he sold was unique and left a paper trail.

"'You say your mother's name is Sophie?' he asked. I walked right into the trap. Say what you will about the man, but he was no dummy. He'd seen both sets of identity documents that night on the mountain with Mama standing right in front of him as he compared the photos. And he still remembered the name Liane Terwiel.

"Instead of apologizing, he threatened to 'tell the world . . . and the authorities,' as he put it, about the false pretenses Mama used to enter the country. The publicity could have ended my career in those days, but the stress Mama would have experienced explaining to the authorities why she used false papers to enter the United States was the real reason I paid him off. I wouldn't let him put her through any more pain. That's when we moved to Switzerland. I never trusted that he would keep his word, but he surprised me." Grandmother's tone is bitter. "But if he kept a file lying around, then I was right about him all along."

"By the way," I say to change the subject before her mood sours further, "I need to teach you how to work a scanner. You only sent part of the letter from your mother."

"You really think I don't know how to work a scanner, Lucinda?" Grandmother's voice is laced with offense. "I didn't send you the rest because it's private."

"You're not going to tell me her secret?"

"Haven't you guessed?"

"She didn't name you Sophie after herself?"

"I asked her once, and she told me, 'Men name sons after themselves all the time. Why not me?'"

"In the letter, she came clean?"

"She did. From what you say about this letter to Samuel, it must have been the way she liked to communicate the things she couldn't say," Grandmother says. "I don't know when she wrote it. Possibly years before she died because she was still lucid in those pages, and she wasn't at the end. We never spoke about her lie, but I figured it out long before I found the letter in her things.

"When I changed my name, Mama begged me not to, but I didn't know anything about the real Sophie." Grandmother's tone is contemplative. "If I had, then I'd probably be Sophie Saint today. I think Sophie was the person my mother loved most in the world. Giving me her name was a gift."

We are silent for a long moment, thinking our own thoughts.

"I have something to tell you." I've saved this good news until the end. Grandmother cries when I tell her about Samuel. I'd like to say that I have no reaction, that I stoically comfort her with verbal "there, theres," but the truth is that I have to pull the car over so that I can sob too.

"He'll want to meet you," I tell Grandmother, and I hope that when the time comes, I can go with her.

By then I am out of Ortisei, and the connection starts to fissure. There are so many more questions and things to say, especially about my mother, but now I know there will be time.

Does it matter that I only lied because I love you? Grandmother had asked that last day I saw her in Switzerland.

I didn't reply then, couldn't reply, but through a tightness in my chest, I feel sure that it does. The truth is complicated. And not every lie is created equal.

"I'd like to see you," Grandmother says. "Do you think we could try—" She starts but can't finish the sentence.

Trying is all we can ever do, Little Voice says.

"Do you feel like a trip out to Reno?" I ask.

Grandmother laughs. She actually laughs. It's the most joyful thing I've heard in days. "I'd love that, Lucinda." There is a power when someone who loves you says your name, a filament of gold in the river of mattering.

When we end the call, the sun is dipping below the horizon, coloring the Dolomites pink. *Enrosadira*, Adam said it was called. I savor the sight, and then I start the car again and pull back onto the road.

I have a playlist ready. I start off with Selena Gomez, rhapsodizing about "dance floor therapy" in "Let Me Get Me," which is apropos even if my dance floor is a car. Tapping in time to the music on the steering wheel, I move my body in a (maybe?) safe version of car movement therapy, if such a thing exists. The narrow road curves beneath me, trees and the occasional house whipping by, and I wish I had a convertible and a scarf tied around my head with its silk tails flapping in the wind.

The best I can manage is lowering all the windows, my hair flying into my face like Medusa's snakes. The last of the light is in my eyes as I witness my final Italian sunset. Here and then gone. In a moment, the sun will sink behind these giant mountains, guarding secrets new and old as they have done for centuries.

I can already picture myself narrating this scene to Adam, how he'll roll his eyes and call me melodramatic for timing my departure to drive off into an actual sunset. But I've been through hell for this sunset, and I'm not apologizing to anyone for seizing the moment.

The world is vast and infuriating and surprising and magical. Full of ugliness but also moments of shockingly pure beauty. I crank the volume of the tinny rental car stereo as loud as it will go and sing along with such gusto that I'm almost screaming into the wind and the wild and the world. *I guess this is what it feels like to be free.*

Before I left the bar, Hilde had slipped the photograph into my hand. "Show your grandmother and then send it back to me."

Two girls, trapped in a moment in time, holding on to one another for dear life. On the back of the photo, written in German, the ink faint but still legible: *Sophie + Liane. It is always us. We are the stars.*

AUTHOR'S NOTE

While Sophie and Liane are entirely fictional characters, I used the last name Baum as a tribute to Marianne Baum, the cofounder of a Communist Jewish resistance group in Berlin who was executed at the age of thirty by the Nazi regime for treason. The first name Sophie is in honor of Sophie Scholl, a student murdered at the age of twenty-one for distributing anti-Nazi leaflets at the University of Munich for the nonviolent resistance group White Rose, which she cofounded.

The name Liane is a tribute to Liane Berkowitz, who, after giving birth in prison, was murdered at the age of nineteen for her activities as part of the Berlin Red Orchestra resistance group (her baby was reputedly also murdered by Nazis later that year). The last name Terwiel honors Maria Terwiel, murdered at the age of thirty-three, also for her activities with the Red Orchestra.

The initials M. H. for the fictional Flower Girl are a tribute to Mildred Fish-Harnack, an American woman who was arrested for her leadership in resistance efforts in Berlin, including with the Red Orchestra. Her initial six-year prison sentence was reversed by Hitler himself, and she was executed by guillotine in 1943 at the age of forty. The last name Schmitz honors Elisabeth Schmitz, who survived the war but was largely unrecognized during her lifetime for her work vocally criticizing the Nazi regime and hiding Jews throughout the war. In 2011, she was recognized as "Righteous Among the Nations" by the Commission of Yad Vashem.

Hilde is named to honor Hilde Coppi, who was pregnant when arrested for her resistance work and executed shortly after giving birth when Hitler refused a petition for clemency. Finally, Giovanna commemorates Giovanna Zangrandi, the pseudonym used by Italian resistance fighter Alma Bevilacqua, who used her knowledge of the Dolomiti terrain to hide partisan fighters and keep them supplied (and in 1948 built a rifugio in the area where she operated, which still exists today: Rifugio Antelao).

These are but a few of the remarkable women of all faiths and backgrounds who risked or gave their lives to actively work against the evil of the Nazi regime. I hope that their stories inspire you as they have inspired me.

While the story presented within these pages is a work of fiction, I have done my best to accurately depict historical events where they are referenced, including the timeline and troop movements at the end of World War II and resistance efforts in, and the fall of, Berlin, including the mass rape of German women and girls. However, despite my best efforts, I can't promise that I got everything right. All errors are mine alone, and certain liberties have been taken to suit the needs of the fictional storyline.

I also did my best to represent historical figures authentically. La Païva, for example, was a Jewish woman born into poverty as Esther Lachmann in Russia. She amassed fame and fortune after moving to France and reinventing herself as a high-class escort called La Païva (a name that—with her chosen accent over the *i*—has no meaning I could find in any language and was entirely her own invention). She was so loved by her last husband, Count Guido Henckel von Donnersmarck, that he purportedly embalmed her corpse and kept it in the attic of his castle. The castle still stands in modern-day Poland. La Païva's only known son, Antoine, died while in medical school in 1862, without descendants as far as I know. You can still see La Païva's Parisian mansion, built with funds from Count Guido, on the Champs-Élysées.

Count Guido's second wife, Princess Katharina Henckel von Donnersmarck, really did own a tiara auctioned by Sotheby's and made with emeralds from French Empress Eugénie's crown jewels. I used this tiara as inspiration for the provenance of the emerald necklace, which is a figment of my imagination. Empress Eugénie was, however, known for her love of Colombian emeralds and had all manner of emerald jewelry, so one can certainly imagine there was a necklace in the mix. When she left France after its defeat by Prussia in the War of 1870, the empress took her extensive jewelry collection with her into exile in England and proceeded to sell off jewels piece by piece, and Count Guido was among her customers (though the claim that she used tax proceeds from the French people to buy her jewelry was, as far as I know, a fictional invention on my part).

The forger in this book is fictional, but I was inspired by Cioma Schönhaus, a Jewish man who survived most of World War II in Berlin and then escaped to Switzerland by bicycle after saving countless lives with his forged documents.

The popular song "Bella Ciao" really did originate as a folk song by women to protest working conditions in the paddy fields in the late nineteenth century but went on to become a theme song of sorts for Italian liberation, including for the Italian partisans fighting fascism and then the occupying Nazis. It is still sung in many parts of Italy on Liberation Day (and also viewed by some Italians as an unseemly reminder of painful wartime years).

The reference made to Adam's fear for his safety were he to be turned over to the authorities in Uganda is factual. Uganda's 2023 Anti-Homosexuality Act allows for imprisonment for "promotion" of homosexuality and the death penalty for "aggravated homosexuality." According to Human Rights Watch, at the time of this writing, Uganda is joined by the following countries in authorizing the death penalty as punishment for same-sex relationships: Brunei, Iran, Mauritania, Qatar, Saudi Arabia, and Yemen.

The Department of Lost Things is (to the best of my knowledge) entirely my invention.

Finally, for those wishing to learn more about Berlin during and after World War II, the following memoirs and biographies, listed alphabetically, helped shape my perspective, and I recommend them wholeheartedly: *All the Frequent Troubles of Our Days* by Rebecca Donner, whose meticulous research into the life and death of her great-great-aunt Mildred Fish-Harnack, referenced earlier, was an invaluable source of information on life in Berlin and the activities of various resistance groups before and during World War II; *The Forger* by the aforementioned Cioma Schönhaus, in which the author shares his firsthand account as a forger in Berlin on the run from discovery by the Nazis; *Gone to Ground* by Marie Jalowicz Simon, who shares her remarkable story of survival in Berlin as one of approximately 1,700 "U-boats" (German Jews who survived the war "submerged" beneath the Nazis' noses); and *A Woman in Berlin* by Anonymous, in which the author—later identified as German journalist Marta Hillers—chronicles her experience in Berlin under Russian occupation after the end of World War II.

ACKNOWLEDGMENTS

I started the novel that became BOBN (rhymes with robin) during the bleak days of the Covid-19 pandemic. World events since then have continued to feel dark, and I wrote BOBN to rail against that feeling of despondency. I wanted to laugh but also to remind myself of the best of humanity—the stars that shine on the darkest nights in the form of bravery to do the right thing, generosity even at great personal cost, and above all, kindness. Enough of us believing in and practicing these things keeps the darkness in the world at bay, and the research I did on the characters that inspired the World War II portion of this book affirmed this for me more than ever. Good people of the world, don't lose hope! It is, after all, our world, and we each have the opportunity to shape it into the one we want by how we show up and treat each other. Don't stop putting your light out there!

And now the part where I try and fail to adequately convey my appreciation for everyone who generously gave their time and talent to make BOBN a reality. You know who you are, and I am thankful from the bottom of my heart.

In particular, a huge thanks to my friends and family for years of support and a special shout-out to:

Ann and Debby, for incredibly insightful input as BOBN's first and most enthusiastic readers;

Alexandra, Bola, Julia, Mary-Anne, Robynne, Sara, and Tova, for their invaluable feedback and plot-hole spotting on the full manuscript;

Beti, Carol, Katie, Michelle, Sarah, Summer, and Vanessa, for reading snippets and otherwise providing cheerleading and motivation;

Dolomiti Sara (and her aunt), for introducing me to Giovanna Zangrandi and providing useful context on World War II–era life in the Dolomites;

Sophie, first and foremost, as well as Jenny, Olivia, and Orly, for the incredibly hard work in finding BOBN all the right places to land;

Molly, for liking the laugh emoji and all the fantastic editing, as well as everyone on the amazing Gallery team: Jennifer, Aimée, Sally, Matt, Lucy, Tianna, Christine, Linda, Diane, Tracy, Caroline, Emily, Angel, Kathryn, Lexi, Lisa, Min, and Vi-An;

Felix, for the hugs and belief in me (and BOBN);

My parents, for all the things, including joining in the trip to the Dolomites that gave BOBN the perfect setting; and

YOU, most of all, for reading, because a book without a reader is the proverbial tree in the forest that falls without anyone to hear it.

With love and gratitude,
Elisabeth

ABOUT THE AUTHOR

Elisabeth Dini is a lawyer and former prosecutor of war crimes and crimes against humanity at the International Criminal Court. Born in Nevada, she is a graduate of Brandeis University and Stanford Law School. Elisabeth currently lives in the Netherlands with her husband and a bevy of mostly well-adjusted houseplants. *Bearer of Bad News* is her first novel.